THE
OBSESSION

Series

Irish Born Trilogy

BORN IN FIRE
BORN IN ICE
BORN IN SHAME

Dream Trilogy

DARING TO DREAM
HOLDING THE DREAM
FINDING THE DREAM

Chesapeake Bay Saga

SEA SWEPT
RISING TIDES
INNER HARBOR
CHESAPEAKE BLUE

Gallaghers of Ardmore Trilogy

JEWELS OF THE SUN
TEARS OF THE MOON
HEART OF THE SEA

Three Sisters Island Trilogy

DANCE UPON THE AIR
HEAVEN AND EARTH
FACE THE FIRE

Key Trilogy

KEY OF LIGHT
KEY OF KNOWLEDGE
KEY OF VALOR

In the Garden Trilogy

BLUE DAHLIA
BLACK ROSE
RED LILY

Circle Trilogy

MORRIGAN'S CROSS
DANCE OF THE GODS
VALLEY OF SILENCE

Sign of Seven Trilogy

BLOOD BROTHERS
THE HOLLOW
THE PAGAN STONE

Bride Quartet

VISION IN WHITE
BED OF ROSES
SAVOR THE MOMENT
HAPPY EVER AFTER

The Inn BoonsBoro Trilogy

THE NEXT ALWAYS
THE LAST BOYFRIEND
THE PERFECT HOPE

The Cousins O'Dwyer Trilogy

DARK WITCH
SHADOW SPELL
BLOOD MAGICK

The Guardians Trilogy

STARS OF FORTUNE

eBooks by Nora Roberts

Cordina's Royal Family

AFFAIRE ROYALE
COMMAND PERFORMANCE
THE PLAYBOY PRINCE
CORDINA'S CROWN JEWEL

The Donovan Legacy

CAPTIVATED
ENTRANCED
CHARMED
ENCHANTED

The O'Hurleys

THE LAST HONEST WOMAN
DANCE TO THE PIPER
SKIN DEEP
WITHOUT A TRACE

Night Tales

NIGHT SHIFT
NIGHT SHADOW
NIGHTSHADE
NIGHT SMOKE
NIGHT SHIELD

The MacGregors

THE WINNING HAND
THE PERFECT NEIGHBOR
ALL THE POSSIBILITIES
ONE MAN'S ART
TEMPTING FATE
PLAYING THE ODDS
THE MACGREGOR BRIDES
THE MACGREGOR GROOMS
REBELLION/IN FROM THE COLD
FOR NOW, FOREVER

The Calhouns

SUZANNA'S SURRENDER
MEGAN'S MATE
COURTING CATHERINE
A MAN FOR AMANDA
FOR THE LOVE OF LILAH

Irish Legacy

IRISH ROSE
IRISH REBEL
IRISH THOROUGHBRED

BEST LAID PLANS
LOVING JACK
LAWLESS

SUMMER LOVE
BOUNDARY LINES
DUAL IMAGE
FIRST IMPRESSIONS
THE LAW IS A LADY
LOCAL HERO
THIS MAGIC MOMENT
THE NAME OF THE GAME
PARTNERS
TEMPTATION
THE WELCOMING
OPPOSITES ATTRACT
TIME WAS
TIMES CHANGE
GABRIEL'S ANGEL
HOLIDAY WISHES
THE HEART'S VICTORY

THE RIGHT PATH
RULES OF THE GAME
SEARCH FOR LOVE
BLITHE IMAGES
FROM THIS DAY
SONG OF THE WEST
ISLAND OF FLOWERS
HER MOTHER'S KEEPER
UNTAMED
SULLIVAN'S WOMAN
LESS OF A STRANGER
REFLECTIONS
DANCE OF DREAMS
STORM WARNING
ONCE MORE WITH FEELING
ENDINGS AND BEGINNINGS
A MATTER OF CHOICE

Nora Roberts & J. D. Robb

REMEMBER WHEN

J. D. Robb

NAKED IN DEATH
GLORY IN DEATH
IMMORTAL IN DEATH
RAPTURE IN DEATH
CEREMONY IN DEATH
VENGEANCE IN DEATH
HOLIDAY IN DEATH
CONSPIRACY IN DEATH
LOYALTY IN DEATH
WITNESS IN DEATH
JUDGMENT IN DEATH
BETRAYAL IN DEATH
SEDUCTION IN DEATH
REUNION IN DEATH
PURITY IN DEATH
PORTRAIT IN DEATH
IMITATION IN DEATH
DIVIDED IN DEATH
VISIONS IN DEATH
SURVIVOR IN DEATH
ORIGIN IN DEATH
MEMORY IN DEATH
BORN IN DEATH
INNOCENT IN DEATH
CREATION IN DEATH
STRANGERS IN DEATH
SALVATION IN DEATH
PROMISES IN DEATH
KINDRED IN DEATH
FANTASY IN DEATH
INDULGENCE IN DEATH
TREACHERY IN DEATH
NEW YORK TO DALLAS
CELEBRITY IN DEATH
DELUSION IN DEATH
CALCULATED IN DEATH
THANKLESS IN DEATH
CONCEALED IN DEATH
FESTIVE IN DEATH
OBSESSION IN DEATH
DEVOTED IN DEATH
BROTHERHOOD IN DEATH

Anthologies

FROM THE HEART
A LITTLE MAGIC
A LITTLE FATE

MOON SHADOWS
(with Jill Gregory, Ruth Ryan Langan, and Marianne Willman)

The Once Upon Series

(with Jill Gregory, Ruth Ryan Langan, and Marianne Willman)

ONCE UPON A CASTLE   ONCE UPON A ROSE
ONCE UPON A STAR   ONCE UPON A KISS
ONCE UPON A DREAM   ONCE UPON A MIDNIGHT

SILENT NIGHT
(with Susan Plunkett, Dee Holmes, and Claire Cross)

OUT OF THIS WORLD
(with Laurell K. Hamilton, Susan Krinard, and Maggie Shayne)

BUMP IN THE NIGHT
(with Mary Blayney, Ruth Ryan Langan, and Mary Kay McComas)

DEAD OF NIGHT
(with Mary Blayney, Ruth Ryan Langan, and Mary Kay McComas)

THREE IN DEATH

SUITE 606
(with Mary Blayney, Ruth Ryan Langan, and Mary Kay McComas)

IN DEATH

THE LOST
(with Patricia Gaffney, Mary Blayney, and Ruth Ryan Langan)

THE OTHER SIDE
(with Mary Blayney, Patricia Gaffney, Ruth Ryan Langan, and Mary Kay McComas)

TIME OF DEATH

THE UNQUIET
(with Mary Blayney, Patricia Gaffney, Ruth Ryan Langan, and Mary Kay McComas)

MIRROR, MIRROR
(with Mary Blayney, Elaine Fox, Mary Kay McComas, and R. C. Ryan)

DOWN THE RABBIT HOLE
(with Mary Blayney, Elaine Fox, Mary Kay McComas, and R. C. Ryan)

Also available . . .

THE OFFICIAL NORA ROBERTS COMPANION
(edited by Denise Little and Laura Hayden)

THE
OBSESSION

Nora Roberts

BERKLEY BOOKS, NEW YORK

BERKLEY

An imprint of Penguin Random House LLC
375 Hudson Street, New York, New York 10014

This book is an original publication of Penguin Random House LLC.

Library of Congress Cataloguing-in-Publication Data

Roberts, Nora.
The obsession / Nora Roberts. — Berkley hardcover edition.
pages ; cm
ISBN 978-0-399-17516-9 (hardcover)
1. Man-woman relationships—Fiction.   2. Fathers and daughters—Fiction.   I. Title.
PS3568.O243O25 2016
813'.54—dc23
2015025894

International edition ISBN: 978-1-101-98862-6

PUBLISHING HISTORY
Berkley hardcover edition / April 2016

PRINTED IN THE UNITED STATES OF AMERICA

10   9   8   7   6   5   4   3   2   1

Cover photos by Babaroga / Shutterstock Images.
Endpaper graphics sourced from Shutterstock Images.
Cover and endpaper design by Rita Frangie.
Text design by Laura K. Corless.

Penguin
Random
House

For:

Elaine, Jeanette, JoAnne, Kat, Laura, Mary, Mary Kay, Nicole, Pat, Sarah.
And the one fabulous week a year when we're all together.

EXPOSURE

For now we see through a glass, darkly.

CORINTHIANS 13:12

One

August 29, 1998

She didn't know what woke her, and no matter how many times she relived that night, no matter where the nightmare chased her, she never would.

Summer turned the air into a wet, simmering stew, one smelling of sweat and drenching green. The humming fan on her dresser stirred it, but it was like sleeping in the steam pumping off the pot.

Still, she was used to that, to lying on top of summer-moist sheets, with the windows open wide to the relentless chorus of cicadas—and the faint hope even a tiny breeze would slither through the sultry.

The heat didn't wake her, nor did the soft rumble of thunder from a storm gathering in the distance. Naomi went from sleep to awake in an instant, as if someone had given her a good shake or shouted her name in her ear.

She sat straight up in bed, blinking at the dark, hearing nothing but the hum of the fan, the high pitch of the cicadas, and the lazy, repetitive *hoo* of an owl. All country summer sounds she knew as well as her own voice, and nothing to put that odd little click in her throat.

But now, awake, she felt that heat, like gauze soaked in hot water and wrapped around every inch of her. She wished it were morning so she could sneak out before anyone was up and cool off in the creek.

Chores came first, that was the rule. But it was so *hot* it felt like she'd have to part the air like a curtain just to take a step. And it was Saturday (or would be in the morning) and sometimes Mama let the rules slide a little on Saturdays—if Daddy was in a good mood.

Then she heard that rumble of thunder. Delighted, she scrambled out of bed to rush to her window. She loved storms, the way they whirled and swung through the trees, the way the sky went spooky, the way lightning slashed and flashed.

And maybe this storm would bring rain and wind and cooler air. Maybe.

She knelt on the floor, her arms folded on the windowsill, her eyes on the bit of moon hazed by heat and clouds.

Maybe.

She wished for it—a girl who'd turn twelve in just two days and still believed in wishes. A big storm, she thought, with lightning like pitchforks and thunder like cannon fire.

And lots and lots of rain.

She closed her eyes, tipped her face up, tried sniffing the air. Then, in her Sabrina the Teenage Witch T-shirt, she pillowed her head on her hands and studied the shadows.

Again she wished for morning, and since wishes were free, wished it were the morning of her birthday. She wanted a new bike so *bad*, and she'd given out plenty of hints.

She knelt, wanting morning, a girl tall and gawky, who—though she checked daily—was not yet growing breasts. The heat had her hair sticking to her neck. Annoyed with it, she pushed it up, off, let it hang over her shoulder. She wanted to cut it—really short, like a pixie in the fairy-tale book her grandparents had given her before they weren't allowed to see one another anymore.

But Daddy said girls were supposed to have long hair, and boys short.

So her little brother got a crew cut down at Vick's Barbershop in town, and all she could do was pull her sort-of-blonde hair back in a ponytail.

But then Mason got spoiled silly, in her opinion, being the *boy*. He'd gotten a basketball hoop *and* a backboard, with an official Wilson basketball for his birthday. He got to play Little League baseball, too—something that by Daddy's rules was only for boys (something Mason never let her forget)—and being younger by twenty-three months (something *she* didn't let *him* forget), he didn't have as many chores.

It wasn't fair, but saying so only added on more chores and risked losing TV privileges.

Besides, she wouldn't care about any of that if she got the new bike.

She caught a dull flash—just a shimmer of lightning low in the sky. It would come, she told herself. The wish storm would come and bring the cool and wet. If it rained and rained and rained, she wouldn't have to weed the garden.

The idea of that excited her enough that she nearly missed the next flash.

Not lightning this time, but the beam from a flashlight.

Her first thought was someone was poking around, maybe trying to break in. She started to stand up, run for her father.

Then she saw that it *was* her father. Moving away from the house toward the tree line, moving quick and sure in the beam of the light.

Maybe he was going to the creek to cool off. If she went, too, how could he be mad? If he was in a good mood, he'd laugh.

She didn't think twice, just grabbed up her flip-flops, stuck her tiny flashlight in her pocket, and hurried out of the room, quiet as a mouse.

She knew which steps creaked—everybody did—and avoided them out of habit. Daddy didn't like it if she or Mason snuck downstairs for a drink after bedtime.

She didn't put the flip-flops on until she reached the back door, then eased it open just enough—before it could creak—to squeeze out.

For a minute she thought she'd lost the trail of the flashlight, but she caught it again and darted after. She'd hang back until she gauged her father's mood.

But he veered off from the shallow ribbon of the creek, moving deeper into the woods that edged that scrap of land.

Where could he be going? Curiosity pushed her on, and the almost giddy excitement of sneaking through the woods in the dead of night. The rumbles and flashes from the sky only added to the adventure.

She didn't know fear, though she'd never gone this deep into the woods—it was forbidden. Her mother would tan her hide if she got caught, so she wouldn't get caught.

Her father moved quick and sure, so he knew where he was going. She could hear his boots crunching old dried leaves on the skinny trail, so she kept back. It wouldn't do for him to hear her.

Something screeched, made her jump a little. She had to slap her hand over her mouth to muffle the giggle. Just an old owl, out on the hunt.

The clouds shifted, covered the moon. She nearly stumbled when she stubbed her bare toe on a rock, and again she covered her mouth to smother her hiss of pain.

Her father stopped, making her heart pound like a drum. She went still as a statue, barely breathing. For the first time she wondered what she'd do if he turned around, came back toward her. Couldn't run, she thought, for he'd surely hear that. Maybe she could creep off the path, hide in the brush. And just hope there weren't snakes sleeping.

When he moved on she continued to stand, telling herself to go back before she got into really big trouble. But the light was like a magnet and drew her on.

It bobbled and shook for a moment. She heard something rattle and scrape, something creak like the back door.

Then the light vanished.

She stood in the deep, dark woods, breath shallow, and cold prickling over her skin despite the hot, heavy air. She took a step back, then two, as the urge to run fell over her.

The click came back to her throat, so sharp she could barely swallow. And the dark, all the dark seemed to wrap around her—too tight.

Run home, run. Get back in bed, close your eyes. The voice in her head pitched high and shrill like the cicadas.

"Scaredy-cat," she whispered, clutching her own arms for courage. "Don't be a scaredy-cat."

She crept forward, almost feeling her way now. Once again the clouds shifted, and in the thin trickle of moonlight she saw the silhouette of a ruined building.

Like an old cabin, she thought, that had burned down so only the jags of foundation and an old chimney remained.

The odd fear slid away into fascination with the shapes, the grays of it all, the way the thin moonlight played over the scorched bricks, the blackened wood.

Again she wished for morning so she could explore. If she could sneak back there in the light, it could be *her* place. A place where she could bring her books and read—without her brother nagging at her. And she could sit and draw or just sit and dream.

Someone had lived there once, so maybe there were ghosts. And that idea was a thrill. She'd just love to meet a ghost.

But where had her father gone?

She thought of the rattles and creak again. Maybe this was like another dimension, and he'd opened a door to it, gone through.

He had secrets—she figured all adults did. Secrets they kept from everybody, secrets that made their eyes go hard if you asked the wrong question. Maybe he was an explorer, one who went through a magic door to another world.

He wouldn't like her thinking it because other worlds, like ghosts and teenage witches, weren't in the Bible. But *maybe* he wouldn't like her thinking it because it was *true*.

She risked a few more steps forward, ears cocked for any sound. And heard only the thunder, rolling closer.

This time when she stubbed her toe, the quick cry of pain escaped, and she hopped on one foot until the sting eased. *Stupid rock*, she thought, and glanced down.

In that pale moonlight she saw not a rock, but a door. A door in the ground! A door that would creak when opened. Maybe a magic door.

She got down on all fours, ran her hands over it—and got a splinter for her trouble.

Magic doors didn't give you splinters. Just an old root cellar, or storm cellar. But though disappointment dampened her spirits as she sucked her sore finger, it was still a door in the ground in the woods by an old burned-out cabin.

And her father had gone down there.

Her bike! Maybe he'd hidden her bike down there and was right now putting it together. Willing to risk another splinter, she put her ear to the old wood, squeezing her eyes tight to help her hear.

She thought she heard him moving around. And he was making a kind of grunting noise. She imagined him assembling her bike—all shiny and new and red—his big hands picking the right tool while he whistled through his teeth the way he did when he worked on something.

He was down there doing something special just for her. She wouldn't complain (in her head) about chores for a whole month.

How long did it take to put a bike together? She should hurry back home so he didn't know she'd followed him. But she really, really, *really* wanted to see it. Just a peek.

She eased back from the door, crept over to the burned-out cabin, and hunkered down behind the old chimney. It wouldn't take him long—he was good with tools. He could have his own repair shop if he wanted, and only worked for the cable company out of Morgantown to provide security for his family.

He said so all the time.

She glanced up at the snap of lightning—the first pitchfork of it—and the thunder that followed was more boom than mumble. She should've gone home, that was the truth, but she couldn't go back now. He could come out anytime, and he'd catch her for sure.

There'd be no shiny red bike for her birthday if he caught her now.

If the storm broke, she'd just get wet, that's all. It would cool her off.

She told herself he'd just be five more minutes, and when the minutes passed, he'd just be five more. And then she had to pee. She tried to hold it, ignore it, squeeze it back, but in the end, she gave up and crept her way farther back, back into the trees.

She rolled her eyes, pulled down her shorts, and crouched, keeping her feet wide to avoid the stream. Then she shook and shook until she was as dry as she was going to get. Just as she started to pull her shorts back up, the door creaked open.

She froze, shorts around her knees, bare butt inches off the ground, her lips pressed tight to hold back her breath.

She saw him in the next flash of lightning, and he looked wild to her—his close-cropped hair almost white in the storm light, his eyes so dark, and his teeth showing in a fierce grin.

Seeing him, half expecting him to throw back his head and howl like a wolf, she felt her heart thudding with the first true fear she'd ever known.

When he rubbed himself, down there, she felt her cheeks go hot as fire. Then he closed the door, the quick slam of it echoing. He shot the bolt home—a hard, scraping sound that made her shiver. Her legs trembled from holding the awkward position while he tossed layers of old leaves over the door.

He stood a moment more—and oh, the lightning sizzled now—and played the beam of his light over the door. The backwash of it threw his face into relief so she saw only the hard edges, and the light, close-cropped hair made it look like a skull, eyes dark, soulless hollows.

He looked around, and for one terrible moment she feared he looked right at her. This man, she knew into her bones, would hurt her, would use hands and fists on her like the father who worked to provide security for his family never had.

With a helpless whimper in her throat, she thought: *Please, Daddy. Please.*

But he turned away, and with long, sure strides, went back the way he'd come.

She didn't move a trembling muscle until she heard nothing but the night song, and the first stirring of the wind. The storm was rolling in, but her father was gone.

She hiked up her shorts and straightened, rubbing the pins and needles out of her legs.

No moon now, and all sense of adventure had dropped into a terrible dread.

But her eyes had adjusted enough for her to pick her way back to the leaf-covered door. She saw it only because she knew it was there.

She could hear her own breath now, wisping away on the swirl of wind. Cool air, but now she wanted warm. Her bones felt cold, like winter cold, and her hand shook as she bent down to brush the thick layers of leaves away.

She stared at the bolt, thick and rusted, barring the old wood door. Her fingers traced over it, but she didn't want to open it now. She wanted to be back in her own bed, safe. She didn't want that picture of her father, that wild picture.

But her fingers tugged on the bolt, and then she used both hands as it resisted. She set her teeth when it scraped open.

It was her bike, she told herself even while a terrible weight settled in her chest. Her shiny red birthday bike. That was what she would find.

Slowly, she lifted the door, looked down into the dark.

She swallowed hard, took the little flashlight out of her pocket, and, using its narrow beam, made her way down the ladder.

She had a sudden fear of her father's face appearing in the opening. That wild and terrible look on his face. And that door slamming shut, closing her in. She nearly scrambled back up again, but she heard the whimper.

She froze on the ladder.

An animal was down here. Why would her daddy have an animal down . . . A puppy? Was that her birthday surprise? The puppy she'd always wanted but wasn't allowed to have. Even Mason couldn't beg them a puppy.

Tears stung her eyes as she dropped down to the dirt floor. She'd have to pray for forgiveness for the awful thoughts—thoughts were a sin as much as deeds—she'd had about her father.

She swung her light around, her heart full of wonder and joy—the last she would feel for far too long. But where she imagined a puppy whimpering in his crate was a woman.

Her eyes were wide and shined like glass as tears streamed from them. She made terrible noises against the tape over her mouth. Scrapes and bruises left raw marks on her face and her throat.

She wasn't wearing any clothes, nothing at all, but didn't try to cover herself.

Couldn't, couldn't cover herself. Her hands were tied with rope—bloodied from the raw wounds on her wrists—and the rope was tied to a metal post behind the old mattress she lay on. Her legs were tied, too, at the ankles and spread wide.

Those terrible sounds kept coming, pounded on the ears, roiled in the belly.

As in a dream, Naomi moved forward. There was a roaring in her ears now, as if she'd gone under the water too long, couldn't get back to the surface. Her mouth was so dry, the words scraped her throat.

"Don't yell. You can't yell, okay? He might hear and come back. Okay?"

The woman nodded, and her swollen eyes pleaded.

Naomi worked her fingernails under the edge of the tape. "You have to be quiet," she said, whispering as her fingers trembled. "Please be quiet." And pulled the tape away.

It made an awful sound, left a raw, red mark, but the woman didn't yell.

"Please." Her voice sounded like a rusty hinge. "Please help me. Please, don't leave me here."

"You have to get away. You have to run." Naomi looked back toward the cellar door. What if he came back? Oh God, what if the wild man who looked like her father came back?

She tried to untie the rope, but the knots were too tight. She rubbed her fingers raw in frustration, then turned away, using her little light.

She saw a bottle of liquor—forbidden by her father's law in their house—and more rope, coiled and waiting. An old blanket, a lantern. Magazines with naked women on the covers, a camera, and oh no, no, no, photographs of women taped to the walls. Like this woman, naked and tied up and bloody and afraid.

And women who stared out with dead eyes.

An old chair, cans and jars of food on a shelf nailed to the wall. A heap of rags—no, clothes, torn clothes—and the stains on them were blood.

She could smell the blood.

And there were knives. So many knives.

Closing her mind, just closing her mind to everything else, Naomi grabbed one of the knives, began to saw at the knot.

"You have to stay quiet, stay quiet."

She nicked flesh, but the woman didn't cry out.

"Hurry, please hurry. Please, please." She bit back a moan when her arms were free, and those arms shook as she tried to lower them. "It hurts. Oh God, God, it hurts."

"Don't think about it, just don't think about it. It hurts more when you do." It hurt, yes, it hurt to think. So she wouldn't think of the blood, the pictures, the heap of torn and terrible clothes.

Naomi went to work on one of the ankle ropes. "What's your name?"

"I— Ashley. I'm Ashley. Who is he? Where is he?"

Couldn't say it. Wouldn't say it. Wouldn't think it. "He's home now. The storm's come. Can you hear it?"

She was home, too, Naomi told herself as she cut the other rope. Home in bed, and this was all a bad dream. There was no old root cellar that smelled of musk and pee and worse, no woman, no wild man. She would wake in her own bed, and the storm would have cooled everything.

Everything would be clean and cool when she woke.

"You have to get up, get out. You have to run."

Run, run, run, into the dark, run away. Then this will never have happened.

Sweat rolling down her battered face, Ashley tried to get up, but her legs wouldn't hold her. She fell to the dirt floor, her breath wheezing. "I can't walk yet—my legs. I'm sorry, I'm sorry. You have to help me. Please, help me get out of here."

"Your legs are asleep, that's all." Naomi grabbed the blanket, wrapped it around Ashley's shoulders. "You have to try to get up."

Working together, they managed to get Ashley to her feet. "Lean on me. I'm going to push you up the ladder, but you have to try to climb. You have to try."

"I can do it. I can do it."

Rain whipped in on the slow, sweaty climb up, and twice on that short journey, Ashley nearly slipped. Naomi's muscles twanged from the strain of holding the weight, of pushing. But on a last sobbing grunt, Ashley dragged herself out, lay panting on the ground.

"You have to run."

"I don't know where I am. I'm sorry. I don't know how long I've been down there. A day, two. I haven't had any food, any water since he . . . I'm hurt."

Tears streamed, but she didn't sob, just stared at Naomi through the flood of them. "He . . . he raped me, and he choked me, and he cut me and hit me. My ankle. Something's wrong with it. I can't run on it. Can you get me out of here? To the police?"

Rain pounded, and the lightning lit the sky like morning.

But Naomi didn't wake.

"Wait a minute."

"Don't go back in there!"

"Just wait."

She scrambled down, into the terrible place, and picked up the knife. Some of the blood on it wasn't fresh, wasn't from the nicks. No, some was old and dry, and from more than nicks.

And though it sickened her, she pawed through the heap of clothes and found a tattered shirt, a torn pair of shorts.

She took them with her as she climbed back out. Seeing them, Ashley nodded.

"Okay. You're smart."

"I didn't see shoes, but it'll be easier for you with the shirt and shorts. They're torn, but—"

"It doesn't matter." Ashley bit down hard as Naomi helped her into the shorts, as she carefully lifted Ashley's arms into the shirt.

Naomi paused when she saw that the movement opened thin slices on Ashley's torso, saw fresh red blood seeping.

"You have to lean on me." Because Ashley shivered, Naomi wrapped the blanket over her shoulders again.

Just do, she told herself. *Don't think, just do.*

"You have to walk even if it hurts. We'll look for a good thick stick, but we have to go. I don't know what time it is, but they'll look for me in the morning. We have to get to the road. It's more than a mile into town after that. You have to walk."

"I'll crawl if I have to."

She got to her knees, levered herself up with Naomi's help. It was slow, and Naomi knew from Ashley's labored breathing that it was painful. She found a downed branch, and that helped a little, only a little, as the trail went to mud in the storm.

They crossed the creek—running fast now, from the rain—and kept going.

"I'm sorry. I'm sorry, I don't know your name."

"Naomi."

"That's a nice name. Naomi, I have to stop for a minute."

"Okay, but just for a minute."

Ashley braced against a tree, breathing hard, leaning heavily on the broken branch while sweat and rain ran down her face. "Is that a dog? I hear a dog barking."

"It's probably King. The Hardy place is right over that way."

"Can we go there? We can call the police, get help."

"It's too close." Mr. Hardy was a deacon at church with her father. He'd call her father before he called the police.

"Too close? It feels like we've walked miles."

"Not even one."

"Okay." Ashley closed her eyes a moment, bit down on her lip. "Okay. Do you know the man? The one who took me, the one who hurt me?"

"Yes."

"You know his name, where they can find him."

"Yes. We have to keep going now. We have to keep going."

"Tell me his name." Wincing, Ashley pushed off the tree, began her hobbling walk. "It'll keep me going to know it."

"His name is Thomas Bowes. Thomas David Bowes."

"Thomas David Bowes. How old are you?"

"Eleven. I'm going to be twelve on Monday."

"Happy birthday. You're really smart and strong and brave. You saved my life, Naomi. You saved a life before your twelfth birthday. Don't ever forget it."

"I won't. I won't forget. The storm's passing."

She kept to the woods. It took longer that way than it would have if she'd gone out to the road. But she knew fear now, and kept to the woods until the edge of the little town of Pine Meadows.

She went to school there, and to church, and her mother shopped in the market. She'd never been inside the sheriff's office, but she knew where it was.

As dawn lightened the sky to the east, and the first light glimmered on puddles, she walked past the church, over the narrow bridge that arched over the narrow stream. Her flip-flops made soggy flaps on the street, and Ashley limped, the branch clomping, her breath a raw pant with each step.

"What town is this?"

"It's Pine Meadows."

"Where? I was in Morgantown. I go to college at WVU."

"It's about twelve miles from here."

"I was training. Running. I'm a long-distance runner, believe it or not. And I was training like I do every morning. He was parked on the side of the road with the hood up, like he'd had a breakdown. I had to slow a little, and he grabbed me. He hit me with something. And I woke up in that place. I'm going to have to stop again."

No, no, no stopping. No thinking. Just doing.

"We're almost there. See, right down the road, that white house—see the sign out front?"

"Pine Meadows Sheriff's Department. Oh thank God. Oh thank God." Ashley began to weep then, racking sobs that shook them both as Naomi tightened her arm around Ashley's waist, took more weight, and trudged the rest of the way.

"We're safe now. We're safe."

When Ashley collapsed on the narrow porch, Naomi wrapped the blanket closer around her, then knocked hard on the door.

"Is someone going to be there? I didn't think. It's so early."

"I don't know." But Naomi knocked again.

When the door opened, Naomi had a vague recognition of the young face, the tousled hair.

"What's all this?" he began, and then his sleepy eyes shifted by her, landed on Ashley. "Well, Jesus."

He shot the door open, jumped out to crouch beside her. "I'm going to get you inside."

"Help. Help us."

"You're all right. You're going to be all right."

He looked scrawny to Naomi's eyes, but he hefted Ashley like she was nothing—and flushed a bit when the blanket slipped and the torn shirt exposed most of her left breast.

"Honey," he said to Naomi, "hold the door open now. Y'all have an accident?"

"No," Naomi said. She held the door open, had one instant to think whether she should run away, just run, or go inside.

She went inside.

"I'm going to set you down right here. All right now?" His eyes studied the bruising on Ashley's throat, and knowledge came into them. "Sweetheart, you see that water fountain over there. How about you get— What's your name now?"

"Ashley. Ashley McLean."

"You get Ashley some water, would you?"

He turned as he spoke, then spotted the knife Naomi held at her side. In that same easy tone, he said, "Why don't you give that to me, all right? There you go."

He took the knife from Naomi's limp hand, set it up on a shelf out of reach.

"I need to make some calls, and one to the doctor who'll come and examine you. But we're going to have to take some pictures. Do you understand?"

"Yes."

"And I'm calling the sheriff in, and there'll be questions. You up to that?"

"Yes."

"All right now. Drink a little water. That's a good girl," he said to Naomi, running a gentle hand over her wet hair as she brought the paper cup to Ashley.

He grabbed a phone from a desk, punched in numbers.

"Sheriff, it's Wayne. Yeah, I know what time it is. We got a woman here who's hurt. No, sir, not an accident. She's been assaulted, and she's going to need a full exam." He turned away, spoke quietly, but Naomi heard the words *rape kit*.

"Kid brought her in. I think it's Tom and Sue Bowes's girl."

Ashley lowered the cup, stared into Naomi's eyes. "Bowes."

"Yes. I'm Naomi Bowes. You need to drink."

"So do you, baby." But Ashley set the cup aside and drew Naomi to her. "So do you."

When she broke, when everything finally broke inside her, Naomi laid her head on Ashley's shoulder and wept.

Ashley met Wayne's eyes over Naomi's head. "It was her father who did this to me. It was Thomas David Bowes who did this. And it was Naomi who saved me."

Wayne let out a breath. "Sheriff, you better get in here right quick."

Two

When the sheriff came, Wayne took Naomi into another room, bought her a candy bar and a Coke. She'd never been allowed such indulgences, but she didn't argue it. He got a first-aid kit and began to doctor the cuts and scratches she hadn't realized she'd inflicted on herself on that long hike through the woods.

He smelled of Juicy Fruit gum—she saw the yellow pack of it sticking out of his breast pocket.

And she would always, from that morning on, associate the gum with simple kindness.

"Honey, you got a favorite teacher?"

"Um. I don't know. I guess Miss Blachard maybe."

"If you want, I could call her, ask her to come in, be with you."

"No. No, that's okay. She's going to know. Everybody's going to know." It made her chest hurt, so she looked away. "But I don't want to be there when they do."

"All right. We got a nice nurse coming in to be with Ashley, to go with her when she goes to the hospital. Do you want somebody like that? Maybe who doesn't know you."

"I don't want anybody. What's going to happen?"

"Well, the sheriff's talking to Ashley right now for a little bit, and then they'll take her into the hospital in Morgantown and fix her up."

"She hurt her ankle."

"They'll fix it, don't you worry. You want a different kind of candy bar?"

Naomi looked down at the Snickers she hadn't opened. "No, sir. I just never had candy first thing in the morning."

"How about Easter?" Smiling, he put a Band-Aid on a small, deep scratch.

"That's a holy day. It's for praying, not for candy rabbits."

Even as she echoed her father's words, she saw the pity in the deputy's eyes. But he only patted her legs. "Well. We'll get you a hot breakfast soon as we can. You be all right here for just a minute?"

"Am I under arrest?"

Not pity now, but that Juicy Fruit kindness again as he laid a hand on her cheek, gentle as a mother. "For what, honey?"

"I don't know. You're going to arrest my daddy."

"Don't you worry about that right now."

"I saw him. I saw him when he came out of that cellar in the woods, and he looked wrong. I was afraid."

"You don't have to be afraid anymore."

"What about my mama, and my brother?"

"They're going to be fine." He glanced over as the door opened. She knew Miss Lettie—she went to their church. But she'd forgotten she worked in the sheriff's office.

Lettie Harbough came in with a red tote bag, and a sad smile on her plump face.

"Hey there, Naomi. I got some dry clothes for you here. They're my girl's, and she's not as tall as you, and not so slim, but they'll be clean and dry."

"Thank you, Miss Lettie."

"You're more than welcome. Wayne, the sheriff wants you. Naomi and I'll be fine. You can change right out in the washroom, all right?"

"Yes, ma'am."

The clothes were too big, but there was a belt so she could cinch the jeans.

When she came out Lettie sat at the tiny table sipping coffee out of a big blue mug. "I've got a brush here. Would it be all right if I brushed your hair out? You got it all tangled."

"Thank you."

Naomi made herself sit, though she wasn't sure she wanted to be touched. Still, after the first few strokes of the brush, she relaxed.

"Such pretty hair."

"It's dishwater."

"No, indeed. It's like deer hide, all the tones of blonde mixed up, and all sun-streaked now from summer. Nice and thick, too. I'm going to ask you a couple of things, maybe hard things, sweetie. But they're important things."

"Where's Ashley?"

"They're taking her to the hospital now. She asked after you, asked if we could bring you in to see her. Would you want to?"

"Yes, ma'am. Please, I want to."

"All right. But now, I have to ask you if your father ever hurt you. I know that's a hard thing to ask."

"He's never laid a hand on me or Mason. My mama gives out the hidings if we need it, and they don't count for much. She doesn't have the heart for a real hiding, so we pretend, all three of us. Because Daddy says, 'Spare the rod, spoil the child.'"

"I never liked that one myself. The harder one is asking if he ever touched you in a bad sort of way."

Naomi stared straight ahead while Lettie ran the brush through her hair. "You mean like he did to Ashley. He raped her. I know what rape is, ma'am. They raped the Sabine women in the Bible. He never did that to me. He never touched me wrong."

"All right, then. Did he ever hurt your mama?"

"I don't think so. Sometimes . . ."

"It's all right." In practiced moves, Lettie used a little band to pull Naomi's hair back into a tail. "All you have to do is tell me the truth."

"Sometimes he looked like maybe he wanted to hurt her, but he didn't. If he got really mad, he'd just go off for a day or two. Cooling off, Mama said. A man needs to cool off on his own time. She didn't know, Miss Lettie. Mama didn't know he hurt people, or she'd have been afraid. More afraid."

"People?"

When Lettie came back around to sit again, Naomi stared straight ahead. "Ashley said she thought she'd been down there for a day or two. There was more rope down there, and pictures. There were pictures on the wall of other women, tied up like she was. Worse than she was. I think some of them were dead. I think they were dead. I'm going to be sick."

Lettie tended to her, holding her hair back as she hugged the toilet, bathing her face with a cool cloth when she was done.

She gave Naomi something minty to rinse out her mouth, brushed a kiss over her forehead.

"You've had enough. Maybe you want to rest awhile."

"I can't go home, can I?"

"Not right now, I'm sorry, honey. But I can take you to my house, and you can use the guest bed, try to sleep."

"Can I just stay here until Mama and Mason come?"

"If that's what you want. How about I get you some toast, we see how that settles. You save that Snickers bar for later."

"Thank you."

Lettie rose. "What you did, Naomi? It was right. And more, it was brave. I'm awful proud of you. I'm only going to be a couple minutes. How about some tea with honey to go with the toast?"

"That'd be nice, thank you."

Alone, Naomi laid her head on the table, but she couldn't rest. She sipped at the Coke, but it was too sweet. She wanted water—just cold and clear. She thought of the water fountain, rose.

She stepped outside the little room, started to call out, ask if it was all right.

She saw the deputy hauling her father across the room toward a big metal door. His hands were in cuffs behind his back; a raw bruise bloomed on his right cheek.

He didn't look wild now, or upset or sorry. He had a sneer on his face—the sort he got when somebody said maybe he was wrong about something.

He saw her—and she braced for his fury, his hate, his wrath.

All she got was an instant of indifference before he walked to the metal door, and through. And away.

The room was crowded with people, noise, and something that sparked darkly on the air. She felt she floated in it, as if her legs had just gone somewhere else and her body hung suspended.

She heard words, disjointed, tinny to her ear.

FBI, serial killer, forensics, victims.

Nothing made sense.

No one noticed her, a gangly girl with eyes too wide, too bright in a face pale as a ghost, swimming in too-big clothes and shock.

No one glanced her way, and she wondered, if they did, would their eyes pass over her—through her—just as her father's had.

Maybe none of it was real. Maybe *she* wasn't real.

But the pressure on her chest, that felt real. As if she'd fallen from the high limb in the old oak tree out back and knocked away her breath. So far away she couldn't get it back.

The room took a slow, sick spin, and the light faded. A cloud over the moon.

With Bowes secure, Wayne came out in time to see Naomi's eyes roll back in her head. He shouted, and he leaped toward her. He was fast, but not fast enough to catch her before she hit the floor.

"Get some water! Where's the damn doctor? What the hell's she doing out here?" He gathered her up, cradled her. Gently tapped cheeks he thought looked pale enough for his hand to pass through.

"I'm sorry. Ah, merciful God. She needed food. I just came out to see about getting her something." Lettie crouched down with a cup of water.

"Did she see him? Did she see me bring that bastard in?"

Lettie only shook her head. "I wasn't gone for more than three minutes. She's coming around. There you are, baby. Naomi, honey, just breathe easy now. You just had a faint. I want you to sip some water."

"Have I been sick?"

"You're all right now. Take a sip."

It came back to her, all of it. Her eyes—what her mother called medicine bottle green—closed. "Why isn't he mad at me? Why doesn't he care?"

They urged water on her. Wayne carried her into the back again. They brought her sick food—the tea and toast. She ate what she could, and found it made the worst of that floating feeling go away.

The rest passed in a blur. Dr. Hollin came in and looked her over. Somebody stayed with her all the time—and Wayne snuck her in another Coke.

The sheriff came in. She knew him—Sheriff Joe Franks—because she went to school with Joe Junior. He had wide shoulders on a sturdy body, and a tough face on a thick neck. She always thought of a bulldog when she saw him.

He sat across from her.

"How you doing, Naomi?"

His voice was like a gravel road.

"I don't know. Um. Okay, sir."

"I know you had a hard night, and you're having a hard day on top of it. Do you know what's going on here?"

"Yes, sir. My daddy hurt Ashley. He tied her up down in that old cellar in the woods by this burned-out cabin place. He hurt her really bad, and he hurt other people, too. There were pictures of them down there. I don't know why he did those things. I don't know why anybody would do what he did."

"Did you ever go out there to that cellar before last night?"

"I didn't know it was there. We're not supposed to go into the woods that far. Just to the creek, and only when we have permission."

"What made you go out there last night?"

"I—I woke up, and it was so hot. I was sitting by my window, and I saw Daddy go out. I thought maybe he was going to the creek to cool off—and I wanted to go, too. I got my flashlight and my flip-flops and I snuck out. I'm not supposed to."

"That's all right. So you followed him."

"I thought maybe he'd think it was funny. I could tell if he did before I let him know I was there. But he didn't go to the creek, and I just wanted to know where he was going. And I thought when I saw the old place, and the cellar, maybe he was putting a bike together for my birthday."

"Is it your birthday, honey?"

"Monday is, and I asked for a bike. So I waited—I was just going to take a peek. I hid and I waited until he came out, but—"

"What?"

For a moment, she thought it would be easier if she floated again, just kept floating. But the sheriff had kind eyes, patient ones. He'd keep those kind eyes on her even if she floated away.

And she had to tell somebody.

"He didn't look right, Sheriff. Sir. He didn't look right when he came out and it scared me. But I waited until he was gone, and I just wanted to see what was down there."

"How long'd you wait?"

"I don't know. It felt long." She flushed a little. She wasn't going to tell him she'd peed in the woods. Some things were private. "There was a bolt on the door, and I had to work some to push it, and when I opened the door I heard something like whimpering. I thought maybe it was a puppy. We weren't allowed to have a dog, but I thought maybe. But then I saw Ashley."

"What did you see, honey? It's hard, but if you can tell me exactly, it's going to help."

So she told him, exactly, and sipped at the Coke even though her stomach jittered with the retelling.

He asked more questions, and she did her best. When he was done, he patted her hand.

"You did real good. I'm going to bring your mama back."

"Is she here?"

"She's here."

"And Mason?"

"He's over at the Huffmans' place. Mrs. Huffman's keeping an eye on him, and he's playing with Jerry."

"That's good. He and Jerry like to play together. Sheriff Franks, is my mama all right?"

Something shuttered down over his eyes. "She's had a hard day, too." He said nothing for a moment. "You're a steady girl, Naomi."

"I don't feel so steady. I got sick, and I had a faint."

"Trust me, honey, I'm an officer of the law." He smiled a little. "You're a steady girl. So I'm going to tell you there are going to be other people asking questions. The FBI—you know what that is?"

"Yes, sir. Sort of."

"They're going to have questions. And there's going to be reporters wanting to talk to you. You're going to have to talk to the FBI, but you don't have to talk to any reporters."

He hitched up a hip, took a card out of his pocket. "This is my phone number—the number here, and the one at home I wrote on the back. You can call me anytime—doesn't matter what the time. You need to talk to me, you call. All right?"

"Yes, sir."

"Put that away safe. I'm going to go get your mama now."

"Sheriff Franks?"

He paused at the door, turned back to her. "Yes, honey?"

"Is my daddy going to jail?"

"Yes, honey, he is."

"Does he know?"

"I expect so."

She looked down at her Coke, nodded. "Okay."

Her daddy was going to jail. How could she go back to school, or church, or to the market with her mother? It was worse than when Carrie Potter's daddy went to jail for two months for getting in a fight at the pool hall. Even worse than when Buster Kravitt's uncle went to jail for selling drugs.

She'd be going into seventh grade in just another week, and everyone would know what happened. What her daddy did. What she did. She didn't see how she could—

Then the door opened, and there was her mother.

She looked sick, like she'd been sick for days, and bad sick so it had eaten away at her. She looked thinner than she had when Naomi had gone to bed the night before. And her eyes were all red, swollen, and tears still stood in them. Her hair was every which way, like she hadn't taken a brush to it, and she wore the baggy, faded pink dress she mostly wore for garden chores.

Naomi got shakily to her feet, wanting nothing more at that moment than to press her face to her mother's breast, find comfort there, find promises she'd pretend to believe there.

But the tears just rolled out of her mother's eyes, driven by guttural sobs. She sank right down to the floor, covered her face with her hands.

So the child went to the mother, gathered her in, stroked and soothed. "It'll be all right, Mama. We'll be all right."

"Naomi, Naomi. They're saying terrible things about your daddy. They're saying you're saying them."

"We'll be all right."

"They can't be true. This can't be true." Susan pulled back, grabbed Naomi's face in her hands, and spoke fiercely. "You imagined it. You had a bad dream."

"Mama. I saw."

"No, you didn't. You have to tell them you made a mistake."

"I didn't make a mistake. Ashley—the girl he had—she's in the hospital."

"She's lying. She has to be lying. Naomi, he's your daddy, he's your *blood*. He's my husband. The police, they're going all over our house. They put your daddy in handcuffs and took him away."

"I cut the ropes off her myself."

"No, you didn't. You're going to stop this lying right *now*, and tell everybody how you made it all up."

A dull throb filled Naomi's head so her own voice sounded flat and hollow through it.

"I pulled the tape off her mouth. I helped her get out of the cellar. She could hardly walk. She didn't have any clothes."

"No."

"He raped her."

"Don't you say such a thing." Her voice pitching high, Susan shook Naomi. "Don't you dare."

"There were pictures on the wall. A lot of pictures, of other girls, Mama. There were knives with blood dried on them, and rope, and—"

"I don't want to hear this." Susan clamped her hands over her ears. "How can you say all this? How can I believe all this? He's my husband. I lived with him for fourteen years. I bore him two children. I slept in the same bed, night after night."

The fierceness shattered, like glass. Susan dropped her head on Naomi's shoulder again. "Oh, what are we going to do? What's to become of us?"

"We'll be all right," Naomi said again, helplessly. "We'll be all right, Mama."

They couldn't go home. Not until the police and now the FBI cleared it so they could. But Lettie brought them all clothes and their own toothbrushes and so on, and made her guest room theirs—hers and her mother's—with Mason bunking in with her son.

The doctor gave her mother something to make her sleep, and that was good. Naomi took a shower, put her own clothes on, tied her hair back, and felt more herself.

When she walked across the hall from the bathroom and cracked open the door to check on her mother, she saw her little brother sitting on the bed.

"Don't wake her!" Naomi hissed, then felt bad for the sharp order when he turned his head to look at her.

He'd been crying, too, and his face was splotchy from it, his eyes red-rimmed on the outside, lost on the inside.

"I'm just watching her."

"Come on out, Mason. If she wakes up, she'll start crying again."

He did what she said without arguing—a rare thing—and then walked straight into her, wrapped his arms tight.

They didn't hug much anymore, but it felt good to have somebody to hold on to, so she hugged back.

"They came right into the house, and we were still sleeping. I heard Daddy yelling, and other people, and I ran out. I saw Daddy fighting with the deputy, and they pushed him against the wall. Mama was screaming and crying, and they put handcuffs on Daddy, just like on the TV. Did he rob a bank? Nobody will tell me."

"No, he didn't rob a bank."

If they went downstairs, Miss Lettie would be there, so instead she sat down with her brother on the floor.

"He hurt people, Mason. Ladies."

"Why?"

"I don't know, but he did."

"Maybe it was their fault."

"No, it wasn't. He took them to a place in the woods, and locked them up and hurt them."

"What place?"

"A bad place. They have to put him in jail for it."

"I don't want Daddy to go to jail." The tears started up again. All she could do was wrap an arm around his shoulders.

"He did bad things to people, Mason. He has to go to jail."

"Does Mama have to go to jail?"

"No, she didn't hurt anybody. She didn't know he was hurting people. Don't go pestering her about it. And don't go fighting either. People are going to say things about Daddy, and you're going to want to fight about it, but you can't. Because what they're going to say is true."

His face went belligerent. "How do you know what's true?"

"Because I saw, because I know. I don't want to talk about it anymore right now. I talked about it enough today. I wish it was over. I wish we were someplace else."

"I wanna go home."

She didn't. She didn't ever want to go back to that house again, knowing what was back in the deep woods. Knowing what had lived in those same rooms, eaten at the same table.

"Miss Lettie says they've got Nintendo down in their family room."

Belligerence changed to a look of hope mixed with doubt. "Can we play it?"

"She said we could."

"Do they have Donkey Kong?"

"We can find out."

They didn't have video games at home—or a computer—but they both had enough friends who did to know the basics. And she knew Mason dearly loved video games. It was simple to set him up in the family room with Miss Lettie's help—and better yet when she hard-eyed her teenage son into playing with Mason.

"I'm going to make some lemonade. Why don't you come in the kitchen with me, Naomi, give me a hand with that?"

The house was so nice. Clean and pretty, with lots of colors on the walls and in the furniture. She knew Mr. Harbough taught English and literature at the high school, and Miss Lettie worked for the sheriff. But the house looked *rich* to her.

And the kitchen had a dishwasher—which was her name at home—and a counter of snowy white in the middle with a second sink right in it.

"Your house is so nice, Miss Lettie."

"Why, thank you. It makes me happy. I want you to be comfortable while you're here."

"How long will we be here, do you think?"

"A day or two, that's all." Lettie put sugar and water in a pot to boil. "You ever made lemonade from scratch?"

"No, ma'am."

"It's a treat. Takes a while, but it's worth it."

Lettie puttered around. Naomi noted she didn't wear an apron but just tucked a dish towel in the waist of her pants. Daddy didn't like Mama to wear pants. Women were supposed to wear skirts and dresses.

Thinking of it, of her father, hearing his voice in her head, made her stomach tie itself up again. So she made herself think of something else.

"Miss Lettie, what do you do at the sheriff's office?"

"Why, honey, I'm the first woman deputy in Pine Meadows, and still the only one after six years."

"Like Deputy Wayne."

"That's right."

"So you know what happens next. Will you tell me what happens next?"

"I can't say for certain, as the FBI's in charge now. We assist them. They're going to gather up evidence, and take statements, and your daddy will have a lawyer. A lot of the next depends on the evidence and the statements, and what your daddy says and does. I know it's hard, but it'd be best if you try not to worry about all that just yet."

"I can't worry about Daddy." She'd already figured that out. But . . . "I have to take care of my mama, and Mason."

"Oh, baby girl." Lettie sighed, and after giving the pot a stir, she came around the counter. "Somebody's got to take care of you."

"Mama won't know what to do without Daddy telling her. And Mason won't understand what Daddy did. He doesn't know what rape is."

On another sigh, Lettie pulled Naomi into a hug. "It's not for you to hold everybody else up. Where's your mother's brother now? Where's your uncle Seth?"

"In Washington, D.C. But we're not allowed to have anything to do with him because he's a homosexual. Daddy says he's an abomination."

"I knew your uncle Seth. He was a couple years behind me in school. He didn't seem like an abomination to me."

"The Bible says . . ." It made her head and her heart hurt, what the Bible said—or what Daddy said it said. No, she couldn't worry about that now. "He was always so nice to us. He has a nice laugh, I remember. But

Daddy said he couldn't come visit anymore, and Mama wasn't to talk to him on the phone."

"Would you like him to come?"

Just that, just those words made Naomi's throat slam shut so she could only nod.

"All right, then. When I take the syrup off the stove to cool, I'll see about getting in touch with him. Then I'm going to show you how to squeeze lemons. That's the fun part."

She learned how to make lemonade from scratch and ate a grilled cheese sandwich—a combination that would forever become her comfort food of choice.

As her mother slept through the day, Naomi, for the first time in her life, begged for chores. Lettie let her weed the flower garden out back, and the vegetable patch, and put fresh seed in the bird feeders.

When she was done, Naomi gave in to fatigue, stretched out on the grass in the shade, and slept.

She woke with a start, just as she had in the night. Something, there was something.

She sat up fast, heart pounding, half expecting her father to be standing over her with a rope in one hand, a knife in the other.

But the man who sat in the shade with her on a summer chair wasn't her father. He wore khaki pants and loafer shoes without any socks, and as her gaze traveled up, a bright blue shirt with a little man on a horse where a pocket might have been.

He had her eyes, that medicine bottle green, in a face smooth and handsome as a movie star, all topped with waving brown hair under a Panama hat.

"I fell asleep."

"Nothing better than a nap in the shade on a summer afternoon. Do you remember me, Naomi?"

"Uncle Seth." Her heart hurt, but not a bad kind of hurt. She feared she might faint again, though it didn't feel the same as before, but everything felt light and bright.

"You came. You came," she said again, then crawled right into his lap, weeping and grasping. "Don't leave us. Please don't leave us, Uncle Seth. Please, please."

"I won't, I won't leave you, baby girl. I promise you. You stop worrying right now, because I'm here, and I'll take care of you."

"You gave me a pink party dress."

He laughed, and the sound eased the ache in her heart even as he pulled a snowy white handkerchief out of the pocket of his khakis and dabbed at her tears.

"You remember that? You weren't more than six."

"It was so pretty, so fancy and fine. Mama's sleeping. She just keeps sleeping."

"It's what she needs right now. Look how tall you are! Those long legs. Got 'em scratched up some."

"It was dark in the woods."

His arms tightened around her. He smelled so good, like lime sherbet. "It's not dark now, and I'm here. As soon as we can, you're coming home with me. You, Mason, your mama."

"We're going to Washington, D.C., to stay with you?"

"That's right. With me and my friend Harry. You'll like Harry. He's in playing Donkey Kong with Mason, getting acquainted."

"Is he a homosexual?"

Something rumbled in Seth's chest. "Why yes, he is."

"But a nice one, like you."

"I think so, but you'll judge for yourself."

"I'm supposed to start back to school soon. Mason, too."

"You'll go to school in D.C. Is that all right with you?"

Relief nearly made her faint again, so she only nodded. "I don't want to be here anymore. Miss Lettie, she's been real nice. And Deputy Wayne. And the sheriff, too. He gave me his number so I could call if I needed. But I don't want to be here anymore."

"As soon as we can, we won't be."

"I don't want to see Daddy. I don't want to see him. I know that's bad, but—"

He drew her back. "It's not bad, and don't ever think that. You don't have to see him if you don't want to."

"Will you tell Mama? She's going to want me to, me and Mason. I don't want to see him. He didn't see me. Can we go to Washington, D.C., now?"

He cradled her again. "I'm working on it."

It took more than a week, though they didn't spend even one night at Miss Lettie's. The reporters came—the sheriff was right on that. And they came in herds and packs, with big vans and TV cameras. They shouted questions and swarmed any time someone went outside.

No one remembered her birthday, but she didn't care. She wanted to forget it herself.

They ended up in a house, not nearly so nice as Miss Lettie's, outside Morgantown. And FBI people stayed there, too, because of the reporters, and because there had already been threats.

She heard one of the FBI people talking about it, and how they were moving her father, too, to somewhere else.

She heard a lot, because she listened.

Mama arguing with Uncle Seth about going to D.C., about not taking the children to see their father. But her uncle kept his promise. When her mother went to see her father, she went with the FBI lady.

The second time she went, she came back and took the pills. And slept more than twelve hours.

She heard her uncle talking to Harry about how they'd change things around so three more people could live in their house in Georgetown. She did like Harry—Harrison (like Indiana Jones) Dobbs. Though it had surprised and puzzled her that he wasn't white. Not exactly black either. He was like the caramel she liked so much on ice cream when she'd earned a special treat.

He was really tall and had blue eyes that seemed so special against the caramel. He was a chef, which he told her with a wink was a fancy cook. Though she'd never known a man who knew his way around a kitchen, Harry made dinner every night. Food she'd never heard of, much less tasted.

It was like a movie again, such pretty food.

They bought a Nintendo for Mason, and got her and Mama some new clothes. She thought she could stay right there in the not-so-nice house if Harry and Seth stayed, too.

But one night, late, on a day her mother had gone to visit Daddy, she heard the argument. She hated when her uncle and her mother argued. It stirred fear that they'd make him go away again.

"I can't just pick up and leave, take the children away. They're Tom's children."

"He's never getting out of prison, Susie. Are you going to drag those kids to visiting days? Are you going to put them through that?"

"He's their father."

"He's a fucking monster."

"Don't use that language."

"A fucking monster, deal with it. Those kids need you, Susie, so stand up for them. He doesn't deserve a minute of your time."

"I took vows. Love, honor, obey."

"So did he, but he broke them. Jesus Christ, he raped, tortured, killed over twenty women—and that's what he's confessed to. Bragged about, for God's sake. Over twenty young girls. He'd come to your bed after he was done with them."

"Stop it! Stop it! Do you want me to say he did those things? He did those terrible things? How can I live with it, Seth? How can I live with it?"

"Because you have two children who need you. I'm going to help you, Susie. We're going to get away from here where you and the kids feel safe. You, and they, are going to get counseling. They're going to go to good schools. Don't put me in the position of telling you what to do, the way he did. I will for now, if I have to, to protect you and the kids. But I'm asking you to remember who you used to be, before him. You had a spine and plans, and a light."

"Don't you understand?" That terrible plea in her mother's voice, that awful rawness, like a cut that wouldn't heal. "If I go, I'm saying it all happened."

"It did happen. He's admitted it."

"They *made* him."

"Stop it. Just stop it. Your own daughter, your own baby saw what he did."

"She imagined—"

"Stop. Susie, stop."

"I can't just . . . How could I not have known? How could I have lived with him nearly half my life and not known? The reporters, they shout that at me."

"Screw the reporters. We're leaving tomorrow. God, where's your anger, Suze? Where's your anger for what he did, what he is, what he put you and your kids through? What Naomi went through? I hope to hell you find it, but until you do, you're going to have to trust me. This is the best thing. We can go tomorrow, and you can start building a life for yourself and the kids."

"I don't know where to start."

"Pack. And we'll take it a step at a time from there."

She heard her mother crying when Seth left the room. But after a while Naomi heard drawers opening, closing.

Packing sounds, she thought.

They were leaving in the morning. Leaving all of this.

Closing her eyes, she said a special prayer of thanks for her uncle. She understood that she'd saved Ashley's life. Now she thought Uncle Seth was saving hers.

Three

Naomi lived in D.C. for five months, two weeks, and five days. That narrow slice of time brought so many highs and lows, so many jolts and joys she couldn't keep track.

She loved the house in Georgetown with its high ceilings and deep, rich colors, with its pretty backyard patio and little fountain with its own tiny pool.

She'd never lived in a city before, and could spend hours sitting at the window in her room watching the cars and cabs and people. And her room was so beautiful. The old cherrywood dresser—an antique, not a hand-me-down, because there was a difference—had a big oval mirror framed in the same wood, and with little curlicues. She had a double bed, a luxury that had her rolling around in it or stretching her arms wide just because she could. The sheets were so soft and smooth she'd stroke her fingers over the pillowcase to lull herself to sleep.

The walls were sunset gold and had pictures of flowers grouped together in their own little garden.

She liked her room even better than Mama's, which was fancier with a pale green canopy draped over the big bed, and a chair with strange and beautiful birds flying over it.

Mason slept on a pullout sofa in what her uncle called the upstairs parlor, but most nights in the first few weeks, he'd end up crawling into bed with her or curling up on her rug like a puppy.

Harry took them to his restaurant with its tablecloths and candles and flowers, and gave them a tour of the big kitchen that was all noise and rush and heat.

Starting school brought nerves and excitement. A new school, a new place, where no one knew her. That was both scary and wonderful. She got to use a new name, too. Here she'd be Naomi Carson—the new girl—and some made fun of her accent. But none of the other kids knew her daddy was in prison.

She didn't much like going to the therapist. Dr. Osgood was nice— young and pretty, and she always smelled really good. But it felt wrong, at least at first, to say things to a stranger about her parents, and her brother, and more than anything about what had happened that night in the woods.

Mason went to another doctor, a man, and liked it fine because his doctor let him talk about video games and basketball. At least Mason said he did, and after a few weeks of talking about video games and basketball, he stopped coming in to sleep in Naomi's bed.

Her mother went to another doctor altogether, when she went. A lot of times she said she wasn't feeling up to it, and went to bed with one of her headaches.

Once a week she borrowed Uncle Seth's car and drove to the prison— United States Penitentiary, Hazelton—on visiting day. It took nearly eight hours for the trip up and back, for the little bit of time she had to visit through the glass. And she always came back looking beaten up and with one of her headaches.

But she wouldn't stop going.

Still, everything settled into a kind of routine, with school for her and

Mason, the restaurant for Harry, the office where Seth worked on investing other people's money, and her mother working part-time as a waitress.

Then Seth came home from work one night with a tabloid paper in his hand, and there was hell to pay.

Naomi cringed. She'd never seen her uncle angry, never heard him raise his voice. Now she didn't know what to do as she was making chicken and rice like Harry had shown her on the big gas cooktop while Mason sat at the eating counter dawdling over his homework, and Mama sat staring off into space and pretending to help.

Her mother jumped up to stand when Seth slapped the paper down on the counter. And Naomi saw that the front of it had a picture of her father and, oh God, one of her from picture day back at Pine Meadows Middle School.

"How could you? How could you do this to your children, to yourself?"

Susan clutched at the little gold cross around her neck. "Don't yell at me. I didn't say hardly anything."

"You said enough. Did you give them this picture of Naomi? Did you tell them you were living here in D.C.?"

Now her shoulders hunched together, the way, Naomi thought, they used to when Daddy gave her a mean look.

"They paid me five thousand dollars. I've got to earn my way, don't I?"

"Like this? Selling your daughter's picture to the tabloids?"

"He could've gotten it without me, you know it, and they've been writing about all this for weeks now. It never stops."

"They didn't have her picture, Susan." As if weary, Seth pulled the knot of his red tie loose. "They didn't know y'all were living here."

When the phone rang, he held up a hand to stop Naomi. "Don't answer it. Let it go to the machine. I had six calls at my office already. It wouldn't take long to dig up an unlisted number. Unlisted to protect you and the children, Suze, from what's going to happen now."

"They're always at the prison, pestering at me." With her shoulders still hunched, Susan pressed her lips together.

There were lines deep around her mouth, Naomi noted. Lines that hadn't been there before that hot summer night.

"And Tom said we could make some good money. He can't do it himself, it's the law, but . . ."

"You can funnel it to him."

Susan flushed deeply, the way she did when deeply embarrassed or angry. "I've got a duty to my husband, Seth. They got him locked up, and in what they call the special area. He said how he needs money to pay the lawyer to work out getting him in general population."

"Ah, Christ, Suze, that's just bullshit. Don't you know bullshit when you hear it?"

"Don't use that language."

"The language bothers you, but this doesn't?" He slapped a hand on the tabloid as the phone began to ring again. "Did you read it?"

"No, no, I didn't read it. I don't want to read it. They—they kept pestering me, and Tom said he'd start getting more respect if he could tell his story, and I could back him up."

"Nobody respects tabloids. Even he'd know . . ." He paused, and Naomi snuck a look, thought he seemed more sick than angry now. "Who else pestered you? Who else have you talked to?"

"I talked to Simon Vance."

"The writer. True crime."

"He's a professional. His publisher's going to pay me twenty-five thousand dollars. It says so right in the contract."

"You signed a contract."

"It's professional." Eyes glazed, lips trembling, Susan threw her arms out as if to ward off an attack. "And there'll be more when they make the movie deal. He said."

"Susan." Naomi knew despair now, and heard it in her uncle's voice. "What have you done?"

"I can't get by waiting tables. And that doctor you make me go to, she said how I need to work on my self-confidence. I need to get a place closer to the prison so I don't have to take your car and drive so far. Tom wants me and the kids closer."

"I'm not going there."

Susan spun around at Naomi's voice, and the heat of anger seared through the tears. "Don't sass me."

"I'm not sassing, I'm saying. I won't go. If you take me, I'll run off."

"You'll do what your daddy and I tell you." Hysterics—Naomi had heard them often enough in the last four months to recognize them—spiked into Susan's voice. "We can't stay here."

"Why is that, Susan?" Seth spoke quietly. "Why can't you stay here?"

"You live with a man, Seth. You live in sin with a man. A black man."

"Naomi, honey." Seth's voice stayed quiet, but his eyes—full of noise—stayed on Susan's face. "You and Mason go on upstairs for a bit, will you?"

"I got dinner on."

"Smells good, too. Just take it off the heat for a bit, all right? You go on up, help Mason finish his homework."

Mason slid off the stool, wrapped his arms around Seth. "Don't make us go away. Don't let her take us away. Please, I want to stay with you."

"Don't you worry now. Go on upstairs with your sister."

"Come on, Mason. We're not going anywhere but upstairs." Naomi looked back as she gathered up Mason's books and papers. "Harry's not a sin, but I think it's one for you to say so."

"You don't understand," Susan began.

"I understand. I started understanding that night in the woods. It's you who doesn't understand, Mama. Come on, Mason."

Seth said nothing as Susan began to cry, just opened the wine fridge, chose a bottle. He let her stand, hands over her face, while he opened it, poured himself a glass.

He turned off the ringer on the phone that hadn't stopped.

While she wept he took two careful sips.

"You've known I was gay since I was fourteen. Probably longer, but that's when I got up the nerve to tell you. It took me a little longer to come out to Mom and Dad, and they took it pretty well, all things considered.

But I told my big sister first. Do you remember what you said—well, after you asked if I was sure?"

When she just kept crying, he took another sip of wine. "You said, well, don't go putting the moves on anybody I've got my eye on. Where's that girl, Suze, the one who could say just the right thing to me when I was so scared I had jelly in my knees? The girl who made me laugh when I'd be trying not to cry. The one who accepted me for what I am."

"I'm sorry. I'm sorry."

"That's fine, Susan. But I'm going to say this to you, and you hear me. You hear me, Susan. Don't ever talk about the man I love that way again. You understand me?"

"I'm sorry. I'm so sorry. Harry's been everything kind and good to me and the kids. And I can see how good he is for you. I'm sorry. But . . ."

"We're still an abomination? Is that what you really think? Is that what your heart tells you?"

She sat again. "I don't know. I don't know. I don't *know*! Fourteen years. He wasn't so strict at first. It all came on so gradual I didn't notice. He didn't want me to work anymore, and I was just pregnant with Naomi, so I thought that would be fine. Being able to make a real nest, and stay home with my baby. Then he didn't want to go see Mom and Dad—had excuses. Then he didn't want me going. We were a family, and he was head of the house. Then he didn't like them coming to our place either. Holidays maybe—at first."

"He was cutting you off from everyone who loved you."

"He said how we were what was important. We needed to make our own lives, and then Mason came along, and he was so strict about how things had to be. But he worked hard, and paid the bills. He never laid a hand on me, I swear it. Or on the children. How he thought, what he wanted, what he said, it just seeped in. I missed Mom and Dad. I missed you so much, but . . ."

He got out another glass, poured wine, set it in front of her.

"I haven't had anything but church wine since I was carrying Naomi. I used to be like her, didn't I? Strong and brave and a little bit fierce."

"You were, yeah."

"I lost that, Seth. I lost all that."

"You can find it again."

She shook her head. "I'm so tired. If I could sleep, just sleep until it all went away. She meant what she said, Naomi did. She wouldn't go with me. Or if I made her, she'd run off—take Mason with her. She wouldn't leave him. Not like I left you. She'd make me choose between my children and my husband."

"You chose him over your family once before."

"A woman cleaves to her husband." On a sigh she picked up the glass, drank. "Oh, that's good. I'd forgotten. I did take vows, Seth. I know he broke them, I know he did unspeakable things—at least sometimes I know. But it's hard for me to break those promises, to accept that the person I made them to is the man in prison now. I'm just so tired. All the time. If I could, I'd sleep the rest of my life."

"It's depression, honey. You have to give the therapy and the medication time. You have to give yourself time."

"It feels like years already. Seth, every time I drive up to Hazelton, I tell myself it's the last time. I don't want to see those walls, to go through those guards. Sit there, talk to him through the glass. To have those reporters and the others who wait for me to come, try to talk to me. They yell out things. You don't know."

"Then stop being their target."

She only shook her head. "But then . . . Tom's got a way of turning me around, of making me doubt myself. I'll end up doing just what he says to do. I knew talking to those reporters was wrong. I knew signing that contract was wrong. But I'm not strong and brave and fierce, so I did just what he told me. He said, take that money, sign those papers. I was to put money on his prison account and get a house close by. I was to keep coming every week, and bringing the children once a month to start."

"I'd fight you on that. I might lose, but I'd fight you on taking those kids there."

"She'd fight me. My girl." On a half sob, Susan knuckled a fresh tear away. "She wouldn't go and she'd fight me like a tiger to keep Mason away. I've got to do better by them. I know it."

"Don't go back." He laid a hand over hers, felt hers stiffen. "Get stronger. Take a few weeks, then see. Talk to the therapist about it."

"I'll try. I swear. I'm so grateful to you and Harry. I'm so sorry I did what Tom told me, after all you've done for us."

"We'll get through it."

"I'm going to go up, talk to the kids for a minute. Then we'll come down, finish making dinner."

"That's a good start. I love you, Suze."

"God knows you must." She rose, reached for him. "I love you. Don't give up on me."

"Never happen."

She gave him a hard squeeze, then walked out, walked up the stairs. The hardest walk of her life, she thought. Even harder than that horrible walk through the prison to the visiting area.

She stepped to Naomi's door and looked at her children, sitting on the floor with Mason frowning over his pencil and worksheet.

He'd been crying, and that broke her heart because she'd brought those tears on.

But not Naomi. Her eyes were dry and hot when they lifted, met hers.

"I want to say first I was wrong. What I said down there about your uncle and Harry. It was a wrong and ugly thing to say. I hope you'll forgive me. And I want to say you were right. Both of you were right. We won't be moving away from Seth and Harry. I was wrong about talking to those people. The paper, and the magazine, and the book writer. I can't go back and not do it, but I'll never do it again. I'm so sorry, Naomi, for letting them have your picture. I don't know how to make it up to you. But I'm going to try to do better. I promise, I'm going to try. It's easy to say that. What I have to do is show you. You need to give me a chance to show you I'll do better."

"I'll give you a chance, Mama." Mason sprang up, ran into her arms.

"I love you so much, my little man." She kissed the top of his head, then looked at Naomi. "I understand it's going to take longer for you."

Naomi only shook her head and ran to her mother.

She did better, though there were dips, and some of them deep. She'd opened a door her brother had tried to close by giving the interviews, selling the photographs.

It engendered more, with side stories on the serial killer's gay brother-in-law, and with reporters stalking him to and from his office. Paparazzi captured photos of Naomi leaving school for the day, one of Mason on the playground.

TV talk shows fueled the machine with discussion, with "experts," and the tabloids were relentless.

Word leaked that Pulitzer Prize–winning author Simon Vance had a book deal in cooperation with Thomas David Bowes and his wife, and the media circus began anew.

As the new year began they all sat together in the front parlor, with a fire snapping, and the glittering holiday tree shining like hope in the window.

Harry made hot chocolate, and Mason sat on the floor with his fondest wish: a puppy that had greeted him on Christmas morning. He'd named the pup Kong after his favorite game.

It should have felt good, Naomi thought. The puppy, the hot chocolate, and the tree Harry said would stay up until Twelfth Night.

But something was wrong, and she felt it deep inside. So her chocolate sat, going cold in the tall mug.

"Harry and I have some news," Seth began, and Naomi's stomach knotted.

They'd be sent away. Too much trouble, all the reporters, and the people who walked or drove by to stare.

Someone had egged the house on Halloween, and worse, written on Seth's car:

KILLER'S FAG KIN

Mama lost her job at the café because they found out where she worked, and the manager let her go.

"It's big news," he continued, taking Harry's hand.

Naomi couldn't look up, couldn't stand to see his face when he said they had to live somewhere else.

"Harry and I are opening a restaurant."

She looked up then, stunned. Felt the knots begin to uncoil.

"We found a great space, and figured it was time to have our own." Harry winked. "We've even got the name. The Spot."

"Spot's a dog," Mason said, and wrestled with the deliriously happy puppy.

"Not this spot. It's The Spot because that's just what it's going to be. *The* spot everyone wants to go."

"Where is it?" As delirious as the puppy, Naomi picked up her chocolate. "Can we go see it?"

"You bet. The thing is, it's in New York."

"You're moving away."

"We're all moving. To New York City. The West Village. New place, new house, new start."

Naomi looked at her mother, who only sat with her fingers twisted together.

"But you have this house. This is your house."

"The one in New York will be our house. All of us." Still smiling, Seth patted Harry's leg. "Wait until you see it. It's fabulous."

"You're moving because of us. Because of the people who won't leave us alone."

Before Seth could speak, Harry shook his head. "That's not altogether wrong, not altogether right. I've wanted my own restaurant for a long time, and this feels like the right time, the right place. The fact is, it's been hard for Seth to work while being bothered, and we both feel the house here? It's closed in now."

"We've talked it all out, Harry, me, your mama. This is best for all of us. If you don't object to it, we'll have your names changed legally to Carson. I've given my notice at work, and so has Harry. I'm not pretending when I say I'm pretty excited about this. I know you'll have to change schools again."

"It doesn't matter." Naomi sent Mason a sharp look in case he said different.

"And therapists," Seth continued, "but we have good recommendations there."

"I don't need to go anymore. I don't," Naomi insisted. "I'd say if I did. If this is a new place and all that, I can be new, too. I want to cut my hair."

"Oh, Naomi," Susan said.

"I want to. I don't want to look like the girl they've been taking pictures of. I can do it myself."

"Oh, no, you don't!" Seth gave his good laugh. "I draw that line. We'll take you to the salon, and get it done right. She's heading toward thirteen, Suze. It should be up to her."

"They can still find us. But maybe they won't if I don't look the same. Mason already looks some different than he did, 'cause he's bigger and his hair's longer now. And it's darker than it was. I don't care what my name is, as long as it's not Bowes. I'm sorry if that hurts your feelings, Mama."

Susan said nothing, only continued to stare down at her hands, fingers twisting in her lap.

"Can Kong go to New York? I can't leave him."

"Mason, my man." Harry snatched the puppy up from where it waggled. "This here is one urban-canine-to-be. Of course he's going."

"I know this is uprooting everyone, and it's my doing."

"No, Susie. I think they would have run us to ground sooner or later anyway. We didn't take enough precautions. Now we will. New place, new start." Seth grinned at Naomi. "New look."

"When?" Naomi asked.

"The house goes on the market tomorrow, and the agent is champing at the bit. One way or the other, we move over your spring break. It's a four-bedroom, so, Mason, you'll have your own room. How about that?"

"Me and Kong!"

"You and Kong."

"Can we have bunk beds?"

"Bunk beds it is. Naomi? You okay with this?"

"I'm fine with it. You can have friends over again. You'll have to make some new ones, but you can have parties again. You couldn't have your annual Christmas party this year or go out on New Year's like you always do."

Harry gave the wiggling dog to Seth. "Do you hear everything?"

"Mostly, I do. And Mama won't go to the prison from New York. I know you've only been a few times since . . . since you signed those papers, but when you did you came back sad. New York's farther away. The farther away, the better."

"I'm trying, Naomi."

"Mama, you're doing so much better. Just like you said." Out of love, and out of duty, Naomi got up to squeeze into the chair with her mother, wrapped around her. "This will be even better. I just know it."

"New York, here we come?" Seth said.

"New York, here we come!" Mason shook his fists in the air. "Can we go to see the Knicks? Can we?"

"Nick who?" Seth said, and made Mason laugh and laugh.

The house sold within two weeks, and for ten thousand over asking price. They stayed busy packing up. And Naomi heard how Seth paid the movers extra to come at night, take things off in small trucks, a bit at a time.

In March, when spring break came with sweeping winds and some spitting snow, they left Georgetown in the middle of the night, like thieves.

She watched the house recede through the windows, felt a hard tug. But then she faced forward, flipped her fingers through the hair Seth had dubbed "Naomi: The Short and Sassy."

A new look, she thought, a new place, a new start.

She wouldn't look back.

Four

New York, 2002

At sixteen Naomi Carson lived a life Naomi Bowes could never have imagined. She had a pretty room in a lovely old brownstone in a city full of color and movement. Seth and Harry spoiled her with a generous allowance, shopping trips, tickets to concerts, and most of all with trust that gave her freedom.

She did her best to earn the indulgences. She studied hard, got exceptional grades—with an eye focused on Providence College in Rhode Island and a degree in photography.

They'd given her a little point-and-shoot Fuji for her first Christmas in New York, and her love affair began. Her interest blossomed, her skill improved—and netted her a serious Nikon for her sixteenth birthday.

With it, she'd joined the yearbook committee and newspaper at her high school as official photographer, and racked up experience and an impressive portfolio she hoped to use to get into the college of her choice.

She'd worked hard to lose her accent, wanting more than anything to be just like the other girls, to have nothing left of those first twelve years. Hints of it could slip through, but by the time she'd started high school, the slips were rare.

She had friends, dated now and again, though unlike most of her contemporaries she didn't want a steady boyfriend. Too much drama, from what she'd observed.

And while she liked kissing—if the boy was any good at it—she wasn't ready to be touched. Thought maybe she never would be.

She had let Mark Ryder touch her breast—she'd finally grown some, but accepted that they were never going to amount to much. She'd wanted to see what it felt like, but instead of making her excited, it just made her nervous and uncomfortable.

Mark hadn't been happy that was all she let him do—and not much of that. Naomi figured that was his damage and ignored him when he accused her of being a tease, being frigid, being a freak.

At sixteen she hit five-ten—most of it leg—and was willow slim and pretty enough that boys wanted to touch her breasts. She'd let her hair grow to shoulder length, mostly so she could tie it back when she took pictures.

When she won a photography competition, Seth rewarded her with a trip to the salon for highlights and lowlights in her dark blonde hair.

Mason hit a growth spurt around twelve and was first-string center of his school's basketball team.

Sometimes it irritated her to know that her little brother was smarter than she was. Sometimes it made her proud. Either way, he was whip-smart, good-looking, and affable. So he enjoyed the attention and admiration of the girls who fluttered around him, and he had a core circle of guys to hang with.

Days could go by without her giving Pine Meadows and all that had happened there a thought. For days she was just a regular teenager, worrying about her grades, her wardrobe, listening to music, meeting friends for pizza.

She kept in touch with Ashley, mostly through email. Ashley had never gone back to Morgantown and lost a whole year before she'd transferred to Penn State.

When she'd graduated, Naomi sent her a card and a framed photo she'd taken herself of a cherry tree full of pink blooms and promise.

On her twenty-first birthday, in the first spring of the new century, Ashley gave herself a gift. She took the train to New York to spend a whole day with Naomi.

Whenever she looked back at that day, Naomi remembered her own nerves—what should she wear, what should she say—and the speechless pleasure of seeing Ashley waiting, as promised, on the observation deck of the Empire State Building.

So pretty, Naomi thought, with long, long blonde hair dancing in the crazy spring breeze. All the nerves, the sudden shyness, vanished the instant Ashley saw her, rushed to her, arms wide.

"You're so tall! You're taller than me. Half of everybody is, but I— Naomi." She held tight, swayed back and forth, back and forth.

"You came. It's the most special birthday there is, and you came here."

"I'm having the most special birthday there is because of you. I wanted to spend it with you. I wanted to meet you here, even though it's awesome corny, because I wanted to say that everything I can see from here is because of you. And I wanted to give you this."

Ashley took a small wrapped box out of her purse.

"But it's *your* birthday. I have a present for you."

"Let's save mine for later—over lunch maybe. I really want you to have this now, and here, high in the sky. You brought me out of the ground, Naomi, and now we're standing high in the sky. Open it, okay?"

Overwhelmed, Naomi opened the box and stared at the pendant. Three thin silver chains held an oval with a purple iris suspended in its center.

"It's beautiful. It's just beautiful."

"I have to say it was my mom's idea. She said how flowers have meanings. This one, the iris, it has a couple of them. One of the meanings is valor, and another is friendship. You qualify for both. I hope you like it."

"I do. I love it. Ashley—"

"Let's not cry. I want to cry, too, but let's not cry today. Let's put the necklace on, and then you have to show me some of the city. I've never been to New York."

"Okay. Okay." It was as hard, she learned, to hold back happy tears as tears of misery. "Where do you want to go first? It's your special day."

"I'm a girl. I want to go shopping!" Ashley laughed as she helped Naomi fasten the necklace. "And I want to go someplace where I can have a glass of champagne at lunch. I'm legal!"

"I love you," Naomi blurted out, then flushed. "That sounds weird, I—"

"No, no, it doesn't. We've got something between us nobody else does. We're the only ones who really understand what it took for both of us to get right here, right now. I love you back. We're going to be friends forever."

The therapist—she had gone back for nearly a year after her mother hit one of those deep dips—asked Naomi how she felt when she saw Ashley; Naomi said it made her remember the light.

Her mother worked as a waitress in Harry's restaurant. She did all right—except when she didn't. Her mother sometimes went into the dark, and forgot to remember the light. But she had a job, and when she went into the dark, Harry held the job for her.

Her doctor called it depression, but Naomi knew that as bad as depression could be, the dark times were worse.

In the dark times her mother took too many pills. Once when she'd taken too many she'd had to go to the hospital. She'd taken the too many pills right after Simon Vance's book came out, and there were big ads for it all over the city.

He'd titled it *Blood in the Ground: The Legacy of Thomas David Bowes*, and all the bookstores had big displays. Vance, a serious man with a polished, academic style, hyped it all over the talk shows, did in-depth interviews in magazines and newspapers. In those interviews, on those talk shows, Naomi's name came up as often as her father's.

That tie, that blood and bloody tie, brought back the nightmares.

Whenever Naomi saw those ads, those displays, she knew a terrible part of her life beat inside them.

It made her afraid, and it made her ashamed.

So she understood her mother's fear, her mother's shame, and trod carefully.

But when her mother remembered the light, things were good, even simple. Her favorite picture was one she'd taken of her mother dancing with her uncle, at a party in the summer. The light had been good, inside and out, and her mother had looked so pretty laughing into her brother's face. She'd given it to Susan, along with one she'd taken with a timer of her mother, her brother, and herself sitting on the patio of the brownstone in the springtime.

When the dark came back, and her mother needed to stay in bed with the curtains shut tight, Naomi would take her food on a tray. She'd know how deep the dark was if she saw those pictures lying facedown, as if her mother couldn't bear the sight of her own happiness.

Still, weeks would go by—sometimes even months—when everything seemed as normal as normal could be. When it was all about studying or fretting over a test; bickering with Mason, who could be the bane of her existence; or wondering what she should wear to a movie date.

She was at the movies—not on a date, but with a big group of friends (and Mason with a group of his) getting ready to see *Spider-Man*. She had popcorn and an orange soda and settled down to enjoy the previews when the houselights dimmed.

Her friend Jamie immediately started making out with her boyfriend of the moment, but Naomi ignored them—and the smacking noises Mason's group made in the row behind her.

She loved movies, and truth be told she liked movies like *Spider-Man* and *The Lord of the Rings* more than the love stories her girlfriends sighed over.

She liked movies where people had to *do* something, overcome something. Even if it meant getting bitten by a radioactive spider to do and overcome.

The screen filled with the point of view of someone driving a truck. She knew about point of view from studying photography. A man's point of view, she noted—one wearing a wedding ring.

She liked noticing the details.

Then others began to catch her eye—catch her by the throat.

She knew those roads. She knew that truck. When he veered off into the woods, bumping over a rough trail, she felt that crushing weight in her chest.

Scenes flashed—the root cellar, the photographs, a woman bound on the mattress, eyes full of terror.

She couldn't breathe.

Flash to a house near the edge of the woods. And it *was* their house. God, God, their house. A long-legged girl, thin with long hair, looking out the window on a hot, storm-waiting night.

Quick splice to the family in church—father, mother, gangly girl, little boy. And the next of the girl reaching for the lock on a rough wood door.

She couldn't watch. The popcorn fell out of her hand, spilled everywhere; the soda landed with a wet slap as she jumped up. Her friends called out:

Hey, watch it!

What the hell, Naomi!

But she was bolting for the doors.

She heard the announcer blare behind her.

A story of depravity. A story of courage. Daughter of Evil. *Coming November.*

Her knees buckled as she stumbled into the lobby. She fell on all fours while the room spun and her chest burned.

She heard Mason's voice, miles away, as he shook her.

"Get up. Come on, Naomi, you have to get up."

He pulled her up and half dragged, half carried her out into the hot, heavy air of September, the too-bright lights of Times Square.

"Look at me. Look at me."

He was nearly as tall as she was, and he had their father's eyes. A deep golden brown. They held both worry and shock.

"Can't breathe."

"Yes, you can. You are. Just take it slow."

"It was—"

"Don't say it. Don't say it here. Anybody asks, you got sick. You felt sick, and we went home. Let's walk. Come on."

She managed two shaky steps, then had to stop, brace her hands on her knees and lean over, afraid she would be sick. But the queasiness passed, the dizziness eased.

"Did you know? Did you?"

He took her hand in a firm grip, pulled her down Broadway. "I knew they were making it. I didn't know they'd finished everything or that they'd show the damn preview during *Spider-Man*."

"That was our house."

"They filmed a lot of it on location."

"How do you know?"

"I look stuff up sometimes. I just thought it would take longer to get out, but it's already getting, you know, buzz from the critics and online."

"Why didn't you *tell* me?"

He stopped, shot her a cool look of disdain only a sibling can manage. "Because you don't want to hear it. Nobody talks about it, nobody tells me anything. So I look shit up for myself. I read Simon Vance's book."

Now she felt hot and sick all over again. "We have to put it behind us. It's been four years."

"Have you? Have you put it behind you?"

"Yes. Most of the time. A lot of the time."

"Mama hasn't. Remember when she said she was going for a weekend with that friend of hers? To some spa deal? She didn't. She took the bus and went to see him, in prison."

"How do you know that?"

He shrugged, then pulled her inside a coffee shop, wound through to a table. "She's done it before. When the rest of us went to Hilton Head for a week, and she said she had a stomach virus? She went to see him then, too. I found the bus tickets in her purse, both those times, and one other."

"You went through her purse?"

"That's right." He didn't miss a beat. "Two Cokes, please," he said with remarkable ease to the waitress. "And I go through her room, so that's how I know she's been writing to him. She has letters from him that come to a P.O. box."

"You can't disrespect her privacy," Naomi began, then covered her face with her hands. "Why is she doing this?"

"She's submissive and dependent—he's dominated her the whole time. It's like emotional abuse and battering."

"Where do you get that?"

"I look shit up, like I said. He's a psychopath, for Christ's sake, Nome. You should know. And he's a narcissist. That's why he gives the cops another name and location every couple years. Another victim, and where he buried her. It keeps him in the news, keeps getting him attention. He's a liar and he manipulates Mama. He twists her up because he can. Remember when she OD'd?"

"Don't say it like that, Mason."

"It's what happened. Thanks." He sent the waitress a quick smile when she set their drinks down. "He'd talked her into giving more interviews to Vance—the writer. I don't know how he got in touch with her right off, but he talked her into that, and when the book came out, she couldn't handle it."

"He knows where we are."

"I don't know, but he sure as hell knows we're in New York." Then Mason shrugged. "He doesn't care about us, and never did. Mama's his target."

"He cared about you."

"I don't think so. Do you think I wanted a buzz cut every freaking month? If he made it to one of my Little League games I could *feel* his eyes on my back when I came up to bat. I knew if I struck out, fouled out, he'd give me that sneer—that *I'm raising a pussy* sneer."

"But . . ."

"He watched me for signs of 'Carson blood.' That's how he put it. When I was eight he told me if I ever showed any fag tendencies, he'd beat the fag out of me."

Shocked, she grabbed Mason's hand. "You never told me."

"Some shit you don't tell your sister. At least when you're eight. He scared the crap out of me—you, too. We just got used to being scared of him, like that was normal."

"Yes." She let it out on a shaky breath. "Yes, what kind of mood will he be in? Will he be in a good mood? Everything circled around him. I've gotten some of that out of therapy. I just didn't know you felt that, too."

"Same house, same father."

"I thought . . . I thought it was different for you because he wanted a son. It was so clear he wanted a son more than a daughter. More than me."

"He wanted himself, and I wasn't."

"I'm sorry," Naomi murmured.

"For what?"

"I was jealous because I thought he loved you more. And it's horrible to think that, feel that, because he's . . ."

"A psychopath, a sexual sadist, a serial killer."

Each almost-flippant term made Naomi wince.

"He's all that, Nome. But he's still our father. That's just fact. So forget it. I guess I was jealous some, because he let you be more. You were Mama's deal; I was his. Anyway. Mama talked to the movie people, too. He pushed her into it, just kept asking and making it like it was the best thing for us—you and me."

They kept their hands linked, leaned toward each other over the table now. "Why would he want it?"

"The attention, the fame. He's right up there with Bundy, Dahmer, Ramirez. Serial killers, Naomi. Pay attention."

"I don't want to pay attention. Why do they want to make a movie about him? Why do people want to see it?"

"It's as much about you as him. Maybe more." He turned his hand over, gripped hers harder. "The title's you, not him. How many eleven-year-old kids stop a serial killer?"

"I don't want—"

"True or false? He'd have killed Ashley if you hadn't gotten her out."

Saying nothing, she reached for the pendant Ashley had given her on top of the world. Nodded.

"And when he'd finished with her, he'd have gotten another. Who knows how many he'd have killed.

"I look like him a little."

"No, you don't! Your eyes are the same color. That's all."

"I look like him some."

"You're not like him."

"No, I'm not like him." And the determination, the bright intelligence in those eyes spoke as truly as the words. "I'm never going to be like him. Don't you be like Mama. Don't let him twist you up. He tried to do that to us all our lives, just like with her. It's praise and punish. It's how they get you to do what they want, how they train you."

She understood it, or some of it. And yet. "He never hit us."

"He'd take things away—promise something, then if we didn't do something just the way he said, he'd say how we couldn't go or couldn't have. Then he'd show up with presents, remember? He put up the basketball hoop for me, brought you that American Girl doll. I got that brand-new catcher's mitt, you got that little heart locket. Stuff like that. Then if we did anything even a little out of line, he'd take what he'd given us away. Or we couldn't go to a party we'd been counting on, or the movies."

"He said we were going to Kings Dominion, and we were so excited. I didn't get my room picked up all the way, so he said we weren't going because I didn't respect what I had. You were so mad at me."

"I was seven. I didn't get it wasn't you. He didn't want me to get it wasn't you. Maybe we'd give Mama a little sass when he wasn't around because we knew she wouldn't tell him, but we never bucked him. Never. We lived by his moods, just like you said, and that's how he liked it."

She'd never left so much as a pair of socks out of place in her room after that, she remembered. Yes, he'd trained her.

"What are you reading to come up with all this?"

"A lot of books in the library on psychiatry and psychology. A lot of stuff online, too. I'm going to study and be a psychiatrist."

From her vast advantage of twenty-three months, she smiled a little. "I thought you were going to be a pro basketball player."

"It's what Seth and Harry, and Mama, need to hear now. And I like basketball. I'll play my ass off if it helps me get into Harvard."

"Harvard? Are you serious?"

"They don't have scholarships, but they have like incentive programs. I'm going to get into Harvard, study medicine, get my degree. And maybe I'll use it to get into the FBI, into behavior analysis."

"God, Mason, you're fourteen."

"You were three years younger when you saved a life." He leaned forward, those golden brown eyes intense. "I'm never going to be like him. I'm going to be somebody who helps stop people like him, who learns to understand so they can. You stopped him, Naomi. But he's not the only one."

"If you do all that, you'll never put it behind you."

"You put something behind you, Nome, it's got its eyes on your back. I'd rather keep it in front of me, so I can see where it's going."

It scared her, what he'd said, and more the coolheaded logic behind it. He was her baby brother, often a pain in her butt, regularly goofy, and a slave to Marvel comics.

And he not only had aspirations, he had lofty ones he spoke of as if he'd already checked them off a list.

He'd spied on their mother. Naomi could admit to watching her mother—and closely. Living with Susan was like carrying around something delicate. You watched every step so you didn't stumble, drop the delicate so it shattered.

She could admit to herself, and now to Mason, a huge sense of disappointment with their mother. Mixed in with the sincere effort to make some sort of a life had been lies and deception. And over a man who'd taken lives, ruined others.

Was it love that drove her? Naomi wondered.

If it was, she didn't want any part of it.

She'd try sex, because whatever the books and songs and movies said, she knew one didn't have to walk arm in arm with the other. She considered the best way to go about it, knew there was no way she'd discuss birth control with her mother. And as much as she loved Seth and Harry, such a conversation would be mortifying.

So the next time she went to the doctor, she'd ask. Then when she decided to have sex, she'd be prepared.

Maybe Mason was right, and if she put it, or tried to put it, all behind her, it meant the whole ugly business could rush up to nip at her heels anytime it wanted.

Like with the movie.

So as fall came to New York, she set it aside. She didn't like the idea of keeping it straight in front of her—couldn't you just trip over it then? But setting aside seemed like a good compromise.

And for right now her mother got out of bed every day, got dressed, went to work. Naomi kept busy with school, her yearbook and school paper assignments, and considering which boy it made the most sense to have sex with when the time came.

But she made it a point to get her uncle alone and speak to him about the movie.

"It's coming out in just a few weeks now."

"Honey, I know. Harry and I planned to talk to you and Mason about it."

"But not Mama?"

"I'll talk with her. I hate having to. She's doing so well right now. But the movie doesn't change anything. Your lives are here now. That part of your lives is over."

"Not for her. You need to talk with Mason."

"Why?"

"You need to talk with him. It's his to tell."

Naomi didn't know what her uncle said to her mother, but after a couple of dark days, Susan came out again.

She took Naomi shopping for a new dress for homecoming, insisted on making a day of it. A rare thing.

"Anything looks good on you, honey, you're so tall and slim, but don't you want something with some color?"

Naomi turned in the dressing room, checked front and back on the short black dress with its cinched waist and square-necked bodice.

"I'll be taking pictures more than dancing. The black's better for that than the pink."

"You ought to have a date," Susan insisted. "Why aren't you going out with that nice boy anymore? Mark."

"Oh." Naomi just shrugged. Her mother wasn't the type you told a boy hadn't been satisfied just touching your breast. "He's all right, but I didn't want a date for homecoming."

"Well, when I was your age, having a date for homecoming was the most important thing in the world. So maybe you're smarter than I was. But I just love the pink, and it has that sparkle on the skirt."

"I don't know if I'm a sparkle-pink girl."

"Every girl deserves some sparkle pink. You want the black, that's fine. Gosh, you're so grown-up it takes my breath. But we're getting the pink, too."

"Mama, you can't buy both."

"I can. You can wear the black since you'll be taking pictures, and save the pink for something special. I haven't given you and Mason enough special."

"Sure you have."

"Not nearly enough, but I'm going to. We're going to buy those dresses, and have a fancy lunch. Then we're going to hunt up the perfect accessories."

Naomi laughed, happy to see some sparkle—not on the pink but in her mother's eyes. "My camera's my accessory."

"Not this time. You'd probably be better off with Seth and Harry there, but we'll find just the right things. Shoes and a bag, and earrings. I know you wanted to go shopping with your girlfriends today, but—"

"Mama, I love doing this with you."

"It all went so fast. I see that now. It seemed so slow, and some days— and nights—lasted forever. But I see now, looking at you, so grown-up, how fast it all went. I wasn't with you."

No, no, the sparkle was dying out. "You always were."

"No." Susan laid her hands on Naomi's cheeks. "I wasn't. I'm really going to try to be. I . . . I'm sorry about the movie."

"It doesn't matter. Don't worry."

"I love you so much."

"I love you back."

"I'm going to take the pink dress out to the saleslady, have her get started. You go on and change, then we'll have lunch."

They bought the dresses, and shoes, and a pretty bag that sparkled— and made her mother smile again. At Naomi's urging Susan bought herself a red sweater and suede boots. They came home flushed and exhausted, modeled everything all over again.

When Naomi dropped into bed that night, she thought she'd had the best day of her life.

October turned brisk, and the light Naomi loved best slanted gold over the burnished trees of the parks.

To please her mother she wore the pink instead of the black to homecoming, and though it wasn't a date, she asked Anson Chaffins, a friend—and the editor of the school paper—to pick her up.

And saw the glimmer of tears in her mother's eyes from joy instead of sorrow when she and Anson dutifully posed for pictures before she could get out of the house.

On Halloween Susan dressed up as a flapper, coordinating with Seth and Harry in their zoot suits to hand out candy to the ghosts, goblins, princesses, and Jedi knights. As it was the first time Susan had dressed up for the holiday, Naomi browbeat Mason into spending part of the evening at home instead of out with his friends doing God knew what.

"It's like she's turned a corner, and she's really moving forward now."

Mason, who'd made himself into a vampire hobo, shrugged. "I hope you're right."

Naomi gave him an elbow in the ribs. "Try to be happy because I am right."

But she wasn't.

The third week of January, in a quick cold snap that blew in some thin snow, she rushed home at lunch. Anson came with her.

"You didn't have to come," she said as she dug out her keys.

"Hey, any excuse to get out of school for a half hour."

Anson Chaffins was a senior, gawky and on the geeky side, but he was, to Naomi's mind, a good editor and a really good writer. Plus, he'd done her a favor at homecoming.

He'd put what she thought of as half-assed, clumsy moves on her that night, but hadn't pushed anything.

As a result, they got along just fine.

She let him in, turned to the alarm pad to key in the code.

"I'll go up, get my camera bag. Which I'd have had with me if you'd told me you wanted shots of the drama club rehearsing."

"Maybe I forgot so we could get out for thirty." He grinned at her, shoved up his dark-framed glasses. He shoved them up constantly, as if his eagle-beak nose served as their sliding board.

Behind them his eyes were pale, quiet blue.

He glanced around. "Maybe you've got like a Coke or whatever. No point leaving empty-handed."

"Sure, we've always got Cokes. Do you remember where the kitchen is?"

"Yeah. This house is totally cool. You want a Coke while I'm at it?"

"Grab two." She yanked off her gloves, stuffed them in the pocket of her coat.

He gave her that half-smirking grin, the one that curled the side of his mouth. "Maybe you got chips?"

She rolled her eyes, plucked off her cap. "Probably. Get whatever. I won't be long."

"Take your time—we got twenty-five left on our pass. Hey! This yours?"

He walked up to a black-and-white photo study of an old man dozing on a park bench with a floppy-eared mutt curled beside him.

"Yeah. I gave it to Harry for his birthday a couple weeks ago. And he put it up right in the foyer."

"*Excelente* work, Carson."

"Thanks, Chaffins."

Amused—he called everyone by their last name, insisted everyone use his—she started upstairs.

It surprised her to see Kong sitting outside her mother's bedroom door. His habit was to wait in Mason's room, or, in better weather, belly out through the dog door to sun on the patio—or do what he had to do in the corner designated for it.

"Hey, boy." She gave him a quick rub as she passed, glanced back when he whined. "No time. Just passing through."

But he whined again, scratched at her mother's door. And Naomi felt something flutter and drop in her belly.

"Is Mama home?" Had the good stretch come to a dip?

Her mother should be at work, with Harry and Seth. There was, she knew, a party of twenty-two coming in for a retirement lunch, so it was all hands on deck.

Naomi eased the door open, saw that the curtains had been drawn closed—a bad sign. And saw in the dim light her mother lying on top of the bed.

"Mama."

She wore the red sweater they'd bought on their shopping spree rather than her white work shirt and black vest.

Kong jumped on the bed—something he was only allowed to do in Mason's room—licked her mother's hand, and whimpered.

Her mother lay so still.

"Mama," Naomi said again, and switched on the bedside lamp.

So still, so pale—and her eyes weren't quite shut.

"Mama. Mama." Naomi gripped Susan's shoulder, shook. Took her hand, found it cold. "Mama! Wake up. Wake up!"

The pills were right there, there by the lamp. No, not the pills, the bottle. The empty bottle.

"Wake up!" Gripping her mother's hands, she pulled. Susan's head lolled, fell forward. "Stop it. Stop it." She tried to get her arms around Susan, pull her off the bed.

On her feet, on her feet, make her walk.

"Hey, Carson, what the hell are you shouting about? You need to chill— What . . ."

"Call an ambulance. Call nine-one-one. Hurry, hurry."

He stood frozen for a moment, staring as Susan's limp body fell back on the bed, and her eyelids opened like shades to show the staring eyes behind them. "Wow. Is that your mom?"

"Call nine-one-one." Naomi laid an ear to her mother's heart, then began to press on it. "She's not breathing. Tell them to hurry. Tell them she took Elavil. Overdosed on Elavil."

Staring, he fumbled out his phone, punching in 911 with one hand, shoving up his glasses with the other, while Naomi did CPR, puffing out her breath as she worked.

"Yeah, yeah, we need an ambulance. She overdosed on Eldervil."

"Elavil!"

"Sorry, Elavil. Crap, Carson, I don't know the address."

She called it out while tears ran down her cheeks, mixed with sweat.

"Mama, Mama, please!"

"No, she's not awake, she's not moving. Her daughter's doing CPR. I-I-I don't know. Maybe, um, like forty."

"She's thirty-seven." Naomi shouted it. "Just hurry."

"They're coming." Anson dropped down beside her, hesitated, then patted Naomi's shoulder. "She—the operator—she said they were on the way. They're coming."

He swallowed, moistened his lips, then touched his fingers to Susan's hand.

It felt . . . soft and cold. Soft like he could push his fingers through it. Cold like it had lain outside in the winter air.

"Um, oh jeez, Carson. Ah, man, look, hey." He kept one hand on

Susan's, put his other on Naomi's shoulder again. "She's cold, man. I think . . . I think she's dead."

"No, no, no, no." Naomi laid her mouth on her mother's, blew in her breath, willed her to breathe back.

But there was nothing there. Like the pictures of the women in her father's cellar, there was nothing left in the eyes but death.

She sat back. She didn't weep, not yet, but smoothed back her mother's hair. There was no weight pressing on her chest, no churning in her belly. There was, as in her mother's eyes, nothing.

She remembered the feeling—the same as when she'd swum through the air toward the sheriff's office on that hot summer dawn.

In shock, she thought. She was in shock. And her mother was dead.

She heard the bell, got slowly to her feet. "I need to go let them in. Don't leave her alone."

"Okay. I'll, um . . . Okay."

She walked out—sort of like sleepwalking to Anson's eyes. He looked back at the dead woman.

They wouldn't get back to school in thirty.

Five

She wore the black dress to her mother's funeral. She'd never been to a funeral before, and this was more a memorial as there would be no burial.

Seth sat down with her and Mason to talk about that. Did they want to take their mother back to Pine Meadows to bury her?

No, no, no.

Did they want to find a cemetery in New York?

It surprised her how firm Mason had been. No cemetery here either. If she'd been happy in New York, she'd still be alive.

So they'd had her cremated, and in the spring, they'd rent a boat and send her ashes to the air and the sea.

There were tears, of course, but for Naomi they came from rage as much as grief.

She had to talk to the police. For the second time in her life, the police came to her home, went through her home, asked questions.

"I'm Detective Rossini. I'm so sorry for your loss. I know this is a very difficult time, but I have some questions. Can I come in, talk to you?"

Naomi knew that some cops on TV and in the movies were female and pretty, but she'd assumed that was mostly made up. But Rossini looked like she could play a detective on TV.

"Okay."

She'd gone to her room because she didn't know what else to do, not with all the police, with Seth and Harry talking to them. And with her mother . . .

Rossini came in, sat on the side of the bed, facing Naomi, who sat in her desk chair with her knees folded up to her chin.

"Can you tell me why you came home today, why you and your friend weren't in school?"

"We got a pass to come home, get my camera. We work on the school newspaper. I'm supposed to take pictures of rehearsal—the drama club. Is he still here? Is Chaffins—Anson—here?"

"My partner already talked to him. We had him taken back to school."

"He'll tell everybody." Naomi pressed her face to her knees. "He'll tell everybody about my mother."

"I'm sorry, Naomi. Can you tell me what happened when you got home?"

"Chaffins wanted a Coke, so I told him to go get a couple of them while I went up for my camera. And Kong—our dog—Kong was outside my mother's room. He kept whining. He usually stays in Mason's room or in the courtyard when we're at school, but . . . Her door was closed, and I opened it. I thought . . . I thought she was sleeping or not feeling well. I couldn't wake her up, and I saw the pills. I mean the empty bottle. Chaffins came upstairs, and I told him to call nine-one-one. I tried CPR. We took a class, and I knew how. I tried, but I couldn't make her breathe."

"She was on the bed when you went in."

"I tried to get her up, to wake her up enough to walk. If she'd taken too many pills, I could make her walk, and get her to the hospital."

"She'd done that before? Taken too many pills?"

Naomi just nodded with her face pressed against her knees.

"When did you see her last, before you came home from school?"

"This morning. Harry fixed breakfast, but she didn't come down for it. I went upstairs, and she was just getting up. She seemed fine. She said she had some errands to run before she went to work, and she'd get breakfast later. She said, 'Have a good day at school.'"

She looked up then. "My brother. My brother, Mason."

"Your uncle's gone to the school to get him. Don't worry."

"Do you know who my father is?"

"Yes, Naomi, I do. And I know that for the second time in your life you had to face something no one should ever have to."

"Will everyone know now? Even though we changed our names, will everyone know?"

"We're going to do the best we can to keep that out of the press." Rossini waited a moment. "Do you know how often your mother and your father communicated?"

"She wrote to him, and went to see him a few times, too, since we moved to New York. Mason found out, and he told me. She pretended she wasn't, but she was. We didn't tell Uncle Seth or Harry. The movie—she talked to the movie people because he wanted her to. Mason found that out, too. But she'd been trying really hard, and for a couple months or more, she'd been doing good. She'd been happy. Happier. I don't guess she's ever been happy since that night I found . . ."

"All right. Your uncle said he'd call your grandparents, and Mr. Dobbs is right downstairs. Do you want me to have him come up, stay with you?"

"No, not right now. Ma'am? You asked about them communicating. Did Mama talk to him today? This morning?"

"I don't believe your mother and father spoke today."

"But there's something. He wrote something to her, didn't he? Something that had her coming home, after she'd been doing so well, and taking those pills."

"We're asking questions so we can give you answers," Rossini said as she rose.

"You have some. I didn't see a note in her room. I wasn't looking. I was trying to . . . I didn't see a note, but she had to write one. She had to say good-bye." The sob wanted to rip out of her chest. "However sad she was, she loved us. She did. She'd say good-bye."

"I'm sure she loved you. She did leave a note, addressed to all of you. It was in your uncle's room. She put it on his dresser."

"I want to see it. I have a right to read it. It was addressed to me. I want to read what she wrote before she took those pills and left us."

"Your uncle said you would. Wait here."

What had he done? Naomi wondered, and the rage began to root. What had he done to make her mother so sad, so fast? So fatally?

She stood up when Rossini came back in. She wouldn't read this last thing her mother said to her curled in a chair, but on her feet.

"You'll need to read it through the evidence bag. It still needs to be processed."

"It doesn't matter." Naomi took the bag, stepped to the window and the thin winter light.

I'm so sorry. I made so many mistakes, so many bad choices, told so many lies. I told lies to the people who deserved me to tell the truth. I told them because he said I should. No matter how many times I tried to break free, I just couldn't. Now he has, after all the mistakes I made, all the hurt I caused because Tom said I should. He's divorcing me so he can try to marry some other woman. One who's been writing him and coming to see him for more than two years. He sent me papers from a lawyer for a divorce, and a letter that said such cruel and awful things. But some of those things are true. I am weak and stupid. I am useless. I didn't protect my children when I had the chance. Seth, you did that. You did that, Harry. You gave us a home, and I know you'll look after Naomi and Mason, do right by them as I never have. Mason, you're so smart, and you made me proud every day. I hope one day you'll understand why Mama had to go away. Naomi, I'm not strong and brave like you. It's so hard to try to be. I'm so tired, honey. I just want to go to sleep. You'll look after Mason, and both of you will listen to Seth

and Harry. You'll have a better life now. One day you'll know that's
true. One day you'll forgive me.

"Why should I forgive her? She left us because he didn't want her
anymore? She came home and took all those pills because she was *tired*?"

"Naomi—"

"No, no! Don't make excuses. You're the police. You didn't know her,
you don't know me or any of us. But you know what this is?" She threw
the bag on her bed, fisted her hands as if she could fight something. "It's
what a coward does. He killed her. He killed her just like he killed all
those other women. But they didn't have a choice. She did. She let it
happen. She let him kill her when we were all right here."

"You're right. I think you're right. But there are other means of torture
besides physical. I can't tell you how to feel, but I can tell you I think you
have a right to be angry. You have a right to be mad as hell. When some
of the mad wears off, I hope you'll talk to someone."

"Another therapist. I'm done with that. Done. A lot of good it did her."

"You're not your mother. But if you don't want to talk to a therapist,
to a friend, to a priest, to your uncle." She took a card out of her pocket.
"You can talk to me."

"You're the second cop who's given me a card and said that."

"Did you talk to the other cop?"

"We moved away."

"Well." Rossini set the card on Naomi's dresser, then walked over and
picked up the evidence bag. "Cops are good listeners. Detective Angela
Rossini. Anytime."

So three days later, Naomi put on the black dress. She used the curling
iron because her mother had liked it best when she wore her hair long
with some waves in it. She didn't give any of her angry words to Seth—he
looked sickly and shaken. She didn't give them to Mason, not with the

hollow look in his eyes. Or to Harry, who seemed to need to tend to all of them at once.

She kept them inside, where they crawled through her like fiery ants, and went to the restaurant.

They'd closed for the day to hold the memorial. Harry had done most of the work—insisted on it. Putting out flowers and photos, choosing music, preparing food.

Her grandparents came. She and Mason saw them several times a year since they'd moved out of Pine Meadows, and it hadn't taken long to understand that all the hard things their father had said about their mother's parents had been more lies.

They were kind and loving—forgiving, she thought. They'd forgiven the daughter who'd cut them out of her life and kept their only grandchildren from them. They'd paid for all the therapy, and never—at least not in her hearing—said an unkind word about their daughter.

They never spoke of Thomas David Bowes.

Everyone who worked at the restaurant came, and so many of Seth's and Harry's friends. Some of her teachers, some of Mason's came. Some parents brought some of their friends, at least for a short time.

And Detective Rossini came.

"I didn't know the police came to funerals like this."

"I wanted to pay my respects. And to see how you were doing."

"I'm all right. It's hardest, I think, on my uncle. Even harder than it is on my grandparents. He thought he could save her. He thought he had. He tried, every day. Harry, he tried, too. But right now he's mostly worried about his Seth. About Mason and me, too, but mostly about his Seth. Harry worked hard to put all this together, to make it look so nice, to try to make it that celebration of life people talk about. But she didn't have much of a life to celebrate."

"I think you're wrong. She had you and Mason, and that's a celebration."

"That's a nice thing to say."

"It's a true thing. Did you take that picture?"

Naomi glanced at the photo of her mother dancing with Seth. "How did you know?"

"I'm the police." Rossini smiled a little. "It's a happy moment, and you knew how to capture it. But that's my favorite."

Rossini stepped over to the photo Naomi had taken with a timer. Her mother flanked by her children. Harry had set it in front of a big vase of pink roses, because her mother had favored pink.

"You can see she was proud of you and your brother."

"Is that what you see?"

"Yes. Cops are good listeners, and they're trained observers. She was proud. Hold on to that. I have to get back to work."

"Thank you for coming," Naomi said, as she'd said to everyone.

Surprised, she stood where she was as Mark Ryder came up to her.

"Hey," he said.

"Hey."

He was tall, great-looking with big brown eyes, glossy hair that curled just the right amount at the ends.

"I'm really sorry about your mom and all."

"Thanks. It's nice you came. It's nice."

"I'm sorry, you know? My mom died when I was a baby."

"But . . . I met your mom."

"My dad married her when I was about three. She's great—and she's, like Mom, but my, you know, *mom* died."

"I didn't know. I'm sorry, Mark."

"Yeah, well, it's hard, you know, and I wanted to say I'm sorry."

Touched, she stepped closer, hugged him. Realized the mistake when he hugged her back—with a hand sliding down to her butt.

She pulled back. "It's my mother's memorial."

"Yeah, yeah, sorry. I just thought . . ." He shrugged, managed a half laugh. "Whatever."

"Thanks for coming," she told him. "You can get a soft drink at the bar, if you want."

"Yeah, maybe. See you around."

Alone, Naomi turned. She could sneak into the storeroom, get some quiet, get some time alone before anyone noticed she wasn't there.

But she nearly walked into Anson Chaffins.

"Um. Hey." He shoved up his glasses, then stuck his hands in his pockets. "I guess it's weird but I was, like, you know, there, so I thought I should come and say . . . whatever."

"Let's go sit over there. People won't bug me if I'm sitting down with somebody."

"I saw some of the guys from school. But I kind of hung back until they went off. It's weird, like I said. People want to know, you know, what it was like, and don't want to ask you. Well, plus, you haven't been back to school. Are you coming back?"

"Yeah, next week."

"It'll be weird."

She gave a half laugh—he wrote better than he talked, she thought. "I need to keep up my grades—Mason, too. We have to think about getting into college."

"I'm heading to Columbia next fall."

"You got in?"

"It looks good for it. I got a couple backups, but it looks good. I'm going to study journalism."

"You'll be good at it."

"Yeah." He shifted. "So. I heard a couple of the cops talking. You know they had to take my statement and all that? And I heard a couple of them talking about Bowes. Your mother being his wife. Thomas David Bowes."

Naomi clutched her hands together in her lap, said nothing.

"I knew the name, because of the movie. And I read the book, too. You're that Naomi."

"Does everyone know?"

"Like I said, I heard the cops talking, and I knew who they were talking about, and I'd read the book. I did some research—more, I mean. You're Naomi Bowes."

"Carson. That's my legal name."

"Yeah, I get that. Look, I didn't say anything to anybody."

"Don't. I just want to finish school. Mason needs to finish school."

"I haven't told anybody, but look, other people can do research, especially now that the movie's such a big hit. Hell, lots of kids who don't read go to the movies. What are you going to do?"

"I'm going to finish school. I'm going to go to college."

"I won't tell anybody, right?" He shoved his glasses back up his nose. "It's just between you and me, okay? I want you to tell me the story. Hold on."

He held up a hand, edged closer with his glasses sliding down again. He just took them off.

"From your point of view, *your* story, Carson. We can keep where you live and all that out of it. I won't tell anybody—and that's a lot, right, because I want to be a journalist and this is a really big story. But I'll hold back some details."

He picked up his glasses, sat back, pushed them on. "I don't have to do that."

"My mother just died."

"Yeah. Otherwise I wouldn't have put it together. I don't tell anybody, and you give me the whole story—first person. We'll go out a few times, somewhere quiet, and I'll record your story. It's a big deal, and if I do it right, it could land me an internship at the *Times*. You've never talked to anybody, not Simon Vance, not the scriptwriter, the director, the actors. Your father did. Your mom, too, but not you. I did my research."

They were friends—she thought they were friends. He'd been with her when she'd found her mother. He'd called the ambulance. And now . . .

"Simon Vance and the screenwriter beat you to it, Chaffins. Nobody's going to care."

"Shit, are you kidding me? Everybody's going to care. Look, we'll meet up. You can come to my place during the day, after school. My parents will be at work, and nobody has to know. I gotta split. I'll text you when and where."

When he rushed off, she sat a moment, a little stunned, a little sick.

Why was she surprised? she wondered. Because she'd thought he was, at least a little bit, a friend? Should she be grateful he hadn't already published what he knew in the school paper?

The hell with it, she thought. Just the hell with all of it.

She got up—before someone could sit down and try to comfort her—and made her way back to the kitchen. She could slip into the storeroom from there for the belated alone.

But Harry was right behind her.

He pointed to a stool. "Sit." And sat himself on a stack of boxes. "Now tell me what that boy said to upset you."

"It wasn't anything."

"Don't lie to me."

She jerked back. He never used that sharp, angry tone. "Harry."

"We're going to stop lying to each other. I knew your mother was lying about going to the prison, about keeping in contact. I knew, and I kept it from Seth. I didn't tell him because it would upset him. And that's a lie. Omission is a lie."

"You knew?"

"And maybe if I'd said something . . ." He rubbed his tired eyes. "We'll never know."

"We knew. Mason found out and told me. We didn't say either."

"Well, where did all that get us, baby? Look where we are now. No more lies, no more omissions." He leaned forward, took her hands. His eyes, so blue against the caramel, held that innate kindness he showed her every day. "When Seth asked me about taking you, your brother, your mother into the home in D.C., I said of course. But I thought, It won't be for long. Of course we have to help—Seth needs to help his family—but they'll get on their feet and get their own in, oh, six months or a year. I could open our home for a year. I did it because I love Seth."

"I know you do."

"What I didn't count on was falling in love with you. With Mason. With your mother. That's what happened. When we talked about selling the house, moving to New York, I didn't do it just for Seth. I did it for all

of us. Because we'd become a family. You're my girl, Naomi. Same as if
we were blood. I mean that."

"I love you, Harry. I do, so much." The tears came then, hot but clean.
"I know how much you've done for us, all you've given us."

"I don't want to hear about that. I could tell you what you've done for me,
what you've given me. I bet it balances out pretty square. What I want, and
need, I think what we all want and need from today on, my baby, is truth.
Let's start right here. What did Anson say to put that look on your face?"

"He knows who we are. He heard some of the police talking, and he
figured it out. He wants to be a journalist, and he wants the story. From me."

"I'll have a talk with him."

"No, sir. No, Harry. What's the point? He knows, and you can't make
it so he doesn't. He said he wouldn't say where I—we are, would leave out
some details, but—"

"You don't trust him. Why should you?"

She thought of Mark's hand sliding down to her butt, of Chaffins's
blind ambition. "I don't trust anybody but you, Seth, and Mason."

"We can put you and Mason in private school."

"It'll just happen again. We can move again, and it'll happen again.
Mama's gone, and it was hardest on her. We couldn't protect her from
him or herself."

"Nobody's going to hurt my baby girl."

"I thought he was a friend. But nobody stays your friend when they
find out who you are."

"If they don't, they weren't worth your friendship."

"But how do you know, ever, who is?" She remembered the card the
policewoman who looked like she could play one on TV had given her,
and took it out of her bag. "Detective Rossini."

"What about her?"

"I think, maybe, she's a friend. He smokes pot—Chaffins—sells it a
little, too."

Harry sighed. "Naomi, I understand peer pressure and the need for
experimentation, and this isn't the time to—"

"I don't do drugs. Neither does Mason." She frowned at the card as she spoke. "He wants Harvard and the FBI—Mason won't take any chances with that. Chaffins wants Columbia, and the *New York Times*. It wouldn't look good for him to get arrested for possession, maybe suspended from school."

Harry's eyebrows lifted. "Blackmail?"

"That's what he's doing. I'd be ratting him out to the cops—and I'm not proud of it. But I think Detective Rossini would go have that talk with him, and it might work, long enough for me to write the story."

"What? What story?"

"I'm not as good a writer as Chaffins, but I can do this." It came to her, like a lightning flash on a hot summer night. "If I write the story—as Naomi Bowes—and sell it, maybe even to the *Times*, he's got nothing. I just need some time, and Detective Rossini could get me that. I write the story, like Chaffins said—from my point of view. And then he can't. No one would care after that what some jerk writes about me. Mason? He won't care."

"Honey, are you sure?"

"No one's going to do this to me, to us. I'm sure."

"Talk to the detective. If you decide this is really what you want to do, well, we're going to be behind you."

S he went back to school, forced herself to continue with the yearbook committee, the school paper. She ignored the furious stares from Chaffins—and completed the crap assignments he handed her. Because whatever Rossini had said to him kept him quiet, and she could comfort herself that in four months, he'd graduate and be out of her life.

After the Oscars, where the screenwriter for *Daughter of Evil* took home the gold, and the now-fifteen-year-old actress who'd played Naomi Bowes walked the red carpet in Alexander McQueen, after the movie-tie-in release of the book hung for sixteen weeks on the bestseller list, the *New York Times* ran a three-part article on consecutive Sundays.

She wasn't at all surprised to receive an angry email from Anson Chaffins.

First you sic that cop on me, now this! You're a lying bitch, and I'll tell everybody who you are, where you are, what you are. I gave you the idea. You stole my article.

She wrote back only once.

My life, my story, and I never agreed to your *deal*. Tell anyone you want.

But he didn't tell anyone. On her own she sent Detective Rossini flowers as a thank-you. She changed her email address, her phone number, and buckled down to focus on her schoolwork, her photography, and her family.

She told herself she'd put the past in the past now, where it needed to stay. And she'd really begun her life as Naomi Carson.

DEPTH OF FIELD

Ends and beginnings—there are no such things.
There are only middles.

ROBERT FROST

Six

Sunrise Cove, Washington State, 2016

It hadn't been impulse. Naomi assured herself of that as she roamed the rambling old house on the bluff. A little rash, maybe. A gamble, absolutely. She'd taken plenty of gambles, so what was one more?

But holy shit, she'd bought a house. A house older than she was—about four times older. A house on the opposite side of the country from her family. A house, she admitted, that needed work. And furniture.

And a serious cleaning.

An investment, she told herself, wincing at the grimy kitchen with its dated appliances—surely older than she was—and cracked linoleum floor.

So she'd clean it up, fix it up, paint it up. Then she could put it back on the market, or rent it out. She didn't have to live there. That was a choice—something else she'd made plenty of before.

It would be a project. Something to keep her busy when she wasn't working. A home base, she considered, and tried the faucet of the chipped porcelain sink.

It coughed, banged, and then spewed out fits of water.

A home base with bad plumbing.

So, she'd make a list. Maybe it would've been smarter to have made a list before buying the house, but she'd make one. *Plumber* went straight to number one.

Gingerly, she opened the cabinet under the sink. It smelled a little dank, looked dingy, and the ancient bottle of Drano didn't inspire confidence.

Definitely find a plumber.

And a whole bunch of cleaning supplies.

She blew out a breath, pulled her phone out of a pocket of her cargo pants, opened an app.

Hire plumber went on first.

She added more as she wandered back out, through a dining room with a wonderful fireplace of carved black wood. A chimney sweep. Did people still become chimney sweeps? Somebody must inspect and clean chimneys, and since there were five fireplaces in the old house, *chimney sweep* definitely went on the list.

Why had she bought a house with five fireplaces? And ten bedrooms? And six and a half baths?

She wouldn't think about that now. Now she'd work on what to do about it.

The floors were solid. They needed refinishing, but the real estate agent had really sold the wide-planked ponderosa pine. She could do some research, see if she could refinish them herself. Otherwise, *flooring guy*.

And then there was *tile guy*—would that be the same person?

What she needed, Naomi thought as she started up the creaky stairs, was a contractor. And bids. And a plan.

What she needed, she corrected, as she stood on the landing where the hallway shot left and right, was her head examined. How the hell could she manage a house this size, and one in this shape?

Why in God's name had she tied herself to this remote dot of land in Washington State? She liked to travel—new places, new views, new ideas. Just her and her equipment. Free to go anywhere. And now she had this anchor of a dilapidated house weighing her down.

No, it hadn't been impulse. It had been lunacy.

She walked past dingy walls and, okay, gorgeous old doors, by far too many rooms for one solitary woman, and felt that old, familiar pressure in her chest.

She would not have an anxiety attack because she'd been an idiot.

Breathing slowly, deliberately, she turned in to what the real estate agent had billed as the master.

It was big and bright, and yes the floors needed work, and the walls were an awful faded blue that looked like cloudy pool water, and the old glass slider needed to go.

But she pulled and tugged it open on its rusted runners and stepped out onto the wide, sturdy deck.

And this was why, she thought as all the pressure lifted into sheer bliss. This was why.

The inlet, deep gleaming blue, curved and widened, split around knots of land green with the earliest whispers of spring. Shorelines climbed up, upholstered with trees, as the water traveled out through a narrow channel into deeper blues. In the distance just west, mountains rolled up against the sky to back a thick forest of green shadows.

And straight out, beyond the inlet, the channel, the knots and knuckles of land, spread the deeper blue of the sound.

Her bluff wasn't particularly high, but it afforded a pure, unobstructed view of water and sky and land, and for her, an indescribable sense of peace.

Her place. She leaned against the rail a moment, breathed it in. She'd known it was her place the moment she'd stepped out here on that breezy February afternoon.

Whatever needed to be done to make the house habitable would be done. But no one could take this view, this sense of *hers* away.

Since she'd left her equipment downstairs, she took her phone, switched to camera mode. She framed in a shot, checked it, took another. She sent it to Mason, Seth, Harry—what she listed in her contacts as *My Guys*—with a simple message.

This is why.

She tucked her phone away, thought the hell with lists. She was going into town and buying supplies. She'd figure out the rest as she went.

The little town made most of its living off the water with its marina, dive shop, the kayak and canoe rentals, the fish market. On Water Street—naturally—gift shops, coffee shops, restaurants, and the Sunrise Hotel faced the curve of the marina with its bobbing boats.

She spent a couple nights in the hotel when she'd followed her nose into Sunrise Cove. She'd wanted to add to her portfolio of stock photography, beef up her portfolio of fine photography, and had found plenty of studies for both.

She'd caught sight of the house—just a piece of it—outside her hotel window, and found herself amused and intrigued by the way it angled away from the town, its people, toward the water and the wood.

She'd wanted some photos of it, had asked for directions. Before she knew it, she was heading out to what the locals called Point Bluff with John James Mooney, Realtor.

Now it belonged to her, Naomi thought, and parked in front of the grocery store.

A few hundred dollars later she loaded up food, cleaning supplies, paper products, lightbulbs, laundry detergent—which was stupid, as she didn't know if the old washer worked—plus a basic set of pots and pans, a coffeemaker, and a vacuum cleaner she'd purchased at the neighboring hardware store.

She'd also gotten the name of a contractor from both places—the same name, so obviously a popular guy. Deciding there was no time like the present, she called him then and there, made an appointment to meet him for a walk-through in an hour.

She headed back, pleased it took a solid ten minutes on winding roads to reach the house. Far enough away for privacy, close enough for convenience.

Then she opened the back of her 4Runner, looked at the haul, and swore the next trip in she'd make a list.

That list, she realized when she started unloading groceries, would have included cleaning the refrigerator *before* buying food to go in it.

By the time she'd cleaned it, filled it, and started out for the next load, she saw the black truck winding up the road toward her.

She slipped a hand in her pocket, closed it over her pocketknife. Just a precaution.

The truck pulled up. A man in a ball cap and sunglasses leaned out one window. A big black dog with a polka dot bandanna leaned out the other.

"Ms. Carson?"

"That's right."

"Kevin Banner." He said something to the dog that had its head retreating before he got out of the truck.

She judged him early thirties, sandy hair curling out from under the cap. A good strong jaw, a compact build. He held out a hand.

"It's nice to meet you."

Workingman's hand, she thought, and relaxed. "Thanks for coming."

"I heard somebody from back east bought the place. It's something, isn't it?"

"It's something."

He grinned, shifted his weight. "It's been sitting empty about ten years now—I guess Mr. Mooney told you—since Mr. Parkerson died, and Mrs. Parkerson had to let it go. They ran it as a B-and-B for more than twenty years. She just couldn't keep it up, and ended up moving to Seattle to live with her daughter. Rented it out for a while here and there, but . . ."

"A big place, a lot of maintenance."

He hooked his thumbs in his front pockets, rocked back on his heels as his gaze traveled over the long rectangle of building.

"You got that. I threatened to buy it a while back—it's got history and that view—but my wife threatened to divorce me. Now maybe I'll get my hands on it, and get to keep my wife."

"Let's take a look. Is your dog okay in the truck?"

"She'll be fine."

The dog rested her head on the dash, sent Naomi a soulful look.

"I like dogs. You can bring her if you want."

"Thanks. She's a good dog, used to job sites. Come on, Molly!"

The dog leaped straight out of the window, landed neat as a gymnast, then pranced over to sniff Naomi's boots.

"Nice jump, pretty girl." When Naomi stroked Molly's head, the dog did a full-body wag.

"Maybe you can give me an idea what you're looking to do."

"Bring it into the twenty-first century. I don't mean the look," Naomi added. "But the plumbing, the lighting, the kitchen, bathrooms. I'm hoping a lot of it's cosmetic," she said as they started inside. "I can paint and handle simple DIY, but there's a lot of clunking and hissing when you use the water. And I don't know if it's safe to use any of the fireplaces. I considered tackling the floors myself—refinishing—but realize that would probably take me two or three years."

"Windows?"

"What about them?"

"Replacing them with double-paned, low-E glass, that's going to be more energy efficient, and while it costs now, it saves you in utility bills. It gets drafty in here during the winter."

"That can go on the list, and we'll see."

"I'm going to want to take a look at the wiring, make sure it's safe and up to code. We can look at the chimneys, make sure you're good there. You want to keep them wood burning?"

"I hadn't thought about it."

The dog wandered around, sniffing, exploring. It struck Naomi that Kevin did nearly the same.

"You've got some fireplaces upstairs, right? If you don't want to haul wood upstairs, you could think about gas logs on the second floor."

"That is a thought—cleaner."

"You thinking of a B-and-B?"

"No, I'm not. Not right now."

He nodded, made notes, muttered a little to himself as they toured the first floor. When they came to the kitchen, he took his cap off, scratched his head, fixed it back on again.

"I'm going to tell you straight, this kitchen's a pure gut job."

"If you'd said different, I'd wonder why everybody I asked recommended you."

"All right then. Now I'm betting the hardwood runs right on through, under this ugly-ass linoleum."

"Really? Do you think so?" The idea balanced out against the notion of needing to replace a zillion windows. "Can we check?"

"If you don't mind me messing up a corner."

"You can't make ugly-ass more ugly."

He chose a corner, pried it up with his own pocketknife. "Oh yeah, got your ponderosa pine."

"Hot damn. Take this crap up, sand, refinish, seal, right?"

"That's what I'd do."

"That's what I want."

"All right then." With his sunglasses hooked on the breast pocket of his T-shirt, Kevin ran steady hazel eyes over the space. "I can work up a couple designs for you in here."

"I'll take a stab at it. I haven't designed a kitchen, but I've shot plenty of them. Photography," she explained. "For catalogs, websites, stock photos." Hands on hips, she walked the room, imagined it down to the bare walls and floor.

"It's roomy, and that's a plus. I'd want an island, good size, for prep and for eating. I don't want sleek, but I don't want country either. More contemporary rustic, so dark cabinets, glass-fronted, go light on the countertops, figure out an interesting backsplash, and have fun with the lighting. There's room for double wall ovens there—I don't know what I'll do with double ovens, but my uncles swear by them. Gas cooktop and a snappy exhaust—like a focal point. Farm sink under that window, and that bathroom's awkward anyway. Take that out, make it a walk-in pantry. And get rid of this poky little back door. Open it up to that deck, that view. Big-ass double doors—full glass, no panes."

He'd been making notes, nodding, but looked up now.

"Ms. Carson?"

"Naomi."

"Naomi. I love my wife."

She sent him a careful smile as she turned. "That's good."

"I fell for her when I was sixteen, and didn't get up the courage to ask her out for nearly a year. I might still be thinking about kissing her for the first time if she hadn't taken that bull by the horns, so to speak. I was twenty-three when we got married—she took that over, too, or I'd be working up the nerve to ask her. We got two kids."

"Congratulations."

"I'm just saying I love my wife, and I tend to move slow in some areas. But if you and I had a longer acquaintance I'd kiss you right on the mouth."

"Should I anticipate that for later?"

He grinned again. "It could happen if you keep realizing my hopes and dreams. It was taking out that skinny door there that did it. It needs the view. Why have that view, and keep it outside? If you let me take out that wall there, I'd give you open concept into the dining room. It would make it more of an entertaining space. Living room's at the other end of the house, but you'd have this area here so people could gather when you're cooking."

"It could go on the list."

They went through, bottom to top, and then Kevin went out for his tape measure and went through it again.

By the time he'd finished, she'd put her supplies away and poured them both Cokes. They drank them on the front porch, watching the sun burn its way down through the trees.

"I'll work up an estimate. You might want to be sitting down when you read it over."

"I already got that picture."

"Once you do, we can talk about priorities, what you want done right off, what can maybe wait some. I can give you the name of a good landscaper while you're reeling from estimates."

"I'll take it, but I'm going to tackle some of that myself."

"All right. Thanks for the Coke." He handed her the empty glass. "I appreciate the chance to look the place over. If you give me the job, I'll do good work for you."

"I believe you would."

"I'll be in touch. Let's go, Molly."

She watched him drive off, felt the silence fall just like the sun behind the trees.

She'd do good work here, too, she thought. And went inside to make herself a temporary nest and work space.

She spent mornings taking pictures: sunrises—all those holy colors blending—the water, trees, birds. In the afternoons she hunted up second-hand stores, flea markets. She bought a desk and chair, a couple of lamps, and the happy prize of an old metal glider and matching chair.

Evenings, she'd put together a sandwich or scramble some eggs, pour some wine, and work on the photos she'd taken that morning.

She could and did sell some fine photography through her website and through a gallery in New York, but her real bread and butter came from the royalties on stock photos.

She'd learned she could work anywhere—in her car, in a campground, in a motel room. But this, working in her own house, with the quiet every-where and the light playing on the water, felt like a gift, one made possible by her grandparents and the trust funds they'd set up for her and Mason.

Grateful, she sent them regular emails with photos. Since college she'd called them every week, no matter where she'd been, what she'd been doing.

They'd lost their daughter—twice, to Naomi's way of thinking. She'd made certain they never lost their granddaughter.

She took before photos of the glider and chair, playing up the texture of the rust, the peeling paint, the square lines—and the pop from the bucket of purple pansies she'd planted and set on the deck with them. She'd take after shots, too, send both home—but she'd play with the before shots on her computer, put them up on her website for sale.

It took nearly a week for Kevin to bring the estimate. This time he had his six-year-old son, Tyler, as well as Molly. The boy was a mini version of his father, and so cute Naomi wished she had cookies.

"We're on our way to pick up pizza, and figured we'd drop this off. You might want to have a stiff drink and sit down before you read it over."

"Uh-oh."

"Yeah. Well. Like I said, you can figure out priorities. I gave you my mind on that in there. And if you want to take on some DIY, we can save you some money. Take some time, think about it. Just let me know. I got another name in there, too. You might want another bid, and I know that company does good work. They're out of Hoodsport."

"Thanks."

"Let's go, team." The boy raced back to the truck with the dog. Kevin paused. "Don't forget that stiff drink."

Naomi tapped the manila envelope on her palm, took it back inside to the kitchen. A glass of wine couldn't be wrong, she thought, and poured one, and since other than her desk chair it was her only option, she went out on the deck and sat in the half-sanded glider.

She sat a moment, drinking wine, watching the water and the bright red kayak that slid along it toward the shore.

She set the wine down on the drop cloth, opened the envelope.

"Holy shit. Oh hello, six figures." She wished she'd gone for stronger than wine. Like a few tequila shots. She hadn't bought any tequila as yet, but that would be rectified.

She took another deeper drink of wine, blew out a breath, and read over the estimate.

So much work. The kitchen—she'd expected that price tag. And in fact, he'd bid a little under what she'd been braced for. The windows—there were so many windows, and replacing them added up. She'd done some research there, and his price was, again, slightly under what she'd calculated.

Contractor's discount, she mused. He was passing some of that on, and that was more than fair.

She got up, walked up and down the deck, sat down. Read on.

The plumbing, the electrical, spray insulation in the attic. Nothing sexy there, but necessary. God, the floors. So much square footage. Why had she bought such a big house?

To answer her own question, she looked up at the view. The sun hung low, sparkling over the blue. A bird, white and wide-winged, just sailed over it.

She read through the estimate again. She could take on at least some of the painting. She wasn't afraid of hard work. There was bound to be something else she could handle. And corners she could cut.

But she didn't want to cut corners.

She leaned back, gliding slowly. She could get a lot of photos out of the demo, the rehab. Photos of workers, of broken tiles, of tools and lumber. If she played it right, she could pull in some income even while coughing up the outlay.

She had savings, she reminded herself. She'd lived carefully, didn't need a lot to live. Her biggest expenses before the house had been her Hasselblad and her 4Runner. She could do this.

She looked out over the water again. She needed to do this. She'd been to every state, working her way. She'd been to Europe twice, working her way.

And nowhere had ever drawn her like this spot, this place.

She took out her phone, called Kevin.

"Do you need an ambulance?"

He made her laugh. She didn't make friends easily, but he made her laugh. "I wished for tequila shots, but I toughed it out. When can you start?"

"What? Sorry, what?"

"Let's go for it. When can you start?"

"I might need an ambulance. Wow. Wow. Listen, I'm kicking myself as I say this, but don't you want to get that other bid?"

"I bought this place because it spoke to me, it said words I needed. You get that. I'm going to try to do some of this—like the painting. I might be able to help with demo or something, to cut it down a little. But I'm going for it. When can you start?"

"Monday. I'm going to draw up a contract, and I'll put in that you're taking on the painting. That doesn't work out, we'll sub it for you. I drew up the kitchen design you outlined, but—"

"Yeah, I saw it. We'll go with it, and you can tell me where I look for the countertops, the cabinets, and all that so I can figure out what I want."

"It's a lot to figure."

"Yeah, so let's get started."

"Naomi, I might have to kiss you on the mouth. My wife will understand."

She hoped his wife was as, well, adorable as he was. "We'll cross that bridge."

"I'll come by with the contract tomorrow."

"And I'll give you a check for materials, like it says here."

"I'd appreciate it. You got a favorite color?"

"Sure. All of them."

"Good enough. See you tomorrow. And thanks, Naomi."

She went inside, topped off her wine. And toasted herself in her soon-to-be-gutted kitchen.

He brought the contract, along with his wife—the very pretty Jenny—Tyler, and four-year-old Maddy, a sweet, towheaded version of her father.

And he handed her a pot of rainbow tulips along with the contract.

"You said all of them. Favorite color."

"They're great."

Then he took her by the shoulders, kissed her. Tyler covered his eyes; Maddy giggled. Jenny just beamed.

"He's had ideas about what needed to be done to this place longer than I can remember. And he said yours ran right down the same lines. Kevin's the best. He's going to make it beautiful for you."

"Jenny's biased." Kevin wrapped an arm around her shoulders. "But honest. I've got a Dumpster coming first thing Monday morning. The crew will be here by seven thirty. We're going to be loud."

"I'll deal."

"See you Monday then."

They piled into a minivan, and like the dog, Kevin stuck his head out the window. "We're going to rock this place!"

Naomi put the coffeemaker in her bedroom on the desk, filled her cooler with soft drinks, lunch meats, some fruit. She could set her Coleman stove on the deck. She'd put meals together in much less cozy circumstances.

Monday, she gave herself the day off and joined in gutting the kitchen and adjoining bathroom. She swung a sledgehammer, wielded a pry bar, helped haul out old counters, old cabinets.

And exhausted, aching, fell dead asleep before the forest swallowed the sun.

Every morning the hammering started. She'd get coffee, a granola bar, her camera. The crew got used to her, stopped posing.

She took pictures of callused hands, hands bleeding at the knuckles. Of sweaty torsos, steel-toed work boots.

Evenings, in the blessed quiet, she ate sandwiches and worked. She cropped a study of the kitchen floor, the linoleum jagged against the exposed hardwood. She played with filtering, considered other compositions, spent time updating her site, punching up her marketing.

She chose which studies belonged on her site, which should be exclusive to the gallery, which should be put up as stock.

There were dozens of decisions to be made, and she would have sworn not as many hours in the day as there'd been a week before.

She took more time off to look at slabs of granite, and ended up spending more than an hour taking pictures—those raw edges, the graining, the dapples and colors. Tired of cold meals or soup over the Coleman, she stopped and picked up pizza in town on the way home.

She'd sit on her pretty slate blue glider, breathe in the quiet, and eat loaded pizza on her bedroom deck. Then she'd treat herself to a movie on her laptop. No more work that day. And thank God the king-size mattress she ordered would be delivered in the morning. She'd spend her last night on her air mattress.

Twilight shimmered in the west as she followed the snaking ribbon of road.

The deer leaped out of the trees. She had time to see that it was a massive buck before she cut the wheel to avoid the collision. She hit the brakes, fishtailed.

She felt more than heard her tire blow, and cursed as she tried to fight the wheel back.

She ended up thudding into the shallow ditch alongside the road with her heart pounding between her ears.

The buck merely turned his head, gave her a regal stare, and then leaped into the shadows.

"Damn it, damn it, damn it. Okay, okay. Nobody's hurt, including fricking Bambi." She shoved open the door to see the damage.

Tire shot, she noted, but she didn't think she'd damaged the wheel. She could change a stupid tire, but it was going to be tricky with the way she'd angled into the ditch. And dusk was falling fast now—with her on the curve of the switchback.

She opened the back, pulled out the emergency kit, lit a flare, set it several feet behind the truck, set another several feet in front, eased into the car, turned on her flashers.

Resigned to the annoyance, she hauled the jack out of the trunk.

She caught the headlights, worried they came too fast. But the truck— she made out the shape of a truck—slowed, then swerved gently to the shoulder between her car and the back flare.

Naomi set down the jack and took a good grip on the tire iron.

"Got some trouble?"

"Just a flat. I've got it, thanks."

But he sauntered forward, in silhouette with the headlights glaring at his back.

"Got a spare?"

Deep voice, deeply male. Tall—long legs and arms.

"Of course I have a spare."

"Good. I'll change it for you."

"I appreciate that." Her hand tightened on the tire iron. "But I've got it."

He just hunkered down to take a closer look. She could see him better now—a lot of dark, windblown hair, a sharp-boned profile under some scruff. A battered leather jacket, big hands on the knees of long legs.

"You're at a bad angle for the jack, but it's doable. I've got emergency lights in the truck."

He looked up at her now. A hard and handsome face, a tough-guy face with the scruff, with the thick, windblown hair, a firm, full, unsmiling mouth.

She couldn't see the color of his eyes, but didn't detect any mean in them. Still . . .

"I've changed a tire before."

"Hey, me, too. In fact, you can make a living. Xander Keaton. Keaton's Garage and Body Works—name's on the side of my truck. I'm a mechanic."

"I didn't call a mechanic."

"Aren't you lucky one just came along? And I'd appreciate the hell out of it if you didn't smack me with that tire iron." He goose-stepped over, picked up the jack, got to work. "Killed this tire good. You're going to need a new one. I can order one for you."

He picked up the lug wrench. "How'd it blow? It doesn't look worn."

"A deer—it jumped out in front of me. I overcompensated."

"That'll happen. Heading home? Just making conversation," he said when she remained silent. "I can smell the pizza. You're coming from town, so you're not staying in town. I haven't seen you before, and given you're a serious looker, I'd remember if I had."

"Yes, I'm going home."

"New around here—because I know everybody—heading home on this road. Killer blonde. Are you Naomi?"

She stepped back.

"Settle down." He said it calmly as he got up to get the spare. "Kevin Banner. He's rehabbing the old Parkerson place up on Point Bluff for you. Best pals, birth to earth. Well, earth's a ways off, unless you kill me with that tire iron, but we've known each other since before we could walk. You can call him, get my bona fides if it'll loosen the grip you've got on that thing."

"He never mentioned you." But her grip did loosen, a little.

"Now that hurts. He was my wingman, I was his best man. I'm Tyler's godfather. His cousin Mark's doing your plumbing, and Macie Addams— who I was madly in love with for about six weeks in junior year—is one of your carpenters. Does that clear me?"

"I'll know when I ask Kevin tomorrow."

"That's a cynical and suspicious nature you've got. I have to like it."
He tightened the lug nuts on the spare, gave it a testing spin. "That'll do."

As he lowered the jack, he looked up at her again. "How tall are you?"

"Five-ten. And a half."

"You know how to wear it." He rose, fitted the jack and the tools back
in their compartments.

"Do you want me to take the tire with me, order you another?"

"I . . . Yes, actually, that would be great. Thanks."

"No problem. Hold on a minute." He took the tire to his truck, got out
a bucket of sand, picked up the flare. "Wanna get the other one?"

"You're prepared."

"Part of the job." He doused the flares in the sand, shook his head as Naomi
dug in her pockets. "You want to pay me? Give me a slice of that pizza."

"What? Seriously?"

"That's Rinaldo's pizza. I've got a weakness."

"You want a slice of pizza?"

"It doesn't seem like much to ask after I risked a concussion and possible brain damage to change your tire."

She opened the door, opened the box. "I don't have anything to put it on."

Xander held out a hand. "How about this?"

With a shrug, Naomi set the slice of pizza on his wide palm.

"Thanks for the assist."

"Thanks for the pizza. You drive safe now."

She got in, strapped in, watched him saunter away—that was what he
did. Saunter. She eased out of the ditch, bumped back onto the road.

He gave his horn a friendly honk as she drove away.

He sat a moment, getting in a couple bites of pizza so he could drive
one-handed. He found it, as always, delicious.

But it didn't hold a candle to the leggy blonde with suspicious eyes.

Seven

She'd come for peace, quiet, solitude. And ended up with a houseful of people and noise. There were days when even the view didn't balance it out.

When she asked herself why she hadn't settled for just the basics—like reliable plumbing and a decent refrigerator—she couldn't quite remember the answer.

The house was torn to pieces, full of dust—with the biggest Dumpster known to man sitting in her front yard. After three solid days of rain that made heading out with her camera unappealing, Naomi was ready to throw her things in the car and run.

She bought paint instead.

On the first day of rain, she cleaned and primed the master bedroom walls. On the first night of rain, she studied paint chips, created palettes and schemes with her computer. On the second day, she convinced herself it was just paint, and if she didn't like it on the wall, she'd just paint it again.

She bought the amount of color Kevin recommended, and semigloss white for the trim—along with rollers, brushes, pans. She forgot a stepladder—next time—so again she borrowed one from the crew.

Dressed in the sweatshirt, jeans, and Yankees fielder's cap already speckled with primer, she got to work cutting in. Since she couldn't block out the Skilsaw buzzing, the nail guns thwacking, and the headbanger rock pounding from the first floor, she plugged in her earbuds and painted to her own playlist.

Xander drove up thinking the old house looked like it was made to loom on the bluff on rain-washed days. The day sloshed along gloomily, so the lights glinting against some of the windows added to the atmosphere. Maybe the giant Dumpster out front took some of that away, but he imagined Kevin and his crew were having a hell of a good time filling it.

He got out, hunched against the wet, strolled up to the house.

Inside the noise was amazing, but you'd have that on job sites. He smelled sawdust, coffee, wet dog—which meant Molly'd been out running around. Drop cloths and cardboard paths covered the floor.

The interior, as far as he could see, just looked sad. Dim, dingy, neglected. Maybe the high ceilings gave it some class, the natural stone fireplace some character, but he saw a lot of space to fix and fill.

He thought of the long, tall blonde with the sexy pixie hair and the don't-make-me-kick-your-ass attitude. He couldn't see the connection. She said city to him. Big city.

It made her and her choice of living arrangements all the more interesting.

He made his way back, following the noise. He saw stacks of lumber, tools, cords, wheels of wiring.

He wondered what people did with all these rooms. What the sexy blonde meant to do with them.

When he reached the kitchen, he had a partial answer. Here, at least, she meant to start from scratch.

They'd gutted the place, taken it right down to the studs, were now putting up new ones. A blue tarp shuddered from the windy rain over a big hole in the back wall. He knew enough about plumbing to read the rough-ins, get a sense of where things would go. Just as he could read that at one time there'd been a john in the far left corner.

"Hey, Kev, you planning on putting both kids through college on this place?"

Kevin, hunkered down with the plumber, glanced back. "It's going to help," he called over the noise.

He pushed up, crossed the tarped floor. "What brings you out here?"

"New tire for that FourRunner."

"Right. I'd've picked it up for her, saved you a trip."

"No problem. I wanted to see the place anyway."

Satisfaction covering his face, Kevin looked around. "It's coming along."

Shoulder to shoulder, Xander looked around the same space. "To what?"

"You need vision, man. You just need vision." He crooked a finger, stepped over to the dining area and the plywood set on sawhorses. "It's coming to this."

Hands in pockets, Xander studied the blueprint of the projected kitchen. "That's what the hole's for. What was there before?"

"Standard door. Total waste. I knew Naomi had that vision when she said to open it up."

"Vision and deep pockets."

"Lucky for both of us. Lucky for this place. She's got an eye—you know, photographer and all that. And she gets the feel of the place, the character. She's not looking to go all sleek and polished. This space here and the master bath, those are the biggest projects. You add in new windows—got them coming in tomorrow—refinishing the floors, the plumbing, the wiring, trim—she wants crown molding here and there, and some of the original trim needs to be replicated—painting, installing, it's all mostly cosmetic, but it's a lot of that."

"How many rooms in this place?"

"Eighteen, plus five and a half baths now that we took the one out in here. Not counting a granddaddy of all basements—unfinished."

"She's single, right? Lives alone?"

"Some people like space, some people like to live in three rooms over their garage."

"Some people drive a minivan."

Kevin gave him a light punch. "Wait till you have kids."

"Yeah, let's wait on that. Where is she anyway?"

"She's up in the master, as far as I know, painting."

"She's painting—like walls or with an easel?"

"Walls. She did all right on the prep and priming up there, but I expect we'll be calling Jimmy and Rene in to handle the rest."

He could've handed Kevin the bill, put the tire in her car, and gone on his way. But since he was here anyway . . .

"I'm going to go on up."

"You can take the back stairs." Kevin wagged a thumb. "Corner room, facing the inlet."

"Buy you a beer when you knock off?"

"I wouldn't mind it. Yeah, I'll swing by."

He went up the back way—and having Kevin for a friend all his life, he recognized good craftsmanship in the new stairs, the sturdy rail. The light looked like it had come out of someone's cabin in the fifties, but that was an easy fix.

Then he reached the second floor and just stood, staring down the hallway. It looked like something out of *The Shining*. He half expected to see some kid on a Big Wheel pedaling along. Or a decomposing corpse leaking its way under a doorway.

He wondered how she slept in this place at night.

He knocked on the door of the corner room, considering his options when no one answered. He went with the simplest and opened the door.

She stood on a stepladder in paint-splattered clothes and ancient Converse high-tops, carefully cutting in the wall at ceiling height. She'd nearly finished, he noted, and couldn't fault her work.

He started to rap his knuckles on the open door, but as she dipped her brush she picked up the chorus of "Shake It Off."

"'Cause the players gonna play, play, play, play, play."

Decent voice, he thought, and noticed the earbuds.

By the time she got to "Baby, I'm just gonna shake, shake, shake," he'd crossed over, tapped her shoulder.

She spun around so fast, leading with the brush, he barely dodged the paint swipe across his face. He said, "Wow," and then, because she over-balanced, put a firm hand on her ass to keep her on the ladder.

With that he smiled—all smug male. "Nice."

"Back off."

"Just keeping you and that bucket of paint off the floor." But he dropped his hand. "I knocked, but you and Taylor were too busy shaking it off to hear."

Very carefully, she set down her brush. "When you knock and nobody answers, the logical and polite thing to do is go away."

"That's fifty-fifty, don't you think?" She had green eyes. He hadn't been able to tell in the dark on the side of the road, but she had incredibly deep green eyes. And they were pissed. "A lot of people open the door, take a look."

"What do you want?"

"Nice to see you again, too. I dropped off your tire—the replacement."

"Oh. Thank you."

"No problem." He took a folded invoice out of his back pocket, held it out. "It cost more than a slice of pizza."

"I bet. Will you take a check?"

"Sure. Cash, check, credit card." He took an electronic swipe out of his jacket pocket. "Your choice."

"We'll use my card then. Isn't that high-tech for a garage?"

"I like tech, plus it's handy when people need roadside assistance. I can fix them up, swipe their card, send them on their way."

She nodded, took a slim wallet out of her back pocket. Xander just cocked an eyebrow as she slid out a credit card. Every woman he knew carted around a purse the size of a Shetland pony, filled with the mysterious.

"I appreciate you bringing the tire all the way out here."

"It's not that all the way. I'll put it in the spare compartment when I leave. Kev's got it torn up down there."

"Yes. Yes, he does."

"You've got a big hole in the wall."

"At the end of the day it'll be a door. Please, God."

He swiped her card. "Nice color—the paint."

"Yeah. I think." She worried over it as she signed her name. "Does it read warm to you?"

He handed her back her card and studied the soft, watery blue seriously. "Yeah. It's warm, and calm, right? You're picking up the tones of the water, early morning before it goes deep."

"That's it. I almost went a little more gray. More spa-like. Maybe I should've . . . It's just paint."

"It's walls," he corrected. "You've got to live with them."

"Crap."

"You hit warm and calm if that's what you were after. And whatever it is, you'll get used to it. I can email you a receipt."

"That's all right. I don't need one."

Didn't want him to have her email, more likely. Xander pocketed the reader, the phone. "That's a lot of wall to paint. You ought to open those doors, get some air in here."

"It's raining. And you're right." She stepped over, fought the slider open an inch. "This stubborn, ugly bastard's going."

Xander put a hand above hers, gave the slider one good shove. Then looked out as she did.

"Walls don't mean dick when you look at that."

"I keep telling myself."

In the rain the world outside was dreamy, with gloom adding a fanciful edge, just touches of fog and mist floating like gossamer birds.

"Makes you forget the second floor looks like part of the Overlook Hotel."

"Well, thanks for that. I'm going to imagine *Redrum* written in blood on that horrible wallpaper now."

He grinned. "Points for getting the reference. I gotta get going. Good luck with this."

"Thanks."

She stood when he walked out, watching the cool spring rain.

He'd scared her, she could admit that. The quick, firm tap on her shoulder when her mind had been on painting and music. The equally quick and firm hand on her butt.

She'd have caught her balance, probably.

He'd backed off when she'd told him, easily, signaling he was harmless.

But he wasn't harmless. Despite the easy talk about paint and wall-paper, he wasn't harmless. He had strong blue eyes, very direct—and something behind them warned that he wasn't a man to trifle with.

She had no intention of trifling with Xander Keaton.

He might have had a runner's build, but there was a toughness in there. She knew how to judge who might be an easy companion for a night or two, if she had the need.

No question he was attractive, in a rough and sexy sort of way, and though she'd learned not to let it matter, it was a bonus that he had a good four inches over her in height. She wouldn't deny she'd felt a tug in the belly, but if and when she had that need, she'd steer clear of Keaton.

Keep it simple, she thought as she went back to the stepladder. Because her life, her nature, would always be complicated.

Instinct told her Xander Keaton was anything but simple.

When the soaking rain finally moved off and the sun sparkled again, Naomi had the sheer delight of folding outswing doors off her kitchen. After they'd been installed and the crew left, she opened and closed them half a dozen times just for the fun of it.

With the turn of weather, she donned her boots and a light jacket and grabbed her camera. Stock photos of flowers always provided a decent revenue, and the burgeoning bulbs and wildflowers offered her a treasure trove. She could ramble the woods looking for the interest of rough bark, nurse logs, the charm of a narrow stream running fast with snowmelt. The surprise of a little waterfall running faster yet to a tumble of rocks below.

And she got an unexpected shot of a bear when they encountered each other in the silvery quiet of dawn.

After ten days of working for a living, the tedium of painting, the stress of selecting cabinet hardware and kitchen appliances, she sat on her new king-size mattress with her laptop.

Hello from Construction Central, loves of my life.

I did it. This room is painted, every square inch of wall, ceiling, and trim. I have wonderful atrium doors leading out to my deck, and intend to sit out there—on the chair I sanded and repainted—in the morning and wallow with coffee over my view. It'll be a short wallow as the crew comes early, and the indescribable noise comes along with them. But I can see the kitchen coming together. I remember when you had the kitchen redone about—what—six years ago. I was home for a couple weeks and it was chaos. This is chaos times infinity.

But I think I like it—the process of it.

I saw a bear this morning. Don't worry, I was more interested in him than he was in me. Picture attached. I couldn't get one of the whale— I'm sure it was a whale—sounding way out. By the time I got my camera, zoomed out, it was gone.

I'm happy here. They're getting to know me in town—enough to say hello when I'm at the market or hardware—my two favorite places right now. Oh, and the pizza place. It's not New York pizza, but it's not crap either.

I'm happy here, despite the daily noise, the deluge of decisions. Kevin says I really have to decide on the tile for the master, and the backsplash for the kitchen. Both terrify me more than a little. But that's for later.

Write me back soon—and that goes for you, too, Mason, with more than an all's good, how's it going. I'm about to start picking color and designs out for the rooms I've earmarked as yours when you visit.

Before pictures also attached.

Miss you, love you,
Naomi

Once she sent the email off, she ordered herself to work. She had to update her Facebook page, do the Tumblr thing, the Pinterest deal, and write something for the blog. All chores she'd have put off for the rest of her life if they weren't part of the job.

An hour later, she took her laptop back to the desk to plug in the charger. And saw the moon riding over the water.

She grabbed her camera, filters, a second lens, and went out on her deck in the deep night chill.

She caught the moon along with its reflection in the water. *Mirror Moon*, she thought, already composing as she took more pictures, changed filters, angles. She'd make a series—cards, which always sold well off her site. If they turned out as well as she thought, she'd set up her mat cutter and board and start sending some art to the gallery.

But she was doing one for herself. She rose, drew in the quiet, the light, the sense of lovely, lovely solitude.

She'd hang the best of the best on the wall she'd painted herself.

Her moon over her inlet.

It didn't get better than that.

Three weeks after demo, Kevin stayed late to finish installing the hardware on the kitchen cabinets. Overwhelmed, Naomi grabbed tools and worked with him while Molly napped by the doors.

"I can't believe how it looks."

"It's coming along."

"Coming along? Kevin, it's amazing. I didn't make a mistake, right, changing up from the idea of the dark cherry cabinets for this sage green?"

"They're classy, have character, and don't look like a showroom—in a good way. With the gray granite, those veins of green in it? You've got an eye, Naomi. The beveled glass fronts set it all off."

"I think so. I guess I'm going to need something better than paper plates and plastic cups to go in them. I've never bought a set of dishes in my life."

"Didn't you have like an apartment or something before?"

"Oh, here and there, but mostly I stayed on the move. Have camera, will travel. And it was paper, plastic, or secondhand. I never intended to settle."

Overwhelmed definitely, she thought, glancing up at her empty cabinets. "It looks like I have, so I'd better think about dishes and glassware. I don't know where I'm going to find the room in my head for that with faucets and light fixtures and tile."

"You should talk to Jenny. That woman loves playing with new dishes."

"Maybe I'll just go with restaurant white, so I don't have to think about it."

"You should talk to her. You know what?" He nudged back the bill of his ball cap. "You should come on out tonight, have a drink with us at Loo's."

"That's the bar, right, off Water Street?"

"Yeah, it's a nice place, though. Good food, friendly. Music tonight, too. Jenny and I have a sitter, so we're going for a while. Why don't you meet us?"

"That sounds like date night to me, Kevin."

"Yeah, sort of. The thing is, Jenny's been after me to ask you over to dinner, and I figure you've had enough of all of us by the end of the day."

Good instincts, she thought, because truer words.

"You come out tonight, have a drink, talk dishes with her some, it's a compromise. Seems like you could use a night off and out, too."

"Maybe."

He didn't push, so they fell back to companionable silence as they worked. When it was done, they bumped fists.

"I'll see you at Loo's if you make it," he said, and she just waved him off.

She didn't intend to leave her nearly finished, wonderful kitchen with its empty cabinets and pale gray (hinting toward green) walls. She had dozens of things to keep her busy, including reading the owner's manuals on her new appliances.

Settling in, she reminded herself. If she really meant to settle in, no matter how innately unsociable, it required minimal doses of friendliness.

Otherwise she was that weird woman up on Point Bluff. That just asked for talk and attention. Normal people had a drink with friends now and then. She didn't really know Jenny, but she definitely considered Kevin a friend.

Harry would have deemed them simpatico.

So why not? She'd throw on some halfway decent clothes, slap a little makeup on, and drive into town. Have a drink at the local bar, talk with her friend's wife about tableware. She'd stay for one set since there was music, and consider any and all social obligations met for at least a month.

Good deal.

She opted for black jeans, and because it ran cool at night, a sweater. Not black, she ordered herself, as that was her first choice. She chose the one Seth and Harry had given her for Christmas—worn only once—and in nearly the same shade as her kitchen cabinets. She considered changing her habitual silver studs for something more fun and frivolous, then decided that worrying about earrings was too much for a simple drink with a friend and his wife.

She took some trouble with her makeup mainly because those needs could come calling—and maybe there was a local boy who could meet them at some point.

No reason to scare him off, whoever he might be.

Night had fallen when she set out, so she left the porch light on—new fixture yet to come—and locked up. Alarm system, she thought, installed very soon.

When she glanced back at the house, she nearly went back inside. It looked so appealing sitting there, so quiet. One drink, she ordered herself, and pushed herself to drive away from solitude.

She'd never been into town this late—no reason to—and saw that Friday night hopped a bit. She imagined that those strolling along the boardwalk by the marina were tourists, but it was likely a mix with those on the street, poking into shops open late, sitting out with heaters at outdoor tables.

She knew Loo's sat a block off Water Street, tucked between a seafood restaurant and a snack shop. She spotted Kevin's truck, found a parking spot half a block down from it.

She needed to come back at night with her camera, get night shots of the marina, the old character homes, the bold red door and the blue neon curl of *LOO'S* over it.

Music pumped against the door before she opened it.

She'd pictured a little bar, but it proved bigger—even boasted a small dance floor, packed now as crowd-pleasing rock beat out. She smelled beer and fried food, perfume, sweat. The bar itself dominated one wall in dark, aged wood backed by more than a dozen taps. She heard the whirl of a blender and immediately decided on a foamy frozen margarita. As she scanned, Kevin waved from a table near the dance floor.

She wound her way through, found her hand caught in Jenny's.

"I'm so glad you came! Kevin didn't think you would."

"Couldn't resist."

"Sit, sit. Kevin, get Naomi a drink."

"What'll you have?"

"I hear the song of a frozen margarita—with salt."

"I'm going to get that going for you. It takes a while for them to get to the tables. Jenny?"

"I'm still nursing this one."

As Kevin moved off, Jenny swiveled in her chair. "God, you're so beautiful."

"I . . ."

"I'm on my second glass of wine. I get loose easy. It's just I always wanted to be tall, and look what happened."

"I always wanted to be petite. What are you going to do?"

"I looked up your website, your photos. They're wonderful, really. There's this one of a water lily, just one water lily with these ripples around it where it floats? I felt like I'd been on vacation just looking at it. And this one of an old gravestone in a cemetery, and you can see the shadow of the church. The dates? She was a hundred and two when she died, and it still made me tear up. I can't remember the name on the stone."

"Mary Margaret Allen."

"That's right." Jenny's eyes, nearly the same soft doe brown as her hair, smiled. "What I'm saying—I take a good snapshot. Slices of life, the kids and all, I mean. And it's important to have the record, those memories. But what you do, it just grabs emotions right out."

"Best compliment ever."

"It's a true one. Kevin said you needed dishes and glassware and such."

"I do. I was thinking white and clear, and done."

"Well, going that way you can jazz it up with napkins and so on. The thing is . . . He took some pictures of the kitchen with his phone, and showed me. I just love the soft green of the cabinets, and the pewter tones of the hardware, the gray of the walls. It's like you're pulling the tones and colors from outside in."

"I can't resist that either."

Jenny sipped her wine, gave her long, loose hair a push back. "I think it's just right, if that matters. And it struck me how if you went deep, deep blue with the dishes, like cobalt blue, you'd have that pop behind the glass, and keep with that scheme."

"Cobalt blue. It would look great."

"I think it would, then you go for color in the glassware, softer, like blues and greens—a mix, just tie it in. I can give you sites to look at, and I've got a stack of catalogs. And before Kevin comes back, because I'll embarrass him, I'm going to ask you to ask me to come over and look at the place, at his work, and what you're up to. I know he said you took this old glider and chair and redid them. I love doing that kind of thing, finding something someone's gotten rid of and making it new."

"Sure you can come by, have a look."

"I swear I won't be a pest or take advantage." She beamed at Kevin when he came back with a jumbo margarita.

"I've talked her ear off. Stop me."

He set the drink down, sat, kissed his wife's cheek. "Shut up, Jenny."

"I will. Plus I love when they do this number."

"I could take a bath in this," Naomi commented. She took a sip. "But I'll drink it instead."

She angled to look at the band as she recognized the Springsteen classic—and the voice lit the suggestive lyrics of "I'm on Fire" like a slow-burning match.

He wore black—jeans and a T-shirt, worn motorcycle boots. He stood, the guitar slung low, his fingers working the frets and strings while that voice wrung every drop of sex out of the words.

She should've known.

"Xander and the band play here every few weeks," Kevin told her. "They're the Wreckers."

She said, "Oh."

And deep inside as those bold blue eyes met hers, as that voice sent out lures and warnings, something inside her said, *Oh damn.*

She figured she'd need every drop of that margarita to cool off.

Eight

He came over on the break with a bottle of water and an easy swagger. Jenny pointed a finger at him.

"You know what that song does to me."

"You can thank me later," Xander said to Kevin, and sat—slouched, with his long legs stretched out. "So." He gave Naomi a slow smile. "How ya doing?"

"Good. I'm good." She felt like someone had started a brush fire under her skin. "You're good, too. My uncles are huge Springsteen fans. They'd have approved your cover."

"How many uncles?"

"Just the two. They took my brother and me to the E Street Band's reunion tour at Madison Square. Have you ever seen him in concert?"

"In Tacoma, same tour. Blew the roof off."

She relaxed enough to smile. "Yeah, they did."

A blonde in a tight pink shirt came up, circled Xander's neck from behind. "Are you doing 'Something from Nothing'?"

"Last set."

"How about coming over, having a beer? Patti and I are right over there."

"Working, Marla." He wagged his water bottle.

She wasted the sexy pout, in Naomi's opinion, as Xander couldn't see it with her chin resting on the top of his head. "You could come over anyway. Hi, Jenny. Hi, Kevin."

Her gaze tracked over to Naomi. "Who's your friend?"

"Naomi," Kevin said, "Marla."

"Visiting?" Marla asked.

"No, I live here." And didn't that sound odd, Naomi realized. She lived here.

"Haven't seen you around before. You must . . . Hey, are you the one who bought the old place on the bluff? You're working there, right, Kevin?"

"That's right."

"You must be rich or crazy."

"I'm not rich," Naomi said, adding a half smile because the pouty blonde's statement struck her as more baffled than needling.

"You know it's haunted, right? They should've told you it was haunted."

"I don't think anyone mentioned it."

"I'd be scared out of my mind staying there alone. You take pictures, right? Patti figures you're looking to open a photography studio."

"No. I don't do studio photography."

"What other kind is there?"

"How much time do you have?"

"What?"

"I'll come over next break." Xander gave the hand currently stroking his clavicle a pat.

"Okay. Then maybe . . ." She leaned down, put her mouth on his ear, and whatever she whispered had Xander's lips curving.

"That's a hell of an offer, Marla, but I don't want Chip coming after me with a hammer."

She did the pout again. "We're divorced."

"And still."

"Well, you think about it."

"Hard not to," he murmured as she hip-swiveled back to her table.

"What was the offer?" Kevin wanted to know.

"I'll tell you later."

"She just can't help it." Jenny glanced at Naomi, apology in her eyes. "She doesn't mean any harm. She's just a little clueless."

"Did she do any harm?" Xander wondered.

"Not to me." Naomi lifted her margarita, sipped. "But then, she didn't make me an offer."

"Ha. She's hoping Kevin will tell Chip she did—"

"Which I wouldn't."

"No, but she's hoping you will, and that would rile Chip up enough he'd go by her place, and they'd fight about it, have pissed-off sex, and she'd kick him out again after."

"That's about it," Kevin agreed. "They have a strange relationship. He wouldn't come after you with a hammer because he knows you—and you're a bud."

"Add in, Chip's sweet," Jenny claimed. "I know he's punched a couple people over her, but she pushed him into it. He's a sweet man."

"She doesn't think she wants sweet. She'd be wrong about that," Xander added. "But that's their problem. You guys want another round? I can let Loo know."

"Another glass of wine and I'll be a wild woman. What the hell?" Jenny decided. "It's Friday night, and we've got a sitter."

"I'll keep up with her," Kevin said.

"Not for me. I'm driving, and I really should go."

"Stick around." Xander sent her a lazy look. "Make a request—something on your playlist. Come on, play stump the band."

She considered. "'Hard to Explain.'" A choice, maybe because it had played in her ear right after he'd walked out of her bedroom the other day.

He grinned, pointed a finger at her, then walked off.

"I don't know that one," Jenny commented. "But I bet Xander does."

He sent over another round—water for Naomi.

And she didn't stump the band, who played the Strokes' old classic as if they'd rehearsed it that morning. She stayed for most of the second set, then realized if she didn't slip out, she'd end up staying until they closed.

"I've really got to go. Thanks for the drink—and for talking me into coming out."

"Anytime. See you Monday."

"I'm going to come by soon," Jenny told her. "If you're busy, Kevin will show me around."

She left with a slow, simmering cover of Clapton's "Layla" following her into the night.

She decided the sex dream with Xander with throbbing bass and mad guitar riffs while the house burned around them was inevitable.

Maybe it left her a little edgy, but she had plenty to do to work off the beginnings of sexual frustration. She wasn't ready to be sexually frustrated, and far from ready to take care of it.

A weekend of quiet, of work, of sun and soft evening rain polished the edges away. As promised, she took morning coffee out on the deck—she *would* buy a better coffeemaker—and soaked in the silence and solitude.

When she FaceTimed New York on Sunday, her mood was high and light.

"There she is!" Seth, sporting the trim goatee he'd decided he'd needed on his forty-fifth birthday, beamed through her iPad screen.

"Hi, handsome."

"You talking to me?" Harry moved into view, draping an arm over Seth's shoulders. The rings they'd exchanged in Boston in the summer of 2004 glinted on their hands.

"Two scoops of handsome."

"Make it three. Guess who's here for Sunday dinner?"

Mason slid on-screen just behind them and grinned at her.

"Why, it's Doctor Agent Carson."

Just look at him, she thought, so tall and—yes, three scoops of handsome now. And best, happy. He was on his way to doing and being just what he'd set out to do and be. "How's the FBI?"

"That's classified."

"He just got back from upstate," Seth told her. "He helped on a kidnapping, helped bring a twelve-year-old girl back home safe."

"It's a living. What's going on with that crazy house you bought?"

"Crazy? Take a look." She panned the tablet, slowly circling the kitchen. "Who's crazy?"

"Naomi, it's beautiful. Look at that range hood, Seth! You went with the Wolf."

"I listen."

"Forget the range hood," Seth said. "The cabinets are fabulous. Why are they empty? Harry, we need to send her some dishes."

"No, no, I've got a line on that. I'll send you the link to what I'm looking at. I'm taking you upstairs. I want you to check out the master bedroom walls—which I painted myself."

"You?" Mason snorted.

"Every inch of them. I may never pick up a paint roller again in my life, but I did every inch of this room."

"And how many rooms in that place again?"

"Shut up, Mason. Now be honest—does the color work?"

Upstairs she did another slow pan.

"Pretty and restful," Seth declared. "Now why don't you have an actual bed?"

"It's on the list." The really long list. "Really, I just finished the paint, and I finally set up a temporary mat room. I have a ton of stuff I've been processing and printing."

"You work too hard, too much," Seth objected.

"You worry too hard, too much. I went out with friends Friday night, had a drink, listened to a local band."

"Seeing anyone?" Harry prompted, and behind him Mason rolled his eyes—mouthed, *Better you than me.*

"I see lots of people. The crew's here eight hours a day, five days a week."

"Any good-looking, single men in that crew?"

"Are you looking for one?"

Harry laughed. "Got all I can handle."

"Me, too, right now. I want to hear how you're all doing. How's the restaurant? What's for Sunday dinner? Is Mrs. Koblowki next door still entertaining gentlemen callers?"

She didn't distract them—she knew better—but they let it go, and for the next fifteen minutes they talked about easy things, funny things, homey things.

When she said good-bye and turned off the tablet, she missed them like a limb.

She worked in the mat room for an hour, tried to settle down at her laptop. But the contact with family left her restless and blue.

Time to get out, she told herself. She'd yet to take real pictures in town, real studies of the marina. What better way to spend the rest of a Sunday afternoon? Then she'd come home and cook something besides scrambled eggs or a grilled cheese sandwich in her gorgeous new kitchen.

Pleased with herself, she drove into town, dumped her car, and just walked. No errands to run, no chores to deal with. Just walk and study and compose shots.

The sailboat called *Maggie Mae*, its paint white as a bridal gown and its sails lowered, its shining brightwork. The cabin cruiser decked out with balloons for a party, the fishing boat of dull gray that made her think of a sturdy old workhorse.

All the masts naked and swaying into blue sky, and reflected blurrily in the water.

And farther out, a couple zipping along on Sea-Doos, their busy speed a perfect contrast to the dreamy waiting of the docked boats.

She treated herself to an orange Fanta—a staple of her teen years—and climbed back in the car with plans to spend the evening working on the prints.

She rounded a turn. Slammed the brakes.

It wasn't a deer this time, but a dog. Not in the road, but limping on the shoulder. She started to drive on—not her dog, not her deal—but it took another couple of steps, then just lay down as if hurt or sick.

"Damn it."

She couldn't just drive away, so she pulled over, even as she asked herself what the hell she was supposed to do.

Maybe it was rabid, or vicious, or . . .

It lifted its head when she got out of the car and gave her an exhausted, hopeful stare.

"Oh well. Okay, hey boy. Nice dog—I hope to God."

Because he was pretty big, she noted. But thin—she could nearly count his ribs. Big, thin, and filthy, a big, skinny, dirty brown dog with shocking blue eyes that looked so painfully sad.

And damn it again, the blue against the brown made her think of Harry.

She didn't see a collar, so no tags. Maybe he had a chip. Maybe she could contact the vet or the animal shelter—she could find the numbers on a quick search with her phone.

Then he whimpered, bellied toward her. She didn't have the heart to leave him, so she walked closer, crouched, and gingerly held out her hand.

He licked it, bellied closer.

"Are you hurt?" Filthy, he—or she—might have been. Naomi gently stroked his head. "Are you lost? God, you look half starved. I don't have anything to eat on me. How about I call somebody to help?"

He laid his head, all floppy eared and dirty, on her leg, didn't whimper so much as moan.

She took out her phone, then heard the sound of an engine—motorcycle—heading out from the direction of town.

She lifted the dog's head, set it gently back on the shoulder of the road, and stood to wave down the rider.

The second she spotted him—long legs in jeans, lean torso in black leather—she thought, of course. It would be. Even with the smoked-glass visor of the helmet, she recognized Xander Keaton.

He cut the engine, swung a leg over the bike. "Did you hit him?"

"No. He was limping along the side of the road, then he just lay there. And I—"

She broke off as he was already hunkered down, running those big, guitar-playing hands over the dog as gently as a mother stroked her baby.

"Okay, boy, just take it easy. I don't see any blood, any wounds. Don't feel any breaks. I don't think he's been hit by a car."

"He's so thin, and—"

"There's some water in the saddlebag. Get it, will you? Thirsty? I bet you're thirsty. Plenty hungry. Been on the road awhile, right? Been traveling."

As he talked to the dog, stroked it, Naomi poked through the saddlebag of the bike, came out with a bottle of water.

"Let's see what we can do here." Xander took the bottle, gestured Naomi down. "Cup your hands."

"I—"

"Come on, come on. It won't kill you."

She did as he asked, cupping them in front of the dog's muzzle. He lapped at the water Xander poured, panted, lapped, then laid his head down again.

"We need to get him off the road. I'll put him in the back of your car."

"Where should I take him?"

"You should take him home."

"I can't take him home." She sprang up as Xander slid his arms under the dog, lifted him.

She saw that the dog was definitely male—unneutered male. "He belongs to somebody."

With the bone-thin, tired, filthy dog in his arms, Xander stood, boots planted, and gave her a long look out of deep blue eyes. "Does this dog look like it belongs to anybody? Open the back."

"He could've gotten lost. Somebody might be looking for him."

"We'll ask around, but I haven't heard about anybody losing a dog. He's full-grown. Mutt. Maybe some husky or Australian shepherd in there with those eyes. Alice will know—the vet. If somebody lost a dog, she'll know. Meanwhile she's closed on Sunday."

"There must be an emergency number."

"The only emergency I see is a dog who needs a decent meal, a good bath, and somewhere to rest."

"You take him home."

"On that?" He jerked his head toward his bike.

"I'll wait."

"You found him."

"You'd have found him two minutes later."

"There you go. Look, take him home, and I'll go pick up some supplies for him. You get him to the vet tomorrow, I'll split the bill with you. You're not taking that dog to the shelter. If they don't find the owners—and I'm betting they're long gone—they'll probably put him down."

"Oh, don't say that." Turning a frustrated circle, she gripped fists in her hair. "Don't say that so I feel guilty and obligated. Wait, wait—he's filthy, and he smells amazing."

Naomi grabbed the old blanket she carried in the back, spread it out.

"There you go. You'll be all right. I'll run back, get what you need. I'll meet you back at your place."

Trapped, as Xander strode back to his bike, swung on, kick-started it to a roar, and zoomed away, she looked back at the dog. "You just better not get carsick."

She drove slowly, eyes flicking to the rearview, but didn't hear any sounds of sick dog.

When she pulled up in front of her house, she wondered if the most excellent work she'd done that afternoon had been worth dealing with a stray, starving dog for a night.

She got out, walked around to open the back. "Yes, that's an amazing smell that will potentially take weeks to dissipate. Not entirely your fault, of course, but you smell disgusting. I don't guess you could just jump out on your own."

He bellied over a little, tried to reach her hand with his tongue.

"Never mind. You're skinny enough I could pick you up and probably carry you a half a mile without breaking a sweat. But you're just too dirty and smelly. We'll wait for Xander. Stay there. Just stay."

She dashed into the house, filled a plastic cup with water, grabbed some flatbread crackers. Best she could do.

When she dashed out again, the dog was whining, sniffing at the edge of the back. "No, no, just wait. A little refreshment, that's all. Here, here's a cracker."

He all but inhaled it, and six others, then slurped and lapped the water from the cup.

"That's a little better, isn't it? He's not going to be long. He really better not be long because every minute you're in there is another week it's going to take to air out the smell."

This time when she broke down to pet him, the dog turned his head, nuzzled her hand. "Yeah, I guess that's a little better."

She went back into the car for the orange Fanta, then followed impulse and pulled out her camera.

"We can make flyers for the vet, for the shelter, for whatever."

She took several photos while he stared at her with those strange blue eyes, so strongly colored against the dirty brown—and felt ridiculous relief when she heard the sound of an engine.

Xander, now in his truck, pulled up behind her.

The dog's tail thumped.

"Fancy crackers?"

"I didn't have kibble handy."

"We got some. Better feed him out here in case he sicks it up again."

"Good thinking."

Xander, obviously not delicate about the dirt or smell, lifted the dog out. The dog stood this time, looked a little wobbly, while Xander hauled an already-open fifty-pound bag of dog food out of the truck.

"Think you got enough food?"

Xander only grunted and poured some into a big plastic blue bowl.

"Hey."

She caught the red bowl he tossed.

"For water."

Naomi went around the side, where she had a hose to water the so-far-imaginary garden.

When she came back, the dog had wolfed down every morsel and appeared capable of doing it again.

His tail swung back and forth with more energy.

"Water first, big guy." Xander took the bowl, set it down. The dog drank like a camel.

"I don't care if you think I'm heartless, but that dog's not coming in the house unless we can deal with that smell."

"Yeah, yeah, can't blame you. Somewhere along the line he rolled in something dead. They just love doing that. So we give him a bath. Probably a couple of them. Hose around there?"

"Yeah. I've got dish soap inside."

"Don't need it." He went back to the truck and came back with a black dog collar and a bottle of dog shampoo.

"You did get supplies."

"You're going to have to hold him. I'll soak him down, suds him up, rinse him off, but he's not going to like it."

"If he bites me, I'm going to hurt you."

"He's not a biter. There's no mean in those eyes. You hold on to him, Slim."

"I've got him."

The dog was stronger than he looked—but then so was she. When Xander ran the water over him, he balked, strained, barked, pulled.

But he didn't snap, snarl, or bite.

Xander pulled a massive dog biscuit out of his back pocket, and the dog settled down to eye it greedily.

"Yeah, you want this. Hold the hose," he told Naomi, then broke the biscuit in half. "Half now, half when we're done. Got it?"

He gave the dog the half biscuit, and poured green liquid from the bottle in his hands. Obviously the dog enjoyed the rubbing and soaping, and stood quietly while Xander scrubbed at him.

He didn't care for the rinsing off, but the second round of soaping had his eyes half closing in bliss. By the end of it, he sat quietly—maybe, Naomi thought, as delighted as she was that he didn't smell like dead skunk.

"Better stand back when I let him go."

"Let him go? What if he runs?"

"He's not going anywhere. Stand back, or you'll get wetter than you already are."

She released the collar, then danced back and out of range of the energetic shaking and storm of water.

"He isn't as ugly as I thought."

"Get some meat back on his bones, he'll be a good-looking dog. Might have some Lab in him—shape of the head. Probably got a lot in him. Mutts make the best dogs."

"Now that he's clean, doesn't look like he's going to collapse, and you've got the truck, you can take him with you."

"Can't do it."

"You know the vet by name. And—"

"I can't. Look . . ." He turned, went back to his truck for a rag of a towel, and began to rub the wet dog. "I had to put my dog down last month. Had him nearly half my life. I just can't take this one. I'm not ready."

The open bag of kibble, the shampoo, the bowls, the collar. She should've put it together. "Okay. I know how it feels. We had a dog—my brother's dog, really. The uncles gave it to him for Christmas when he was ten. He was so sweet, so considerate, we didn't have to put him down. He just slipped away in his sleep when he was fourteen. The four of us cried like babies."

The dog sniffed at Xander's pocket.

"This one's not stupid." Xander took the second half of the biscuit, offered it. This offering was taken politely.

"He's a good dog. It shows."

"Maybe."

"You get him to Alice tomorrow. I'll split the vet bill with you. I'll get the word out."

"All right."

"I've got a leash and a dog bed—it's a little worn, but he won't care. A couple of rawhide bones. I'll bring it in."

Naomi looked at the dog, at Xander, at the enormous bag of dog food. "Want a beer? I'd say you've earned it."

"Hang on." He pulled out his phone, punched in a number. "Hey. Yeah, yeah, I texted I would be. Now I'm going to be later."

"Oh, if you've got a date, don't—"

Xander shifted his gaze—a deeper, bolder blue than the no-name dog's. "Kevin and Jenny. Sunday dinner. Naomi found this dog, I'm just helping her get it cleaned up. Don't know. At least a couple years old, golden brown now that six inches of filth are washed off. Mixed breed."

"I took pictures. I'll send them a picture, in case they recognize him."

"Your boss here's going to send you a picture of the mutt. No, go ahead. Yeah, later." He put the phone away, hefted the bag of dog food over his shoulder. "I could use that beer."

They started toward the house, the dog between them. "He's still limping."

"He's been on the road awhile, I'd say. The pads of his paws are scraped up and sore."

After unlocking the door, holding it open, she watched the dog limp inside, begin to explore.

"You don't think we're going to find his owners."

"I'd lay money against it. You want this back in the kitchen?"

"Yeah." She'd keep him overnight, even for a few days while they tried to locate his owners or found someone who wanted a dog. She got out a beer, a bottle of wine, handed Xander the beer, poured wine into a plastic cup.

"Thanks." As he drank, Xander wandered around the kitchen. "Looks good. Real good. I didn't see how he'd turn this one around, but he always does."

"I love it. Nowhere to sit yet—I have to find stools. And a table and chairs, and according to my uncles, a divan or love seat for that space over there, fronted by a burl-wood table for tension."

"Who are these mysterious uncles who take you to see Springsteen, buy you dogs, and advise you to buy divans—and why do they call it a divan instead of a couch?"

"I think it's size or shape, or maybe geography—on the divan/couch part. My mother's younger brother and his husband. They more or less raised me and my brother."

"You were raised by your gay uncles?"

"Yes, is that a problem?"

"No. It's interesting. It's New York, right?" He leaned back against the counter, as apparently at home as the dog who now stretched out on the floor and slept the sleep of the clean, content, and completely trusting.

"Yes, it's New York."

"Never been there. What do they do? The uncles."

"They own a restaurant. Harry's a chef. Seth is the man of numbers and business. So it works. My brother's with the FBI."

"No shit?"

"He's got degrees in psychiatry, psychology, and criminology. He wants the Behavioral Analysis Unit."

"Profiling?"

"Yes. He's brilliant."

"You four sound tight. But you're three thousand miles away."

"I didn't expect to be. But . . ." She shrugged. "Do you have family here?"

"My parents moved to Sedona a few years ago. I've got a sister in Seattle, and a brother in L.A. Not so tight, but we get along all right when we have to."

"You grew up here—with Kevin."

"Womb to tomb."

"And own a garage, body shop place, own half interest in a bar—Jenny mentioned it—and run a band."

"I don't run the band. But half interest in the bar means we get to play there." He set down the bottle. "I'll get the dog bed. Down here or upstairs?"

She looked at the dog again, sighed. "I guess up in the bedroom. I hope to Christ he's housebroken."

"Most likely."

He hauled the brown corduroy dog bed up the stairs, set it in front of the fireplace, tossed a yellow tennis ball in it.

"Color works," he said.

"I really think so."

"So . . . I wouldn't feed him any more tonight. Maybe one of the Milk-Bones, and maybe give him the rawhide to chew on."

"It better be all he chews on." She glanced over as the dog had followed them out, then back in, then up the stairs, and now had the yellow tennis ball in his mouth.

"I'd better get going or Jenny won't feed me. Uncle's a chef?"

"A terrific chef."

"You cook?"

"I was taught by a master."

"It's a good skill."

He stepped up. She should've seen it coming. She was always, always aware of moods and moves. But he stepped up, pulled her in before she'd read the warning sign.

He didn't go slow; he didn't ease in. It was one bright, hot explosion followed by shuddering dark. His mouth covered, conquered, while his hands ran straight up her body as if they had every right, then down again.

She could have stopped it. He was bigger, certainly stronger, but she knew how to defend herself. She didn't want to stop—not yet, not quite yet. She didn't want to defend.

She gripped the sides of his waist, fingers digging in. And let herself burn.

It was he who eased back until she stared into those dangerous blue eyes. "Just like you look."

"What?"

"Potent," he said. "You pack a punch."

She saw the move this time, laid a hand firmly on his chest. "So do you, but I'm not up for a bout right now."

"That's a damn shame."

"You know, right at the moment, I couldn't agree more. But."

"But." He nodded, stepped back. "I'll be in touch. About the dog."

"About the dog."

When he went out, the dog looked after him, looked at Naomi. Whined.

"You're with me for now." She sat on the foot of the bed—such as it was—because her legs felt shaky. "He's completely the wrong choice. I'm absolutely sure of it."

The dog came over, laid his paw on her knee. "And don't think you're going to charm me. I'm not getting tangled up with Xander, and I'm not keeping you. It's all temporary."

A night or two for the dog, she promised herself. And absolutely not with Xander Keaton.

Nine

The dog didn't like the leash. The minute Naomi snapped it on, he pulled, tugged, tried to turn around and bite it. She ended up dragging him out of the house, using a Milk-Bone as a bribe.

He also didn't like the vet's office. The minute she got him into the waiting room, he quivered, shook, strained to get back out the door. A grizzled old man sat in one of the plastic chairs with a grizzled old mutt sprawled at his feet. The old mutt's lips curled as if in disdain. A cat in a carrier stared out with feral green eyes.

It was hard to blame the dog for dropping down on the floor, refusing to budge. He trembled the whole time Naomi filled out the paperwork, even when the old man took the dog, who walked obediently even if he cast a look back—disdain again—as they went into the back.

While they waited, and Naomi had to be grateful they'd squeezed her in, a woman came in with a red-gold ball of fur and fluff. The fluffball stopped dead when it spotted Naomi's stray, then went into a wild series of high-pitched yips punctuated by throaty little growls.

The dog did his best to crawl into Naomi's lap.

"Sorry! Consuela's very high-strung." The woman plucked up Consuela and tried to quiet and soothe her while Naomi struggled to keep the dog's nose out of her crotch.

When they called her name, the relief was so huge she didn't mind being forced to half drag, half carry her charge into the exam room.

He quivered in there, too, and looked at her with such abject terror that she crouched down to hug him.

"Come on now, pull yourself together."

He whined, licked, then laid his head on her shoulder.

"Somebody's in love. Alice Patton."

The vet, maybe five-two with a sturdy, compact build, had her gray-streaked brown hair pulled back in a short ponytail and black, square-framed glasses over eyes of soft, quiet brown. She came in briskly, wearing a short white lab coat over T-shirt and jeans, and crouched down.

"Naomi Carson."

"It's nice to meet you. And this is the handsome guy you picked up on the side of the road."

"I made up some flyers to help find his owner. Your receptionist took a few."

"We'll put them out, but I haven't seen this boy before. Let's get him on the scale first, then we'll see what's what."

He didn't much care for the idea, but they weighed him in at seventy-one pounds.

"He could use another ten. Definitely undernourished. Clean, though."

"He wasn't. We bathed him. Twice."

"Xander helped you out with him, right?" And to Naomi's astonishment, Alice hefted seventy-one pounds of trembling dog onto the exam table.

"Yes, he came along a couple minutes after I found the dog."

"Put Milo's collar on him, I see."

"Milo? Was that his dog?"

"Mmm-hmmm." Like her eyes, her voice was soft and calm as she ran her hands over the dog. "Great dog, Milo. Cancer came on fast and hard. We did everything we could, but . . . He had fifteen good, happy years, and that's what counts. This one here, he's about two, and he's been on the road awhile from the looks of his paws."

She got out her light, slipped him a small treat before examining his ears. "I'm going to give you some drops for his ears."

"Drops?"

"He's got an infection brewing in the left one. And I've got some meds you'll need to give him for worms."

"Worms?"

"Stool sample you brought in. He's got worms, but the meds should clear that up quick enough. I'm going to give him a test for heartworm, and I'd like to do a titer to gauge if he needs shots. Seeing as he's a stray, I'm going to discount all this for you."

"I appreciate it. He's got to belong to somebody, right?"

"Hasn't been neutered." Alice stepped away, got a syringe. "As he's a mixed breed, it's not likely he has all his works because someone intends to breed him. He's seriously underweight. Go on and stroke his head, distract him a little. He's got intestinal worms," Alice continued, as she drew blood. "The pads of all four paws are raw. I'm going to be able to tell in about twenty minutes or so if he's had shots for rabies and distemper, if he has heartworm. But he's got a little mange, and ticks and fleas have been at him."

"Fleas."

"Dead now, from the flea bath you gave him. I'm the only vet in town, and he hasn't been in here before. Wouldn't be the first time somebody dumped a dog they decided they didn't want."

"Oh." Naomi looked down to where, despite the needles, the tests, the dog stared into her eyes with absolute trust.

"I'll call the vets I know in the area, and we'll put up your flyer, contact the shelters. It's possible he got lost, and someone's been looking for him."

Naomi clung to the possibility.

It took more than an hour altogether, an unfortunate round of shots, though the dog handled them without more than a look of puzzlement.

She left with a bag of pills, drops, pamphlets, written instructions, and a dog-sized hole in her credit card.

Reeling, she hunted up Xander's garage.

It was bigger than she'd imagined. Cars and trucks scattered around a lot, some of them—such as the hatchback with the crunched front fender—obviously waiting for repairs.

One building about the size of a Quonset hut looked like it held offices. Another spread in a long backward L with the front bay doors open wide. The dog still didn't like the leash, but she was onto him now, and shortened up her grip on it.

She intended to try the offices, but the dog pulled and bulled his way toward the open doors and the noise.

She heard the *whoosh-thump* of an air compressor, a steady banging, and Walk the Moon advising everyone to shut up and dance.

She'd spent a lot of time on the road, so she'd been in her share of garages. The sounds, the smells (grease, oil), the sights (tools, machines, car guts) seemed fairly usual. But they apparently fascinated the dog, who strained on the leash until he got inside.

Then his tail wagged like a flag in the breeze.

He'd obviously scented Xander over the motor oil, gas, lubes, and grease guns, and let out a happy, greeting bark.

Xander stood under a sedan on a lift doing whatever mechanics do to underbellies, Naomi decided. He wore scarred motorcycle boots and faded jeans with a hole in the knee and a dirty red rag hanging out of the back pocket. She couldn't figure out how he made the look sexy.

"Hey, big guy." He stuck the tool he'd used in his other back pocket, then crouched to greet the delighted dog. "You look better than you did yesterday." He glanced up at Naomi. "You always look good."

"We just came from the vet."

"How'd he do?"

"He tried to crawl inside me in the waiting room because he was terrified of a Pomeranian. But she did have attitude. He has an ear infection and worms, and I have a bag full of pills and drops and instructions. He had to have a half million tests, followed by shots as the whatever-the-hell-it-is was low and he probably hasn't had the shots before. He doesn't have heartworm, so yay. And he needs to gain weight. I have dog vitamins, for God's sake.

"Plus."

She dug in her purse, took out the vet bill, held it out.

Xander said, "Ouch."

"And this is the discounted, Good Samaritan rate."

"Well, it's his first, and he needed it. I'm good for half."

"It's not the money, though okay yeah, ouch; it's the very strong sense I get that in her opinion nobody's looking for him. What am I supposed to do with him?"

"Looks like you're doing it."

A man in gray coveralls and a gray cap with the garage's logo wandered out and plugged coins into the soda machine along the wall. "That Chevy's looking good as new, boss. Better."

"Will it be ready by four?"

"She'll be ready."

"I'll tell Syl."

The dog tugged on the leash, and as Naomi had loosened her grip, he slipped free to wag his way to the new guy.

"Hey, boy. Your dog's got a sweet face, ma'am."

"He's not mine. He's not mine," she said almost desperately to Xander, who only shrugged.

"Want another dog, Pete?"

"You know I would, but Carol would skin me. Nice dog," he added, then walked off while the dog wandered around sniffing at everything.

"How'd he sleep?"

"What? The dog? Fine. I woke up at five because he was standing by the bed staring at me—and scared the crap out of me."

"So he's housebroken."

"I guess. So far anyway, but—"

"You live a ways from town," Xander continued. "A dog's good security."

"I'm having an alarm system installed."

"A dog's good company," he shot back.

"I like solitude."

"You're a hard sell, Naomi."

The dog walked back, tail wagging, with a rag hanging out of his mouth and happy eyes as he brought it to Naomi.

"He loves you."

"Because he brought me a filthy rag he found on the floor."

"Yeah. You'll get used to it. Meantime, I'll get you half that bill, and I'll keep asking around if anyone's missing him or interested in taking him."

She dug into her purse again and came out with the flyer she'd printed. "Put this up."

Xander studied it. "Nice shot of him."

"I have to go get some work done. I haven't done anything but dog all morning."

"You could ask me to dinner."

"Why would I?"

"Then you'd have done something else, and I'll give him his evening meds. You said you can cook."

She gave him a long, cool look. "You're not after a meal."

"Man's gotta eat."

"I don't have dishes, or chairs, or a table. I'm not going to sleep with you, and I am *not* keeping this dog." Annoyed with him, with herself, she snatched the leash and began to pull the dog out of the bay.

"You like to gamble, Naomi?"

She looked over her shoulder, still dragging the dog. "No."

"Too bad, because I'd bet you every bit you just said's going to change."

The hell it would, she told herself.

She didn't realize until she got home that the dog still had the disgusting rag. When she tried to get it from him, he decided she wanted to play tug. In the end, she gave up and sat on the top step of her front porch, the dog with the disgusting rag beside her. And the noise of saws and hammers behind.

"What have I done? Why didn't I just pitch a tent in the woods? Why do I have a big house full of all these people? Why do I have a dog I have to medicate?"

Adoringly, he dropped the wet, greasy rag in her lap.

"Perfect. Just perfect."

He went with her when she climbed down the steep, jumbled path to the shoreline. She'd been certain the dog would stay, hang out with the crew, but he'd insisted on going out when she did. Next time, she'd sneak out.

Still, she found he didn't get in the way as she found her shots. Even the one of the dark purple starfish shining in a tidal pool. In fact, after a brief exploration, the dog seemed content to doze in the sun as long as she stayed in sight.

Just as he seemed content to curl up nearby when she sat at her desk working, or worked in her mat room.

If she went downstairs, the dog followed. If she went up, he climbed right up after.

When the house was quiet again, she wondered if dogs could have abandonment issues.

He didn't like the ear drops, and that was a battle—but she won. She knew from Kong the best way to get meds into a dog, and disguised the pills in rolled slices of cheese.

When she sat out on the deck eating her dinner of a grilled cheese sandwich, he ate his—and didn't bolt it down as if starved this time.

And when she got into bed with her laptop to spend the last hour of her day looking for faucets and showerheads, the dog curled into his bed as if he'd done so all his life.

At five in the morning she woke with a start, the dog's eyes gleaming at her, his doggy breath in her face.

Xander sent his half of the vet bill with Kevin, along with the message that he'd split the follow-up, too.

Two days later, he showed up himself with another bag of dog food, another rawhide bone, and the biggest box of Milk-Bones she'd ever seen.

She wondered if he'd timed it to arrive minutes after the crew left, or if it was just coincidence. But it made the dog happy, and he spent some time roughhousing with him.

"He's getting some energy back." Xander winged a tennis ball so the dog could chase it like it was gold.

"Nobody's responded to the flyers. Nothing from any of the vets or shelters."

"You're going to have to face it, Slim. You've got yourself a dog. What's his name?"

"I'm not naming him." If she named him, she was finished.

"What do you call him?"

"The dog."

Xander winged the ball again when the dog retrieved it, and shook his head. "Have a heart."

"Having a heart's what got me into this. If I keep him any longer, I have to have him neutered."

Xander gave the dog a pitying look. "Yeah. Sorry about that, pal. You should try out some names."

"I'm not going to—" She broke off. Why argue? "Alice said your dog was Milo. Where'd you get the name?"

"Milo Minderbinder."

"*Catch-22*? Everybody gets a share?"

"Yeah. I'd just read it, and the pup, he just looked like he'd have all the angles. Name's gotta fit. Are you going to ask me in?"

"I am not. Nothing's changed."

"It's early days yet," he said, then turned as she did at the sound of an approaching vehicle. "Expecting anybody?"

"No."

The dog barked, raced up to stand beside Naomi.

"You've got a guard dog there."

"I can guard myself just fine." And her hand went into her pocket, closed over the folding knife.

The big truck lumbered up the hill—the big truck with New York plates.

The driver—young, sharp-eyed—leaned out the window. "Naomi Carson?"

"Yes."

"Sorry we're so late in the day. We got a little turned around."

"I didn't order anything from New York. Did you drive cross-country?"

"Yes, ma'am. Me and Chuck did it in fifty-five hours, twenty-six minutes." He hopped out of the truck and gave the dog a pat while his companion hopped out the other side.

"Why?" Naomi asked.

"Sorry?"

"I don't understand what you're doing here."

"Delivering your bed."

"I didn't order a bed."

"Shoot. All this way and we forgot. No, ma'am, you didn't order it. It's a gift, sent by Seth Carson and Harry Dobbs. We're to get it here, put it where you want it, and set it up. They paid for the full white-glove delivery."

"When?"

"A little more than fifty-five hours and twenty-six minutes ago, I guess you could say." He grinned again. "There's a couple packages in the back, too. Wrapped. It's a hell of a bed, ma'am."

The one called Chuck handed her a clipboard with the order sheet. She recognized the name of the furniture store her uncles patronized.

"I guess we'll find out."

"Want some help with it?" Xander asked.

The driver gave his shoulders a roll, and Xander a look of pure gratitude. "It's one big mama, so we could use it."

As it was heavily wrapped for shipping, Naomi couldn't say if it was a hell of a bed, except in size. She carted the packages, one at a time, as the men began the more laborious effort of getting the bed inside and up the stairs.

Since the dog stayed with the men, she got a box cutter and opened the first box. Four king-size pillows—down. In the second, more pillows, a gorgeously simple duvet several perfect shades deeper blue than her walls, with matching shams. In the third, two sets of lovely white-on-white Egyptian cotton sheets, and the handwritten note.

> *Our girl needs a bed, and one that gives her sweet dreams.*
> *We knew it was for you the minute we saw it. We love you,*
> *Seth and Harry.*

"My men," she said with a sigh, and carted the first box upstairs.

Since her bedroom was currently chaos and full of other men, and dog, she went back down, got soft drinks out of the fridge, and took them back up.

"'Preciate it. We'll haul all the wrapping and padding away with it. We've got specific instructions. It's going to take a while to get it put together."

"Okay."

"You want it where you got the mattresses, right?"

"I . . . Yes. That's fine. I need to make a call."

She left them to it, called home, and spent the next twenty minutes with Seth as Harry was at the restaurant. His pleasure zipped over every mile.

She didn't tell him she'd narrowed down her choices and styles of bed, had even planned a day trip to Seattle to look some over. Whatever they'd bought her would be treasured just for that.

When she went back into the bedroom she stopped short. They had her mattresses on the frame, had the headboard and footboard on—or heading that way.

"Oh my God."

"Pretty, isn't it?"

She looked at the driver—she didn't know his name—then back at the bed. "It's gorgeous. It's wonderful. It's perfect."

"Wait till we get the posts up."

Mahogany, she thought, with satinwood crossbanding. Chippendale-style—she hadn't been raised by Seth and Harry for nothing. The wood tones, rich and lovely, set off the soft colors of the walls. Fretwork legs, and posts high and turned.

If a woman didn't have sweet dreams in a bed like that, she needed therapy.

"You okay, ma'am?"

She managed to nod. "I'm sorry, I didn't get your name."

"Josh. Josh and Chuck."

"Josh. I'm fine. You were right. It's a hell of a bed."

When they were done, she tipped them generously—the least she could do—and gave them more soft drinks for the road.

When they left, she stood staring at the bed, at the way the early-evening light gleamed on the wood, on the details.

"Some uncles you've got," Xander commented.

"Best ever."

"Need to cry it out?"

She shook her head, pressed fingers to her eyes. "No. I hate to cry. So useless. I talked to them Sunday. They went right out and found this, then had it shipped all the way out here this way—along with sheets and pillows and bedding. And it's just right, just exactly right. For me, for the room, for the house."

She pushed the threat of tears away. "I'm not going to cry. I'm going to cook. I still don't have dishes or a table. But you can eat what I fix on paper plates outside on the deck. That's your tip for helping set up the bed."

"I'll take it. What's for dinner?"

"I don't know yet. But I'm having wine. I'm feeling sentimental and a little homesick."

"Got beer?"

"Pretty sure."

"If you do, I'll go for that."

"Okay." She started out, glanced back at him. "I'm still not sleeping with you."

"Yet." His smile was easy. And dangerous. "Beer and a dinner's a start."

A finish, she thought as the dog trooped down with them.

H e watched her cook. He'd never seen anybody cook by grabbing things, throwing this thing in a pan, that thing in a skillet. Chopping this up, stirring that in.

The dog watched her, too, and wasn't subtle about licking his muzzle when the scents started rising.

"What are you making there?"

"We'll call it Pasta on the Fly."

She laid olives—fat ones—on a cutting board, smacked them with a flat of the knife she'd been wielding, and popped out the pits. Something else he'd never seen anyone do.

"Don't those just come in jars without pits?"

"These are Kalamata olives, friend, and they're worth the extra step. Anything I put in here you don't like, you eat around."

"I'm not fussy."

"Good thing."

Now she took a hunk of cheese and worked it to a blur over a grater. He'd have asked why she didn't buy it already grated but figured he knew the answer.

She tossed little tomatoes in the pan, added some sort of herbs, and stirred—even while muttering how she wished the local produce ran to fresh basil.

"I need to get good cookware before Harry sends me that, too."

"What's wrong with what you've got? Looks like it's working fine to me."

"Hardware store special. He'd be appalled. I'm a little appalled myself, actually. And I definitely need good knives. Something to add to the list."

He liked watching her—quick, sure movement. Liked listening to her—a voice that held just the right amount of smoke.

"What else is on the list?"

"Painting the guest rooms I have earmarked for my brother and for my uncles. The one for my grandparents. After that, I think I'll retire my roller and pan. I don't like painting."

"Have the painters paint."

"I need to buy decent cookware and knives—I can paint two more rooms in this ridiculously big house. And now I have to find furniture worthy of that bed, and so on."

She drained the pasta—the little tube sort—then added it to the skillet, along with the olives, the cheese. Tossed it all around.

"Plates are in that cupboard there, such as they are, as are paper napkins and a box of plastic forks."

"Got it."

She tossed the stuff in the skillet a couple more times, then served it up on the paper plates and added wedges of Italian bread that she'd slathered with butter, sprinkled with herbs, and toasted.

"That looks amazing."

"It would look better on the plates I ordered, but it's good enough." She handed him a plate, took one for herself, and then led the way out. Then she handed him her plate. "Hold this while I feed the dog."

The dog looked at the kibble she dumped in his bowl, then back at Xander with the two aromatic plates of pasta. His tail drooped, and Xander swore the dog sighed in disappointment.

She sat, eyeing the dog, who eyed her. "This is mine, that's yours. That's how it goes."

"Hard-ass."

"Maybe."

Xander sat down and sampled what she'd thrown together magically and a little maniacally in about twenty minutes.

"This is really good. Seriously good."

"It's not bad. It'd be better with fresh herbs. I guess I'll have to plant some."

It didn't feel as odd as she'd expected, to sit there, eating pasta with him while the dog—who'd polished off his own bowl—watched them mournfully. Maybe it was the view—that soft hand of dusk gliding pale and purple over water and the green—maybe it was the wine. Either way, she needed to set the line.

"Do you want to know why I'm not going to sleep with you?"

"Yet," he added. "Is there a list?"

"We can call it that. You live here, and right now, so do I."

"Right now? You've got pots and pans for the right now, but have better ones on your list. It seems to me you're looking at the down-the-road."

"Maybe. I've never lived in any one place for more than a few months since I left New York. I don't know if this will stick. Maybe," she said again, "because it feels right—right now. But in any case, you live here and you're friends with Kevin and Jenny—long-term, serious friends. We start something—and I'm also not looking to start something—and it gets messed up, your friend and my contractor's in the middle of it."

"That's weak," Xander said, and went back to the pasta.

"Not from where I'm sitting, in the heart of a construction zone. Plus you're the only local garage and mechanic, and I might need a mechanic."

Thoughtfully, he crunched into the bread. "Probably get the work done faster if we're having sex."

She laughed, shook her head. "Not if we stop having it, and you're pissed at me. There's work, of which I have to do a lot to pay for this house, and everything that goes into it. I don't have time for sex."

"There's always time for sex. Next time, I'll bring pizza and we can have sex in the time you spent making dinner."

And thoughtfully, Naomi ate pasta. "That doesn't speak well of your . . . stamina."

"Just trying to work on your schedule."

"Considerate, but unnecessary as dinner tonight is a one-off. I don't know you."

"That's the only thing you've said so far that makes sense. But we can go back up your list and I can remind you I'm friends—serious, long-term—with Kev and Jenny. They'd warn you if I was a psychopath."

She kept her eye on the view. "People don't always know people close to them the way they think they do."

There was a story, Xander thought. He could hear it murmuring under her words. Instead of pressing on that, he tried something else.

He leaned over and took her face in his hand. Her mouth with his. Strong and hot and edging onto the fierce.

He knew when a woman wanted—and she did. He knew it by the way her mouth responded, heard it in her throaty hum, felt it in the quick, sexy quiver.

Another woman? All this heat, the mesh of needs would lead them straight up and into that excellent new bed.

But she drew back. Still, she kept her eyes, that deep, fascinating green, on his.

"You make an excellent point," she said. "And I can't argue it, but . . ." She looked directly into his eyes. "Like I told the dog, that's how it goes."

"Tonight."

For the moment he contented himself with the food, the view, the mysteries of the woman beside him. Somebody handed him a puzzle, he thought, he just had to solve it. He'd figure her out, sooner or later.

Ten

She went back to work. Since work ranked high on her list of reasons not to sleep with Xander, she had to make her own point.

When she went out to shoot in the morning, the dog tagged along. For a few days, if she headed into woods or along shorelines, she rigged the leash to her belt. They both disliked the solution intensely.

After those few days, she realized the dog wasn't going anywhere and usually left him off the leash. He explored nearby, chased squirrels, barked at birds, sniffed at deer tracks—and scat—while she composed studies of wildflowers, trees, long channels of water in sunlight and in shadow.

And she ended up with an entire series of dog shots.

He snoozed by the fireplace—gas logs installed and fabulous for cool, gloomy days—while she worked at her computer. Now and again, he'd go down, hang with the crew or with Molly if she'd come to visit, but he always came back in, gave her a long look as if checking if she'd finished. If she hadn't, he curled up again, usually with something in his mouth.

Sometimes the something was a stray work glove, and once it was a hammer.

Steady, focused work paid off. She received a satisfying check from the gallery in New York, and watched her PayPal account blossom.

People, it seemed, really liked pictures of dogs.

Jenny stopped by, as promised, and took the tour. When they got to the master suite, Jenny sighed.

"I don't know which is more impressive, the view or the bed."

"I like having the view from the bed."

"It must be wonderful, waking up to that every morning. Xander said your uncles shipped the bed all the way across the country."

"They did. And if I don't find some pieces to go in here, they'll start finding them, and shipping them."

"Come shopping with me!" Bouncing on her toes, Jenny slapped her hands together. "Let's go."

"What? Now?"

"It's my day off, kids in school. I've got . . ." She pulled out her phone to check the time. "Five hours before I have to pick up Maddy, then Ty. I know it's a workday for you, but you have to have more furniture, and I know a couple of places—especially if you're not afraid of refinishing or having something refinished—that should have pieces that will really suit that bed."

"I really . . ." She thought of the income she'd just banked, turned the automatic refusal on its ear. "Should do that."

"Yes! Maybe we can find your dishes."

"I ordered them. Wait. I'll show you."

They both studied her computer screen as she brought them up. "They're recycled glass, which appealed, and I went with some white serving pieces for the bump. I think—"

"They're wonderful. Perfect. Oh, they're going to look fabulous in that kitchen. And on the table once you get a table."

"The table can wait awhile. Not planning any dinner parties. But I do need stools. Stools, and a dresser. It'd be nice to put my clothes in drawers rather than cardboard boxes."

"Let's go bag one."

The dog came. Naomi had no intention of taking him, but he followed them out, hopped right in her car, then crawled into the back to sit, tongue hanging out in anticipation.

"He's so sweet. A dog's a good thing to have living out here alone, and a sweet dog's a good thing anywhere. Kevin says he and Molly get along fine. What's his name?"

"He doesn't have one."

"Oh, Naomi, you have to name him."

"His owners could still—"

"How long since you brought him home?"

"We're into week three." Naomi sighed, rubbed the back of her neck. "He's going in for neutering tomorrow. If you're looking for a dog . . ."

"We have one, thanks. We are thinking of a puppy, a friend for Molly. And we want the kids to have the experience. Besides, Naomi. That's your dog."

Naomi looked in the rearview mirror, and the dog unquestionably smiled at her.

"He's just living here for now."

"Sure he is."

Naomi narrowed her eyes, put on her sunglasses. "Which way?"

"Just head toward town, and I'll guide you from there."

She couldn't think of the last time she'd shopped with a friend—or allowed herself a friend. For the most part she didn't go shopping so much as go, hunt up what she needed, buy it, and take it home. Which baffled and disappointed her uncles.

Plus, she could hunt up and buy almost everything she needed online.

But since she was out and about, she'd stop by the hardware and buy the paint for Mason's room—a warm mossy green—on the way back.

And she liked Jenny. She decided it was impossible not to like Jenny, who was cheerful and funny and didn't ask probing questions.

She decided she really liked Jenny when her new friend directed her to a huge barn a few miles inland.

"I should've brought my camera."

But she opened the compartment between the seats and took out a case.

"What's that?"

"Lenses and filters for my camera phone."

"Really? I didn't know there were such things."

"Works well in a pinch. And that barn—the texture of the wood, the true barn red with the white trim, that old apple tree, the light. It's good."

"Don't you want to see what's in the barn?"

"Absolutely. This won't take long."

She intended to leave the dog in the car. He had other ideas, so against her better judgment, Naomi pulled out the spare leash she'd stowed in the glove compartment.

"If you go, you wear this."

He tried to stare her down. Failed.

"I'll hold on to him while you take pictures."

"Thanks. He hates the leash."

"Wouldn't you? It's all right, sweetheart. We'll think of it as you leading me."

Perversely, the dog behaved perfectly for Jenny, walked happily beside her, sniffed his way to an appealing spot to lift his leg while Naomi composed shots, added lenses, adjusted filters.

She'd come back with her equipment, she promised herself. She'd love a gloomy day, that barn under gloomy skies.

She found more shots inside. The place went on forever, packed with everything under sun or gloom.

Glassware, tinware, collectibles, mirrors, chairs, desks.

In fact, she paused in front of one of the desks. She'd decided to go with new for a permanent desk—something that looked right with the bed, but had all the modern touches. Keyboard drawer, plugs, file drawers.

But.

It was nearly black from years—probably decades—of varnish, and the drawers stuck. It needed new hardware. It wasn't at all what she'd decided on.

And it was perfect.

"The shape's terrific," Jenny said beside her. "Just enough curve at the corners. Plenty of drawers. It needs work." Lips pursed, Jenny checked the tag. "And some bargaining."

"It's solid, sturdy. Mahogany. It needs to be stripped down to the original finish. It's not what I was going for. And I really love it."

"Don't say you love it to Cecil—his place. Look doubtful when you ask him about it. You need a good chair—a new one—ergonomic, lumbar support. Kevin says you spend a lot of time at your desk."

"Kevin's right. The computer's the darkroom today. Though I want to put an actual darkroom in. I still get the urge to shoot film sometimes. Is that a mermaid floor lamp?"

"It appears to be."

"A bronze mermaid floor lamp." Struck, she pulled out her phone again. "I need that for my portfolio."

"No-name and I are going to wander."

"I'll catch up."

She fell for the mermaid floor lamp, which she told herself was stupid. She wasn't looking for a floor lamp, much less a bronze mermaid with sly eyes and sleek breasts. But she wanted it.

"Don't tell Cecil," she reminded herself, and tried to find Jenny and the dog in the maze of fascinating things.

Jenny found her. "Don't hate me."

"Does anybody?"

"Kevin's old high school girlfriend."

"Because she's a slut."

Jenny beamed. "I didn't realize you knew Candy."

"Candy? Definitely a slut. A pink-wearing slut."

"Actually, I have a cousin named Candy, and she's not. She's wonderful. But to circle back, don't hate me, but I think I found the dresser."

"Why would I hate you for that?"

"It's expensive, but I really think it's perfect, and maybe we can team up and drive the price down, especially if you get the desk, too."

"And the mermaid lamp."

"Really?" Jenny threw back her head and laughed. "I love it. I figured you'd see it as a novelty, just for photos, but I think it'd be fabulous in your house."

"So do I. Let's see this dresser. If I hate you, you have to walk home."

There were advantages, Naomi discovered, to shopping with a friend—a friend with a sharp, creative, and discerning eye. It was more gentleman's chest than dresser—which really hit a note for her. Not female and fussy, but gorgeous and dignified without the stuffiness. In good condition, which surprised her, the finish glowing with that lovely reddish gold undertone. She'd change the hardware—get rid of the ornate brass handles—and one of the drawer bottoms had a long diagonal crack, but that was it.

The price made her hiss and shudder.

"We're going to talk him down. You wait and see." Jenny gave Naomi a bolstering pat.

Cecil might have been a scrawny man in bib overalls, a straw hat, with a grizzled beard—and he wouldn't see eighty again—but he had a gimlet eye and a hard line.

But so, Naomi discovered, did the sweet and cheerful Jenny.

She poked her oar in a time or two, just to say she did, but it was primarily Jenny who did the bargaining and, with tenacity and guile, shaved a full twenty percent off the dresser where Naomi had hoped for ten.

The three of them managed to load the dresser in the 4Runner—Cecil was old, but he proved ox-strong.

"Kevin's going to pick up the other pieces," Jenny told Cecil.

"He is?" Naomi wondered.

"Sure. He'll get them after work or in the morning. And remember, Cecil, Naomi has that big house to furnish so we'll be back. And expect good prices."

The dog sprawled out content enough beside the dresser, and Jenny settled in the passenger seat.

"That was fun."

"I'm dazzled by your Arabian marketplace skills. Thank you, really. I can come back and get the other pieces. Kevin doesn't have to come all the way out here."

"It's fine. Plus, if you hire me to refinish that desk, he'll just bring that home to my little workshop."

"You have a workshop?"

"I refinish and reimagine furniture and decorative pieces on the side. I didn't want to say anything, make you feel obligated or awkward. But boy, I want to do that desk. I'm good, I promise. I'll make it gorgeous."

"I bet you will." And she could cross off the hours it would take her to do it. "You're hired."

"Really? Yay! If you came over for dinner Sunday—Kevin said not to bother you, but I've been dying to have you to dinner—you could see the workshop. I've got a bench I'm working on that's perfect for the deck outside your bedroom. An old wire garden bench with a big, curved back. And you can bring the dog. The kids would love him."

Naomi started to make an excuse—knee-jerk. But curiosity won. "I'd love to see your workshop. You don't have to feed me."

"Come to dinner. We eat a little early most Sundays. Come by anytime after four. Time to see my shop, for the kids to play with the dogs."

"I'll be there. I'll bring dessert."

B right and early she took a long-sleeved T-shirt and leggings out of boxes. She refused to use the dresser until she had Kevin fix the drawer and she'd replaced the hardware.

When she walked casually out to the car, the dog followed, jumped right in, gave her that smug-dog grin.

He didn't know what he was in for.

But he got at least part of the picture when she pulled into the parking lot at the vet's.

He quivered, shook, tried to glue his nicely healed paws to the floorboards.

"This time you've got a reason, but you don't know that. Come on, grow a spine." She pulled, hauled, bribed—with a tennis ball, as food was off the table until after the surgery.

"You won't miss them," she told him, then shook her head. "How do I know? I'd miss pretty much anything somebody snipped off me. But it has to be, okay? It's just how it goes."

She got him through the waiting room—empty, as she'd arranged to be the first surgery or appointment of any kind of the day.

"Hey, boy." Alice greeted him with a good rub, relaxed him so he leaned on her. "We'll take him from here. The procedure's routine—sometimes a little tougher on a grown dog, but still routine. We'll keep him a few hours after, to make sure everything's good."

"Okay. I'll come get him when you call." She gave the dog a pat on the head. "Good luck."

When she turned to go he howled—long and mournful, as he'd done a few times when he heard a siren. She glanced back, saw his blue eyes full of sorrow and fear.

"Shit. Just shit."

"Just let him know you're coming back," Alice advised. "You're his alpha."

"Shit," she said again, and walked back to crouch in front of the dog. "I'm coming back to get you, okay?" She took his head in her hands, felt herself battered with the love his gaze sent out. "Okay, all right. I'm coming back to get you, take you home. You just have to do this first. I'll go—hell—I'll go buy you some good dog-sans-balls presents."

The dog licked her cheek, laid his head on her shoulder.

"He'd hug you if he could," Alice commented.

Sunk, Naomi hugged him instead. "I'll be back."

He whined when she rose, cried when she started out.

"He'll be fine," Alice called after her.

And the heart Naomi hadn't wanted to give away broke a little when she heard the dog howl.

She bought him a little stuffed cat, a ball that squeaked—telling herself she'd regret both purchases. She added a sturdy tug rope, a dog brush.

She made herself go home, made herself work. And when she couldn't concentrate for more than ten minutes, she put on her paint clothes. She didn't have to be creative to paint a room.

While she primed the walls, she imagined furnishing it. Maybe a sleigh bed, maybe dark gray. Mason would like it when he came to visit her. Or maybe old and iron—gray again. Gray would work with the green tones she'd paint in here.

Why didn't Alice call?

Annoyed with herself, she broke one of her unwritten rules about poking into whatever the crew was doing unless it was for pictures, and went downstairs.

They'd primed the living room—mostly because she couldn't quite decide what color she wanted there. The fireplace mantel needed refinishing, and made her think of Jenny. If Jenny did a decent job on the desk, she could do the mantel.

She wandered the space, looked out windows at the views. She wasn't ready to throw in the towel and hire a landscaper, but most of the outside rehab just had to wait until the bulk of the work was done inside, and men—and women—weren't tromping all over the place.

She moved on, stopped at the odd jut of a room she'd decided could be a little library. Maybe she didn't often find or take the time to curl up with an actual book, but she'd imagined doing so there on a rainy day— or in the dead of winter with the fire sparking.

Now Kevin and the buxom Macie set the first of the flanking built-ins in place to the right of the hearth.

"Oh, Kevin."

He glanced back, grinned as he shoved up the bill of his cap. "Go ahead and say it. You were right; I was wrong."

"I didn't know you'd finished them."

"We figured we'd surprise you. You were right. I didn't see it, little room like this. Take out that wall, I told you, and you'd have some space. But you stuck, and you had the eye. What you've got is cozy, and good light, and—what do you say, Macie?"

"Charm. It's gonna have charm, especially when we put up the crown molding."

"It's beautiful wood—the cherry—and beautiful work."

"That's what we do, right, Mace?"

"Damn right."

"You were right about straight open, floor to ceiling, too. Gives it dimension, makes the room seem bigger."

"I'm going to have to send for my books. I usually read on my tablet, but I've got a couple boxes of books back home."

"If you need more you can tap Xander."

"Why?"

"He's got books everywhere," Macie told her.

"Oh yeah." Kevin took a small level out of his tool belt, laid it on a shelf. "Every now and then he'll box some up, donate them, but mostly he hoards them. If you need to fill some of these shelves, you should tap him about it."

"I'll see what—" She jumped when her phone signaled, snatched it out of her pocket. "It's the vet. Yes, this is Naomi. Okay. Okay. Really?" As relief washed over her like a warm wave, she rubbed her hand over her face. "That's great. I'll come now. No, I'll be there in a few minutes. Thanks."

Blowing out a breath, she shoved the phone away again. "The dog—he's out of recovery or whatever. Ready to come home. I'll be back."

"Oh, in case I don't see you—you made the papers."

"The what?" She stopped dead.

"The papers," Kevin repeated. "I got a copy in the kitchen."

She kept her voice even. "What happened?"

"The *Cove Chronicle*. It comes out once a month. Just a few pages, local news and such. It's a nice story about the house, fixing it up."

"Oh."

Local little paper. Nothing to worry about. Nobody but the locals would see it.

"I'll leave you the copy. Jenny's got more at home, as I got some ink, too."

"I'll read it when I get back. Thanks. I better go get the dog."

She'd put off the reporter, editor, publisher—she thought the woman who'd wanted to talk to her wore all three hats. But it didn't matter. Naomi took every precaution to keep her name out of print, to keep her whereabouts out of print.

Nobody beyond Sunrise Cove, or certainly no one outside the county, would read the article. And nobody would connect her with Thomas David Bowes.

And she had more important things to worry about right at the moment.

She dashed into the vet's, muttered a thanks when the receptionist gestured her to go back. She found Alice fitting the dog with a cone.

He looked a little dazed and confused, but he let out a short, happy bark, and his tail wagged madly when he saw Naomi.

"He's okay?"

"Came through like a champ. He has meds, and you have instructions. The cone's to keep him from worrying the site, the stitches. He'll probably sleep more than anything else. He may be a little sore and not want to walk much for a day or two."

"Okay. That's okay." She got down, stroked his ears inside the cone. "You're okay."

She took the meds, the instructions, paid the bill, gave him a boost into the car.

He didn't sleep. He had to sniff at everything in the front yard—though he walked a little stiffly. He had to sniff and wag at the crew. He and Molly had to sniff and wag at each other.

And he bumped into everything. Walls, tools, her.

She helped him upstairs, gave him the stuffed cat—a mistake, she noted as the cone got in the way.

One of the crew called up with a question. She went down, and in the fifteen minutes she was gone, he'd managed to get out of the cone and was licking away where his balls had once been.

"How the hell did you get out of that?"

Pleased, he thumped his tail.

"You can't do that anymore. Those days are over." She fitted the cone back on him—an ordeal, as he seemed to hate it more than the leash.

She got it back in place, gave him a rawhide, and considered the matter settled.

It wasn't.

Xander figured he'd given it some time—and he had the excuse of paying her for half the ball snipping. Maybe, if he played it right, he could get another dinner out of it. And with that, maybe he could get her a few more steps closer to that big, beautiful bed.

It was worth the drive out.

He pulled up on his motorcycle, with the dog barking and wagging in greeting. The dog would've rushed over to finish the hello, but Naomi sat on the porch steps, and had the dog in a death grip.

Holding him in place while she . . . Jesus Christ.

Appalled, sincerely, Xander pulled off his helmet. "What the hell are you doing?"

"What the hell does it look like I'm doing?"

"It looks like you're putting pants on that dog."

"Then that's what the hell I'm doing."

She dragged them the rest of the way on—red shorts with a white side stripe—then let the dog go.

She leaned back on the steps while the dog—looking like an idiot—hurried over for a rub.

"What kind of person puts pants on a dog?"

"The kind who isn't going to keep fighting to keep the damn cone on him. He gets out of it. Kevin duct-taped the thing, and he still got out of it if I took my eyes off him for five damn minutes. And when he was in it, he ran into everything. Including me. I swear on purpose. He hated it."

"Cone of Shame?"

"Yeah, the damn Cone of Shame. So now he's wearing the Pants of Humiliation. But the stupid dog seems to like them."

"Pants of Humiliation." Xander had to grin. "You cut a hole for his tail."

"Kevin had them in his truck. His old running shorts. I got creative."

"Maybe, but how do you expect him to do what he needs to do out here?"

"Why the hell do you think I was dragging them back on him?" She waved her arms, winced, rubbed her right biceps. "I brought him out, took them off so he did what he needed to do. Now they're on, and he can't get to the incision site. In fact, he seems to forget about it when he's wearing them."

"Maybe you should buy him an outfit." Impressed with her inventiveness, Xander sat down beside her, rubbed the dog. "I got my half of the deal. Alice said he did fine."

"Yeah, yeah. He's fine. I'm exhausted."

"I can order a pizza."

"No, thanks, but— Crap, just crap. Yes. Please order. The backs of my calves are covered in cone bruises. My arms ache from painting and from struggling with this dog—who's putting on those pounds just fine, thanks."

The dog brought Xander a ball he'd obviously stowed somewhere outside for easy access.

"Don't throw it. He really shouldn't run yet."

Xander pushed up again. "Anything you don't like on pizza?"

"No anchovies, no pineapple. Anything else is fine."

The dog dropped the ball between Naomi's feet, and when she didn't respond laid his head on her knee.

"What's the dog's name?"

She heaved a sigh. "Tag."

"As in 'you're it'?"

"No. As in he tags along."

"Tag." The dog couldn't have recognized his name yet, but apparently he recognized humor as he looked over at Xander, gave a doggy grin. "It works."

PANORAMA

This visible world is but a picture of the invisible,
wherein, as in a portrait, things are not truly,
but in equivocal shapes.

SIR THOMAS BROWNE

Eleven

O nce or twice a week Xander and Kevin grabbed a beer after work. Sometimes they actually planned it and met up at Loo's, but for the most part it just happened.

It just happened that Kevin swung into Xander's garage after trips to the lumberyard and the tile distributor—and the half an hour huddled with his electrician.

He knew how to juggle jobs. Naomi's was priority, but he had a couple others going, which meant he spent a lot of time traveling from site to site.

And right now he wanted a beer.

The garage doors, lowered and locked, didn't mean Xander wasn't around. Just as his truck sitting in the parking lot didn't mean he was. Taking his chances, Kevin got out of his own truck and headed around the back of the garage, where a zigzag of steps led to Xander's apartment.

He heard the music, classic Stones; he followed it around to the rear bay—Xander's personal bay—and found his friend tending to the love of his life.

The '67 GTO convertible.

Or, as Kevin thought of it, the Date Car.

"Who's the lucky lady?" Kevin asked, pitching his voice to ride over Mick's.

Xander glanced up from polishing the chrome rocker panels. "She is. She needed detailing. I'm just finishing it up."

Xander had what he considered a damn fine crew of his own, but nobody, absolutely nobody, touched the GTO but himself. He loved her from her chain mail grille to her eight taillights, and every square inch of her Coke-bottle body between.

He rose now to take a critical look at his own work.

She shined, sparkling chrome against the red body. That was factory red—just as his grandfather had driven it off the showroom floor.

"Are you going to take her out for a spin? I'm up for it."

"Not today. We got rehearsal in—" Xander checked the old schoolhouse-style clock on the wall. "In about an hour. We got a wedding up in Port Townsend on Saturday. Lelo's cousin."

"Right, right. I remember. Got time for a beer?"

"I can make time." Xander took one last look at his sweetheart and stepped out. "Nice evening. How about we do this on the veranda?"

Kevin grinned. "That works."

They trooped up the steps into the apartment. The main space held the living room, kitchen, and—with the card table and folding chairs—the dining area.

Bookshelves—loaded—rose and spread over an entire wall of the living room. Kevin had built them—and the bookshelves in the skinny second bedroom used as an office, and the bookcase in the bedroom—when Xander bought the property and the business.

Xander opened the old fridge, a cast-off harvest gold number that had been the rage in the seventies, grabbed two bottles of St. Pauli Girl, popped the tops on the wall-mounted opener—a rust-colored naked woman holding the opener in upstretched arms—and tossed the caps in the trash.

They went out the bedroom door onto a postage-stamp porch and sat in two of the folding chairs that went with the card table.

And considered it fine.

"Big wedding?"

"Yeah. I'll be glad when it's done. The bride texts me every five minutes the last few days, screwing around with the playlist. Anyway. It's a living."

"Did you break your ban on the Chicken Dance?"

"Never happen. I took an oath." Xander stretched out his legs. He'd positioned the chairs so he could just stretch them out without his feet dropping off the edge. It worked.

"I saw your built-ins in the big house—library? And the tile work in the half bath. Nice."

Kevin stretched out his legs as well and took his first end-of-the-workday pull. "You were up there?"

"Yeah. The dog was wearing your pants, man. I gotta say, he looked better in them than you."

"I've got excellent, manly legs."

"With bear pelts."

"Keeps me and my woman warm in the winter. It was a smart solution. I don't know how the hell that dog kept getting out of the cone, but once she got the idea for the shorts, and we got them on him, he left his no-balls alone."

Kevin took a second pull on his beer. "And you're still trying to move on that?"

"The dog?" When Kevin just snorted, Xander shrugged. "I will move on that. In time."

"I've never known you to take time on a move."

"She's skittish." At least that word came to Xander's mind. "Don't you wonder why that is? She doesn't act especially skittish, look skittish, but she is under there. I'm curious enough to take time. If I just liked the look of her—and I do like the look of her—but if I just, I wouldn't bother with so much time. Either it's going to happen or it isn't. I like that she's smart. I like the contrasts."

"Contrasts?"

"Skittish, but ballsy enough to buy that old place, live out there on her own. She handles herself—and makes you think she's had to. I like what she's doing to the old place, or paying you to do."

"She's got ideas."

"Yeah. She's damn good at what she does. You've gotta appreciate somebody with talent who knows how to use it. And then . . ." Smiling, Xander took a long drink. "She named the dog."

"He's a good dog. He loves her like you love that GTO. He stole Jerry's hammer the other day."

"A hammer?"

"Naomi brought it, a sandpaper block, two work gloves, and a pipe fitting back down the other day. He takes them up to her like presents."

They sat a moment, in companionable silence, looking out toward the road where a few cars passed, the scatter of houses beyond, and the field where they'd both played Little League what seemed like a million years before.

"Tyler's got a T-ball game on Saturday."

"I'm sorry I'll miss that. It'll probably be more entertaining than the wedding."

"I remember playing T-ball, right over in the field. You and me and Lelo. Remember?"

"Yeah. Dim, but yeah."

"Now I've got a kid playing. Makes you think."

It made Xander think, nostalgically, of Lelo, who'd been scarecrow scrawny with beaver teeth. He'd stayed scrawny, Xander considered, but had grown into the teeth. "We sucked at T-ball, man, both of us. Got a groove on in Little League."

"Kids mostly suck at T-ball, that's part of the charm. Maddy starts kindergarten next fall."

Xander turned his head, gave Kevin a long look. "You're thinking about having another."

"The subject's come up a few times."

"Well, you do good work there."

"Yeah, we do. We always said two, and when we ended up with one of each, hey, that's a nice balance. Now Ty's playing T-ball, Maddy's going into kindergarten, and we're talking about starting another from scratch."

"Three's a magic number. You can look it up," Xander added when Kevin just looked at him.

"It's looking like we're going for the magic number."

"Have fun with that."

"That's the plus side. It sure is fun working on making one. You're not looking for sex with Naomi."

"Are you crazy?"

"I mean not just sex."

Xander contemplated his beer. "Why do married guys think single guys are only after sex?"

"Because they used to be single guys, and remember. Case in point—what was her name. Shit. Ah, Ari, Alli, Annie. The redhead with the rack and the overbite? Worked at Singler's last summer?"

"Bonnie."

"Bonnie? Where'd I get all those *A*'s from? That was just sex. She was built, so there's that. But all the work went into the face and body, none into the brain."

"It was the overbite." Even now, Xander could sigh over it. "I've always been a sucker for an overbite."

"Naomi doesn't have one."

"It's a flaw I'm overlooking. Sometimes it's just sex, as Bonnie illustrates and your memory serves. And sometimes, as you ought to remember, you want some conversation, some meat along with the sizzle. Bonnie had the sizzle, but I knew it wasn't going to be enough, even for the summer, when she picked up a copy of *East of Eden* I had on the nightstand and said she didn't know I was religious."

"Religious?"

"She figured Eden—so it must be a biblical story. She didn't even know who Steinbeck was." And he could still shake his head over that. "Even an overbite can't make up for that."

"It's good to have standards."

"Oh, I've got standards. So far, Naomi's meeting them, so I can take some time."

"What if she's lousy in bed?"

"That'd be both surprising and disappointing, but if so, we can still have conversations. Does she ever talk about her family with you?"

"Her brother, her uncles. Little bits and pieces here and there. Not much elaboration, now that you mention it."

"Exactly. It's interesting—what she doesn't say. It's interesting."

He thought about that, late into the night, long after rehearsal and the cold-cut subs he and his bandmates chowed down on.

In general he liked the company of men more than the company of women. He understood what men didn't say, didn't need or want it all laid out in specific words, expressions, freaking tones of voice. Women, to his mind, were work. Often worth it, and he didn't mind work.

But time spent with women, when it wasn't before, during, or after sex, was entirely different than hanging out with men or working with them.

In general, he preferred the short, straightforward mating dance and considered the extra steps and flourishes a waste of everyone's time.

You wanted or didn't; there was heat or there wasn't.

For some reason he found himself willing to take those extra steps with Naomi. He didn't really mind them; in fact, he enjoyed them, all the stops and starts, the detours.

And in his experience once the mating dance was done, the first rush of sex slowed, interest faded.

He liked being interested.

He turned on the bedroom TV, with the sound low as it was mostly to cover the silence so he didn't miss Milo's snoring so keenly. He picked up his nightstand book—a worn paperback of *Lord of the Flies*.

He never had a first read on the nightstand, not if he wanted to sleep, so he settled in with the familiar and fascinating.

But he couldn't get Naomi off his mind.

On the bluff, Naomi turned off the lights. Her brain was too tired for more work, too tired to pretend to read, even to stream a movie. The dog had already settled down, and it was time she did the same.

Since her tired brain didn't want to turn off, she let it wander, circling around faucets, lighting fixtures, whether she should do that study of Douglas firs she'd taken that morning, the green eerie through thin mists. It would make a solid cover for a horror novel.

She worked on it in her head, played up shadows until she drifted off, drifted away.

When she walked through that eerie green, the wind rolled through the tops of the trees, a *whoosh* and moan that laid a chill on her skin. She followed the path. She wanted to get to the water, to the blue, to the warm. Her footsteps were muffled on the thick cushion of pine needles, and those deep green shadows seemed to shift into shapes. And the shapes had eyes.

She moved faster, heard her breath quicken. Not with exertion, but with an atavistic fear. Something was coming.

Thunder mumbled overhead, over the rolling, muttering wind. The shimmer of lightning tossed all into an instant of relief, and brought a sick heaviness to her belly.

She had to run, had to find the light again. Then the shadow stepped from the shadow, a knife in one hand, a rope in the other.

Time's up, it said in her father's voice.

She tried to scream, and woke with it trapped in her throat, with the weight crushing her chest.

No air, no air, and she clutched at her own throat as if to fight away the hands that circled it.

Her heart thudded, sharp, vicious hammer blows that rang in her ears. Red dots swam in front of her eyes.

Somewhere deep under the weight, the terror, she shouted at herself to breathe. To *stop* and breathe. But the air wheezed, barely squeezed through her windpipe, only burned her starving lungs.

Something wet ran over her face. She saw it, felt it, as her own blood. She would die here in the woods of her own creation, in fear of a man she hadn't seen in seventeen years.

Then the dog barked, hard and fierce, chased the shadows like rabbits. So she lay panting—breathing, breathing, with the terrible weight easing as the dog lapped at her face.

He had his front legs braced on the bed. She could see his eyes now, gleaming in the dark, hear his pants along with her own. Struggling to steady, she raised a trembling hand, stroked his head.

"Okay." She rolled toward him, comforted, let her eyes close, focused on long, slow breaths. "It's okay. We're okay. Just a dream. Bad dream. Bad memories. We're okay now."

Still, she switched on the light—she needed it—brought her knees up to rest her clammy forehead on them.

"Haven't had one that bad in a while. Working too hard, that's all. Just working too hard, thinking too much."

Since the dog remained braced on the bed, she shifted to wrap her arms around his neck, pressing her face into his fur until the trembling eased.

"I thought I didn't want a dog. I'd say the way you were wandering you must've thought you didn't want a human." She eased back, rubbed his ears. "And here we are."

She picked up the bottle of water she always kept on her nightstand and drank half of it before rising to go into the bathroom and splash cold water on her face.

Still shy of five, she noted, early for both of them, but she couldn't risk sleep. Not now.

She picked up the flashlight—also handy on her nightstand—and went downstairs. She'd gotten into the habit of just letting him out in the morning, but this time she delighted him by going out with him. For a while they just walked, around the house, around the quiet.

Tag found one of his secreted balls and happily carried it around in his mouth. When she went back in, he watched her make coffee, let the ball drop when she filled his food bowl, picked it up.

"Let's take it upstairs."

He raced halfway up the back stairs, stopped, looked back to make sure she was coming, and then raced the rest of the way.

With the dog, with the coffee, she settled down, calm and content again, to wait for sunrise to bloom over her world.

When Sunday rolled around she thought of a dozen reasons not to go to Jenny's, and the excuses that would cover it.

Why would she take one of her two days of quiet and solitude a week and spend it *with* people? Nice people, certainly, but people who wanted to talk and interact.

She could drive to the national forest, go hiking—alone. She could work on the yard, or finish painting the first guest room.

She could sit around and fat-ass all day.

Really, she'd agreed to go in a weak moment, in the rush of mermaid lamps and bargains. She should . . .

She'd agreed to go, Naomi reminded herself. What was a couple of hours? If she was going to live here, she needed to be moderately sociable. Hermits and recluses generated gossip and speculation.

And she'd said she'd bring dessert, and had even shopped for what she needed to make the strawberry torte. It was spring, after all— stubbornly cool, often rainy, but spring.

She decided to compromise. She'd make the torte, then see how she felt.

Tag cast suspicious looks at her new stand mixer, as he did the vacuum cleaner. But she loved it, had actually done a little dance when it had arrived two days before.

Cooking soothed her and gave her a chance to spend quality time in the kitchen with the pretty blue dishes behind the glass, her exceptional knives arranged on their magnetic strip.

Tag changed his mind about the mixer when she skimmed her finger over the batter left in the bowl and let him have a lick.

"Damn right, it's good." She slid the jelly roll pan into the oven, got to work on the strawberries.

She put them in one of her blue bowls first, found the right spot, the right light. Ripe red berries in a blue glass bowl—good stock photo. Considering, she added more props—new wineglasses—then put the bowl of berries and the wineglasses on the bamboo tray she'd bought and set it all out on her glider. She took another shot with the pot of pansies in frame.

She wished she had a throw pillow—hadn't bought any yet. Maybe she would then set up this shot again with a colorful pillow in the corner of the—

No, better, a woman's white silk slip or sexy nightgown, draped over the arm of the glider.

She didn't have that either, and had less use for a slip or a sexy nightgown, but—

The oven timer buzzed.

"Crap. I haven't done the berries."

She went back to the kitchen work, composing other shots in her head.

The finished torte looked so beautiful, the making of it so satisfying, she convinced herself she'd be fine for a couple of hours with people she actually liked.

"And how the hell am I going to get it from here to there? Didn't think of that."

She didn't have a cake carrier or a torte carrier or any carrier. In the end she lined a shipping box with foil, tented the torte on its white platter, secured it in the box, and, thinking of the dog, taped the lid shut.

She packed it in the fridge, then went up to dress.

Next problem, she realized. What did people wear to Sunday dinner?

Sunday brunch had been the thing in New York. Seth and Harry hosted elaborate Sunday brunches. Dress code had been casual or colorful, or whatever struck your fancy.

She hated to think about clothes, so she didn't have any to worry about. Eventually she'd send for what was still in New York—the cocktail dresses, the sharp business wear, the artist black. Meanwhile, she had what she had.

The reliable black jeans, a white shirt. After a short debate, she went with the Converse high-tops.

Nobody would care.

She added a red belt to prove she'd given some thought to the whole deal, and remembered to do her makeup.

Anytime after four, she remembered, and as it was now four thirty, she should just go. A couple of hours—three, tops—and she'd be home, in her pajamas, back at her computer.

She loaded the boxed torte onto the floor of the passenger seat and let the dog in the back.

"Don't even think about it," she warned him when he eyed the box.

Armed with the directions Kevin had given her, she set off.

She made the turns, took a road she'd yet to explore, and found a little neighborhood built around a skinny inlet. Docks speared out with boats moored. Sunfish, sloops, cabin cruisers. She saw a girl who couldn't have been more than twelve paddling a butter yellow kayak toward the widening channel with such smooth skill she might have been born in one.

Naomi pulled up behind Kevin's truck and gave Xander's motorcycle a beady-eyed stare. She should've known.

She thought the house charming and decided she should have known that, too, given who lived there. Bold blue trim against weathered cedar shakes, wide windows to bring in the view of the inlet. It stood two stories, with dormers and the enchantment of a widow's walk.

She immediately wanted one.

Flowering bushes, trees, and bedding plants danced in cheerful profusion and made her think of her own scrabbly, neglected yard.

She'd get to it.

Ordering herself to put on her Be-Sociable Suit, she got out and circled around for the torte and the dog. Tag all but glued himself to her side as she walked the pavered path to the covered front porch.

"It's not the vet, so buck up."

Before she could knock, Jenny opened the door—and Tag's tail wagged in relief and joy at the sight of her.

"I saw you pull up." Immediately Jenny moved in to hug, hard. "I'm so glad you came! Everyone's outside running around. It's almost like summer today."

"I didn't realize you lived on the water—and you have a widow's walk. I had instant house envy."

"Kevin built it. And half of everything else. Let me take that." Jenny reached for the box as they stepped into an entranceway cleverly outfitted with a built-in bench and cupboards above, drawers below.

"Sorry about the delivery system. Dessert's inside."

"You made something? I thought you'd just get something from the bakery. You're so busy."

"I needed to try out my new mixer. I love your house. It's so you."

Colorful, cheerful, the bold blue of the trim echoed in a big sink-into-me sofa loaded with patterned pillows. And those were echoed by boldly patterned chairs.

Echoed, Naomi thought, but nothing matching. And everything complementing.

"I like cluttered."

"It's not cluttered. It's clever and happy."

"I really like you. Come on back to the kitchen. I'm dying to see what's in this box."

The kitchen showed Kevin's hand and Jenny's style. It followed the open floor plan with a lounge/play area, more comfortable seating, and the man-size flat wall screen.

Jenny set the box on the long, wide white granite peninsula and tore at the tape.

Naomi glanced toward the dining area, the painted blue table, the mix and match of green chairs with flowered cushions. "I love the dining room—did you paint the furniture?"

"I did. I wanted color—and easy maintenance."

"It's happy, again, and I really love the chandelier."

Distressed iron strips formed a large ball with clear, round bulbs inside.

"Me, too, thanks. Kevin found it on one of his job sites—it was some sort of decoration. He brought it home, I fixed it up, he rewired it."

"Handy couple—and I'm getting so many ideas."

"I'm going to get you a glass of wine in just a minute," Jenny promised, "but— Oh my God, you *made* this?"

"I can't make a chandelier, but I can make a strawberry torte."

Almost reverently, Jenny lifted the torte from the box. "It looks like something out of Martha Stewart. I'd ask for the recipe, but I already know it's beyond me. And it's going to put my lasagna to shame."

"I love lasagna."

"Mostly with two kids and a part-time job, I toss meals together. So Sunday dinner's the day I actually try to cook, take time with it. Shiraz all right?"

"Yes, it's great. I almost talked myself out of coming."

Jenny glanced away from the torte she'd set in the center of the prep counter—like a centerpiece. "Why?"

"I'm easier alone than with people. But I'm glad I came, even if just to see your house."

With a humming sound, Jenny poured Naomi a glass of wine, then picked up her own. "I should tell you, then, I've decided we're going to be really good friends, and I'm just relentless."

"I haven't had a really good friend in a long time. I'm out of practice."

"Oh, that's all right." Jenny wrist-flicked that away. "I've got the skills. Why don't I show you my workshop? I've got your desk stripped down."

They went through a laundry room and straight into a space full of tables, chairs, shelves, workbenches. Though both windows stood open, Naomi caught the scents of paint thinner, linseed oil, polish.

"I keep picking things up," Jenny explained. "It's a sickness. Then I fix them up and talk my boss at Treasures and Trinkets into taking them on consignment. She'll use pieces for display, and if they don't sell, I haul them down to this co-op in Shelton. If they don't sell there, I haul them back. I'm getting some work from people who want a piece redone or fixed up, but most is Dumpster diving, I guess."

Naomi gestured to a three-tiered piecrust table. "You didn't get that out of a Dumpster."

"Job site again. The lady sold it to Kevin for ten dollars—it was broken, the top tier snapped clean off. So he fixed it—you can't even tell it was broken. And I'm—"

"I want it. When you've refinished it, I'll buy it."

Thrown off rhythm, Jenny blinked. "You think fast."

"It's just the sort of thing I want. I'm looking to mix a lot of old pieces, character pieces, through the house. This is perfect."

"I should have you over more often. Will you barter for it?"

"You've already got the torte."

"I mean, would you trade me a picture for it and the work on the desk? You've got this one on your website, and I keep seeing it over our little fireplace in the living room in a white—shabby-chic white—frame. It's sunset, and oh, the sky is just full of red and gold and going to indigo blue, and the trees are reflected on the water. And there's a white boat— sailboat—in the sound. It makes me think that's what heaven could be. Sailing in a white boat on the water into the red and golds."

"I know the one you mean, but it doesn't seem fair—two pieces for one."

"I know what your work goes for. And I know what mine goes for. I'm getting the better deal."

"Depends on where you're standing. Done—but I frame it. Tell me what size you want."

Jenny pointed toward a frame—shabby-chic white.

"About twenty-four by eighteen. I'll take the frame with me."

"Oh boy! And what I really wanted you to see was that bench. It just seems right for your bedroom deck."

Following the direction, Naomi stepped around a couple of projects in progress and saw the high-backed wire bench, done in a distressed forest green.

"No pressure," Jenny said quickly. "If you don't like it—"

"I do. And it would work there. Better, if I ever get the grounds cleared and decently landscaped, it would be wonderful as a garden seat, wouldn't it?"

"In a shady nook," Jenny imagined. "Or in the sun, by a weeping cherry."

"Absolutely. And it would make pretty seating on the bedroom deck in the meantime. Sold."

"Will you trade me the water lily print for it?"

"You make it easy," Naomi agreed.

"I have this frame—distressed silver—and I can just see that print in it, on my bedroom wall. It's fun helping decorate each other's houses."

"Let's see the frame."

"Ah, it's over . . . there."

With Jenny, Naomi started toward it, then stopped. "Oh! My desk."

At her tone, Tag stopped exploring and trotted over. Naomi all but cooed as she ran her hand over the smooth wood. "I know it's just stripped and sanded, but it's already beautiful. Look at the hues, the grain. It's like somebody had dressed a gorgeous woman in a baggy black coat, and you took it off. I think we just made a hell of a good deal, both sides."

"That's what good friends should do." Delighted, Jenny hugged an arm around Naomi's waist. "I'm going to love seeing my work in your space, having your work in mine. And now, why don't we go out the door here so we can walk around outside. I bet Tag wants to see Molly. They're friends, too."

"He decided she wouldn't try to rip his throat out. Now he takes her the tug rope when he sees her. It's sweet."

They stepped out into the side yard.

"It's awful quiet," Jenny commented as she turned to secure the door. "Quiet worries me."

She'd no more than said it before Naomi took a blast of cold water—heart-shot.

Xander swung around the corner, leading with a huge water rifle. Naomi held her hands out to the sides, looked down at her soaked shirt, and looked up.

"Really?"

"Hey, sorry. I thought you were Kevin."

"Do I *look* like Kevin?"

"Can't say you do, but I figured him to double back from this way. Kids broke the treaty, and the three of them are ganging up on me. This would be the fog-of-war sort of situation."

"Fog of war, my ass."

"It's more your—" He broke off when he took a volley of shots in the back.

"Xander's dead!" Tyler did a war dance. "Xander's dead." He wiggled his butt and shook his water gun at the sky.

"Traitors. You're living with traitors and back-shooters," Xander told Jenny.

"You shot an unarmed woman. I'll get you a dry shirt, Naomi."

"Thanks. And thank you for killing him," Naomi said to Tyler. "He ambushed a noncombatant."

"You're welcome."

"You're a really good shot. Could I . . ." She took the gun and shot a stream into Xander's face. "There. That's what we call a coup de grace."

Maddy giggled, then started climbing up her father's leg. "Xander's got cooties."

"That's right." She gave Tyler back the gun, then narrowed her eyes at the gleam in Xander's. "Don't even think about it," she said before walking away with Jenny.

She ate in one of Jenny's T-shirts and enjoyed herself more than she'd thought possible. Good food and good company, two things she rarely took the time for or had the inclination for, proved the perfect end to the day—even when she found herself cornered into playing Xbox.

"You've got game," Xander commented after she'd trounced everyone at the LEGO Movie game—twice.

"Everything is awesome when you have a brother who's still a video game maniac. And now that I remain undefeated"—she added a finger in the belly for Tyler—"I really have to go."

"Play one more!"

"Practice," she advised, "and I'll take you on next time. But Tag and

I have to get home. Everything was great, Jenny, thanks for having me. I can take those frames with me if you want."

"I really want." In her easy way, Jenny stepped up and hugged Naomi. "Sunday dinner, open invitation. I mean it."

"Thanks. And thanks, Kevin. See you tomorrow."

"I'll get the frames. Meet you out front with them," Xander told her.

She hadn't intended to stay so late. But the setting sun painted the sky in the west and the air had cooled enough that she could have used a sweater.

Still, she thought as she walked the dog to the car, she could get some work in, plan out her agenda for the week, and have time to read herself to sleep.

She opened the door to the back; the dog jumped agilely in. Then she sat on the back of the car, facing the water, and took pictures of the sunset over the inlet, the empty docks, the shimmering silence.

"Do you ever quit?" Xander asked as he carried the frames across the lawn.

"I get amazing sunrise shots from my place, but this little spit of water edges west, and that's one champion sunset."

"My place isn't on the water, but I get some worthy sunsets through the trees. You might want to check it out."

"I might."

He propped the frames in the back, gave the dog a rub, and then managed to turn in a way that boxed her in.

"It's still early."

"That depends. Maddy was drooping."

"Maddy's four. Why don't we go into Loo's? I'll buy you a drink."

"I had several glasses of wine."

"Over about four hours. Walk a straight line."

She laughed, shook her head. "I can walk a straight line, and since I want to continue to be able to, I'll pass on another drink. You have terrific friends, Xander."

"Seems like they're your friends, too."

"Jenny won't take no."

"Why say no?"

She shrugged, looked back to the sunset. Going to gold now, she thought. Soft, shimmering gold. "General rule."

"You make it hard not to ask questions."

"I appreciate that you don't. I really have to go."

He ran a hand down her arm, but stepped back. Didn't kiss her, Naomi realized, because she expected it.

He had game, too.

But he walked around, opened the door for her. "Do you like eggplant parm?"

"I do."

"Come to my place Wednesday for dinner. We'll have eggplant parm."

Her eyebrows shot up. "You're going to make eggplant parmesan?"

"Hell no. I'll get takeout from Rinaldo's. They make good eggplant parm."

"Two social outings inside one week? I don't know if I can handle it."

"Try. Bring the dog."

She blew out a breath as Tag shoved his face out her door and pushed his muzzle into Xander's big, callused hand.

"Just dinner."

"I can take no."

"You're going to have to. What time?"

"About seven works best. I'm over the garage. You come around back and take the stairs up."

"All right. Wednesday. Probably."

Still letting the dog nuzzle his hand, Xander grinned. "You like keeping the door cracked open."

"Always. Good night."

Why was that? he wondered when she drove away. What was it she needed to be ready to run from?

Yeah, she made it hard not to ask questions.

Twelve

Creatively, her week sucked. She had to move her workstation from the bedroom into one of the guest rooms—at least she could try it out as her potential studio—as they wanted to demo her bathroom. And since they were doing that, Kevin opted to have them demo all but one of the other baths on the bedroom floor.

The noise, even with earbuds in and music blaring, was horrendous.

She considered moving downstairs, but the painters held court in the living room, with the library next on the slate. She'd end up playing musical workstations, so she tried her best to stick it out.

By midweek she gave up and drove into the national forest with the intent of hiking with camera and dog.

Fresh air, a dry, sunny day, and lovely green-tinged light whipped annoyance away. She wished she'd brought her laptop, as she'd have found a handy stump, sat right down, and done her updates in the serenity of the forest.

She walked—the leash fixed to her belt, as Tag tolerated it now— through a stand of trees that looked as if they'd stood since time began. Towering columns with branches lifted to catch the sea of wind and send dapples and rays of filtered sun to the forest floor.

Wildflowers danced there through fans of young ferns, around moss-carpeted rocks. Snow-white trillium like fairy brides, and calypso orchids their colorful slippers.

She thought about taking a few days, camping out. How would the dog deal with that, now that she had a dog to consider? Two or three days, on her own again, away from the noise she'd brought on herself.

Maybe.

No question Tag enjoyed the forest, puffing himself up by threatening squirrels or prancing along beside her. He even sat patiently enough when she paused to take pictures, no matter how long she took.

"It could be fun. Just you and me, and all this."

As they meandered she began to think getting a dog—or being got by one—had been a fine idea after all.

A couple of hikers came her way, leading a handsome little beagle. Before she could give them the fellow-hiker nod of greeting, Tag let out a yip of terror and literally leaped into her arms. And knocked her flat.

The hikers—a couple of guys up from Portland for a few days—rushed to her aid. But the friendly and harmless beagle only had Tag squirming on top of her as if he could worm his way straight through and under her where it would be safe.

Since her camera was cushioned between her body and the dog's, no damage done. But she'd seen stars—and felt their sharp little points in her ass.

"You're a disgrace," she told the dog as she walked stiffly back to the car. "Definitely no camping for you. A teacup poodle might come along and try to rip you to pieces."

Tag crawled into the back, hung his head, and said nothing.

Since her butt ached, she tried the seat warmer on low and found that it soothed her considerably on the drive back. And with relief she saw only Kevin's truck in front of the house.

He walked out as she gingerly eased out of the car.

"Hey! I just left you a note. We made some good progress today. How was the hike?"

She watched Tag rush over to greet Molly like a long-lost friend.

"He's fine with her."

"Sure."

"If there's a cat or a Pom or Pekinese, whatever, in the vet, he shakes like he's walking into the seventh circle of hell. He runs at squirrels, or barks at them, but we ran into a couple of guys with a damn beagle on the trail, and he freaked. Jumped on me, knocked me flat."

"You okay?"

Automatically she rubbed her sore ass. "It rang my bell, I'll tell you that, and he's all but clawing me open to climb inside, away from the terrifying beagle who licked at my limp hand in sympathy."

To her shock, Kevin stepped straight up and started running his hands over her head. "You've got a little bump. I can run you to the ER."

"It's just bumps and bruises. And extreme pissed-off."

He cupped her chin, looked hard into her eyes, and did something she thought no one could at that moment. He made her smile.

"Bumps and bruises only, Dr. Banner."

"Headache?"

"No. Ass ache."

"Ice bag, warm bath, a couple of Motrin. That'll be two hundred dollars."

"Put it on my account, because that's exactly what I'm going to do."

"A good dinner you don't have to cook over at Xander's should polish it off."

"I . . . It's Wednesday."

"All day, half the night. You take it easy," he added, giving her a gentle poke. "And I know it looks torn up in there, but it's good progress. Tell Xander I'll see him tomorrow at Loo's."

"Right." Fuck, fuck, fuck. She started in as Kevin got into his truck.

She had a perfect excuse—*reason*, she corrected—to cancel dinner at Xander's. Sore, cranky, out of sorts—all for good *reason*, she thought, and headed straight back for that ice pack.

Then she turned straight around and walked back to stand and stare at the living room.

The painting wasn't finished—as the ladders and drop cloths attested—and she could see where touch-up was needed.

But oh, it was going to be just lovely.

She'd gone back and forth, around and around on color, and had worried the soft taupe would come off as dull and boring.

It didn't.

Settled, she thought. For some reason the tone said *settled* to her.

"I keep thinking I've made a mistake with this place." Sighing, she laid her hand on Tag's head as he leaned against her leg. "Then I see the next step or stage, and know I haven't."

She looked down, smiled. Then narrowed her eyes. "I'm mad at you," she reminded them both, and went back for the ice bag.

She argued with herself as she soaked her aching butt in the ugly baby blue tub in the single bathroom left to her upstairs. She could call off dinner without a qualm. She'd had an incident.

But calling it off tonight really equaled postponing.

Better to do it—get it done—and work on a way to shift whatever this was with Xander into the kind of friendship she had with Kevin.

The kind where being touched made her smile instead of tense.

And that, she admitted, would never happen.

Too much heat.

She got out of the tub, pleased the ache had lessened—and displeased to see she had a palm-sized bruise on her posterior.

She opted for leggings—softer on the ass—and a pale gray hooded sweater. She considered skipping makeup altogether but deemed it too obvious, so she kept a very light hand with it.

At quarter to seven she started out—though she felt Tag didn't deserve a second outing. Then she walked back in and grabbed a bottle of wine.

It wasn't a strawberry torte, but she'd been raised too well to go empty-handed.

She made the drive easily, then let the dog out but gave him the cold shoulder. As instructed, she took the steps up and rapped a knuckle on the door.

"Yeah, it's open! Come on in."

Naomi pushed the door open to see Xander in the jut that formed a kitchen, opening a bottle of wine.

Jeans, a chambray work shirt with the sleeves rolled up to the elbow, at least a day's worth of scruff on that toughly handsome face.

She'd break down, she thought, and ask him to pose for her. "I could have been a trained assassin with her vicious hellhound."

"A locked door wouldn't stop a trained assassin or her vicious hellhound."

He had a point. Tag strolled right in and wagged his way over to Xander.

And Naomi stared, with wonder and delight, at the living room wall of books. "Wow, the rumors of book lover are true. That's quite a collection."

"Part of it."

"Part? You're a serious man, Xander."

"About books, anyway."

She glanced around. "Very efficient space, and that is one of the best uses of a wall I've ever seen. Color, texture, dimension."

"Not to mention words."

He walked over, offered her a glass of wine, took the bottle from her.

"Yeah, words. I like to read as much as the next guy—unless you're the next guy."

"That's the plan."

She laughed, waving him off as she walked up and down the wall. "But this is art. You're smart enough to know your furniture is absolute crap. You don't care about that. You've arranged your space for efficiency and high-lighted a passion. And by highlighting it, created art. I want pictures of this."

"Sure, go ahead. I don't care."

"Not now, not with my phone. I mean serious pictures. I want to come back with my camera. And with big daddy Hasselblad."

"Whose daddy is he?"

She laughed, but continued to study the wall of books. "Film camera. Medium format. I could do a nice panorama, too, and—"

"Bring your camera when you want. But why don't we sit outside and have this wine?"

"You're having wine?"

"It's not so bad now and again. You smell great."

He cupped her chin, but not like Kevin had, and took her mouth.

No, she thought, no, not like Kevin. Not in the least.

"Bath salts—it was medicinal."

"Yeah, I heard. Small-dog fear."

"What?"

He took her hand, tugged her into the bedroom, felt her resist. "I've got a deck through the door in here."

And more books, she noted. A big-screen TV, crap furniture, and more books.

He opened the door to the small square of deck with a half-rusted table and a couple of folding chairs. "I can get you a pillow to sit on."

"You talked to Kevin."

"I'm supposed to keep an eye on you, which I'd planned to do anyway."

"I'm fine." She sat, carefully. "Mostly. But to the issue: There's no such thing as small-dog fear."

"Microcynophobia."

On a laugh, she sampled the wine. "You're making that up."

"Cynophobia's fear of dogs—add the micro. You can look it up."

Though she had her doubts, considering his collection of books, she didn't argue the term. "Why would he—and he's eighty-five pounds now, a lot of it muscle, I can attest—have microcynophobia?"

"Can't say. Maybe he was traumatized at an early age by a Chihuahua."

He reached behind her head, gently tested. "Ow."

"That's what I said once I got my breath back. My ass hit harder than my head."

"Want me to check it out for you?"

"I've taken care of that, thanks." She studied his view. "You can sit here and watch the ball game."

"And do, if I'm too lazy to walk over."

"Little League?"

"T-ball, Little League, Pony League, and some sponsored adult leagues. Keaton's sponsored the Whales—currently battling their way out of the basement."

"Do you play?"

"Not much anymore. Not a lot of time for it. You?"

"No, I never did."

"What kind of feminist are you?"

"The non-sport-playing type. My brother played for a while, but basketball was his deal."

"Is that right?"

"He played for Harvard."

"Huh. Crimson. What position?"

"Point guard. I noticed you have a blacktop court and hoop out back."

"Shooting hoops clears the brain. Used to play, back in high school. Mostly pickup games now."

"What position?"

"Same as your brother. We'll have to go one-on-one if he ever gets out here."

"He will." She'd have her family here, she thought, including her grandparents so they could see what they'd helped her have. Maybe by the fall, she'd have her family out.

"Are you any good, because, I can attest, he is."

"I hold my own."

She suspected he did, in many ways.

And he was right about the sunlight through the trees as it dropped toward the horizon.

"It seems like a good spot for a garage. Quick and easy access to the road, close to town, and a quick zip to 101. Is that why you picked it?"

"The place was here already. It used to be Hobart's. He was looking to sell—getting up in age, and his wife took sick. We came to an agreement, and they moved to Walla Walla. Their daughter lives there."

"Was it having your own business, or mechanics?"

"It was both. Is. I like cars. If I wanted a car—and I did—I had to learn how to keep it running. I liked learning how to keep things running. I didn't mind working for Hobart—he was fair. But I like working for myself better. You must feel the same."

True enough, she thought—but she preferred being by herself as much as working for herself.

Still . . .

"I worked as a photographer's assistant for about fourteen months after college. I thought of it like an apprenticeship. He was not fair, by any measure. Arrogant, downright mean, demanding, and prone to toddler-scale tantrums. He was, and is, also brilliant."

"Sometimes the brilliant think they're entitled to tantrums."

"Unfortunately true, but I was raised by a chef—a brilliant one—and brains and talent weren't considered excuses for arrogance, for pettiness, but gifts."

"No throwing spatulas or frying pans?"

The idea made her smile. "Not in Harry's kitchen—home or restaurant. In any case, I'd planned on two years with Julian—the photographer—but fourteen months was all I could take. One of the happiest days of my life was punching him in the face and walking off the shoot."

He glanced at her hand—slender, fine-boned. "That's an interesting way to give your two weeks' notice."

"Two weeks' notice, my ass."

She shifted toward him—he wondered if she knew she rubbed her foot on Tag's back, keeping the dog in quiet bliss. "Major shoot. Advertising—shampoo."

"Shampoo is a major shoot?"

"Let me tell you, friend, there's big money in ad photography. The model has a yard of glorious flame-red hair—she's a joy to shoot. This guy, he's a perfectionist, and I've got no problem with that. He's also a vicious little dick. I'm used to the verbal abuse, at this point. The blame-casting, the castigating, even the throwing of objects. All of which were present during this particular shoot. He actually had the makeup artist in tears at one point. Then he claimed I handed him the camera with the wrong lens, I'd had enough, and pointed out I'd given him what he'd asked for. He slapped me."

Amusement faded. "He hit you?"

"Slapped me like a little girl. So I punched him, just the way Seth—my uncle—taught me. Nothing in my life had ever felt that good. I think I actually said that while he's screaming—again like a little girl—and the other assistants are scrambling around. The model walked over, gave me a high five. He's holding his bloody nose."

"Did you break it?"

"If you're actually going to punch somebody in the face, it's stupid to pull it."

"That's my philosophy."

"I broke his nose, and he's screaming about having me arrested for assault. I told him to call the cops, go right ahead, because I had a studio full of witnesses who'd seen him assault me first. When I walked out I promised myself I'd never work for a vicious little dick again."

"Another excellent philosophy."

Had he thought her interesting? No, not interesting, he corrected. Fascinating.

"So you broke a guy's nose, then started your own business."

"Sort of. Seth and Harry were friends with the owner of a gallery in SoHo, and they convinced him to take a couple of my pieces. They'd have supported me—in every way—while I tried to make a living in art photography. But I knew I could hold my own doing stock photography, getting some work doing book covers, album covers. Food shoots—I already did them for the restaurant. And clip art—it can be fun and creative, and it can generate income. I needed to get beyond New York, so I took the leap. Car, camera, computer."

She stopped, frowned down at her wine. "That was a lot."

"A microcosm," he countered, pleased she'd forgotten her reserve, distrust, whatever it was, long enough to tell the story. "It tells me you've got guts and spine, but I already knew that. You do album covers?"

"I have. Nobody major. Unless you've heard of Rocket Science."

"Retro-funk."

"You surprise me."

"I haven't even started. The band's working on another CD."

"Another?"

"We did one a couple years ago. Mostly for tourists, or when we do a wedding, that kind of thing. How about it?"

"You're looking for a photographer?"

"Jenny's cousin's friend did the last one. It wasn't bad. I figure you'd do better."

"Maybe. Let me know when you're ready, and we'll see. How long have you been playing?"

"With the band or at all?"

"Both."

"With these guys, about four years. Altogether, since I was around twelve. Kevin and I started a band—Lelo on bass, just like now."

Obviously surprised, she lowered her wineglass. "Kevin?"

"Do not ask him to play his Pearl Jam tribute. Trust me."

"Does he play the guitar?"

"You can't really call it playing."

"That's mean," she said with a laugh.

"It's truth. Let's eat." He took her hand again, this time tugging her inside. "We did some local gigs—school dances, parties. After high school, we lost our drummer to the Marines, Kevin did the college thing, Lelo stayed stoned."

"And you?"

He pulled the takeout from the oven, where he'd kept it warm. "I hit trade school, worked here, picked up some gigs. Some with Lelo when he realized he wasn't going to get the girls, and couldn't play worth crap when he was stoned."

She thought of the wall of books, looked over at it again. "No college for you?"

"Hated school. Trade school, that was different. But regular school.

They tell you what to learn, what to read, so I opted out, learned from Hobart, learned from trade school, took some business classes."

"Business classes."

"If you're going to have your own, you have to know how to run a business."

He divided the salad from the take-out box in the fridge into two bowls, transferred the eggplant parm to plates, and added the breadsticks the pizzeria was locally famous for.

"This actually looks great." She sat, and smiled when Xander pulled a rawhide bone out of a cupboard. "Smart."

"It'll keep him busy. What was your first picture? You had to have a first."

"We had a long weekend in the Hamptons—friends of my uncles. I'd never seen the ocean, and oh God, it was so amazing. Just amazing. Seth let me use his little point-and-shoot Canon, and I took rolls and rolls of film. And that was that. What was the first song you learned to play? You had to have a first."

"It's embarrassing. 'I'm a Believer.' The Monkees," he added.

"Oh, sure. Really? It's catchy, but doesn't seem your style."

"I liked the riff, you know . . ." He diddled it out. "I wanted to figure out how to play it. Kevin's mom used to play old records all the time, and that one kept circling around. His dad had an old acoustic guitar, and I worked on it until I could more or less play it. Saved up, bought a secondhand Gibson."

"The one in the bedroom?"

"Yeah. I keep it handy. I figured out, by the time I was fifteen, that if you had a guitar and could even pretend to play it, you got the girls. How's the parm?"

"You were right. It's really good. So you got the girls, being as you can more than pretend to play, but none of them stuck?"

"Jenny might have."

"Jenny?" She set down her fork. "Jenny-Jenny?"

"Jenny Walker back then, and I saw her first. New girl in school, just moved up from Olympia, and pretty as a butterscotch sundae. I asked her out before Kevin. Kissed her first, too."

"Is that so?"

"It's Keaton/Banner history. I was about half in love with her, but he was all the way in love with her."

"And there's bros before hos."

Grinning, he picked up a breadstick. "You said it, I didn't. I ended up playing Cyrano to his Christian, finally got his guts up to ask her out. And that, as we've said, is that. I'm still half in love with her."

"Me, too. And the package along with it. They're like central casting called for a great-looking, all-American family, dog included. If you're waiting for another Jenny, you're going to be out of luck. I'm pretty sure she's one of a kind."

"I've got my eye on a tall, complicated blonde."

She knew it, wished hearing it didn't set off those flutters low in the belly. "It's not smart to aim for the complicated."

"Simple's usually surface anyway, and wears off. Then the complications are annoying instead of interesting. You've got my interest, Naomi."

"I'm aware." She watched him as she ate. "Nine times out of ten I'd rather be alone than with anyone."

"You're here now."

"I'm twenty-nine, and I've managed to evade, avoid, and slip around any sort of serious relationship."

"Me, too. Except I've got three years on you."

"Since I left New York six years ago, I haven't stayed in any one place over three months."

"You've got me there. I've lived here all my life. But I have to repeat myself, you're here now."

"And right now, this feels like my place. Things start up with you, screw up with you, it affects that."

"I don't know how you manage life with that sunny, optimistic nature of yours."

She smiled. "It's a burden."

Knowing the risk, he pushed a bit deeper. "Ordinarily I'd assume you had some crappy relationship or marriage behind you. But that's not it. You've got a solid family under you, and that's foundation."

She nudged her plate away. "Think of it as internal wiring."

"No. I'm good with wiring. You've got enough self-confidence and sense of self-worth to punch an asshole, to head off on your own to go after what you wanted. You're complicated, Naomi, and that's interesting. But you're not wired wrong."

She rose, took both their plates to the counter. "There was a boy who loved me—or thought he did the way you can at twenty. I slept with him, and studied with him, worked with him. When he told me he loved me, asked me to live with him, I broke it off. Right then and there. It was hard for us both to get through the rest of college. Easier for me, no doubt, because I didn't have those feelings for him. So I could just walk away."

"But you remember him."

"I hurt him. I didn't have to."

Maybe, Xander thought, but he doubted anybody got through the labyrinth of life without hurting someone, whether or not they had to.

"I guess you're counting on me falling in love with you and asking you to live with me."

"I'm pointing out the problems with relationships when they go south and people live and work in close proximity."

"Maybe you'll fall in love with me, ask me to live with you in that big house on the bluff."

"I don't fall in love, and I like living alone."

Xander glanced at Tag and decided not to point out that she'd fallen for the mutt and lived with him.

"Then I know that going in—unlike the college boy. I'll get those. I know how it works. Want more wine?"

She turned away from the sink. "Better not. Water's better since I have to drive."

"It's a nice night. Once I clean this up we can take a walk, work off dinner. Let the dog stretch his legs."

"He could probably use it." She took the water he offered, wandered back toward the wall of books. "I really do want to take some shots here. Is there any time that works for you?"

"Why don't you come over Friday—anytime. The door's open if I'm working down below. But if you came later in the day, you could go over to Loo's after. We could grab some dinner before we play."

"You're playing Friday?"

"Nine to midnight. Ish. Kevin and Jenny can probably come, if you want."

Not really a date so much as a get-together, with food and music. And she did like the music. More, she wanted to get back in here with her camera and . . .

Everything went blank and cold as her gaze latched onto a single spine in the wall of books.

Blood in the Ground: The Legacy of Thomas David Bowes, by Simon Vance.

They'd changed the title for the movie—the title and focus—as they'd wanted the drama focused on the young girl who'd discovered her father, who'd saved a woman's life, who'd stopped a murderer.

After her mother's death, once she'd believed she could face it, Naomi read interviews by the director, the screenwriter, so she knew why they'd turned the book into *Daughter of Evil*. But this was where it had started, this held all the horror and the cold-blooded years of one man's murderous secrets.

"Naomi?" Xander tossed the dishcloth aside and started for her. "What's wrong?"

"What?" She turned, too sharply, and she'd gone pale so her eyes burned dark. "Nothing. Nothing. I . . . A little headache. I probably shouldn't have had the wine after rapping my head."

She sidestepped, talking too fast. "This was really great, Xander, but I should go pop a couple more Motrin, make it an early night."

Before she could get to the door, he took her arm, felt it quivering. "You're shaking."

"Just the headache. I really need to go." Afraid the shaking would turn into a panic attack, she laid a hand over his. "Please. I'll come back Friday if I can. Thanks for everything."

She bolted, barely waiting for the dog to catch up.

Xander turned back, eyes narrowed on the books. Was he crazy? he wondered. Or had something there put the fear of God into her?

He walked over, scanned the titles. Then adjusted, estimating where she'd been looking. Her position, her height.

Baffled, he shook his head. Just books, he thought. Words and worlds on pages. He pulled one out at random, put it back, tried another. She'd been looking right about here when he'd glanced back, when he'd seen her freeze as if he'd pointed a gun at her head.

He frowned, drew out the nonfiction book—serial killer, he remembered, back east. It had fascinated him as a teen when it buzzed all over the news. So he'd bought the book when it came out.

West Virginia, he remembered, looking at the grainy photo of the killer in the cover art.

Couldn't have been this. She came from New York.

He started to slide it back in, and then, as he often did with a book in his hand, opened it to skim the flyleaf.

"Yeah, West Virginia, some little podunk town. Thomas David Bowes, cable guy, family man. Wife and two kids. Deacon in his church. How many did he kill again?"

Curious enough, Xander kept skimming.

"Hot August night, summer storm, country dark, blah blah. Eleven-year-old daughter finds his murder room, and . . . Naomi Bowes. Naomi."

He stared at the book, once again saw her pale, stricken face in his head.

"Son of a bitch."

Thirteen

After considerable internal debate, Naomi pushed herself out of the house on Friday night. A compromise of sorts, she thought, as she couldn't and wouldn't push herself to go back to Xander's. Not yet.

Tag wasn't thrilled with the idea of her going out at all, though she left him with his stuffed cat, a rawhide bone, and the promise that she'd be back.

She couldn't take the dog into a bar.

She'd nearly used him as an excuse, at least to herself, but going out was normal, and normal, after the disaster ending Wednesday night, was her current goal.

One drink, she told herself. One drink, one set, easy Friday-night conversation with Jenny and Kevin—and if Xander came over during the break, easy conversation with him.

Normal.

Maybe the thought of reaching for normal exhausted her, but she'd give it a solid attempt.

Conversation posed no issue with Jenny, so she'd just let Jenny take the lead, ride that wave until it was time to go.

Keeping it all light had to help throttle things back with Xander. She'd chosen the house—or it had chosen her—the small town. Which meant that avoiding Xander struck the wrong note. So throttle it back to casual friendship. That was the answer.

How could she have forgotten, allowed herself to forget, what she'd come from and how easily normal could come crashing down?

A book on a shelf, she thought now. It only took that to remind her.

As before, she'd timed it so the band already rocked the small stage. She made her way to Jenny and Kevin, cozied up at the same table. Jenny immediately grabbed her hand.

"Great timing. Sitter was late so we just got here. And they're hot tonight! Kevin's going to get us drinks, then he's going to dance with me."

"My round," Naomi insisted. "Sam Adams, red wine?"

"You got it, thanks. Come on, Kevin."

"Why don't we just—"

But Jenny dragged him to the dance floor while Naomi worked her way back to the bar.

She felt Xander's eyes on her, the responsive flutter in her belly. She needed to acknowledge him, and she would. She would.

She outlined it as she maneuvered.

Get to the bar, order, then lean back on the bar, send Xander a smile.

Two bartenders worked nonstop, so she figured she'd have a wait. But the hot brunette—sassy swing with . . . yes, that looked like magenta streaked through the brown—glanced her way.

She had a face so sharp, cheekbones so keen, she might have been carved with a scalpel.

"Leggy blonde, short hair, long bangs, a boot-in-the-balls face. You're the photographer."

"I . . . Yes."

The woman sized her up with eyes more gray than blue in the dim light. "All right," she said with a slow nod. "You're with Jenny and Kev?"

"Yes."

"Sam Adams, glass of merlot—and what're you drinking?"

"The merlot's fine."

"It's not bad."

The woman wore big silver hoop earrings, joined in the left lobe by a trio of red studs that matched her snug, low-necked T-shirt.

"I used to be married to the guy who pretended to take care of the lawn and yard work up at the old Parkerson place."

"Oh. Pretended?"

"Turned out he was smoking more grass than he mowed. I ended up firing him as a husband before they fired him as groundskeeper. Can't say he wasn't a good-natured sort. Do you want to run a tab?"

"Ah, no. Thanks."

Naomi paid cash, digging bills out of the wallet in her pocket.

"I can have that brought out to you," the woman said.

"I've got it." Competently, Naomi used one hand to cup the two wineglasses, the other to lift the lager.

"You've done some waitressing."

"Yeah, I have. Thank you."

They'd slowed it down with the Stones and "Wild Horses." As she worked her way back, she saw Kevin and Jenny, still on the dance floor, wrapped around each other and swaying.

The sweetness of it struck her straight in the heart.

Love could last, she thought. She'd seen it with Seth and Harry. For some, love could last.

She set the drinks down, sat, and, since the bartender had distracted her from her outline, picked up her wine and looked toward the stage with a smile ready.

Xander's gaze locked on hers. He sang as though he meant it. As if wild horses couldn't take him away. Talent, showmanship, she told herself. And she wasn't looking for love, for promises, for devotion.

Still, where Jenny and Kevin had struck her heart, he gripped it. Just hard enough to make it ache.

She wanted it to stop, just stop. Wanted to empty herself of what he made her feel, made her need. He'd been a mistake, she knew it. Had been a mistake since he'd hunkered down to change her tire on the dark side of the road.

She made herself look away, told herself to watch the dancers. Her gaze brushed over the woman who'd whispered something in Xander's ear the last time she'd been here. Right now the woman looked back at her with something between a sulk and dislike.

Great. Now she had the attention of some jealous groupie.

She should've stayed home with the dog.

The ache stayed lodged in her when they kicked it back up, and Kevin pulled Jenny back to the table.

"Two dances in a row." Bright-eyed, Jenny pumped fists in the air. "That's a record."

"You don't like to dance, Kevin?"

"Did you see me out there?"

She laughed, and spoke absolute truth. "I thought you looked adorable."

He'd known the minute she'd come in—not because he'd seen her, Xander thought as he let Lelo take the lead. But because there had been a change in the air. The way there was before a storm.

She had that inside her, that storm. He knew why now, but the why wasn't the whole story. He wanted the whole of it as much as he wanted her.

Should he tell her he knew? He'd asked himself that question a dozen times and more since he'd picked that book off the shelf. Would telling her help her relax or send her running? She remained too much of a mystery to be sure.

If she trusted him . . . But she didn't.

She didn't want to be here. She covered it well—he imagined she was used to covering—but even in this light he could see that the smile didn't reach her eyes and stay there.

But she'd come, maybe to prove a point to herself, to him. To both.

If he left her alone, just backed away? He suspected she'd be fine with it. And that was likely something else she was good at—making wherever she was, whatever she did, fine for the moment.

She'd be used to that.

And he was damn set on giving her something she wasn't used to.

The hell with fine.

They moved on to Clapton, and Xander ordered himself to concentrate. Even as he watched Naomi and Jenny get up and join the others on the dance floor.

S he couldn't remember the last time she'd danced, but since Jenny had pleaded, Naomi thought dancing might help burn off some of the heat, the tension.

It felt good to move, to let herself go with the music, let her hips clock the beat.

She didn't think anything of it when someone bumped her hard from behind. It was all part of it. But when it happened a second time, she glanced around.

"Am I in your way?" Naomi asked the sulky blonde.

"You're damn right." She gave Naomi a pissy little shove. "And you'd better get out of it."

"Cut it out, Marla," Jenny warned. "You've had too much to drink."

"I'm not talking to you. I'm talking to the bitch in my way. You can't just come around here and try to take what's mine."

"I don't have anything of yours."

Several of the dancers had stopped or slowed, eased back to stare. The attention had spiders crawling over Naomi's skin. To avoid any more, she held up her hands.

"But if you want the floor, it's yours."

She started to back off, and the woman shoved her again, slapped out at the friend who said her name, grabbed at her arm.

"You'll be *on* the floor if you don't stay away from Xander." Eyes gleaming from too much beer, too much frustration, she shoved.

Avoiding attention, sidestepping confrontation—those were hard-learned habits. But defending herself, standing up, those were ingrained.

"You don't want to touch me again."

"What're you going to do about it?"

Smirking, drunk-sure of her ground, Marla planted a hand on Naomi's chest and started to push. Naomi grabbed her wrist, twisted, and had Marla squealing as she dropped to her knees.

"Don't touch me again," Naomi repeated, then released her and walked away.

"Naomi, Naomi! Wait." Jenny caught up with her. "I'm sorry. I'm so sorry. She's drunk and stupid."

"It's all right."

It wasn't, it wasn't all right. She heard the buzzing, felt eyes following her. And she saw Kevin making his way through the crowd toward them, annoyance and concern clear on his face.

"I'm just going to go. Why ask for trouble?"

"Oh, honey. Let's just go outside, take a walk. You shouldn't—"

"I'm fine." She gave Jenny's hand a squeeze. "She's drunk enough to try something again, and I need to get home to the dog anyway. I'll see you later."

She didn't run. She wanted to, but running made it too important. But by the time she got out to her car she felt as if she'd run a mile in a sprint. And the shaking wanted to start, so she just braced herself against the door until she could gather herself to drive.

She straightened quickly and dragged out her keys when she heard someone coming.

Xander just closed a hand over hers before she could hit the lock release.

"Wait."

"I need to go."

"You need to wait until you stop shaking so you can drive without running off the road." He let go of her hand to put both of his on her shoulders, turned her around. "Do you want an apology?"

"You didn't do anything."

"No, I didn't, unless you want to count that I had sex with Marla twice—when I was seventeen. That's about fourteen years ago, so it shouldn't apply here. But I'm sorry she upset you and made a fool of herself."

"She's drunk."

"You know, like brilliance, I never find that a decent excuse for being an asshole."

She let out a short laugh. "Me either, but it's a fact she's drunk. And she's fixed on you, Xander."

"I haven't given her reason to be in fourteen years." Hints of frustration leaked out, but he kept his gaze calm, and on hers. "Plus, for nearly seven of those she's been with or married to someone I consider a friend. I'm not interested."

"Maybe you should tell her that."

He had, more times than he cared to remember. But given the current circumstances, he accepted that he'd have to do it again—and hurt someone he had a fondness for.

No, you didn't get through life's labyrinth without it.

"I don't like scenes," she added.

"Well, they happen. You play in enough bars, at enough weddings, you see every kind of scene there is, more or less get used to it. You handled it, and that's all you can do."

She nodded, hit the lock release.

He turned her around again, pressed her back against the door.

Not fair, not right, she thought, for him to take her over this way when her feelings were so raw, so unsettled.

Not gentle, not soothing, but a struck match to dry timber. And his mouth, just his mouth taking hers, set it all raging.

He took her face in his hands—not gentle there either—as if temper bubbled just under the surface.

"You walked in, and the air changed. I wasn't going to tell you that. It gives you an advantage, and you're enough of a challenge."

"I'm not trying to be a challenge."

"It's one of the things that makes you one. I want you. I want you under me and over me and around me. And you want. I'm a good reader, and I read that from you clear enough. I'm coming by your place when we wrap tonight."

"I don't—"

He took her mouth again, just took it.

"If there's a light on," he continued, "I'll knock. If there's not, I'll turn around and go home. You've got a couple hours to figure out what you'd rather. Text Jenny when you get home. She's worried about you."

He opened the door for her, held it open as she yanked at the seat belt.

"Leave the light on, Naomi," he said, and closed the door.

She'd left a light on for herself, and turned it off, very deliberately, while the dog danced around her in desperate, delirious welcome.

"Just you and me."

Determined not to dwell on the disaster of the evening—and wasn't she racking them up—she went back to the kitchen. She'd make tea, take something for the stress headache banging in her skull. And let the dog out for a last round, she reminded herself, before she locked up and went to bed.

"Sleep's the great escape," she told Tag, who clung to her every word, every move.

Since he wanted her close, and she wanted the air, she went out the back with him, sat watching the moon over the water, drinking soothing tea while he wandered.

She didn't want scenes, she thought. She didn't want complications. This was what she wanted, this right here. The quiet, the peace of moonlight over the water.

It calmed her, settled the jumps the altercation with a drunk, jealous woman had wound up inside her. She'd just stay away from Loo's, from Xander, from everyone else for a while.

Plenty of work to do, and she could take that trip to Seattle. Maybe take two or three days there.

Tag came back, sat beside her.

If she could find a motel that took dogs, she realized, and laid a hand on his head.

She hadn't thought she'd wanted him either, she remembered. And now . . . Now she needed a motel that took dogs if she took a trip.

"Why don't I mind that? I should mind that."

They sat, companionably, for more than an hour.

He rose when she did, walked in when she did, followed her as she checked locks. He walked upstairs with her, darted to his bed to get his stuffed cat, and though he settled down with it, he watched her while she checked her email, her accounts.

As she worked, she'd glance back, see the dog continuing to watch her. Did he sense her restlessness? she wondered.

She got up to put on the fire, hoping that would settle them both.

When it didn't, he walked back down with her, waiting while she turned on the light again.

"This is a mistake, a terrible, stupid, shortsighted mistake."

Still time to change her mind, she thought. But she wouldn't, no, she wouldn't change her mind. So she walked into the kitchen again, this time pouring herself a glass of wine.

And went back outside with the dog again, to wait for Xander to knock.

He caught the tiny glimmer of light up ahead, and everything inside him unknotted. He'd told himself he'd accept the dark—the choice would always be hers—but that glimmer lit inside him like a torch.

She'd left the light on—just one, but one would do.

He parked his bike beside her car, swung off with the guitar case still strapped to his back. He wouldn't leave it out in the air overnight—and he fully intended to stay.

He'd heard the dog bark, approved that. Nothing like a dog for an early-warning system. And his knock brought out another trio of woofs.

When she opened the door, Tag rushed out to wag and lean and wag some more. But Xander kept his eyes on Naomi, with the dark house behind her.

"I'm coming in."

"Yeah." She stepped back. "You're coming in."

When he did, she closed the door behind him, checked the lock.

"I worked out some things to say if the light was on."

"Would you have gone home if it wasn't?"

"I can want, you can want. But unless you open the door, I stay out. Until," he corrected. "Until you open it."

She believed that, realized she could trust that. He might overwhelm, but he'd never force.

"Confidence or patience?"

"It can be both."

"I'd go to the wall telling myself I'm not impulsive. But I have this house, this dog, and I left the light on when I swore I wouldn't."

"You're not impulsive." He unstrapped the guitar case, set it against the wall by the door. "You just know how to make a decision."

"Maybe. All right, I've made a decision. This is just sex."

He didn't smile, just kept his gaze—patience, confidence—locked on hers. "No, it's not. You know that, too. But I'm more than happy to start with that. Tell me what you want."

"Tonight, I want you, and if that doesn't—"

She broke off when he gave her a yank so her body met his. "I'm going to give you what you want."

She let herself take. If this was a mistake, she'd regret it later. Now she'd take, she'd *consume*, she'd let herself gorge on what was offered.

Needy, she dragged at his jacket, fighting it off as the smell of leather surrounded her. As it fell to the floor, he backed her toward the steps, pulled her sweater over her head so fast and smooth it might have been air.

Tag's tail batted against her legs.

"He thinks it's a game," she managed.

"He'll get used to it." Xander pressed her back against the wall on the stairs, turned her blood to lava—molten. "This is mine," he said to the dog. "Settle down."

Reaching back, Xander flicked open her bra, flicked the straps off her shoulders. "You really need to be naked."

"Halfway there."

Hands, big and rough, took her breasts, callused thumbs running over her nipples, stealing her breath while his mouth enslaved her.

He wanted her just like that, desperate, quivering, against the wall. Too quick, done too quick, he warned himself, and pulled her up the rest of the stairs.

The world spun, bursts of light through the dark—heat lightning—shocked sounds she barely realized came from her. She tore at his shirt—where was flesh, she needed his flesh. And when she found it she all but sank her teeth in.

They fell on the bed with streams of moonlight slanting like bars, with the unearthly whisper of wind over the water.

He smelled of leather and sweat—and of the wind over the water. He felt of hard muscle, roughened hands, and bore her down with his weight.

The panic wanted to come but couldn't carve its way through the needs. Desperate to meet those needs, she found his belt, fought the buckle. And his mouth, rough as his hands, closed over her breast.

She arched up, shocked by the bolt of pleasure, the sheer strength of it. Before she could draw the next breath, his hand pressed between her legs.

When she came it was like falling into a hot pool. She couldn't surface, couldn't reach the cool and the air. He only took her deeper, yanking her jeans down her hips, using his hands on her.

Hot and wet, slick and smooth. Everything about her drove him mad. Her nails bit into him as she bowed up. In the dark her eyes were blind and dazed. Her heart, his heart, hammer blows as he fought to free himself.

He couldn't have stopped if the world ended.

When at last he thrust into her, he thought it had.

For an instant it stopped—sound, breath, movement.

Then it all rushed back, a tidal wave that battered and swept and pounded beyond reason.

He lost himself in it, in her, gave himself to it, to her.

When it broke in him, she broke with him.

She lay limp, still, with her heart still raging. Her body felt bruised and used, and so utterly relaxed. Since no coherent thought would form, she let the attempt go.

If she just stayed like this, eyes closed, she wouldn't have to think of what to do next.

Then he moved, rolling off her. She felt the bed dip with his weight. She sensed movement, more shifting.

"Back off, pal," he muttered.

"What are you doing?"

"Getting my boots off. Nobody looks good with his pants around his ankles and his boots on. The dog has your bra if you want it."

"What?"

She blinked her eyes open. In those slants of moonlight, she could see Xander sitting on the side of the bed, see the dog standing there, tail wagging, something hanging out of his mouth.

"That's my bra?"

"Yeah. You want it back?"

"Yes, I want it back." Now she rolled over, reached. Tag did his down-in-front, tail-up move. Wagged.

"He thinks you want to play." To settle it, Xander rose—tall, built, naked—and plucked the stuffed cat out of the dog bed. "Trade you."

Tag dropped the bra. Xander picked it up, tossed it on the bed.

"Is that a naked mermaid?"

Naomi glanced at the floor lamp. "Yes. It doesn't go in here."

"Why not?" And he did what any man would and stroked a hand over a bronze breast.

"It's going in the room I'm doing for my uncles. They'll love it."

All so casual, Naomi thought. That was good. No intense pillow talk.

Then he turned, looked at her. Ridiculous to feel exposed now, she thought, after what they'd just done to each other. But she had to suppress the urge to cover herself.

"We'll call that the fast and the furious."

"The what?"

"I take it you've missed some movies." He walked back over, obviously not bothered by being naked, and sat on the bed. "Still, it would've been faster and more furious without the dog. Being focused on the goal, I'd have banged you against the stairs, but he'd have been all over us. You do that, you tend to miss the finer details. Like how you look, right now, in blue moonlight."

"I'm not complaining."

"Glad to hear it." He skimmed a finger over the little tattoo riding low on her left hip. "Like your tat. Lotus blossom, right?"

"Yeah."

A symbol of hope, he thought, endurance, as it was beauty that grew out of mud.

"What kind of rocker are you?" she asked. "No tats."

"Haven't found anything I want that permanent."

He cupped the back of her head, leaned in to kiss her—softly, a surprise.

"We're going to slow things down some this time."

"We are?"

He smiled, eased her back. "Definitely. I don't want to miss those fine details this time around."

Later, Naomi could attest he hadn't missed a single one.

Fourteen

Xander woke with the dog staring at him from the side of the bed—nearly nose to nose. His cloudy brain registered Milo before he remembered his longtime companion was gone. Still, he handled the interruption of sleep in the same way he had with Milo.

"Go away," he muttered.

Instead of hanging his head, à la Milo, and sulking off to lie down again, Tag wagged his tail and pushed his cold, wet nose into Xander's face.

"Crap." To make his point, Xander nudged the cold, wet nose away, which Tag took as encouragement.

The wet, soggy tennis ball plopped on the bed an inch from Xander's face.

Even the sleep-clouded brain knew better. If he knocked the ball on the floor, the dog would see it as a game and start all over again. So he closed his eyes, ignored the ball and the dog.

Helpfully Tag nosed the ball closer so now the soggy and wet rolled against Xander's chest.

Beside him, Naomi stirred, reminding Xander he had much more interesting games he could play at oh-dark-thirty.

"He won't stop," Naomi murmured beside him, and sat up before

Xander could make his move. And beside the bed, Tag danced in joy. "It's morning ritual."

"It's not morning."

"Five in the morning, like clockwork. He's actually about ten minutes late."

"Where are you going?"

"I'm getting up, which is part of the morning ritual. Getting dressed—also part of the ritual."

To Xander's severe disappointment, she moved away in the dark, rummaged around. He could see her silhouette pulling on some kind of pants.

"You get up at five, every morning?"

"Yes, we do."

"Even weekends? This is America."

"Yes, even weekends, in America. The dog and I are in tune there, at least." She crossed over and opened the doors to the deck. Tag happily raced out. "Go back to sleep."

"Why don't you come back to bed, and we can try out a new morning ritual?"

"Tempting, but he'll be back inside of ten minutes nagging for his breakfast."

Xander considered. "I can work with ten minutes."

He liked her laugh, the smoky morning sound of it.

"Go back to sleep. I need coffee before he comes back."

If he wasn't getting sex, maybe . . . "Is the dog the only one who gets breakfast?"

She was still just a shadow—a long, slim one—already heading for the door. "Not necessarily."

When she walked out Xander lay there a moment. Normally he'd get another hour—maybe seventy minutes more on a Saturday. But he wouldn't get a hot breakfast.

He picked up the tennis ball, judged the distance to the dog bed, tossed it.

So, she was an early riser, he thought as he got out of bed. He could handle that. She wasn't a snuggler—and that equaled bonus points in his score book.

He didn't mind staying tangled up for a while after sex, but when it came to sleep, he wanted his space. Apparently so did she.

Not only amazing in bed, but didn't expect him to cuddle her like a teddy bear for hours after. Big bonus points.

And she cooked.

He found his pants, tugged them up, and when he couldn't find his T-shirt, he turned on the mermaid light. It made him grin. A woman who'd buy a naked mermaid lamp—more points.

The room smelled like her, he realized. How did she do that? And she smelled of summer. Of storms and the sultry.

He found his T-shirt, pulled it over his head.

She still kept some of her clothes in packing boxes. Curious, he crossed over, glanced into them. Organized—and he appreciated at least a sense of organization. Not a lot to organize in there, to his eye.

He studied the opening of what would be a walk-in closet, currently under construction and empty of wardrobe.

Jesus, he had more clothes than she did.

It struck him as both weird and fascinating.

He also spotted a boxed toothbrush in what he'd term her bathroom box, and figured everyone would be happier if he took it.

He crossed over again to use the bathroom, and when he hit the light found it gutted. The rough plumbing told him where things would go—and she'd have a kick-ass shower from the size of it.

He could use a shower.

He went out, found another gutted bathroom, found a bedroom half painted—nice color—and a third gutted bathroom. Just as he decided he'd have to use the great outdoors like the dog, he found one outfitted with baby blue fixtures. Ugly, he decided, but serviceable.

And if the fist-sized showerhead over the blue tub worked, he'd make use of it later. But now, he really wanted coffee.

He wandered down, seeing bits and pieces of Kevin's work. The place would be a showstopper. Not glitzy and fussy—and someone else might have looked for that.

But solid and handsome, with some serious respect for history, location, style.

He paused at the living room. Again, the color worked, and while the gas logs made sense up in the bedroom, he was glad she'd kept the wood-burning original here.

She could use some help with the yard, clearing out the overgrown, pruning back, digging up the weeds. Right now the view from the front was just sad.

He worked his way back, wondering what in the hell one person would do with all the space—then stopped at the library door. For the first time he felt genuine and deep, deep envy.

He'd seen the early stages of the built-ins when he'd dropped by Kevin's shop a couple times, but the finished product beat it all to hell. The natural cherry would glow red-gold in the light, and simmer like the fire in the evenings. And all the space—what he could do with all that book space.

He'd get himself a big leather chair, angle it to face the fire and the view out the window.

Change the chair to a couch? He could live in this room.

The empty shelves and cases stabbed his book-lover's heart. They needed to be filled.

He took one more step toward the kitchen, and the scent of coffee reached him.

She was racking up points like Fast Eddie.

He found her sitting on one of the four stools that hadn't been there on his last visit, drinking coffee and looking at her tablet.

"Help yourself," she told him.

He went for one of the big white mugs rather than the daintier blue cups, poured coffee.

Though it was cool, she'd opened those accordion doors. He could hear the dog chowing down on the deck in the dark that was just starting to thin.

"I found a toothbrush in one of your boxes. I used it."

"That's fine."

"That blue bathroom. Slated for gutting, right?"

She looked up then—just punched him in the gut with those deep, dark green eyes. "You don't like the Boxer Bathroom?"

"Boxer—wait—black and blue. Funny."

"I wasn't sure what to call the pink and black one, but it's gone now. And so is its cabbage rose wallpaper border."

She sipped her coffee as she studied him. He looked rough and rugged, jeans zipped but not buttoned, the slate gray T-shirt bringing out the blue of his eyes, his hair mussed, stubble on his narrow face. Feet bare.

What the hell was he doing drinking coffee in her kitchen before dawn—and making her regret she hadn't taken him up on the offer to come back to bed?

He watched her as steadily as she did him.

She set the coffee down. "So. I'm trying to decide if you get a bowl of cereal, which is my go-to if I go-to breakfast. Or if I really want to try out my new omelette pan."

"Do I get a vote?"

"I believe I know your vote, and lucky for you, I really do want to try out the pan."

"You cook in it, I'll wash it."

"That seems fair."

She rose, went to the refrigerator, began to take out various things, set them on the counter. Eggs, cheese, bacon, a green pepper, those little tomatoes.

This looked serious.

She chopped, sliced, tore up some leaves she got from a pot on the windowsill, whisked, while he drank coffee.

"What makes that an omelette pan?"

"It's shallow with sloping sides." She poured the eggs over the tomatoes and peppers she'd sautéed, crumbled bacon over that, did the cheese-grating thing over that.

She slanted him a look as she eased a spatula around the sides of the cooking egg mix. "I wonder if I still have what it takes."

"From where I'm standing you do."

"Maybe, maybe not." Watching him still, she tipped the pan, gave it a gentle shake. "I'm taking the gamble."

Before his astonished eyes, she jerked the pan so the egg flew up, flipped over. She caught it neatly back in the pan, smiled in satisfaction.

"I've still got it."

"Impressive."

"Could've been a disaster. I haven't made a serious omelette in a couple years." She used the spatula to fold it. "Bread's in that drawer—pop some in the toaster."

She slid the omelette out, set it in the oven she had on warm, and did the whole thing again. Including the flip.

"I officially love this pan."

"I'm pretty fond of it myself."

She sprinkled a little paprika over the plated omelettes, added the toast. "I still don't have a table."

"We aren't far off sunrise."

"My thought, too. Take the plates, and I'll bring the coffee."

They sat on her glider, the hopeful dog sprawled at their feet, and ate while the stars went out and the sun began its golden burn over the water.

"I thought the library was the only thing I was going to envy here. But that . . ." Red, pink, and pale blue joined the gold. "That's another one."

"It never gets usual. I've taken dozens of pictures of sunrises here, and they're all their own. If this place had been a dirt hut, I'd have bought it, just for this."

"And this is where you eat your cereal."

"Or whatever. I probably will even after I get a table. I need to look for one for out here, and some chairs."

"You need books. That library needs books. I haven't seen any around here."

"I use my reader when I'm traveling." She arched an eyebrow. "Do you have something against e-readers?"

"No. Do you have something against actual books?"

"No. I'm sending for mine. I don't have anywhere close to what you do, but I have books. And I have the room now to collect more."

It made him think of the book on his wall, the one that told him things about her she didn't want anyone to know.

"Do you still want pictures of mine—the books?"

He caught the hesitation, though it was brief and well covered. "Yeah, I would. It's a statement."

"What will you do with them?"

"That depends on how they look, if they work the way I see. For the gallery, most likely. And I may do some as notecards for my website."

"You do notecards?"

"It always surprises me how well they sell. People still use notecards. Plenty of book lovers out there to buy them. The wall of books—some angles on that. And a stack of them beside a lamp maybe. One open, being read. I could use your hands for that."

"My hands?"

"You have big hands, big man hands, rough and callused. That's a good shot," she murmured, already seeing it. "Rough hands holding an open book. I could do, say, six shots for cards. One big, arty one for the gallery."

"Do you have anything going tomorrow?"

"Why?"

Always cautious, he thought.

"You could take the pictures tomorrow, and since you'd have your equipment anyway, you'd be in the mode, I should be able to get the guys together. You could take the shot for the CD."

"I don't know what you want there."

"Something that sells some CDs. You're the doctor."

"I'd want to see what you used before."

He boosted up a hip, took out his phone. He noted that he had a half a dozen texts to check, then scrolled through for the CD shot.

The five men, with instruments on the stage at the bar. Done in moody black-and-white.

"It's good."

"She says without enthusiasm."

"No, it's good. It's just not particularly interesting or creative. Nothing here to set you apart."

"What would you do?"

"I don't know yet. Where do you practice?"

"The garage, one of the back bays."

"Well, I'd start there."

He wanted, seriously wanted, to see where she'd start, where she'd finish. What she'd do. "Is tomorrow too soon?"

"No, I guess not. At least I can get a sense. The black T-shirts are okay, but have everybody bring a couple other choices—and some color."

"I can do that. That was a hell of an omelette. I'll get things washed up."

It wasn't much, and easily done. So he still had time to . . .

"Does the shower work up there?"

She did a little wiggle with her hand. "Grudgingly."

"Okay with you if I grab one before I head to work?"

"You work today?"

"Eight to four, Monday through Saturday. Twenty-four-seven emergency towing and road service. When I have a gig, somebody covers until I'm clear."

"Right. Sure, you can use the shower."

"Great." He grabbed her, had her back against the refrigerator, plundering with that hungry mouth, those big, rough hands. "Let's go do that."

She planned to get out early, explore on her way to Cecil's—for pictures and maybe a table.

But his hands were under her shirt, and his thumbs . . .

"I could use a shower."

Naomi blamed the sexual haze in the shower for her agreeing to have pizza with Xander after the workday.

It wasn't a date, she assured herself, and decided to go wild and wear the pewter leggings instead of the black. They were having sex now, so dating was unnecessary.

If she hadn't been hazed, she'd have made an excuse or at the least suggested he pick up the pizza, come to her place.

Her turf. Despite the short span of time since she'd moved in, the house was her turf.

"Then I'm going over there tomorrow," she told the dog. "It's work, yes, but that's still three days running." She topped the leggings with a tunic in a ripe peach color she liked, then belted it so it didn't look as if she wore a bag.

She grabbed what she needed—wallet, keys—and started downstairs with the dog prancing beside her.

She stopped. "You can't go. You have to stay here."

Until that moment she hadn't known a dog could actually look shocked.

"I'm sorry, but you'd just have to sit in the car the whole time, and that's not fair, right? Besides, you're my excuse for coming back in case he suggests, I don't know, a movie, or going to his place. You're my ace in the hole. I'm only going to be an hour or two. Tops two hours, then I'll be back. You have to stay."

He trudged back upstairs—actually trudged, she thought, while sending her forlorn looks over his shoulder.

"You'd think I was locking him in a closet and going out dancing," she muttered. And felt guilty all the way into town.

As he pulled on a fresh shirt, Xander figured he was running right on time. Hitting her up for the pizza had been inspired—especially since she'd been hot and wet and limp in the shower when he'd come up with it.

He also figured it was past time they had an actual date. Pizza always served up a good starter. He'd be on call, but those calls—if any—would go to his cell phone. If luck stuck, he'd get her back to her place and into bed without being called back to tow anything or anyone.

He opened the door, pulled up short. Chip stood, his big, raw-knuckled hand poised to knock. Or punch.

"Hey, Chip."

"Hey, Xander. You're heading out?"

"Yeah, but I got a minute. Do you want to come in?"

"That's okay, I'll walk down with you."

Chip started down the steps on his slightly bowed legs. A big guy—football star in high school—he tended to lumber unless he stood on the deck of a boat, as he did daily for his family business. There, Xander knew, the man had the grace of a Baryshnikov, and his shy, self-effacing nature worked well for the tourists who wanted to do some fishing or sailing.

He'd mooned over Marla as long as Xander had known him, and had finally won her when she'd come back to the Cove after two years of college.

He'd won her by punching the guy she'd taken up with who liked punching her.

It wasn't the first or the last guy Chip had punched over Marla. Xander really didn't want to be the next guy.

But he didn't sense anger, didn't see that hard light in Chip's eyes as they reached the base of the stairs.

"I wanted to, you know, say I was sorry about how Marla acted last night. I heard about it."

"It's no big."

"She's still got that thing for you."

Xander kept a close watch, in case that hard light came calling. "Chip, you know there's nothing there, and hasn't been since high school."

"I know it. I wanted to say how I know it, so you know. Patti, she's making noises like there was something, but I know better. Plenty of other people know better, too."

"Okay then. We're cool?"

"Sure. I want to apologize to the lady—the new lady? It's Naomi, right? But she doesn't know me, so I didn't want to go up there and scare her or anything."

"You don't have to worry about it, Chip. You don't have to apologize to anybody."

"I feel bad about it, all of it. Anyway." He put those ham-hock hands in his pockets, gazed out at nothing special. "You don't know where she is, do you?"

"Naomi?"

"No, not her, not Naomi. Marla."

"Sorry, no."

"She's not at her place, the place she has now, and doesn't answer the phone. Patti said she got mad at her last night, because Patti said she was embarrassed and all. She just took off—and she'd been drinking."

"Was she driving?"

"Seems Patti was, but it's not a far walk back to the place she has now. She didn't go to work today at the market either. They're that pissed at her now."

Hungover, mortified, mad, probably in bed with the covers over her head.

"I'm sorry to hear that."

"If you see her, maybe you can give me a call, so I know she's okay and just in one of her moods."

"I can do that."

"I'll let you go. Maybe if you see the lady—Naomi . . . If you see her, you could tell her I'm sorry about the trouble."

"I'll do that. You take it easy."

"It's the best way to take it." Chip smiled a little, then climbed into his truck.

Since it was close, and he was running a bit late now, Xander got into his own truck and drove to Rinaldo's.

She was already there, sitting in a booth, looking over the menu. He slid in across from her. "Sorry. I got into a thing just as I was leaving."

"That's all right. I was just trying to decide if I'd have room for this calamari starter."

"I'll split it with you, then you would."

"Then I would." She set the menu aside. "Busy place on Saturday night."

"Always has been. You look good."

"Better than I did a few hours ago?"

"You always look good. Hi, Maxie."

The waitress, young and fresh with doe eyes and sunny blonde hair streaked with a pretty shade of lavender, pulled out a pad. "Hi, Xander. Hi," she said to Naomi. "Can I get you some drinks?"

"A glass of chianti, thanks, and some ice water on the side."

"You got it. Xan?"

"Yuengling. How's that hatchback running?"

"It gets me where I'm going and back, thanks to you. I'll be right back with your drinks."

"I guess you get a lot of people where they're going and back."

"It's what I do. Listen, if a big, lumbering sort of guy comes up to your place—"

"What? What guy?"

Xander waved a hand. "Harmless guy. Chip. He's Marla's ex. He came by just as I was leaving."

As she straightened, Naomi's shoulder blades went to iron. "If he's mad about last night, he should be mad at who started it."

"It's not that. He's a nice guy—too nice most of the time. He wanted to apologize for her. He said he wanted to apologize to you, too, but he was afraid he'd scare you if he just showed up."

"Oh. It's not his fault. What's a nice guy who'd apologize for something that's not his fault doing with someone like her?"

"It's impossible to love and be wise."

"Who said that?"

"Francis Bacon. Anyway, I told him I'd tell you he was sorry."

Maxie brought their drinks and took their order.

Maybe it wasn't so bad, coming out, Naomi thought. The place was noisy, but in a good, happy way. And the calamari would've met with Harry's approval.

"I hear you met Loo."

"I did?"

"At the bar last night. The bartender."

"Is that Loo?" Sharp-looking brunette with sexy magenta streaks. "I expected her to be older, sort of businesslike, sitting in some back office with ledgers."

"Loo likes to keep her hand in. She liked you."

She caught a bright peal of laughter, noted that the comfortably built brunette behind the counter let out another as she rang up an order.

"That's flattering, since we talked over the bar for about two minutes."

"She knows what she knows, as she likes to say."

"She mentioned her ex-husband used to be the groundskeeper when my house was a B-and-B."

"Right, the stoner. He's long gone. But it reminds me I could give you a hand with some of the heavy yard work. Kevin said you didn't want to hire a landscaper, at least not yet, but if you decide otherwise, you might talk to Lelo."

"From the band?"

"His family runs the local nursery. He's actually pretty good at the whole lawn-and-garden thing."

"And having a stoner is tradition up there?"

After a gesture with his beer, he took a drink. "A former stoner in Lelo's case. You can size him up tomorrow for yourself."

"Maybe I will." More, maybe she'd just have to. "I wanted to deal with it myself, but so far I've managed to hack away the worst, plant a couple of pots and some kitchen herbs."

"No landscaping in New York?"

"Not like this. We've got a pretty back courtyard garden, simple and easy to maintain. And that's mostly Seth anyway. So maybe I'll think about getting some help with it."

"We could barter some labor for the photo shoot."

"Hmm. Let's see how the shoot goes. That could work all around."

"Why don't you come by, take a look at the garage?"

"I've got to get back for the dog." Ace in the hole, she reminded herself.

"Ten minutes won't matter. It's basically on the way. You take a look tonight, get that sense you wanted."

It would help, she thought. And she still had the dog for her ace in the hole. No matter how tempting, she couldn't end up in Xander's bed— not with a dog pining away at home.

"All right. Let's do that."

Of course, night had fallen so she couldn't judge the light, but she could get a sense of the space, a feel for what she'd have to work with if she shot in their practice area.

Floodlights popped on as she pulled around back behind Xander.

She saw now he had the bays locked and secured with some sort of keypad alarm as well as the motion lights.

"I hadn't thought about the security you'd need."

"A lot of tools, cars, car parts, and sometimes the band equipment."

He opened the bay door and hit the lights.

A good-sized space, she mused, stepping in. The place smelled of oil, and the concrete floor was stained with it. It held a lift, bright orange. She scanned tools: compressors, grease guns, hydraulic jacks, rolly boards, a couple of enormous tool chests—one black, one red.

Yes, she could make this work.

"Where do you set up?"

"Pretty much like we do onstage. If the weather's good, and we start early enough, we set up outside on the pad. It's nice."

Maybe, but she wanted them inside, with those clashing colors, those big, bulky tools.

"I'm going to want your motorcycle in here."

"For the shoot?"

"Yeah, maybe. I want to try that."

And parts, she thought. An old engine would be great, maybe a broken windshield—all those spiderwebs. A steering wheel. Tires.

Yes, she could make this work.

She stepped back out, looked at the space, walked back in, studied it.

"Okay, I want some wardrobe choices—things you're all comfortable in, but like I said, not just black. Get some ball caps, bandannas. Cowboy hat, maybe a duster. Leather. Definitely leather."

"Okay."

She heard the doubt in his voice and smiled. "Trust me. You're going to like what I do here."

But it was a big garage, and maybe there were other possibilities.

"What's in the next bay?"

"The love of my life."

"Is that so?"

"It is. Do you want to see her?"

"Absolutely."

He went out, left the first bay open in case she wasn't done, opened the next. Hit the light.

He'd heard her gasp like that before, he realized. When he'd been inside her.

"This is yours?"

"It is now."

"You have a sixty-seven GTO convertible, in factory red."

He stood in reverent silence for ten full seconds. "I think you have to marry me now. You're the first woman besides Loo who's seen her and known what she is. I'm pretty sure we're engaged."

"It's beautiful." She moved closer, skimmed her fingertips lightly over the hood. "Absolutely pristine. Did you restore it?"

"*Maintain*'s more like it. My grandfather bought her right off the showroom floor, treated her like a baby. The mechanic gene skipped my father, so Grandpa showed me the ropes, and when I turned twenty-one, he gave her to me."

She reached for the door, glanced at him. "Can I?"

"Sure."

She opened it, brushed her hand over the seat. "It still smells new. That's some detailing. Oh, it has the push-button radio."

"My dad talked about getting an eight-track put in, in his day. My grandfather nearly disinherited him."

"Well, it's blasphemy, isn't it? Your grandfather would be pleased at how well you've kept it."

"He is."

"Oh, he's alive?"

"And well, and living with my grandmother—well, stepgrandmother technically, but they've been married close to forty years—in Florida. Sanibel Island."

"Gorgeous place."

"How do you know about classic cars?"

"I only know some. I did a shoot—one of my first on my own. A friend of a friend of Harry's and Seth's."

She circled the car as she spoke. It really was absolutely perfect. And if Xander maintained it, she imagined it ran just as beautifully.

"He had classic cars and wanted photos of them," she continued, "inside and out. I was so nervous about the shoot, especially since I didn't know anything about cars, especially classic cars. I got a list of the cars he had, studied them—actually had Mason quiz me. And one of them was a sixty-seven GTO—not the convertible—but factory red, like this. A beauty."

"Want to take a ride?"

"Oh. I would." She sighed it. "I really would, but I have to get back for the dog."

He recognized lust, and knew how to use it.

"How about this? We take a ride in it to your place. You leave your car here, I stay there. Tomorrow, we load your equipment in her, come back so you can do what you do."

She shouldn't. She shouldn't. Shouldn't sleep with him two nights in a row. It was the next thing to a commitment.

And the car shined under the garage lights, luring her.

Xander stood, hipshot and sexy, finishing her off.

"I can agree to that, but only if you put the top down."

"Deal."

Fifteen

There had been a time in his life when Xander had been more apt to fall into bed at five in the morning than stumble out of it. He really hoped that time wasn't completely at an end.

But when part of the reward for early rising equaled pancakes—and not from a box mix like his mother made—he could see the benefit.

The bigger benefit sat beside him on the old glider smelling of summer while the stars went out.

"So those are the chairs and the table for out here."

"They will be."

Xander studied the old spring chairs. Even in the dark he could see the rust. "Why?"

"I'm going for a theme here, and they were a bargain. And because I have vision. I also dropped off a chest of drawers and a coffee table at Jenny's. Cecil's holding a couple more pieces I want her to look at."

"He must love you, Slim."

"I'm going to pay for this patio furniture, and more, with the pictures I took over there yesterday. I got one of his barn. God, the light was perfect, and the clouds—just a roll of gray. And I talked him into standing in the open barn doors, in those bib overalls he wears. He's leaning on a pitchfork. He grumbled about it, but he liked doing it—and he signed the release in exchange for a print. Good deal all around. Then I— Wait!"

She jumped up, ran inside. Xander exchanged a look with the dog, shrugged, and went back to his pancakes as the first light bloomed at the edge of the world.

She ran back, with her camera and a bag.

"Stand over by the rail," she ordered.

"What? No. I'm eating. It's too dark for pictures anyway."

"Do I tell you how to overhaul an engine? Come on, be a pal. Stand by the rail—with your coffee mug. Come on, come on, I don't want to miss the light."

"Isn't any light," he muttered, but rose and went to the rail.

"Call the dog over."

Since otherwise Tag might take too personal an interest in the plate he'd left on the glider, Xander called the dog.

"Just drink your coffee, watch the sunrise. Pay no attention to me. Just look out—no, turn a little more to your right—and lose the scowl. It's morning, you've got coffee and a dog. You just rolled out of bed after spending the night with a beautiful woman."

"Well, that's all true."

"Feel it a little, that's all. And watch the sun come up."

He could do that, he supposed. It was a little strange doing it while she moved around him with the camera. But the dog, apparently used to it, leaned against his leg and looked out over the water with him.

It was a hell of a show, those first trickles of light, the promise of them, the slow blur of rose hitting the water. Then the shimmer of gold rising up, edging the clouds.

Plus she made damn good coffee in that fancy machine of hers.

He'd just enjoy it, ignore the way she muttered to herself, pawed through her bag for something.

Oh, it was perfect. He was perfect. Hardly more than a silhouette, the tall, sleep-rumpled, barefoot, sexy man with the loyal dog at his side, watching the new day whisper over the water.

Long legs, long arms, big hands, white coffee mug, dark stubble on a sharp profile at the break of dawn.

"Great. Great. Thanks. Done."

He glanced back—and she couldn't resist one more.

"Now done."

"Okay." He went back to the glider and his pancakes, and when she joined him, ignoring her own plate to view the shots, he held out a hand. "Let's see."

She didn't give him the camera, but scooted closer, angled the screen, scrolled through.

He didn't know how she got so much out of the light—or the lack of it—how she'd tossed him into relief, managed to make him look moody and content at the same time. Or how she'd managed to capture every shade of sunrise.

"You're good."

"Yes, I am. I'll print out a release."

"What are you going to do with them?"

Still scrolling, she stopped on one, did something that zoomed in on his profile. "I need to take a closer look at them on my computer, pick the one I think is best for the sexy, moody gallery print I have in mind, then work on it some. Pick another—probably the one where you started to turn, look back at me with the sunrise behind you—for a stock print. You're going to end up on a book cover."

"What?"

"I know what sells there," she said. "One of these days, you can add yourself to your collection. That's a good, and unexpected, morning's work."

She leaned over, kissed him—something she'd never done before. And stifled his instinct to object.

"Are you going to start on that this morning?"

Now she zoomed in on the dog's profile. "That and some other work."

"Okay, I'll get going on the yard."

"The yard?" Distracted, she looked over at him. "My yard?"

"No, I thought I'd just drive around until I found one that appealed to me, and dig in. Yeah, your yard."

"You don't have to do that."

"I'm up, and I like yard work."

"Says the man without a yard."

"Yeah, that's a downside." To Tag's bitter disappointment, Xander polished off the pancakes. "But I give Kevin and Jenny a hand now and then. And Loo. Where are your tools?"

"I have a shovel, a fan rake, and this set of garden tools—you know, little spade, clippers, the fork thing."

He sat for a moment. "And you expect to deal with that yard with a shovel, a rake?"

"So far. What else?"

"You need loppers, a wheelbarrow, you can use some of the empty drywall buckets around here, a pickax. You need both a fan rake and a garden rake, shears—"

"I need to make a list."

"I'll see what I can do with what you've got, and we'll go from there."

Since she'd planned on a full morning's work, she settled down at her temporary station. He could play in the yard, she thought, though she imagined he'd get tired and bored with the sheer grunt work of it and come back in, nudge at her to knock off.

Have sex, take a ride, do something she didn't have on her morning agenda.

That was the problem with having someone around. They so often wanted to do something you didn't have time for.

She took care of some basics first, some bread-and-butter shots. Pleased with the barn studies, she uploaded them before spending time on the one she'd chosen of Cecil.

But since the pictures she'd just taken tugged at her, she shuffled back the other work she'd intended to finish and studied them—frame by frame—on the big screen.

She started on the last shot—the lucky, impulse shot where he'd been half turned toward her, with a half smile, good and cocky, on his face.

God, he was gorgeous. Not slick and polished—nothing slick or polished about him. It was all raw and rough, and only more so with that morning stubble, the ungroomed hair.

She went to work on the background first, burning in the clouds for a little more drama. Yeah, big drama for the backdrop—hot, sexy guy, half turned, looking over his shoulder at a lover.

No mistaking the half-cocked smile and smoky look aimed at anyone but a lover.

As a stock photo it would sell, and for years. In the short term, she calculated she'd sell dozens in under a week. For fun, and the mystery, she titled it *Mister X.*

Yes, an excellent morning's work.

She fussed with it more, zooming in, refining small details, and then, satisfied, uploaded it to her site. Once that was done, she reviewed the two shots she'd come down to for the gallery.

She lost track of time. This work was more exacting, more detailed. She wanted to stress the moment where everything stilled between night and day, just the first hints of light, the drama still below the surface.

And the man, hardly more than a shadow, with the dog lightly leaning against him.

Bring out his eyes more, she decided, so the blue played hot.

She might do a second, she considered, black-and-white—with color pops. Yes, with his eyes boldly blue, and the growing light just as boldly red. The white mug.

She made a note of the number she wanted for that, went back to the first.

She toggled between the two, each time studying the previous work with a critical and fresher eye.

"They're good. They're really good," she murmured, and sent both to the manager of the gallery for preview.

Then she sat back to study them both again.

"Really good."

She rose, rolled her stiff shoulders, circled her head on her stiff neck—and reminded herself she'd vowed to do at least thirty minutes of yoga daily to keep loose.

"Starting tomorrow."

The least she could do was go check on Xander, offer him something cold to drink. Make sure the dog had something, too, as Tag had opted to hang with Xander instead of sprawling beside her while she worked.

She went down, opened the front door.

She saw him, stripped to the waist, torso gleaming with sweat, throwing a stick—more like an entire branch—for the wild-eyed dog.

More sticks, more debris, filled a wheelbarrow. A large swatch of lawn sat patchy, bumpy, and clear of weeds, tangling brush, and the thorny vines that seemed to grow a foot every night.

She spotted a pile of rocks, a chain saw, an ax, a pickax, those drywall buckets, plastic tarps with piles of leaves and pine needles centered on them.

She said, "Holy crap," and got Xander's attention.

"Hey. We got a good start here."

"A start? Where did all this come from?"

"The yard trash from the trashy yard. The tools? Tag and I rode into town, got the truck, stopped by the garden center and the hardware. I left the bills on the kitchen counter. There's half a cold-cut sub in the fridge if you want it. We got hungry."

Slowly she walked down, stepped on grass—pathetic grass, but still. "I never expected you to do all this."

"We had some fun with it. If I were you, I'd get rid of those foundation bushes." He pulled a bandanna out of his back pocket and swiped the sweat off his face with it. "Lelo'd rip them out for you—or tell you if they're worth saving."

"Did I buy a chain saw?"

"No, that's mine. You shouldn't need one now that things are more under control. Once that Dumpster's gone, you can figure out what you want to do over there."

As he spoke, he threw the stick for Tag again. "I'd sure as hell plant myself a good tree."

"I . . . I thought maybe I'd plant one of those weepers. A cherry or . . . whatever."

"That'd be good." He pulled off thick work gloves.

"Xander, how long— What time is it?" She dug for her phone to check, realized she didn't have it.

He pulled out his own. "It's about one."

"In the afternoon?"

"It ain't morning, baby." Laughing, he kissed her. "Where do you go when you work?"

"I just never expected you to . . . You worked *hours*. Thank you, so much."

"It's just yard work, but you're welcome. I need to get cleaned up so we can get going. If you still want those book pictures."

"Yes, I do—and yes, you do. You're all sweaty." Stepping closer, she trained a finger down his chest. "And pretty dirty. You look . . . hot and thirsty."

Since the look in her eyes invited it, he hauled her against him. "Now you're sweaty and dirty, too."

"Then I guess we both need a shower."

H e took her under cool water, running hard, soap-slick hands over her. Eager, avid, her mouth met his so he swallowed those gasps and moans as he took her higher.

When he pinned her against the wall, drove into her, her fingers dived into his hair, clutched there. Her eyes clung to his as, with lips close, their breath tangled.

The green of her eyes went opaque as she peaked, as she said his name as he'd wanted her to say it.

But he held back, denied himself that quick release, slowed the rhythm until her head lolled back.

She could feel nothing but pleasure, all so ripe, so full it should burst. But it only spread, engulfed her like warm, wet velvet.

The tiles, cool on her back, his body hot, pressed to her, in her. The air so thick that breathing it in, letting it go, was a moan. She tried to hold on, to give back, but felt as soft and pliable as wax in sunlight. His lips toyed with hers, conquering by torment rather than force.

She said his name again as her eyes closed.

"No, no, look at me. Open your eyes and see me, Naomi."

"I see you. Yes. God."

"A little more. A little more until there's nothing left. I'm going to take more."

"Yes."

He took more, kept them both swaying on that high wire between need and release, until it built beyond the bearing, until he let the wire snap beneath the weight.

Because she felt a little drunk, Naomi took great care packing her equipment. He'd taken her beyond her own boundaries of control, and somehow she'd allowed it. She'd need time and space to decide, to understand, what that meant.

And now wasn't the time, not when everything in her felt so soft and vulnerable. When she could still feel his hands on her.

She packed her tripod, a camera bag, a case, a light stand, diffuser.

He walked in, smelling of her soap. "All that?"

"Better to have everything than leave behind the one thing you realize you need."

She started to swing on a backpack.

"I've got it. Christ, does everything include bricks?" He picked up her tripod case, the light stand, started out.

As she picked up the rest, Tag barked as if dragons burned down the gates.

"Car's coming," Xander called back. "I've got it."

"He's got it," she murmured. "That's the problem. Why am I mostly okay that he's got it?"

"Easy, killer," Xander told the dog, and opened the front door. He recognized the official vehicle just pulling up beside his truck, and the chief of police behind the wheel.

"Relax, he's one of the good guys." Xander stepped off the porch, carted the equipment to his truck. "Hey, Chief."

"Xander. Is that the stray I heard about?"

"Yeah. That's Tag."

"Hey there, Tag."

Chief of police Sam Winston, a toughly built man with a smooth face the color of walnuts and a Waves cap on his close-cropped hair (the high school football team where his son stood as quarterback), crouched down.

Tag, nervous, crept close enough to sniff.

"He's a good-looking dog."

"Now, he is."

Tag accepted the head scrub, then immediately ran back to Naomi when she came out.

"Ma'am." Sam tapped the brim of his cap. "I'm Sam Winston, chief of police."

"Is something wrong?"

"I'm not sure about that. I've been meaning to come up, introduce myself. It's good someone's back on the bluff, and from what I hear—and can see for myself—you're giving the old girl a face-lift. She needed one. You got Kevin Banner and his crew on it, I hear."

"Yes."

"You couldn't do better. Looks like I caught you two on the way out."

"Naomi's going to take some pictures of the band."

"Is that so?" Sam hooked his thumbs in his thick Sam Browne belt, gave a little nod. "I bet they'll be good ones. I don't want to keep you, and it saves me time to find you both here. It's about Marla Roth."

"If she's trying to push an assault charge, I'll push back. Again," Naomi said.

"I can't say if she'd go there. We can't seem to find her."

"Still?" Xander put in, turned back from stowing the equipment.

"Nobody's seen or heard from her, the way it looks, since Friday night. Not long after your scuffle with her, Ms. Carson."

"If she's still pissed about that, she could've taken off for a few days," Xander began.

Worn boots planted, Sam gave the bill of his cap a little flick up. "Her car's at her house, and she isn't. Chip finally broke in the back door this morning, then came back to see me. She didn't go in to work yesterday, isn't answering her phone. She could be in a snit, and it's most likely she is, but Chip's worried sick, and I need to look into it. Now, the story I'm getting is she went at you at Loo's on Friday night."

Missing could mean anything, Naomi assured herself. *Missing* didn't mean an old root cellar in the deep woods. More often, *much* more often, it just meant a person had gone somewhere no one had looked yet.

"Ms. Carson?" Sam prompted.

"Sorry, yes. That's right. She knocked into me a couple of times, then shoved me a couple of times."

"And you clocked her one?"

"No, I didn't hit her. I took her wrist, gave it a twist—leverage, pressure point, so she went down. So she stopped shoving me."

"Then what?"

"Then I left. It was annoying and embarrassing, so I left and came home."

"By yourself."

"Yes, I came home alone."

"About what time do you think that was?"

"About ten thirty." Just doing his job, Naomi reminded herself, and took a deep breath. "I let the dog out, walked around with him for a while. I was angry and upset, and couldn't concentrate on work."

"And I got here about twelve thirty." Though Xander leaned negligently back on his truck, irritation edged his voice. "The dog got us up just after five, and I left about seven thirty, maybe a little before. Come on, Chief."

"Xander, I've got to ask. Patti's been screeching about Ms. Carson attacking Marla—she's the only one with that take," he added before Xander could speak. "And even she's backed off that mark. But the fact is, Marla stormed out of Loo's in a temper about twenty minutes after Ms. Carson, and as far as I can determine, that's the last anyone saw her."

Sam huffed out a breath, petted the dog, who now apparently found him delightful. "Did either of you see her with anybody, somebody she might've taken it into her head to go off with?"

"She was sitting with Patti." Xander shrugged. "I try not to notice Marla too much."

"I saw her at her table, with her friend, earlier in the evening." Tense now, Naomi rubbed her neck. "I was sitting with Kevin and Jenny. I really wasn't paying attention to her, until Jenny and I got up to dance and she . . . I don't even know her."

"I understand that, I do, and I don't want you to worry about this. She probably went off with somebody she met at the bar, to lick her wounds and get Chip worked up."

Naomi shook her head. "A woman who's pissed off and upset? She's going to talk to her girlfriend."

"They had a bit of a falling-out after the incident."

"Regardless. Even if she called this Patti to argue, or at least send her a bitchy text."

"We'll be looking into it. I'm not going to keep you, but I'd like to come back sometime, see what you're doing inside."

"Yes, sure."

"You have a good day. I'll be seeing you around, Xander."

Naomi's insides twisted as Sam got back in his cruiser.

"Will he really look?"

"Yeah, of course. He's the chief."

"Has anyone else ever gone missing?"

"Not that I know of, and I would. Hey." Xander put a hand on her arm. "Marla's the type who looks for trouble, likes to cause it. It's just the way she is. The chief will do his job. Don't worry about this."

He was right, of course. Marla was a troublemaker and had very likely hooked up with some guy for the weekend to boost her wounded ego.

Not every woman who went off that way ended up raped and murdered. It had never happened here before, Naomi reminded herself. Hadn't she checked into just that after she'd fallen for the house?

Low crime rate, even lower violent-crime rate. A safe place. A quiet place.

Marla would probably show up before nightfall, pleased she'd worried her ex-husband, her friend, had the police out looking for her.

She put it out of her mind, as much as she could, as Xander pulled away from the house in the truck, with the dog riding with his head out the window and his ears flying in the breeze.

LIGHT AND SHADOW

Where there is a great deal of light,
the shadows are deeper.

JOHANN WOLFGANG VON GOETHE

Sixteen

When he'd realized she was serious about taking pictures in his place, Xander had considered pulling the Simon Vance book off the shelf. He'd done so long enough to read it again, refresh himself, then had nearly tossed it into the box he kept for donations.

He didn't want to see that dull, stricken look on her face again.

In the end, he decided pulling it off gave it too much importance. She knew it was there, and would wonder why he'd taken it away.

Weighing the stress factor, he figured it at fifty-fifty, and opted to leave it alone.

She'd tell him when she was ready. Or she wouldn't.

He helped her haul her equipment up the steps, where she paid more attention to the equipment than what she intended to shoot. She pulled a tripod out of a case, telescoped it, did the same with a light stand.

"I've still got that wine you like if you want."

"Thanks, but not when I'm working."

As he subscribed to the same rule, he got them both a Coke.

She nodded, ignored it as she pulled out a light meter. "Can I have one of those chairs over here for the laptop?"

"I'll get it."

She attached a camera to the tripod, eyes narrowed now on the wall of books.

"That's an impressive camera."

"Hasselblad, medium format. Larger media, higher resolution. I'm going to shoot digital first."

She took a back from her case, attached it to the camera. When he looked in the case, the bag—the lenses, backs, cables, attachments—he understood why everything was so damn heavy.

How the hell did she haul all that stuff around?

He didn't ask because he recognized focused work mode.

She peered through the viewfinder, used a remote to switch on the light, switch it off. She popped an umbrella out of the bag, screwed it onto the light stand, then shielded that with a screen.

She checked everything again, changed the angle of the tripod, walked it back about an inch.

If she thought about the book, she didn't show it.

He figured it took her a good thirty minutes to set up and take a couple of test shots. Halfway through it, he decided she didn't need him, got a book out of his office, and settled down at the table to read while she worked.

"Is there a system to the way you shelve the books?"

He glanced up. "Where they fit, why?"

"You have Jane Austen beside Stephen King."

"I don't think either one of them would mind, but if you do, you can move books around."

"No, that's part of the point. It's a wall of stories. Take out any one, go anywhere. It's . . . Storyland."

She pulled him into watching her again. Shoot, study, adjust, test, shoot. Curious now, he got up to take a look at the laptop screen.

The colors bloomed deeper, the light a little dreamy. Somehow she made some of the tattered spines appear interesting rather than worn.

Another popped on. He couldn't see the difference, but apparently she could as she squinted at it, said, "Yeah, yeah."

She took half a dozen more, making minor adjustments, then crouched down to slideshow through all the shots.

"How come it looks better in the picture than in reality?"

"Magic. This one, yeah, this is the one, I think. It looks great in reality. Light, shadow, angle, that's just atmosphere."

"You made art."

"I captured art," she corrected. "I want to take some film." She took the back off the camera and switched it with something out of her bag.

"That camera does both—digital and film?"

"Yeah. Handy."

He wanted to ask how—wanted to *see* how. But she had that in-the-zone look about her again.

She went back to work; he went back to reading.

She pulled him out of his book when she switched backs again, changed lenses, and took the camera off the tripod. She moved to the side, took a picture of the books from a sharp angle. Checked the result, adjusted the light, took a few more.

When she lowered the camera, moved to the shelves, he thought for a moment she meant to pull off the book about her father. But she pulled one from a higher shelf, carried it to the table.

"I want you with the Austen. Can you bookmark what you're reading?"

"I've read it before. I can pick it up where I left off if I want." He felt more than a little foolish. No one would ever term him shy, but the idea of taking pictures of his hands?

Weird.

"You're serious about the hand thing."

"Deadly. Tough man's hand with classic novel written by a woman, one a lot of people consider a woman's book."

"A lot of people are stupid."

"Either way, it should work." She took out her light meter. "And the light's good right here for what I want. Good, natural light through that window. Especially if you just . . . scoot your chair to the right, just a couple inches."

Once he had, she checked the light meter again. Apparently satisfied, she went back for her laptop, set it on the postage-stamp corner of counter.

"Just hold the book open, the way you would if you were reading it. Not the first page—you've been reading it awhile. About a third of the way through."

He felt ridiculous, but he did it. He'd give her five minutes to play around.

She shot over his shoulder so that sultry summer scent spilled over him.

Maybe ten, he considered, while she shifted behind him, leaned in closer.

"Turn a page—or start to, don't turn it all the way. Just—stop, hold it. Good. It's good. But . . ."

She straightened, frowned at the laptop image. He had to twist around to check it himself, and what he saw surprised him.

"I thought you were crazy, but it looks like an ad in a high-class magazine or something."

"It's good, but it's not quite there. It needs . . . Of course."

She pulled open his refrigerator, took out a beer. When she spotted the opener, she popped the top, then to his shock, poured a good third of it down the sink.

"What? Why?"

"Tough hands, a beer, and *Pride and Prejudice*." She set the beer on the table, framed it, moved it closer to the top right edge of the book.

"You didn't have to pour it down the sink."

"It needs to look like you're drinking a beer and reading Austen."

"I have a mouth, and a throat. We could have poured it in there."

"Sorry, didn't think of that. Left thumb under the page, turning it, right hand on the beer. I need you to cover the label—I'm not looking for product placement. Hand on the beer like you're about to pick it up, maybe even lift it a half inch off the table."

Since there was no use crying over spilled beer, he followed instructions. Picking up the beer, setting it down, turning a page, not turning a page, until she lowered the camera again.

"Perfect. Just exactly right."

He turned to see for himself, saw the beer had been inspired. It gave the shot a cheerful edge, and added balance.

"Real men read books," Naomi said. "I'm going to offer poster size."

He felt weird all over again. "Posters."

"Brick-and-mortar bookstores, adult learning centers, college dorms, even some libraries. You've given me some damn good work today, Xander. I'm going to tell Kevin it's a go on the steam shower."

"You're putting in a steam shower."

"I am now." Nodding, nodding, she scrolled through the shots on her computer. "Yes, I am now. I'd talked myself out of it, but when I get this much good work on a Sunday? I'm steaming."

He pointed at her. "I earned time in that."

"You definitely did."

She didn't resist when he pulled her onto his lap, but did hesitate when he started to take the camera.

"I'm not going to bounce it off the floor. It's got weight," he commented.

"Just over nine pounds. I'm mostly going to use the tripod with it, and it's worth the weight. It's tough and reliable, and you can see just how sharp."

"And this deal on the back makes it shoot digital?"

Nodding, she removed it. "Excellent system—no pins to catch on anything, and it has its own integrated software. It's not something I'm going to take on a hike, but for what I wanted here, and for what you want with the band, it's the machine."

He had to admit he'd like to play with it himself, just to see how the mechanics worked. But he didn't see that happening, any more than he'd let her under the hood of his GTO.

"I use my phone if I take a picture."

"Very decent cameras on phones today. I've taken some nice shots I've been able to manipulate and sell. And now, I wouldn't mind a half a glass of that wine while I break this down and we set up in the garage."

"I can take care of that. I've already got most of a beer."

"Thanks." She hesitated again, then kissed him. "Thanks," she repeated.

"No problem."

She rose, went over to carefully replace her camera in its case. And as he rose to get her wine, he saw her gaze shift back to the books.

"So, it's a classic therefore a clichéd question, but have you read all of these?"

"Everything out here, yeah. There's some in my office, in the bedroom I haven't gotten to yet."

She pulled off casual, he thought, compacting her tripod, sliding it into its soft case.

"Mostly fiction, right? But you've got some nonfiction mixed in. Biographies, histories, books on cars—surprise—true crime."

He could pull off casual, too. "Nonfiction, written well, is a story."

"I tend to only read nonfiction that's work related. How do you know if something based on true is written true?"

"I guess you don't."

"Sometimes it must be perception or personal agenda, or just enhancing or adjusting for creative effect. Like a photograph. I take an image that's real, but I can manipulate it, change tones, enhance or soften or crop out to meet my own agenda."

He brought the wine to her. Fifty-fifty, he'd thought. She'd done the work she'd come to do on the first fifty. Now, he could see, she'd tied herself up in the second half.

"I'd say the person in the original image knows what's true and what's manipulated."

"That's the thing about words and images." She took a slow sip of wine. "Once the words are on the page, the image printed, it becomes what's true."

She turned away then, set her glass aside to break down her lighting. "They're not so different, words and pictures. Both freeze moments, both stay with you long after the moment's over."

"Naomi."

He didn't have a clear idea what to say, how to say it, and decided it would be nothing as the sound of an old truck with a rusted-out muffler boomed outside.

"That'll be Lelo and his muffler from hell."

"If he had a friend who was a mechanic, he could get that fixed."

"I'll have to suggest that. For the millionth time. At least he can help us haul all this down."

She liked Lelo—and it generally took her longer to like. And Tag loved him at first sight. Man and dog were all over each other in an instant, like long-lost friends (possibly brothers) thrilled with the reunion.

"That's a good dog. That's some good dog." Crouched, Lelo rubbed Tag all over and got licked lovingly in the face with every stroke. "I heard you found him out of gas on the side of the road."

"That's right."

"Not out of gas now, are you, boy? Not out of gas now."

Tag rolled over, exposing his belly. His hind leg pumped like a piston in time with the rubbing.

Lelo had straggly hair halfway to his shoulders the color of a Kansas cornfield. He came in about an inch shorter than Naomi with a skinny build and ropey muscles set off in a tie-dyed T-shirt and jeans frayed at the knees and the hems. An emerald green fire-breathing dragon rode sinuously up his right forearm.

"How are you doing up there on the bluff?"

"I like it." Naomi set up her lights as she considered ideas and options for the shoot.

"Needs help with the landscaping," Xander said as he brought in—as ordered—his guitars, both his ax and his old acoustic.

"Oh yeah. They sure let that place go. Never did have much what you'd call creativity with the landscaping. And Dikes never gave a shit."

"Loo's ex," Xander explained.

"Stayed stoned most of the time. I should know since I got stoned with him. I don't do that so much anymore," he said to Naomi. "I could take a look up there, if you want. Give you some ideas."

"I could probably use the ideas."

"No charge for thinking. Here comes Dave and Trilby."

Dave the drummer, Naomi remembered. Broad shoulders, compact build, brown hair worn in a kind of modified Caesar. Jeans, a faded Aerosmith T-shirt, banged-up brown hiking boots. Trilby—keyboards—made a striking contrast. Smooth dark skin, wide dark eyes, a head full of dreads. Cargo pants and a red tee on a gym-ripped body.

They hauled in their equipment while Xander called out introductions. It helped that everyone had full hands and tasks. She always had a problem meeting so many people at once.

Of course the dog eased any awkwardness, happily roaming from one to another after he'd sniffed enough to reassure himself they were okay.

"I took a look at your website," Dave said to Naomi as he set up his drums. "Slick. I'm in charge of the band's. Not so slick. Techwise, it rocks—that's what I do—but the look doesn't hit it hard."

Since she'd taken the time to view it herself, she couldn't disagree. "It's really thorough, and easy to navigate."

He grinned. "Which is saying yeah, the look blows. I was wondering if we could get some shots today I could use there, juice it up."

"I've got some ideas."

"Good, because in that area I'm fresh out. My wife said maybe we should go more retro."

"You're married?"

"Eight years, two kids."

She couldn't say why she'd assumed he, and the rest of the band, would be single.

At the serious engine roar, Dave adjusted the angle of his snare. "That'll be Ky. Lead guitar," Dave added, as she watched the big, black, tricked-out Harley roar up.

Tall, dark, and dangerous, she thought. You couldn't say handsome, not with the narrow face, the scruffy goatee, the hawkish nose and just overly generous mouth.

But he made you look.

He aimed eyes as dark as his hair at Naomi. "Hi there, Slugger."

Xander glanced over from setting up the speakers. "Naomi, Ky."

"Yeah, I saw you put Marla on her knees the other night. She'd earned it."

"Nobody's seen her for a couple days," Lelo said.

"Yeah, I just heard about that." With a kind of practiced shrug, Ky swung his guitar case off his back. "Hooked up with somebody at the bar. Wouldn't be the first time. You had a lost weekend with her back when, didn't you, Lelo?"

"A half a weekend, in a weak moment."

"We all have 'em. Got beer, Keaton?"

"Cooler, outside the bay."

He gave Naomi a lazy smile. "Want one, Rocky?"

"No, thanks."

"Water and soft stuff in there, too."

"I'd take a water."

She put her hands on her hips, looked around.

Yeah, she had ideas.

"I'm going to take some basics, just to warm everybody up, test the waters. You're set up like you are onstage, so go ahead, play something."

She pulled out her Nikon, changed the lens, checked her light meter as they got in position, decided what to play.

"Dave's got his Aerosmith on, so let's go there," Xander suggested.

"Don't look at me unless I tell you to," Naomi ordered, and began to shoot.

Standard, she thought. Good, solid, but standard. She got some decent head shots, some wide angles, some where she let the motion blur.

When the last chord crashed down, she lowered the camera.

"Okay. Now, we're not doing any of that. I need to see the wardrobe options. Lelo, I want to stick with what you've got on, but let's see what else there is."

Men, she thought as she pawed through the choices, should learn how to be more creative.

"I bet you've got more stuff in your trucks, your trunks."

Lelo came up with an old, oversized army jacket. She tossed it at Dave. "You."

"Seriously?"

"Trust me." She pulled out a white T-shirt. "You've had this awhile, right?" she asked Xander.

"Yeah."

"Okay then." She took it over to a grease stain, dropped it, rubbed it in with her foot. "Better," she decided when she picked it up. "Better yet, smear some motor oil on it."

"You want me to smear oil on the shirt."

"Yeah, like you got some on your hand, swiped your hand over the shirt." She demonstrated. "Do that, put it on. Trilby, is that red T-shirt new?"

"Kind of."

"Then I'm sorry, but I need to rip it."

"Why?"

"Because you're built, and I want to see some skin and muscle."

Lelo let out a hoot.

"Across the pecs, okay? Xander, I need some chain—not too heavy."

"Christ," he muttered as he ruined a perfectly good T-shirt.

"Chains for me?" Ky grinned at her. "You want to chain me up, Legs?"

"That's what women will wonder when they look at the picture." She gave him a mirror of his cocky grin. "Stud."

"What kind of picture is this?" Trilby asked, holding his red shirt.

"Hot, sexy, rock-and-roll. If you don't like it, we can go with the basics I already shot, and more along those lines. But let's try this. I want that compressor over here, and that grease-gun thing. I want some old tires piled up, right about there. You wouldn't happen to have a broken windshield."

Xander tugged the stained and dirty shirt over his head. "I replaced one last week, haven't taken it to the junkyard yet."

"Perfect. Bonus round. Haul it in here."

"I don't get this," Dave muttered, and sniffed at the sleeve of the army jacket.

"I do." Lelo rubbed Tag, grinned at her. "Open it up, guys. We're the Wreckers, right? We're a fucking garage band. We're in a garage. Let's use it."

"Now you're talking. I want some tools." Lips curved, eyes focused, Naomi nodded. "Big, man-sized tools."

Xander didn't want to think about how long it would take to put everything back where it belonged. The bay turned into a jumble of car parts, tools, and musical instruments.

He thought he had fairly good vision, but it seemed too art house, over the top, and out of the box.

And he was sitting on a freaking air compressor, with his beloved Strat in one hand and a cordless drill in the other. Ky wore chains bandolero-style, and Dave looked baffled in Lelo's grandfather's ancient army jacket. She'd had Trilby lay his keyboard against a stack of tires.

The only person, besides Naomi, who seemed to think it was a fine idea was Lelo, sitting cross-legged on the concrete floor, with his bass in his lap, a grease gun held like a rifle.

She had their own music banging out on playback, and the fancy camera on a tripod. She took some shots, shook her head.

No one spoke as she pulled a bandanna out of the pile of clothes she'd rejected, dipped it into the can of motor oil, then walked to Dave.

"Come on, really?"

"Sorry. You're just too clean-cut." She dabbed and smeared some oil on his cheek.

She stepped back, angled her head.

"Lelo, lose the shoes. Just toss them to the side—beside you, a little in front. I need a hubcap."

"I got one in the bed of my truck."

When Lelo started to rise, she motioned him down. "I'll get it."

Dave turned to Xander when she went out. "What the hell have you gotten us into?"

"I have no idea."

"She's hot." Lelo lifted his shoulders. "Just saying. If you hadn't seen her first, Xan, I'd make some major moves."

"I just bought this shirt." Trilby looked down at the tears. "I only washed it once."

"Let her do what she does," Ky suggested. "Xander's bound to get lucky and owe us."

"He already got lucky," Naomi said. "You had two." She arranged the hubcaps, stepped back. "Tag! Those aren't yours."

He'd nearly reached the discarded shoes, and now slunk back again.

"For now, everybody look straight at the camera. Badasses, give me some badass. Come on, let's see you steam up the lens."

She should've gotten a few beers in them first, she thought.

Still, it worked. The light, the setup, the *arrangement* worked.

She stepped to the side. "See me?"

"You're right there," Xander pointed out.

"So everybody sees me. Hold that thought." She went behind the camera, looked through the lens. "Imagine me naked."

And there we go.

"Again. Don't lose it. Imagine me imagining you naked. Yeah, that's got you thinking."

She came out again, picked up one of the hubcaps, handed it to Dave. Went back.

"Ky, wrap one of the loose ends of chain around your fist. Go with the music, play."

"I've got a hubcap," Dave pointed out.

"And drumsticks. Play the hubcap. Play the tools, play the instrument, whatever strikes. Play. You're onstage, you know how to interact onstage."

She took them from play to war—instruments and tools as weapons.

Out of the corner of her eye she saw the dog slinking back, caught him in the frame.

"Tag!" she called out just as he grabbed one of the shoes.

Lelo just laughed, hooked an arm around Tag. "Hey, he can be in the band."

She took the shot, took two more while the mood held. Then stepped back.

"That's a wrap, gentlemen."

"That's it?" Dave blinked at her.

"It takes her twice as long—more," Xander corrected, "to set things up than to take the pictures."

"You can see if it was worth it. I'll set the laptop on slideshow. If you like the group shots, I've got time to take individuals—you'd want to change again."

"It's nice of you to offer," Dave began, "but I should probably . . . Hey, that's a nice shot."

She'd started with the basic band shot. "Yeah, it's not bad."

"No, these are really good. Tons better than what we have now. You see this, Trilby?"

"Sweet." In his ruined shirt, he braced a hand on Dave's shoulder, leaned in to study. "You got some individuals right here."

"Nice." Ky unwrapped the chain. "We can really use these."

"Aces, but the others are going to be better." Still barefoot, Lelo squeezed in. "Are they coming up?"

"These are with the Nikon. I'll switch cards when they run through."

"Can you email these to me?" Dave asked her.

"You're not going to want all of them, and the files from the Hassie are huge. I'll send you a sample of the best of them once I go through."

She switched cards, waited to see if she'd gone wrong.

"Told ya!" Lelo punched Dave's shoulder when the shots began to slide on-screen.

"These are— We look—"

"Super cool!" Lelo punched Dave again.

"I thought it was crazy, even stupid." Dave glanced up at Naomi. "Big apologies."

"Not necessary. Worth the shirt?" she asked Trilby.

"And then some. These are great. Really great."

"That's talent, and that's vision." Ky nodded at the screen. "Shouldn't have doubted you. Xander's got a knack for spotting talent and vision."

"That one! Gotta have that one, the one with the dog." Lelo scrubbed at Tag, who still had the shoe in his mouth. "Band mascot."

"How about that wine now?" Xander asked her when the slideshow started again.

"I could have a glass—one—before I set up for individuals."

He took her hand, drew her outside the bay. "And after that, stay."

"Oh, I really should get back, take a better look at these, start to weed through them."

He leaned down, kissed her, warm and long in the quieting spring evening. "Stay anyway."

"I . . . I don't have my things, or Tag's food, or . . ." She should take a breath, take some room. Then he kissed her again. "Come home with me," she said. "When we're done, come home with me."

He went home with her, and late into the night when whatever dream chasing her made her whimper and stir, he did what he never did. He wrapped her close, and held her.

While Xander shielded Naomi from the nightmare, Marla lived one.

She didn't know where she was, how long she'd been in the dark.

He hurt her, whoever he was, and when he did, he whispered how he would hurt her more the next time. And he did.

She tried to scream, but he'd taped her mouth. Sometimes he pushed a rag over her face, and the terrible fumes of it made her sick, then made her go away.

She always woke in the dark, woke cold and scared, and wishing with all her heart for Chip to come save her.

Then he'd rape her again. He cut her, and he hit her. He cut her and he hit her even if she didn't fight the rape. Sometimes he choked her until her lungs burned, until she passed out.

She couldn't remember what had happened, not exactly. When she tried to think, her head hurt so bad. She remembered walking home, being mad, so mad. But couldn't remember why. And she remembered— or thought she did—having to stop and puke in some bushes.

Then the big car with the camper—was that it? She walked by a camper, and then something hit her. Something hurt her. And those awful fumes took her away.

She wanted to go home, she needed to go home. She wanted to go back to Chip. Tears leaked out of her swollen eyes.

Then he came back. She felt the movement. Were they on a boat? She felt, as she had before, the space tilt, and creak. His footsteps. She struggled, tried to scream, though she knew it was useless.

Please, please, somebody hear me!

He gave her one hard slap. "Let's see if you've got one more night in you."

Something flashed, blinding her. And he laughed.

"You sure aren't much to look at now. But I can always get it up."

He cut her first so she screamed against the tape. He punched her with a fist cased in a leather glove, then slapped her to bring her around again so she'd cry when he raped her.

It was always better when they cried.

Then he used the rope to choke her. This time he didn't stop when she passed out. This time he finished it, and took her out of the nightmare.

When he raped her, when he choked her, he called her Naomi.

Seventeen

Soaking, sopping spring rains blew in. They made for muddy boots, wet dog, and some dramatic photos.

Naomi worked in the unfinished bedroom with the ugly blue bathroom and learned to block out the scream of tile cutters.

She spent the rainy Monday and started the rainy Tuesday refining the weekend's work. She'd added the Wreckers to her playlist, used their music while she worked on the band shots.

She switched off to blues when refining the shots of Xander on her deck, went random on the book-in-hand.

If she put off working on what she thought of as Storyland, she'd get to it. Inside, she knew she had to get past the upset of seeing that damn book tucked in with all the others on Xander's book wall. And right now, she was experiencing something new and different.

She was happy. Not just satisfied, content, or engaged. Happy in a way that stuck with her right through the day—rainy or not. The house, the progress on it, the work—because, God, she did good work here. Even the dog gave her a sense of happiness.

And still, this was more. However it had happened, however it ran contrary to ingrained habit and what she considered good, sensible judgment, she was in a relationship. And in one, she had to admit, with an interesting man. One who engaged her, mind and body, who worked as hard as she did, and enjoyed it as she did.

Who could blame her for wanting to hold on to it as long as it lasted?

She matted the manipulated shot of him on the deck. Toned black-and-white, his eyes boldly blue, the dog's crystal. Bright white mug, and the red-gold streak of sun an arrow over the horizon where sky met water. She'd debated between white mat or gray, and saw now she'd been right to go with the gray. It popped the colors out, didn't distract as the white might have. Pewter frame, she decided, not black. Keep those edges soft.

She propped the matted print against the wall, stepped back to study it.

The start of a good day, she thought, remembering. She only had to eliminate the visit from the chief of police, and it had been the start to a most excellent day—that ended as it began, with Xander in her bed.

She hooked her thumbs in her pockets, giving the prints ranged against the wall a critical study, called out a *come in* at the knock on the door.

"Sorry."

"It's okay," she told Kevin. "Perfect time to break."

"Good, because Lelo's downstairs."

"He is?"

"Yeah, he wanted to . . . Wow." He came all the way in, leaving the door open so the sounds of hammers and saws echoed from downstairs, and the tile cutter screamed down the hall. "Those are great. That's Cecil's barn—and Cecil. And Xander. Mind?" he asked, and crouched down before she answered. Tag padded over to nose under Kevin's arm for a hug.

"This one? Man, you can smell morning. That minute before it bangs open and it's day."

"You make me wish you were an art critic."

"It's how it hits. The black-and-white with the bits of color, that's dramatic, right? And seriously cool. But this one, it's the quiet and the . . . possibilities?"

"Definitely wish you were an art critic."

"I'm not, but I've got to say Cecil's barn never looked so good. Where are you going to hang them?"

"I'm not. They're going to the gallery in New York. In fact, I need to do a second print of what seems to be your favorite. The gallery owner wants one for his personal collection."

"Hah." Visibly tickled, Kevin pushed up to stand. "Xander's going to New York. You know, the shop where Jenny works would go nuts for those smaller ones there—the flowers and the barn door, the old tree."

She'd matted them for herself, but . . . maybe. The commission, if they sold, could carve nicely into the cost of the old cedar chest she had her eye on at Cecil's.

"I might take some of them in, see about that. Did you say Lelo's downstairs?"

"Hell, got off track. Yeah, he said he'd look at the yard, work up some ideas. But he's poking around with the guys downstairs—or was when I came up."

"We talked about him looking at the yard, but it's pouring rain."

"It's Lelo." Kevin's shrug said it all. "If you're going to break for a bit, I've got some things to talk to you about downstairs. The laundry room deal, and up here, the studio."

"Okay. Let me talk to Lelo, then I'll find you."

"We appreciate you don't breathe down our necks when we're working. I mean that. But you might want to take a look at the work on the master bath before you close off again."

"All right."

Kevin peeled off in the direction of the master, and the dog started down with her. Tag paused on the stairs, sniffed the air. If a single bark could signify utter delight, his did before he all but flew down the stairs.

She heard Lelo laugh. "Hey, there he is! How's it going, big guy!"

She found them, already wrestling over the painter's tarp. Lelo wore a wet cowboy hat and a yellow rain slicker.

"Hi. Figured it was a good day to take a look around since we're rained out on this patio job."

"So you want to slosh around outside here instead?"

"Rain's gotta rain. I didn't want to go poking around without letting you know."

"Let me get a jacket."

"I can just make some notes and all if you don't wanna get wet."

"Rain's gotta rain."

He grinned. "There you go. Meet you out there. Okay if Tag tags with me?"

"I'd have a hard time stopping him. I'll be right out."

She grabbed her rain jacket, a ball cap, and took the time to change her sneakers for boots.

When she got out front, Lelo wandered in the steady rain, tossed a sodden tennis ball for the delirious dog.

"Got a good start on the cleanup," he called out.

"Xander did. I'd barely started on it."

"He likes the work. My dad's always saying he'd hire Xander in a heartbeat, but then who'd fix his truck? I want to say right off, I hope you're not in love with those old arborvitaes because they gotta go."

"I'm not in love."

"Excellent. Anything you especially want?"

"I thought an ornamental weeper, like a cherry. Over there."

"Uh-huh." He stood, rain dripping off the brim of his hat, studied. "That'd work. Have you ever seen a weeping redbud?"

"I don't know."

"It's not red. It's lavender."

"Lavender."

"Awesome color, and just a little less usual. And it's got heart-shaped leaves."

"Heart-shaped."

"You maybe want to look it up."

"I'm going to."

"You could maybe do some pavers, you know? Kind of winding, not straight-arrow-like. And set off the house with native shrubs and plants. You like birds and butterflies? Like that?"

"Sure."

"You gotta have a mock orange. It smells good, looks pretty, and it'll draw the birds and butterflies. And Juneberry. It's got white starry flowers, and it fruits. Purple fruit about this big." He circled his thumb and finger. "You'll get the songbirds with that. You can eat it—it's pretty good. And you want some rhodos."

He walked, gesturing, tossing the ball, rattling off names, descriptions. And painted a picture of something fanciful and lovely.

"I was going to plug in a tree, a couple of shrubs, do some bedding plants and bulbs."

"You could do that. It'd look fine."

"Maybe it would, but now you've got me thinking about plants I've never heard of and trees with heart-shaped leaves."

"I could draw it up for you, give you a better picture."

"Okay, let's do that."

"Can I see around back?"

"We're already wet."

As they started around the side, he reached into the pocket of his slicker. "Want?"

She glanced down, saw the classic yellow pack, caught just the drift of that comforting scent as he drew out a stick of Juicy Fruit.

Though she shook her head, deemed herself foolish, the simple pack of gum cemented her initial impression of him.

Kind, sweet, loyal. No wonder the dog adored him.

"You get afternoon shade here," Lelo continued as he folded a stick of gum into his mouth. "It's a nice spot for a hammock or a bench, some shade lovers. You wind those pavers around, you'd be able to walk clear around the house barefoot."

"You're killing me, Lelo."

They circled to the back, where he set his hands on his skinny hips and looked up the deck steps, out to the narrow ribbon of scrubby lawn to the stone wall.

"You've got a basement, right?"

"A big one. Storage and utility. It's not finished. I don't need the room."

"Might want it when you have kids. And you'd want to build up that wall more when you do. For now, you might want to put some hemlock over there, naturalize some daffodils, give you a foresty feel on that far side. And some shrubs fronting the wall. Keep them low 'cause you don't want anything blocking the view. When you ever decide to finish the basement, you do yourself a walk-out, and you've got a nice shady patio area under the decks, then a sunny little backyard."

"I wanted to put some herbs, some vegetables in. Not a huge space, but enough for a kitchen garden."

"You could do that." Nodding, he walked up the short steps to the first-floor deck. "It's a ways from your kitchen, but you could do that. Or you could have yourself a container garden up here. You got the sun, you got the room on a deck this size. Build them out of the same wood as the house, make them look built-in, you know? Do yourself herbs, some cherry tomatoes, maybe some Romas, some peppers, whatever. Containers are easy to maintain."

"And steps away from the kitchen." More practical, she thought, more efficient. And pretty. "You know what you're doing, Lelo."

"Well, I've been working the business since I was about six."

"It's a lot of work."

"Whatever you do, you can do some here, some there, some down the road."

"But you can draw it up, give me an estimate—on each section?"

"Sure. And there's this other thing."

"Am I going to have to sell the family jewels?"

He grinned, shook his head, and shot out raindrops. "Maybe you could take pictures of the work—you know, before, during, after. We could use them in the business. Like a trade."

Bartering again, she thought. The popular commerce of Sunrise Cove. "That's a smart idea."

"I can't claim it. It's my dad's. I haven't seen what-all you sent to Dave yesterday. I'm swinging by his place after he gets off work—may be able to mooch dinner, too. But my dad took a look at your website, and he came up with it."

She'd want pictures in any case, she thought. She'd been documenting the progress on the house, for herself, for Mason and her uncles and grandparents.

"We'll work that deal."

"Solid." They fist-bumped on it. "I'll get you some drawings and some figures. You're really pretty."

"Ah . . . thank you."

"I'm not hitting on you or anything. Xander's like my brother. It's just you're really pretty. And I like what you're doing with the house. Like I said, I used to hang up here sometimes with Dikes. Even though I used to think working in the business was bogus, I'd end up planting stuff in my head."

"Now you'll plant it for real."

"That's something, isn't it? I should book. Xander's on my ass about the muffler. I guess I'll take it in, let him fix the damn thing. I'll come by when I've got everything worked up."

"Thanks, Lelo."

"Sure thing. You be good." He rubbed the wet dog. "Later," he said, and jogged down and away.

Xander stood under an aging Camry, replacing brake pads that should've been replaced ten thousand miles earlier. Some people just didn't maintain. It needed an oil change and an all-around tune-up, but its owner—his ninth-grade American history teacher—still didn't believe he knew what he was doing. About any damn thing.

And never let him forget he'd been suspended for hooking school.

Something that made no sense to him then or now. Suspension for hooking was like a damn reward.

Speaking of suspension, her shocks were about shot—but she wouldn't listen there either. She'd wait, drive the car into the ground until he ended up towing it in.

He had a transmission job after this and had given a clutch replacement to one of his crew, a simple tire rotation to another.

He had two cars out in the lot, towed in from a wreck on rain-slick roads the night before—a call that had pulled him out of Naomi's bed at two in the morning.

The drivers got off with mostly bumps, bruises, some cuts—though one of them ended up being taken in by the deputy when he didn't pass the Breathalyzer.

Once the insurance companies finished wrangling, he'd have plenty of bodywork to deal with.

But he'd missed waking up with Naomi and the dog, having breakfast.

He'd gotten used to those sunrises. Funny how fast he'd gotten used to them, and unused to sleeping and waking alone in his own space.

Even now he had a low-grade urge to see her, to hear her voice—to catch a drift of her scent. That wasn't like him. He just wasn't the sort who needed constant contact—calling, texting, checking in, dropping by. But he'd caught himself thinking up excuses to do any of that, and had to order himself to knock it off.

He had work—and later in the afternoon a quick meeting with Loo about the bar. He had books to read, sports to watch, friends to hang with.

And the paperwork he should've done Sunday night to clear up.

Xander shook his head when he heard the unmistakable cough and rattle of Lelo's shitty muffler.

"Get that thing out of here!" Xander shouted. "It's bad for business."

"I'm bringing you business, man. And half a jumbo Diablo sub."

Xander paused long enough to glance over as Lelo, dripping rain, walked in. "Diablo?"

"I went by, saw your chick, and she is hot. She is *smoking* hot. Made me want some hot."

"You went up to Naomi's?"

"Still think of it as the old Parkerson place. Not for long if she hires us. Trade you the sub for a Mountain Dew."

"Two minutes." Xander went back to the brake pads. "So you went up, took a look at the yard?"

"I've been dreaming about that place since I sat up there smoking dope with Dikes. Now I find your smoking-hot chick's pretty open and flexible about landscaping. She listens. She's got the vision, man, just like with the photos."

Lelo boosted himself up to sit on a workbench, unwrapped the sub. "We get a job like that? That place is a landmark—sad one these last few years, but still. Showing how we can turn it around's got my parents doing the bebopping boogie. Going to try to work a deal for pictures we can use for promotion, keep her outlay down some. How come you let Denny play that country shit in here?"

"It's all right, and it keeps him happy." Finished, Xander walked over to the soda machine, plugged in coins for a Mountain Dew and a ginger ale.

He grabbed paper napkins—Diablos were hot, and messy—then joined Lelo on the bench.

"Is that Mrs. Wobaugh's Camry?"

"Yeah, she's driving it into the ground."

"I had her for American history."

"Me, too."

"About bored me brainless."

"Me, too."

"Who said that shit about history repeating itself?"

"There are a lot of people who said that shit," Xander told him. "A favorite is: 'History, with all her volumes vast, hath but one page.' That's Byron."

"Cool. So, why do we have to study it, be bored brainless, if it's got one page?"

"We keep thinking if we do, we'll change the next page. Not so much,"

Xander decided. "But as somebody else said, hope springs. So high school kids get bored brainless."

"Guess that's it."

They ate in the easy, companionable silence of old friends.

"Saw you got a couple banged up good in the lot."

"Wreck last night on 119. Driver of the Honda blew a one-point-one."

"D-W-fricking-I. Hurt bad?"

"Busted up some, and the other driver, too. Didn't sound major. Cars have it worse."

"Cha-ching for you."

"Should be." As he ate, Xander studied Lelo's truck. "Are you bringing that piece of shit in here for me to fix?"

"Yeah. I can leave it if you can't get to it, hitch a ride home."

"I can get to it. I bought the damn muffler a month ago, figuring you'd come to your senses eventually. I can shuffle you in next."

"Dude. Gratitude. The chief stopped me this morning on my way out of town—let me off when I told him I was coming back here after some business, and you were taking care of it."

Unsurprised, Xander washed down fire-hot Diablo with ice-cold ginger ale. An excellent combo. "That's one way to come to your senses."

"I'm going to kind of miss the noise."

"Only you, Lelo."

"The chief told me they haven't found Marla."

Xander paused with the can of ginger ale halfway to his mouth. "She's not back?"

"Nope, not back, nobody's seen or heard from her. Since he had me pulled over, he asked if I had, if I noticed her with anybody Friday night. Saw anybody go out after her. It's gotten serious, Xan. It's like she poofed."

"People don't poof."

"They run off—I tried that when I was pissed at my mother over something. Packed up my backpack and set off to walk to my grand-parents'. I figured it only took about five minutes to get there—by car—and being eight I didn't calculate the difference on foot so well. I got halfway there when my mother drove up. I figured I was in for it big-time, but she got out and cried all over me."

He took a hefty bite of his sub. "Not the same, though, I guess."

"We can hope it is. She took off on a mad, and she's sitting somewhere sulking." But the odds of that now, Xander thought, weren't good. "It's too long for that. Too damn long for that."

"People are thinking she got taken by somebody."

"People?"

"They were talking about it in Rinaldo's when I got the sub. Local cops are talking to everybody now, from what I can see. Seems she hasn't used her credit card since Friday either. And she didn't take her car, any clothes. They had Chip and Patti look at that, to see if they could tell if she grabbed up some clothes. Everybody there saw her walk out of the bar, and that's it.

"I can't say I like her. I know I had sex with her a couple times, but Jesus, she has a mean streak. But it's scary, man, thinking something really happened to her. A lot of people are fucked-up, you know? And do fucked-up things. I don't like thinking about it."

Neither did Xander.

But he couldn't put it away. By the time he had Lelo's truck on the lift—and Lelo, with a yen for ice cream, had wandered off to get some—he had a twist in his belly.

He got a clear picture of the look she'd tossed him when she'd come out of the bathroom—where Patti had dragged her on Friday night. The look she'd shot him, full of hot fury, before she shot up her middle finger and stormed out.

That was his last image of her—a girl he'd known since high school. One he'd had sex with because she was available. One he'd blown off countless times since because, like Lelo, he didn't really like her.

She could have walked home in under five minutes, he calculated. And at the pace she'd stormed out, more like three. A dark road, he considered, even with some streetlights. A quiet road that time of night with nearly anybody out and about in the bar for the music and the company.

He tried to see the houses on the route she'd have taken, the shops if she'd cut across Water Street. Shops closed. People would have been awake—or some of them—but those at home most likely sitting and watching TV, playing on the computer. Not looking out the window after eleven at night.

Had somebody come along, offered her a ride? Would she have been stupid enough to get in the car?

Three-to-five-minute walk, why get into a stranger's car?

Didn't have to be a stranger, he admitted, which tightened the twist in his belly. And there, she'd have hopped right in, glad to have an ear to vent her temper to.

Nearly two thousand people made their home in the Cove, in town and around it. Small town by any measure, but no one knew everyone.

And a pissed-off, drunk woman made an easy target.

Had someone followed her out? He hadn't seen anyone, but he'd shrugged and looked away after she'd shot him the look and the finger.

He couldn't be sure.

Even people you knew had secrets.

Hadn't he found black lace panties in the Honda of the very married Rick Graft—whose wife wouldn't have been able to wish herself into panties that small—when he'd detailed the interior?

Graft came off as a happily married father of three, who coached basketball for nine- and ten-year-olds and managed the local hardware store.

Xander had tossed the panties, figuring it was better all around that way. But he couldn't toss away the knowledge.

Or how Mrs. Ensen had smelled of weed and cheap wine, and the mints and spray cologne she'd used to try to mask it, when he'd answered the breakdown call and gone out to change her tire.

And she a grandmother, for Christ's sake.

No, you couldn't know everyone, and even when you did, you didn't.

But he knew Marla wouldn't sulk alone for going on four days.

He was very much afraid that when they found her, it would be too late.

Eighteen

Having a houseful of men had some advantages. Xander and Kevin carted out her shipping boxes and the smaller box of prints she'd framed for potential sale locally.

It left her free to carry her camera bag.

"Thanks. I'll get these shipped off this morning."

"You're heading to New York, Xan."

"Weird," was his thought on it. "Gotta go." He tapped Naomi's camera bag. "Going to work, too?"

"I am. I'll take an hour or two before I head to town."

"Where?" When her eyebrows raised, he kept it casual. "Just wondering."

"Down below the bluff. We'll see if the rain washed in anything interesting. And pretty spring morning. Boats should be out."

"Good luck with that." He yanked her in for a kiss, gave the dog a quick rub. "See you later."

She'd be within sight of the house, he thought as he swung onto his bike. And he'd already had a short, private conversation with Kevin about keeping an eye out.

Best he could do, but he wouldn't be altogether easy until they found out what happened to Marla.

Naomi considered taking the car. She could drive nearly a half a mile closer, then take a track down through the woods—since she wanted shots there first—make her way down to the shoreline.

But quiet area or not, she didn't like the idea of leaving her car on the side of the road with her prints locked inside.

She got the leash, which immediately had Tag racing in the opposite direction. Since she had his number, she only shrugged and started down the curve of road.

He slunk after her.

She stopped, took a dog cookie out of her pocket. "You want this, you wear this until we're off the road." She held out the leash.

Dislike for the leash lost to greed.

He strained against the leash, tugged it, did his best to tangle himself in it. Naomi clipped it to her belt with a carabiner, then stopped to frame in some white wildflowers the rain had teased open like stars on the side of the road.

He behaved better in the forest, occupying himself by sniffing the air, nosing the ground.

Naomi took carefully angled shots of a nurse log surrounded by ferns and blanketed with lichen and moss—yellows, rusty reds, greens on wood studded with mushrooms that spread like alien creatures. A pair of trees, easily ten feet high, rose from it, the roots wrapped around the decaying log as if in an embrace.

New life, she thought, from the dead and dying.

The long rain soaked the green so it tinted the light, seducing wild-flowers to dance in sunbeam and shadow. It scented the air with earth and pine and secrets.

After an hour she nearly headed back, left the shoreline for another day. But she wanted the sparkle of sun on the water after the misty damp of the forest. She wanted the deeper, rougher green of those knuckles of land, the strong gray of rock against the blues.

Another hour, she decided, and then she'd pack it up, run her errands.

Thrilled to be off the leash, Tag raced ahead. She turned onto the bluff trail, one he knew well now. He barked, danced in place whenever she stopped to take other pictures.

"Don't rush me." But she could smell the water now, too, and quickened her pace.

The trail angled down, and proved muddy enough from the rains that she had to slow again. Considering the mud, she realized she'd now have to wash the damn dog before running into town.

"Didn't think of that, did you?" she muttered, and used handy branches to support herself on the slick dirt.

All worth it. Worth it all in that one moment when the water and pockets of land opened up through the trees.

She balanced herself, risked a spill to get shots of the view through low-hanging branches with their fernlike needles.

Down below it would be bright, sparkling, but here, with the angle, the fan of branches, the inlet looked mysterious. Like a secret revealed through a magic door.

Satisfied, she picked her way down to where the dog barked like a maniac.

"Leave the birds alone! I want the birds."

She scraped her muddy boots on rippling rock, climbed over them. Caught the diamond glint she'd hoped for, and happily, just beyond the channel, a boat with red sails.

She blocked out the dog barking until she got what she wanted, until the red sails eased into frame. When he raced back to her, she ignored him, took a long shot of the inlet, of the twin forks of water drifting by the floating hump of green.

"Look, if you're going to tag along, you just have to wait until I'm done before— What have you got? Where did you get that?"

He stood, tail ticking, and a shoe in his mouth.

A woman's shoe, she noted, open toed, long skinny heel in cotton-candy pink.

"You're not taking that home. You can just forget about that."

When he dropped it at her feet, she stepped around it. "And I'm not touching it."

As she picked her way down, he grabbed up the shoe, raced ahead again.

She stepped down onto the coarse sand, the bumpy cobbles of the narrow strip. Tag sent up a fierce spate of barking, a series of high-pitched whines that had her spinning around to snap at him.

"Cut it *out*! What's wrong with you this morning?"

She lowered her camera with hands gone to ice.

The dog stood at the base of the bluff, barking at something sprawled on the skinny swatch of sand. She made herself walk closer until her legs began to tremble, until the weight fell on her chest.

She went down to her knees, fighting for breath, staring at the body.

Marla Roth lay, wrists bound, her hands outstretched as though reaching for something she'd never hold.

The bright, sparkling light went gray; the air filled with a roar, a wild, high wave.

Then the dog licked her face, whined, tried to nose his head under her limp hand. The weight eased, left a terrible ache in its place.

"Okay. Okay. Stay here." Her hands shook as she unlooped his leash, clipped it on him. "Stay with me. God, oh God. Just hold on. Can't be sick. Won't be sick."

Setting her teeth, she pulled out her phone.

She didn't want to stay; she couldn't leave. It didn't matter that the police had told her to stay where she was, to touch nothing. She could have ignored that. But she couldn't leave Marla alone.

But she went back to the rocks, climbed up enough to sit so the air could wash over her clammy face. The dog paced, tugged on the leash, barked until she hooked an arm around him, pulled him down to sit beside her.

It calmed them both, at least a little. Calmed her enough that she realized she could do the one other thing she wanted. She took out her phone again, called Xander.

"Hey." His voice pitched over loud music, noisy machines.

"Xander."

It only took one word, the sound in her voice on a single word, to have his stomach knotting.

"What happened? Are you hurt? Where are you?"

"I'm not hurt. I'm down below the bluff. I . . . It's Marla. She's . . . I called the police. I found her. I called the police, and they're coming."

"I'm on my way. Call Kevin. He can get down there faster, but I'm coming now."

"It's all right. I'm all right. I can wait. I can hear the sirens. I can already hear them."

"Ten minutes." Though he hated to, he ended the call, jammed the phone in his pocket, swung a leg over his bike.

On the rock, Naomi stared at the phone before remembering to put it away. Not in shock, she thought—she remembered how it felt to go into shock. Just a little dazed, a little out of herself.

"We have to wait," she told the dog. "They have to get down the trail, so we have to wait. Someone hurt her. They hurt her, and they must have raped her. They took her clothes off. Her shoes."

She swallowed hard, pressed her face against Tag's fur.

"And they hurt her. You can see her throat. The bruises around her throat. I know what that means, I know what that means."

The panic wanted to rear back, but she bore down, forced herself to take careful breaths. "Not going to break."

The dog smelled of the rain that had dripped from wet trees, of wet ground, of good, wet dog. She used it to keep centered. As long as she had the dog, right here, she could get through it.

When she heard them coming, she drew more breaths, then got to her feet. "I'm here," she called out.

The chief broke through the trees first, followed by a uniformed dep-uty carrying a case. Then another with a camera strapped around his neck.

She couldn't see their eyes behind their sunglasses.

"She's over there."

His head turned. She heard him let out a breath of his own before he looked back at her. "I need you to wait here."

"Yes, I can wait here."

She sat again—her legs still weren't altogether steady—and looked out to the water, to its sparkling beauty. After a time, Tag relaxed enough to sit down, lean against her.

She heard someone coming, too fast for safety on the steep, muddy track. Tag sprang up again, wagged everywhere in happy hello.

"They want me to wait here," she told Xander.

He knelt down beside her, pulled her in.

She could have broken then—oh, it would have been so easy to break. And so weak.

He eased back, skimmed a hand over her face. "I'm going to take you up to the house."

"I'm supposed to wait."

"Fuck that. They can talk to you up at the house."

"I'd rather do it here. I'd rather not bring this into the house until I have to. I shouldn't have called you."

"Bullshit."

"I called before I . . ."

She trailed off as the chief walked back to them. "Xander."

"I called him after I called you. I was pretty shaky."

"Understandable."

"I . . . I'm sorry, the dog . . . I didn't see her at first. I was taking pic-tures, and I didn't see her. He had a shoe—her shoe, I think. I just thought . . . I'm sorry, I know we weren't supposed to touch anything, but I didn't see her at first."

"Don't you worry about that. You came down to take pictures?"

"Yes. I often do. I—we—I mean the dog and I walked from the house, through the forest. I spent some time in there getting photos, but I wanted to take some here. After the rain. There was a boat with a red sail, and Tag had the shoe. A woman's pink heel. I don't know what he did with it."

Sam took the water bottle out of her jacket pocket, handed it to her. "You have a little water now, honey."

"All right."

"You didn't see anybody else?"

"No. He kept barking, and whining, but I didn't pay any attention because I wanted the shot. Then I yelled at him, and turned. And I saw her. I went a little closer, to be sure. And I could see . . . So I called the police. I called you, and I called Xander."

"I want to take her up to the house. I want to take her away from here."

"You do that." Sam gave Naomi's shoulder a light rub. "You go on home now. I'm going to check in with you before I go."

Xander took her hand, kept it firm in his as they started up the track. She didn't speak until they were in the trees.

"I hurt her."

"Naomi."

"I hurt her on Friday night, at the bar. I meant to. And she walked out of there with her wrist aching, her pride ripped up, and her temper leading her. Otherwise, she'd have left with her friend."

"I looked at you instead of her. You want me to feel guilty about that, to try to work some blame up because it was you, not her? This isn't about you and me, Naomi. It's about the son of a bitch who did this to her."

It was the tone as much as the words that snapped her back. The raw impatience with anger bubbling beneath.

"You're right. Maybe that's why I needed to call you. I wouldn't get endless *there-there*s and *poor Naomi*s from you. That sort of thing just makes it all worse. And it's not about me."

"Finding her's about you. Having to see that's about you. You don't want any *poor Naomi*s, I'll keep them to myself, but goddamn I wish you'd gone anywhere else to take pictures this morning."

"So do I. We sat right out on the deck earlier. And she was down there. She had to have already been there." She took a breath. "Does she have family?"

"Her mother lives in town. Her father left I don't know how many years ago. She has a brother in the navy, joined up right out of high school. A couple years ahead of me. I didn't know him really. And she has Chip. This is going to flatten him."

"They don't care about that."

"Who?"

"Killers. They don't care about any of that, they don't think about all the other lives they rip apart. He strangled her. I could see the bruising, her throat. He dumped her clothes near her. I think she was wearing those pink heels on Friday night. I think she was. She must've been with him since then, since she left the bar."

He wanted to pick her up, just lift her up and carry her back to the house. Instead, he kept a solid grip on her hand.

"There's no point in telling you not to think about it, so I'll say yeah, it's most likely he took her after she left the bar. We don't know what happened after that. They've got ways to figure out if she was killed there or somewhere else and dumped there."

"Yes, they have ways."

When they came out of the forest she saw the two patrol cars, Xander's bike.

"If he didn't kill her there, why take her all that way? Why not dump her body in the forest, or bury it there? Or drop her in the water?"

"I don't know, Naomi. But if you hadn't gone down there this morning, it's likely she wouldn't have been found yet. You wouldn't see her from the house, not as close as she was to the foot of the bluff. And from the water? Maybe if somebody came close to shore, maybe. So maybe leaving her there gave him more time to get away."

As they approached the house he looked over at her. "Do you want me to have Kevin pull the crew off for the day?"

"No. No, for once I think I prefer noise to quiet. I think I'm going to paint."

"Paint?"

"The second guest room—my uncles' room. I wouldn't be any good at work, and I don't want to go into town. Errands can wait."

"Okay. I'll give you a hand."

"Xander, you've got a business to run."

"I get not wanting a lot of *there-theres*." He had his arm around her waist now—a step closer to just carrying her—and kept his voice level. "I'd suck at giving them anyway. But I'm not going anywhere, so we'll paint."

She stopped, turned to him, into him, let herself just hold on. "Thank you."

Because it soothed him, and hopefully her, he ran his hands up and down her back. "I'm a crap painter."

"Me, too."

She went upstairs to set up without him. She knew he lingered below to tell Kevin so she wouldn't have to. When he came up, he set down a cooler.

"Some water, some Cokes. Thirsty work, painting."

"Especially when you're crap at it. You told Kevin."

"The chief's going to come up, check on you, so yeah. He'll keep it to himself until then, and the crew will do the same to give the chief time enough to tell her mother, and Chip."

"Mason says that's the worst part, the notifications. I always wonder if it's that hard to give, how much harder it is to get."

"I think it has to be worse not to know. If she hadn't been found, or not for a while longer. It's got to be harder not knowing."

She nodded, turned away. Some of the girls her father had killed had been missing for years. Even now, after all this time, the FBI wasn't sure they'd found all the remains.

Bowes gave them another every few years—for some new privilege. And, as Mason had told her so many years ago, for the fresh attention.

"So . . . you don't like this piss-yellow color?"

She tried to center herself, studied the walls. "I knew it reminded me of something."

He didn't fill the silence with small talk while they worked. Something else to be grateful for. Rolling the primer on the walls, covering something ugly with something clean, soothed.

The dog wandered in and out, and finally settled on stretching himself across the doorway for a nap, so they couldn't leave the room without alerting him.

They'd finished priming two walls, and had begun to debate which of them had a lousier hand at cutting in, when the dog's head shot up and his tail beat on the floor.

Sam stepped up to the doorway.

"Got yourself a guard here."

Naomi clasped her hands together to keep them still. "Are you— I'm sorry, there's nowhere to sit down in here. We can go downstairs."

"I won't be long. I just wanted to see how you were doing."

"I'm all right. I wanted to keep busy, so . . ."

"I hear that. First off, if you're nervous about being alone up here, I can have one of the men sit on the house tonight."

"She won't be alone." As Naomi started to speak, Xander glanced at her. "Consider it the fee for the crap paint job."

"It'd be good to have someone stay with you. I just want to get your timeline, if you remember about what time you left the house this morning."

"Ah. It was maybe quarter to eight. I don't know exactly how long it took me to walk down to where I caught the track. I took some shots, wildflowers, along the way. I can show you."

"I'm not doubting your word," Sam assured her. "Just trying to get a sense."

"I think I was at least an hour in the forest. And I took some shots from where it thins and you can see the channel. And after I went down, I took more from that big flat rock—the first one you come to from the track. That's when Tag ran up with the shoe. I didn't notice the time, but it had to be after nine. Then the dog kept barking and whining and I turned to tell him to knock it off, and I saw her."

"Okay. I'm sorry about this, Ms. Carson."

"Naomi. Naomi's fine."

"I'm sorry about this, Naomi, and I have to say I'm grateful you walked that way today. It might've been another day or two before anyone found her otherwise."

"You're going to tell Chip," Xander put in. "I know he's not next of kin, but you're going to tell him before he hears somebody talking about it."

With a nod, Sam took off his ball cap, scraped fingers through gray-streaked brown hair, set it back on again. "I'm going to see him right after I talk to her mother. If you think of some other details, Naomi, or if you just need to talk it through, you give me a call. This house is looking better than it ever did—well, in my lifetime. I'm a phone call away," he added, and gave the dog a quick rub before leaving.

She woke herself from the nightmare, ripped herself out of the cellar, under a nurse log in the dark, green forest. The cellar where she'd found Marla's body. The fear came with her, and the images of the killing room her father had built, and all the blood and death in it.

Her breath wheezed out, wanted to clog up. She fought to hitch it in, shoved it out again.

Then hands gripped her shoulders. She'd have screamed if she'd had the air.

"It's me. It's Xander. Hold on a minute."

He turned her, one hand still firm on her shoulder, and switched on the light.

One look at her had his hands taking her face, a hard grip.

"Slow it down, Naomi. Look at me, slow it down. You're okay, just slow it down. You're going to hyperventilate and pass out on me otherwise. Look at me."

She pulled air in—God, it burned—fought to hold it, slow it before she let it out. She kept her eyes on his, so blue. A deep, bold blue, like water she could sink into and float.

"Better. You're okay, slower, slow it down some more. I'm going to get you some water."

She lifted her hands, pressed them to his. She needed those eyes, just that deep blue for another minute.

He kept talking to her. She didn't really register the words, just the hands on her face, the blue of his eyes. The burn eased, the weight lifted.

"Sorry. Sorry."

"Don't be stupid. Water's right there, on your nightstand. I'm not going anywhere."

He reached around her, picked up the bottle, uncapped it. "Slow on this, too."

She nodded, sipped. "I'm all right."

"Not yet, but close. You're cold." He rubbed those work-rough hands up and down her arms. He looked over her shoulder, said, "Ease off now."

She glanced over, saw Tag with his front paws on the bed.

"I woke up the dog, too. At the risk of being stupid on your scale, I am sorry. Nightmare."

Not her first, he thought, but the first time he'd seen the full-blown panic. "Not surprising, considering. You should get back under the blankets, warm up."

"You know, I think I'll get up, try to work awhile."

"Nothing much to take pictures of at . . . three twenty in the morning."

"It's not just taking them."

"I guess not. We should go down, scramble some eggs."

"Scramble eggs? In the middle of the night."

"It's not the middle of the night on your time clock. Yeah, eggs. We're up anyway."

"You don't have to be," she began, but he just rolled out of bed.

"We're up," he repeated, and walked over to open the doors. Tag bulleted out. "Up and out. Waffles," he considered, glancing over to study her as he pulled on pants. "I bet you could make waffles."

"I could, if I had a waffle maker. Which I don't."

"Too bad. Scrambled eggs, then."

She sat a moment, bringing her knees up to her chest.

He just handled things, she thought. Nightmares, panic attacks, hurt dogs on the side of the road, dead bodies at the foot of the bluff.

How did he do it?

"You're hungry."

"I'm awake." He picked up the cotton pants and T-shirt he'd gotten off her in the night, tossed them in her direction.

"Do you like eggs Benedict?"

"Never had it."

"You'll like it," Naomi decided, and got out of bed.

He was right. The normality of cooking breakfast soothed and calmed. The process of it, the scents, a good hit of coffee. The raw edges of the dream, of memories she wanted locked away, faded off.

And she was right. He liked her eggs Benedict.

"Where has this been all my life?" he wondered as they ate at the kitchen counter. "And who's Benedict?"

She frowned over it, then nearly laughed. "I have no idea."

"Whoever he was, kudos. Best four A.M. breakfast I've ever had."

"I owed you. You came when I called, and you stayed. I wouldn't have asked you to stay."

"You don't like to ask."

"I don't. That's probably a flaw I like to think of as self-reliance."

"It can be both. Anyway, you'll get used to it. To asking."

"And you brought me out of a panic attack. Have you had experience there?"

"No, but it's just common sense."

"Your sense," she corrected. "Which also had you distracting me with eggs."

"Really good eggs. Nothing wrong with self-reliance. I'd be a proponent of that. And nothing wrong with asking either. It's using that crosses the line. We're in a thing, Naomi."

"A thing?"

"I'm still working out the definition and scope of the thing. How about you?"

"I've avoided being in a thing."

"Me, too. Funny how it sneaks up on you." In a gesture as easy, and intimate, as his voice, he danced his fingers down her spine. "And here we are before sunup, eating these fancy eggs I didn't expect to like with a dog you didn't expect to want hoping there'll be leftovers. I'm good with that, so I guess I'm good with being in a thing with you."

"You don't ask questions."

"I like figuring things out for myself. Maybe that's a flaw or self-reliance." He shrugged. "Other times, it strikes me it's fine to wait until somebody gives me the answers."

"Sometimes they're the wrong answers."

"It's stupid to ask then, if you're not ready for whatever the answers are going to be. I like who you are—right here and right now. So I'm good with it."

"Things can evolve, or devolve." And why couldn't she just let it go, and be right here, right now?

"Yeah, can and do. How long did you say your uncles had been together?"

"Over twenty years."

"That's a chunk. I bet it hasn't been roses every day of the over twenty."

"No."

"How long have we been in this thing, do you think?"

"I don't know. I'm not sure when to start the clock."

"The Day of the Dog. Let's use that. How long ago was it we found the dog?"

"It's been about . . . a little over a month, I guess."

"Well, in the time's-relative area, that's a chunk."

She let out a laugh. "World record for me."

"Look what you've got to work with," he said, gave her that cocky grin. "Let's see what Month Three brings around. For now, when we're done with these really good eggs, we should clean it up, take some coffee up to the deck, wait for sunrise."

When she said nothing, he touched her arm lightly, then went back to eating. "This is your place, Naomi. Nobody can take it or what it means to you away except you."

"You're right. Coffee on the deck sounds perfect."

Nineteen

Brooding, worrying, second-guessing accomplished nothing.

Still, she sat down, wrote a long email to a friend who would understand. Ashley McLean—now Ashley Murdoch—reminded her, always had, always would, that life could go on.

She'd nearly called, just wanting to hear Ashley's voice, but the time difference meant she'd wake her friend before Ashley got out of bed with her husband of ten years come June, got her kids fed and off to school and herself off to work.

And emails came easier—gave her time to compose her thoughts, edit things out. All she really needed was that touchstone.

It helped, it all helped, making breakfast, watching the sunrise with the man she had an undefined thing with, gearing up for a day of errands while construction noise filled the house.

Life had to go on.

With the dog as company—and why had she tried to convince either of them she wanted him to stay home?—she drove into town. At the post office, she unloaded boxes, carted them in, found herself caught for a full ten minutes in that oddity of small-town conversation.

"Check one off the list," she told the dog.

She drove down Water Street. Busier today, she noted. Full-blown spring didn't just bring out the green and the flowers, it brought out the tourists.

They wandered the streets, the shops, with go-cups and cameras and shopping bags. As she looked for parking, she saw boats gliding or putting out of slips, and the kayak/bike rental, with those colorful boats displayed, doing a bang-up business.

She really wanted to try kayaking.

She found her parking spot, pulled in, turned around to the dog.

"You have to wait in the car—I warned you—but we can take a walk around after this stop and before the grocery store. Best I can offer."

He tried to get out when she opened the back to get the box, and the tussle that ensued to deny him illustrated clearly he'd put on weight and muscle. Gone was the weak, bone-thin dog limping down the shoulder of the road.

She got the back closed again, had to lean against it to catch her breath. When she glanced back, he was all but pressed against the rear window, blue eyes devastated.

"I can't take you into the shop. That's how it goes."

She picked up the box she'd had to put down to win the war, started down the sidewalk. Looked back.

Now he had his muzzle out the partially opened side window.

"Don't let him win," she muttered, and aimed her eyes forward.

She knew Jenny worked that morning, as Jenny had called her the night before. Had offered sympathy and comfort. Had offered to bring food, bring alcohol, bring anything needed.

Friendship so easily offered was as unusual for Naomi as ten minutes of small talk in the post office.

She opened the door of the shop to a lovely citrus scent, an artistic clutter of pretty things, and the bustle of business. The bustle made her consider coming back during a lull—if she'd known when and if lulls happened. But Jenny, discussing an old washbasin currently filled with soaps and lotions with a customer, spotted her and gave her a cheerful come-ahead signal.

So she wandered, saw half a dozen things she wanted to buy. Reminded herself she hadn't come to shop, had a house in crazed construction and *shouldn't* shop.

And ended up picking up a set of wrought-iron candle stands that absolutely belonged in her library.

"Let me take that." The minute she could work herself over, Jenny took the box, set it down. "And do this first."

Smelling lightly of peaches, she wrapped her arms around Naomi, tight, tight.

"I'm so glad to see you." She loosened the hug enough to tip back, study Naomi's face. "Are you okay?"

"I'm okay."

"Xander stayed with you?"

"He stayed."

"All right. We're not going to think about it right now. It's all anyone's talking about when they catch a breath, but we're not going to think about it."

"You're awfully busy."

"Tour package." Jenny took a satisfied and slightly calculating glance around the shop. "We've got two busloads in town for the day. The town planner worked the deal months ago. So we're very carefully not mentioning what you and I aren't thinking about in front of tourists. Or trying not to mention."

She bent down to pick up the box again. "I want to show these to Krista. Come with me. She just went in the back, and we're covered out here for a few minutes."

"You're really busy," Naomi reminded her, but Jenny was already nudging her along.

Jenny skirted around tables, displays, all bright chatter, and reminded Naomi of a pretty bird singing as it flitted from branch to branch.

She skirted around a counter and through a door into a storeroom/

office area where a woman with streaky brown hair bundled up and held in place with a pair of jeweled chopsticks sat at a computer.

"Tracked the shipment—it's out for delivery, praise Jesus."

"I've got some potential stock and Naomi Carson for you, Krista."

Krista swiveled on her chair and slid off a pair of purple cheaters. She had a good face with wide brown eyes, a long, full mouth—and the glint of a tiny ruby stud on the left side of her nose.

"I'm so happy to meet you. Pretend there's a seat I can offer you. I really like your work," she added. "I've combed your website several times, and nagged Jenny to get you in here."

"I love your shop—which I've avoided because I'm weak. I've already picked out candle stands, and I probably can't leave without that oval wall mirror with the antiqued bronze frame."

"Jenny's piece."

"Flea market rehab," Jenny confirmed. "Naomi brought us some photos." Jenny set the box on the crowded desk. "I resisted pawing through myself."

"It's good to remember the pecking order around here." Pushing off the chair, Krista opened the box, then put the cheaters back on to take a close look.

She'd gone with small prints, wildflower studies, a series of four of the inlet, one of the marina, another set of nurse logs.

"They're beautifully matted and framed. You do that yourself?"

"Part of the process, yes."

"I can sell these." She propped a pair against the box, stepped back, nodded. "Yes, we can sell these. In fact, with the tour, we can sell some of these as soon as we get them on the floor."

She took off the cheaters again, tapped them against her hand. Then named her price point. "Standard sixty-forty," she added.

"That works for me."

"Good, because I really want them. And I can take more, especially of local flora and fauna, local water scenes, town scenes. I can sell them as unframed prints, too. We can think about that. I'd love the inlet and marina shots as postcards."

"I can do postcards."

Turning, Krista wrapped an arm around Jenny's shoulders in an easy, unstudied way that told Naomi they were good friends. "She can do postcards. Do you know how long I've wanted classy postcards?"

Jenny grinned, slid her arm around Krista's waist. "Since you opened."

"Since I opened. I'll take two dozen postcards right off, as soon as you can get them to me. No, three. Three dozen. I can sell a dozen to the B-and-B in a flash."

"A variety of shots?"

"Dealer's choice," Krista confirmed. "Jen, get these priced and out on the floor. Pick your spot. She's my right hand," she told Naomi. "Even if she's planning to leave me in the lurch."

"Not for months yet. I know just where to put these." Jenny stacked them back in the box, hefted it.

"If you've got a few minutes, Naomi, I'll print out the contract for what we're taking."

"Sure."

"Don't leave without seeing me," Jenny said, and went out to work on the display.

"I'm going to do an order sheet for the postcards while I'm at it. How's work going up on the bluff?"

"Really well, which is why I need those candle stands, the sinuous ones. They need to be in my library. I think the mirror's for the foyer. But . . . it needs to be in there somewhere. And whatever smells so damn good out there."

"That's mock orange in our diffusers today."

"I'm told I need those—the plants. I think I need them in the diffusers, too."

"Tell Jenny you get one—on the house. We're going to make some money together, Naomi."

She left with more than she'd taken in, justified the purchases. The house needed *things*, and Krista was right. They'd make some money together. No question of it, as four of the framed prints sold before Jenny rang her up.

"We've got work to do, Tag."

She clipped the leash on him when he was too distracted with joy to object, loaded her purchases in, got her camera and backpack out.

"Let's take that walk and make some postcards."

B y the time she got home, the crew was knocking off, again proving the advantage of men in the house. The tile team carried her groceries in while Kevin grabbed her gift shop finds.

"I guess you saw Jenny."

"And it cost me. But I also now have art displayed by her hands—and a contract for more." She stopped in the living room, felt the satisfaction of a day well spent kick up another notch. "You finished the crown molding! It just makes the room."

"It's a busy day. Why don't we go up, and you can see what else we finished?"

"If you're talking about my bathroom, I may break down in tears."

With a grin, he tapped her arm. "Grab some tissues."

She nearly needed them.

"You can't walk on it until tomorrow," he warned.

"It's okay. Actually going in might bring me to my knees. It's beautiful, Kevin. It's beautiful work. Everything."

She'd wanted muted and restful, heading toward Zen, and had it with the stone gray tiles, the soft pearly gray of the walls, the gray veining in the white granite counter. She'd added rustic with the big claw-foot tub, gone indulgent with the oversized glass-walled steam shower.

"The brushed nickel was the right choice," he said. "Chrome would've been too shiny. And the open shelving's going to work, too, because you're a tidy soul from what I've seen."

"I'm going to bring some blue in—with towels, some bottles. I saw some old blue bottles at Cecil's. And some green with a plant. Maybe one of those bamboo deals."

"You oughta put some of your pictures on the wall. Some of the ones of the channel."

"Brushed nickel frames, dark gray matting. Good thought. I just love it."

"Glad to hear it. I didn't know if you wanted your desk back in here, and didn't want to move it until you said."

"Maybe tomorrow, when the room's fully functional."

"We made some progress on your studio, if you want to see that."

She wanted to see everything. They spent the next ten minutes going over her choices, discussing timelines. And she began to buy a clue.

"Kevin, are you keeping an eye on me?"

"Maybe. I figured Xander might be coming by shortly."

"And I imagine your wife and kids are home, wondering where you are."

"I've got time. You know, I wanted to ask you about—"

"You're making time," she interrupted. "And I appreciate the thought, but I'm fine. I have a fierce dog."

Kevin glanced back to where Tag lay, studying his own thumping tail as if fascinated, while Molly snoozed beside him.

"Yeah, I see that."

"And I have a brown belt."

"I've got a couple of them."

"In karate. I could've gone for the black, but brown was enough. And that's on top of the self-defense courses I've taken. Single woman, traveling alone," she added, though that hadn't been the primary motivator.

"I'll be careful not to get in a fight with you, but I'd feel better if I hung around until Xander gets here. And I did have a couple of questions about the bathroom off the green room."

He distracted her with talk of tile borders and showerheads, with plans on demo—the black-and-blue bath—until Tag's head reared up, and he raced off barking. Molly yawned, rolled over, and went back to snooze.

"Must be Xander."

"Then you're welcome to stay, have a beer with him, or get out."

"I wouldn't mind a beer."

They walked down while Tag danced and barked at the front door. She wondered if the thing she was in with Xander had progressed to the point of giving him a key and the alarm code.

It seemed a very *big* aspect of the thing, one to think about carefully.

But when she opened the door, Tag raced out and rushed lovingly to Lelo.

"There's that boy. There he is!"

They adored each other for a moment before Lelo straightened. "Hey, Kev. Hi, Naomi. I got those drawings and figures for you."

The Naomi who'd bought the house would have said thanks, taken the packet, and said good-bye. The Naomi she was trying to find took a breath. "Why don't you bring them in? Kevin's going to have a beer. You can have one with him."

"I don't say no to beer after the workday. Want a beer?" he asked the dog.

"He's underage," Naomi said, and had Lelo laughing like a loon.

She went back to the kitchen, opened two beers, then the accordion doors. "I'm going for wine. Those spring chairs out there don't look like much yet, but they're comfortable."

She could hear their voices, muted, quiet, as she poured wine. Curious, she opened the packet out on the counter, began to study the drawings.

When she stepped out, Lelo and Kevin sat in the rusted spring chairs like a couple of guys on the deck of a boat, studying the horizon.

Both dogs sat at the rail, doing the same.

"Lelo, you're an artist."

He snickered, flushed lightly pink. "Aw, well. I can draw a little."

"You can draw a lot. And you've turned the grounds into a garden oasis without compromising the space or the open feel. And the raised beds on the deck, that's inspired."

"Can I have a look?" Kevin took the drawings, paged through, studied. "This is nice, Lelo. It's real nice."

"There's a brochure in there with different pavers, different patterns. We can get you whatever you want in there."

She nodded, sat down on the glider to look over the estimates. He'd done it several ways. The entire grounds and deck—holy shit!—and breaking it down section by section.

And breaking it down yet again with the bartering factored.

"My dad did most of the figuring and math there."

"It's a lot of math and figuring." And would take some of her own, but . . .

"I want the raised beds on the deck. Cooking can relax me after I've worked all day."

"If you ditch Xander, maybe you'd marry me. I can't cook worth shit," Lelo told her, "but I sure like to eat."

"I'll keep you in reserve. I really want the front done, just the way you've drawn it. But I'm going to need another five percent off for the photographs."

"I can text my dad, see what he has to say. I'm thinking he'll go for that."

"And you can tell him if this turns out the way we all want, I should be able to do the rest in the fall. Or next spring. You can't do the whole front until the Dumpster's gone, but I'd love to see some of these trees and shrubs in place."

"Give me a sec."

When Lelo pulled out his phone, the dogs leaped up and raced down the deck steps.

"That must be Xander," Kevin noted. "Dogs are a good early-warning system."

The dogs ran back. Molly settled, but Tag ran away, ran back, all but doing cartwheels until Xander caught up with him.

"Are we having a party?"

"Apparently."

"Good thing I brought more beer." He came up with the six-pack he carried, setting it down long enough to grab Naomi's face and give her a kiss that went from hello to steamy in a heartbeat.

"Just letting them know to get their own woman. Do you want me to top that off?"

She looked down, a little blankly, at her wine. "No, it's good."

"Another round?" he asked Kevin.

"No, one's enough."

He glanced at Lelo, who wandered the deck as he talked on the phone, and held up his three-quarters-full beer.

"Just me, then." Xander took the six-pack inside, came back out with a cold one. "What's all this?"

"My landscape. You didn't tell me Lelo was an artist."

"He's got a knack." After he sat and blew out a cleansing breath, Xander took the first pull.

"Long day?" Naomi asked.

"And then some. Finished now."

Lelo wandered back. "We can start next week."

"Next week?"

"My dad's going to want to come take a look for himself—mostly to meet you, that's the truth. He likes knowing who he's working for, but we can start next week. Probably Tuesday. He's fine with the five percent more." Lelo held out a hand. "We have to shake on it. I'd rather kiss you, but Xander'd pitch me over the deck."

"I'd knock you unconscious first so it wouldn't hurt so much."

"That's a friend." Lelo sat again, scrubbed Tag's head, then Molly's. "You're going to have to teach him not to dig in your beds or lift his leg on the shrubs."

"God. I never thought of that."

"He's a good dog. He'll learn."

Naomi sipped her wine. They were subtle about it—they'd known each other so long, these men. But she caught the signals passing back and forth.

Like Xander, she let out a breath. "Why don't we talk about the elephant on the deck? I'm not the tender sort, and don't need to be shielded. I don't like it either. So has there been anything more about Marla's murder?"

Lelo looked down at the beer he dangled between his legs and said nothing.

"They did the autopsy," Xander said. "And there's some talk leaking out. It could just be talk."

"What could be just talk?"

"That she'd been raped, probably multiple times. Choked multiple times, cut up a little, beat on more than a little."

"I don't get how somebody could do that to somebody else," Lelo murmured. "I just don't. They're saying she wasn't killed down below here, just dumped there that way. I heard Chip about went crazy."

"He loved her," Kevin said. "He always did."

"It couldn't have been anybody from the Cove," Lelo put in. "We'd know if somebody who could do that lived right here."

No, Naomi thought, *you don't always know what lives with you.*

She lost herself in work. She rarely worked on an agenda other than her own, and found it interesting to create photos with Krista's specific wants in mind.

When she talked to or emailed her family, she said nothing of murder.

She didn't give Xander a key—nor did he ask for one. But she thought about it.

Though it brought on a massive stress headache, she attended Marla's funeral. She sat through the short service with Xander, with Kevin and Jenny flanking her other side.

It seemed to her nearly everyone in town had come, wearing sober faces, paying respects to Marla's mother, to Chip.

The church smelled too strongly of lilies—the pink ones draped over the glossy coffin, the pink and white ones rising in sprays from tall baskets.

She hadn't been inside a church in more than a decade. They reminded her of her childhood, of Sunday dresses stiff with starch, of Wednesday-night Bible readings.

Of her father standing at the lectern reciting scripture in his deep voice, so much sincerity on his face as he spoke of God's will, or God's love, of following a righteous path.

Being inside one now, the sun streaming through the stained glass, the lilies clogging the air, the reverend reading all-too-familiar passages, she wished she'd stayed away. She hadn't known Marla, had only had a difficult encounter with her.

But she'd found her, so she'd made herself come.

Relief came like a sharp wind through musty memories when she stepped outside into the clear, uncolored sunlight, the clean, unscented air.

Xander steered her away from where most gathered to talk before the drive to the cemetery.

"You went pale."

"It was so close in there, that's all." And too many who'd come snuck glances at her.

At the woman who'd found the body.

"I need to go to the cemetery," he told her. "You don't."

"I don't think I will. It feels too much like gawking when I didn't know her."

"I'll drive you back, drop you off."

"I should've brought my own car. I wasn't thinking."

"It's not much of a detour," he began, then turned as Chip walked up.

The picture of grief, Naomi thought. Red-rimmed, dazed eyes, pale skin bruised under those dazed eyes from lack of sleep. A big man with a hollow look.

"Chip. Sorry, man."

They exchanged the one-armed hugs men seemed to prefer before Chip looked at Naomi.

"Miss Carson."

"Naomi. I'm so sorry. I'm so sorry."

"You found her. The chief said the way they'd . . . how they'd left her, it might've been a while before anybody did. But you found her so they could bring her back, take care of her."

Tears leaked out of those dazed eyes as he took her hand between his massive ones. "Thank you."

Habitually she avoided touching strangers, getting too close, but compassion overwhelmed her. She drew him to her, held him a moment.

No, killers didn't think of this—or did they? she wondered. Did pain and grief add to the thrill? Did it season it like salt?

As he drew back, Chip knuckled tears away. "The reverend said how Marla's gone to a better place." Chip shook his head. "But this is a good place. It's a good place. She shouldn't have to go to a better one."

He swallowed hard. "Are you coming to the grave site?"

"I am. I'm taking Naomi home, then I'll be there."

"Thank you for coming, Naomi. Thank you for finding her."

As he walked off like a man lost, Naomi turned away.

"Oh God, Xander."

And she wept for a woman she hadn't known.

Twenty

As most of the crew had known Marla, Naomi came home to a relatively quiet house. The noise centered, for now, in what would be her studio, and came in the form of country music and a nail gun.

Still, when she tried to work, she couldn't settle. Whatever images she brought onto her screen, she ended up seeing shattered eyes.

Instead, she took the dog and her camera out front. She'd get those before pictures for Lelo, as simple and routine a task as she could devise. She'd make copies for herself, she thought, maybe put together a book on the evolution of the house.

She could keep it in the library, revisit the process when it would have the charm of distance.

When the dog dropped one of his balls at her feet, she decided to embrace another distraction. She tossed it, watched him joyfully chase after it.

The third time he returned, he spat it out, his ears pricked up, and his gaze shifted with a low, warning growl seconds before she heard the sound of a car.

"Must be the crew coming. Talk about distractions."

But she saw the chief of police's cruiser come up the rise.

Everything in her tensed, balled up in tight, cold fists. She'd seen him at the funeral. If there'd been any progress on the investigation, the odds were high she'd have heard something there. In any case, her finding the body didn't mean he'd feel obliged to tell her anything directly.

There was only one reason he'd come to see her.

To help calm herself, Naomi laid a hand on Tag's head. "It's okay. I've been expecting him."

They started across the bumpy, patchy grass as Sam got out of the cruiser.

"The Kobie brothers," he said, nodded toward the truck.

"Yes. Wade and Bob are upstairs working. The rest of the crew went to the funeral."

"I just left the cemetery myself. I wanted to have a private word with you before the rest of Kevin's crew got back."

"All right." Her stomach in knots, she turned toward the house. "I don't have a lot of seating yet, but it's nice on the deck off the kitchen."

"I heard you hired the Lelos to do some landscaping."

"They plan to start on Tuesday."

"You're making real progress," he commented as they stepped inside.

She only nodded, continued back. Progress, she thought, but for what? She should never have let herself fall in love with the house, with the area. She should never have allowed herself to become so involved with the man.

"This is a hell of a nice kitchen." Hat tipped back, Sam stood, at ease, looking around. "And a view that doesn't quit."

When she opened the accordion doors, he shook his head. "Doesn't that beat all? Did you come up with this, or did Kevin?"

"Kevin."

"They fold right back out of the way, just open it all up. You couldn't have a prettier situation here."

She took one of the spring chairs while Tag poked his nose to Sam's knee.

"I saw you at the service," Sam began. "It was good of you to go. I know you didn't know her, and what you did know wasn't especially friendly."

"I'm sorry for what happened to her."

"We all are." He shifted, turning from the view so his gaze met hers. "I wouldn't be doing my job, Naomi, if I hadn't gotten some background on the person who found her body."

"No. I should have told you myself. I didn't. I wanted to believe you wouldn't look, and no one would know."

"Is that why you changed your name?"

"It's my mother's maiden name, my uncle's name. He raised us after . . . They took us in, my mother, my brother, and me, after my father was arrested."

"You were instrumental in that arrest."

"Yes."

"That's about as hard on a young girl as anything could be. I'm not going to ask you about that, Naomi. I know the case, and if I want to know more, it's easy enough. I'm going to ask you if you're in contact with your father."

"No. I haven't spoken or communicated with him since that night."

"You never went to see him?"

"No. My mother did, and ended up swallowing a bottle of pills. She loved him, or he had a hold over her. Maybe it's the same thing."

"Has he tried to contact you?"

"No."

For a moment, Sam said nothing. "I'm sorry to add to things, but it must have struck you. The similarities. The binding, the wounds, what was done to her, the way she was killed."

"Yes. But he's in prison, on the other side of the country. And the terrible reality is, others rape and kill and torture. Others do what he did."

"That's true."

"But I'm here, and I found her. Like I found Ashley. Only I found Ashley in time. I'm here, and Marla was raped and killed and tortured the way my father liked to rape and kill and torture. So you have to look at me."

"Even if I did, I know you didn't take her, or hold her for two days, and do what was done to her. Even if I did, you were with Xander at times you'd have needed to be with her. I've known Xander all his life and sure as hell don't believe he'd be party to something like this. I don't believe you would either."

She should be grateful for that; she should be relieved. Yet she couldn't find the energy for either.

"But you wondered. When you found out who I was, you had to wonder. Others will, too. And some of them will think, well, Blood tells. It's blood that ties us together, makes us who we are. Her father's a psychopath. What does that make her?"

"I won't tell you I didn't wonder. That's part of my job. I wondered for about ten seconds because I'm small town, that's a fact, but I'm good at my job. I came here to ask you if you're in contact with your father, or if he's in contact with you, on the slim possibility what happened here is connected."

"He didn't even look at me. That morning, in the police station back in West Virginia, when they brought him in."

She could still see it, in minute and perfect detail, down to the sun hitting the water in the water fountain, the dust motes in the air.

"I came out of the room where they had me waiting. I just came out for a minute, and they were bringing him in, in handcuffs. And he looked right through me, like I wasn't there. I think I was never there for him, not really."

"You've moved around a lot in the last few years."

"I made it part of my job. Our uncles shielded us as much as they could from the press, the talk, the stares, the anger. They uprooted their lives for us. But the shield didn't always hold. Every few years, he bargains something, some privilege, something, for the location of another body. It brings it all back—the stories on TV, online, the talk. My brother says it's what he wants more than whatever privilege he's thought up, and I believe that, too. Moving around means you're not in one place long enough for anyone to notice you, or not very much."

"You bought this house."

"I thought I could get away with it. I just fell for it, and convinced myself that I could have this—a real home, a quiet place—and no one would ever know. If I'd walked another way that day, if someone else had found Marla, maybe, but I didn't walk another way. I've got no reason to tell anyone about this."

When she turned her head to meet his eyes again, Sam gave her hand a pat. "It's yours to tell or not."

She wanted relief but couldn't feel it. Couldn't feel. "Thank you."

"It's not a favor. I got background, that was an official act. I don't go around gossiping on people's private business. I needed to ask you the questions I did. Now we can put it away."

"I . . . I just want to find out if I can live here. I want time to try."

"It seems to me you're already living here, and doing it well. I'm going to say something personal now, and then I'm going to go, get back to town. It's clear to me now you haven't told Xander any of this." Sam pushed to his feet. "I'm going to say to you, on a personal level, you're doing him, and yourself, a disservice. But it's your story to tell, or not. Take care of yourself, Naomi."

He walked down the deck steps, left her sitting there staring out at the water, at the white sails of clouds above it, wondering if she'd ever feel again.

Like twin storms, grief and gossip rumbled through the cemetery and left Xander with a low-grade headache. He slipped away as soon as possible, switched the radio off for the drive back to town. He could do with some quiet.

He had enough work, including what he'd postponed that morning, to keep him fully occupied. He stopped into parts and sales, got a ginger ale from the machine, picked up some parts, then headed over to the garage.

After a check of his worksheet, he opted to take the easy first, ease his way into the delayed workday. Before he walked out to drive the Mini Cooper into the bay for its diagnostic, he swung by to see the progress in the body shop.

He considered himself better than good at bodywork, but Pete was a freaking artist. The wrecked Escort would look showroom fine when Pete finished the job.

"Back from the funeral?"

"Yeah."

Frowning, Pete adjusted his safety goggles. "Can't stand funerals."

"I don't think anybody likes them."

"Some do." Pete nodded wisely. "Some people are fucked-up and get off on them. They hunt them up and go even when they don't know who's dead."

"It takes all kinds," Xander said, and left Pete to his work.

Once he'd finished with the Mini, keyed in the worksheet on the shop computer, and sent it to sales, he broke long enough to go up to his apartment, make a sandwich with the slim pickings he had available. With the Mini in the pickup area, he moved on to the next on his sheet.

He put in a solid four hours more—ditched the headache, picked up a stiff neck.

Since he'd told Naomi he'd bring dinner, he called in an order for baked spaghetti before going about the business of closing up.

He'd just started to his bike when Maxie from Rinaldo's pulled in with her flat rear tire bumping.

"Oh, Xander! Please." She actually gripped her hands together as if in prayer as she jumped out of the car. "I know you're closed, but please. Something's wrong with my car, it just started making this noise, and I could hardly steer it."

"You've got a flat, Maxie."

"I do?" She turned, looked where he pointed. "How did that happen? It didn't like blow or anything. It just started thumping. I thought it was the engine or something."

After raking her hand through her purple-streaked blonde hair, she sent him a sheepish smile. "Can you change it?"

He squatted down. "Maxie, this tire's bald as your grandfather, plus you trashed it by driving on it."

"I have to get a new one? Can you change it for now, put the spare on?"

"You don't have a spare, you've got a donut—emergency tire—and you can't drive around on that." He circled the compact, shook his head.

"Your tires lost any excuse for tread about ten thousand miles ago."

Her mouth dropped open; her eyes went to shocked moons. "I need *four* new tires?"

"That's a fact."

"Crap. Crap. Crap. There goes the money I've been saving for a shopping weekend in Seattle with Lisa. And now I'm going to be late for work."

She tried a quick flirt. "Couldn't you just, you know, patch the flat one, just for now, and . . . One more crap," she muttered as he just stared her down. "You've got my father's look on your face."

That stung a little, as he only had about a dozen years on her. But he didn't relent.

"You could have a blowout, end up wrecked. I'll make you the best deal I can, but you've got to replace these. I can have them on for you tomorrow, before noon, and I can run you over to work. I've got a couple of takeouts waiting anyway. Can you get a ride home?"

Resigned, Maxie blew out a breath. "I can just walk over to Lisa's, stay there tonight."

Risking being compared to her father again, Xander shook his head. "No walking alone after closing. Not right now."

"Everybody thinks whoever killed Marla is long gone. Just some horrible pervert passing through."

"I'll make you a deal. You get the tires at my cost, and you make this deal with me. No walking alone after closing."

"All right, all right. I'll get my dad to pick me up." When Xander narrowed his eyes on her face, she rolled hers. "I promise." She swiped a finger over her heart.

"Okay." He got the spare helmet, handed it to her. "You break the deal, I charge you double for the tires."

"Oh, Xander." But she laughed and got on the bike behind him. "A deal's a deal, and at least I get a cool ride to work out of it."

By the time he got to the big house, all he wanted was to sit out on the deck with Naomi, maybe have a beer. And let the entire day shed like dead skin.

By the time he'd unstrapped the takeout, Tag had raced around from the back of the house to greet him as though he'd been off to war.

Appreciating the welcome, he held the food up out of reach with one hand, gave the dog a rub with the other. And when the tennis ball landed at his feet, he gave it a good boot to send Tag joyfully after it.

He noted that Naomi's car sat alone, and wondered why Kevin hadn't waited. Even with the delay, he'd expected Kevin to hang tight until he got there.

He walked around the back, stopping long enough to give the ball another kick.

She sat on the deck alone, working on her tablet, with a glass of wine on the little table beside the glider.

"Got hung up," he said.

She only nodded, kept doing whatever she was doing.

"I'm going to grab a beer, put this in the oven on low."

"That's fine."

He didn't consider himself particularly sensitive to moods—at least, he'd been told by annoyed women he lacked that insight—but he knew when something was off.

In his experience, the best way to handle things when something was off, and you didn't know what, was to just keep going until whatever was off popped out.

Sometimes, if luck held, it just went away.

He came back with his beer, sat beside her, shot out his legs. And Jesus, didn't that feel good?

"Where's Kev?"

"At home with his wife and kids, I imagine."

"I figured he'd hang out until I got here."

"I insisted he go home. I don't need a bodyguard."

It didn't take Mr. Sensitivity to recognize a bitchy mood when it snapped its teeth at him. He took a pull on his beer, let it ride.

The silence lasted maybe twenty seconds.

"I don't like the two of you arranging shifts. I'm not an idiot, and I'm not incapable."

"I never thought of you as either one."

"Then stop hovering, and stop asking Kevin to hover. It's not only insulting, it's annoying."

"Looks like you'll have to be insulted and annoyed."

"You can't decide for me."

"Marla's body, about thirty-five feet straight down from where you're sitting, says I can."

"No one dictates to me, and if you think sleeping with me gives you that right, you're very wrong."

Out of the corner of his eye he saw the dog slink down the steps—looking, Xander imagined, for a safe spot out of the line of fire.

"That's bullshit. It's even weak bullshit. You can either tell me what crawled up your ass since this morning or not, but I know when somebody's looking to pick a fight. I'm not in the mood for one, but that can change."

"You're crowding me, it's as simple as that." She pushed off the glider, picked up her wine, set down the tablet. "I bought this place because I like being alone, and now I never am." She took a long drink from the glass, which he'd bet a week's profits wasn't her first of the evening.

"Yeah, that could change. If you're trying to give me the boot, then be straight about it."

"I need some space."

"And clichés like that are more weak bullshit. You can do better."

"I shouldn't have started this . . . thing with you, and it's moved too fast, gotten too complicated."

Anger, and something he couldn't quite pin down, spiked into her voice.

"I'm tired of feeling surrounded and boxed in. And it just needs to stop. Just stop. You, the house, the yard. God, the dog. It's all too much. It's all a mistake, and it needs to stop."

He wanted to push back, and hard, because, Jesus, she'd hurt him. He hadn't expected the punch or just how completely it flattened him.

Complicated? She had that right. Complications twisted up inside him he hadn't known existed.

But she was shaking, and her breath came just a little too fast. She was working herself up to another panic attack, and he'd damn well know why.

"You want me gone, I'll go. I'll take the damn dog if that's how you want it. I don't force myself on anyone. But give me the truth."

"I just did! This is a mistake. All of this, and I need to correct it."

"By dumping me, the dog, this house, what you've started making here? That's not what you want."

"You don't know what I want." She hurled the words at him, along with a fear-tinted rage. "You don't know me."

"I damn well do."

"You don't! *That's* the bullshit. You don't know me, who I am, or what I am. You know weeks, the weeks I've been here. You don't know anything from before. You don't know me."

It struck him then, clear as glass. That unidentified something under it all, the base of the anger and fear. It was grief.

"Yes, I do." He set the beer aside, rose. "I know who you are, where you came from, what you went through, and what you're trying to make now, away from it."

She shook her head, took a step in retreat. "You can't." He saw her lips tremble before she pressed them together, saw tears glitter before she forced them back.

"Chief Winston told you."

Now he had the match on the fuse. "No, I haven't talked to him, haven't seen him since the cemetery. But you have. He didn't tell me anything. You did."

She crossed her arm over her body, gripped her own shoulder with her hand as if shielding herself.

Not from him, he thought. Goddamn it, not from him.

"I never told you anything about this."

"You didn't have to."

He pushed down his own anger. He'd let it fly later, but for now, for right now, he spoke matter-of-factly.

"The day up in my place, that first time. You saw the book on my shelf. The Simon Vance book. You looked like someone kicked you in the gut. It didn't take much to figure it out from there. There are photos in the book. You were about eleven or twelve, I guess. Just a kid. You've changed your hair, grown up. But you have the same eyes, the same look about you. And Naomi, it's not an everyday name."

"You knew." The knuckles of her hand went white as bone.

"I can wish the book hadn't been there to put that look on your face. But it was."

"You . . . you've told Kevin."

"No." The doubt in her eyes came so clear he waited a beat, kept his gaze level on hers. "No," he said again. "Womb to tomb doesn't mean I tell him what you don't want told."

"You haven't told him," she repeated, and her fingers loosened on her shoulder, her hand slid down. "You've known all this time, known since before we . . . Why haven't you said anything to me, asked me?"

"I didn't know, so the book was there. But once I knew? I wasn't going to put that look on your face again. And okay, I hoped you'd tell me before I had to shove it in your face like this, but you pushed the buttons."

"You didn't." Rubbing the heel of her hand between her brows, she turned away. "You didn't shove it in my face. Others have, so I know exactly what it feels like. I don't know what this feels like."

She set the wine on the rail, pressed her fingers to her eyes. "I need a minute."

"If you need to yell, I can handle it. If you need to cry, I can handle it. Yelling's preferred."

"I'm not going to yell, or cry."

"I think most people would do some of both. You're not most people."

"I'm aware of that."

"Shut up."

The ripe temper shocked her enough to make her turn back.

"Just shut the hell up." Now he let some of that anger fly. "Are you fucking stupid? Maybe I don't know you, because I pegged you as smart. Really smart. But maybe you're stupid enough to believe because you share DNA with a psychotic bastard, you're made wrong."

"He's a monster. He's my father."

"My father doesn't know a carburetor from a brake pad, owns two sets of golf clubs, and likes easy listening."

"That's not the same, at all."

"Why not? Why the hell not? We have blood ties, he raised me—mostly—and we're as different as they come. He reads like one book a year, as long as it's a bestseller. We baffle each other every time we spend more than an hour together."

"It's not—"

"What about your brother?"

He threw her off stride, just as he'd intended.

"I . . . What about Mason?"

"What kind of man is he?"

"He's . . . great. He's smart. Actually, he's brilliant, and dedicated, kind."

"So he can be what he is, with the same gene pool, but you're what? Tainted?"

"No. No, I know better. Intellectually I know better, but yes, sometimes it feels that way."

"Get over it."

She stared at him. "Get . . . over it?"

"Yeah. Get over it, move on. Your father's as fucked-up as it gets. That doesn't mean you have to be."

"My father is the most notorious serial killer of the century."

"It's a young century yet," he said with a shrug, and had her staring again.

"God. I don't understand you."

"Understand this, then. It's insulting and annoying—remember that—for you to think I'd feel differently about you because your father's Thomas David Bowes. That I'd act differently because seventeen years ago you saved a life—no doubt saved a lot of lives. And if this whole fucked-up bullshit is the reason you're trying to kick me to the curb, you're out of luck. I don't kick that easy."

"I don't know what to say to you now."

"If you want me gone, don't use Bowes as the lever to pry me loose."

"I need to sit down."

She sat on the glider. Obviously deciding she needed it, the dog picked his way back, laid his head on her knee.

"I didn't mean it," she murmured, and stroked the dog. "I didn't mean it about the dog, or the house. I didn't mean it about you. I told myself I should mean it; it would be better all around if I could mean it. It's easier to keep moving than to root, Xander, for someone like me."

"I don't think so. I think that's something else you've told yourself until you mostly believe it. If you believed it all the way through, you wouldn't have bought this place. You wouldn't bring it back to life. You sure as hell wouldn't have taken on that dog, no matter how I worked you on it."

He crossed over, sat beside her again. "You'd have slept with me. I saw that the first time you came into the bar."

"Oh, really?"

Not yet settled, but getting there, he picked up his beer again. "I've got a sense about when a woman's going to be willing. But if you believed all that crap all the way through, this wouldn't have turned into a thing."

"It wasn't supposed to."

"A lot of good things happen by accident. If Charles Goodyear hadn't been clumsy, we wouldn't have vulcanized rubber."

"What?"

"Weatherproof rubber—tires, for instance, as in Goodyear. He was trying to figure out how to make rubber weatherproof, dropped this experiment on a stove by accident, and there you go, he made weatherproof rubber."

Baffled, she rubbed her aching temple. "I've completely lost the point."

"Not everything has to be planned to work out. Maybe we both figured we'd bang it out a few times and move on, but we didn't. And it's working out all right."

The sound of her own laughter surprised her. "Wow, Xander, my heart's fluttering from that romantic description. It's like a sonnet."

Yeah, he realized, he was settling again. "You want romance? I could bring you flowers."

"I don't have anything to put them in." She sighed. "I don't need romance, and I don't know what I'd do with it. I like knowing my feet are solid on the ground. And they haven't been, not consistently, since I saw this house. Today . . . the funeral. It hit so hard because it reminded me, again, of all the people my father hurt. Not just the women he killed, but the people who loved them."

"I'd have been sorry you found her no matter what, but I was a hell of a lot sorrier knowing what it would bring back. Have you talked to your brother, your uncles about it?"

"No. No, why bring it back for them? I wasn't going to talk to anyone about it. Not about what it brought back."

"It's yours to tell, or not. You'd find good friends in Kevin and Jenny. Not trusting that? It's a disservice to them, and to you."

"That's what Chief Winston said to me, about telling you. That same word. Disservice."

"Do you want to tell me what else he said?"

"I knew as soon as he drove up."

She closed her eyes, let herself feel the dog at her feet, the man beside her.

"The world just fell out from under me. Just dropped away. I'd expected it—he'd do a background run on me because I found the body. But the world dropped away. He was straightforward, and he was kind. He said he wouldn't tell anyone else, that he hadn't and wouldn't. I've never been around anyone but family who knew. Or if it came out, I left before things changed."

"Left before you knew if they'd change or not?"

"Maybe that's true, but I've been through those changes, and they're awful. They steal everything," she said quietly, "and crush you."

"I'm sitting here having a beer like I'd hoped to do since I closed the garage. There's a hot meal keeping warm in the oven, a nice sunset right out there. Nothing changed or needs to. You'll get used to it."

Nothing needed to change. Could that be true? Was it really possible?

"Maybe we can just sit here for a while longer, until I get used to it."

"That works for me."

H ours later, when all but the bars shut down for the night, and the streets in town went quiet, with pools of light from streetlamps shimmering against the dark, he watched and waited.

He'd taken the time to study the routine along the main street with its shops and restaurants. To study the women who closed up those shops, or walked home from their job as line cook or waitress.

He had his mind on the pretty young blonde, but he wouldn't be picky. At least three young ones worked the late shift at the pizzeria.

He'd take his pick—but the pretty young blonde? She was top choice.

He'd left the camper at the campground a good twelve miles away, all legally set up.

And if they only knew what he'd done inside that home away from home. Just the idea made him want to chuckle.

But the excitement grew, a hot ball in the belly, when the rear door of the restaurant opened.

The hot little blonde, just as he'd hoped.

And all alone.

He slipped out of the car, on the dark edge of the lot, with the rag he'd soaked with chloroform held down at his side.

He liked using chloroform, going old-school. It put them out—no muss, no fuss—even if it tended to make them a little sick. It just added to the process.

She walked along, firm, young tits bouncing some, tight young ass swaying. He glanced back toward the restaurant, making sure no one else came out, started to make his move.

And headlights sliced over the lot, had him jumping back into the shadows. The little blonde waited for the car to turn toward her, then opened the passenger door.

"Thanks, Dad."

"No problem, honey."

He wanted to kick something, beat something, when his desire drove off, left him yearning and hot.

Tears actually gathered in the corners of his eyes. Then the door opened again.

Two more came out. He saw them in the light above the door, heard their voices, their laughter as they talked.

Then one of the boys came out. He and the younger of the women linked hands, strolled off together.

The young girl turned around, walked backward. "Have fun tomorrow! Drive safe."

The lone woman started across the lot. Not young like the others, not so pretty—not blonde like his desire—but she'd do. She'd do well enough.

She hummed to herself as she opened her purse to dig out her key.

All he had to do, really all he had to do was step up behind her. He deliberately gave her that instant to feel fear, to have her heart jump as she turned her head.

Then he covered her face with the cloth, gripped her around the waist while she struggled, while her muffled screams pushed hot against his hand. As she went so quickly, almost too quickly, limp.

He had her in the back of the car, wrists and ankles wrapped in duct tape, more tape over her mouth, a blanket over her, within twenty seconds.

He drove out of the lot, through town, careful to keep to the posted speed, to use his turn signals. He didn't even turn on the radio until he passed the town limits. He opened the windows to cool his hot cheeks, flicked a glance in the rearview at the shape under the blanket.

"We're going to have some fun now. We're going to have one hell of a good time."

FOCUS

The spectator ofttimes sees more
than the gamester.

JAMES HOWELL

Twenty-one

By the time Sunday morning rolled around, all Xander wanted in this world was to sleep until the sun came up. Three road service calls Friday night had pulled him away from practice for a Saturday-night gig, and dragged him out of bed. Twice.

They'd rocked the bar in Union, good exposure, good times, good pay—but he hadn't flopped into Naomi's bed until two in the morning.

He met Tag's five A.M. wake-up call with a snarl.

"I've got it," Naomi told him.

With a grunt of assent, Xander dropped back to sleep.

Mildly disoriented, he woke, alone, three hours later. He thought, *Naomi*, and scrubbed his hands over his face. Christ, he needed a shave—not his favorite sport. Then he remembered it was Sunday, and didn't see why anybody had to shave on Sunday.

The sun shined through the glass doors. Through them he could see the blue lines of water, the quiet spread of it beyond the inlet. A couple of boats—early risers—plied the blue.

He wasn't a fan of boats any more than he was of shaving, but he appreciated the look of them.

But at the moment, he'd appreciate coffee a hell of a lot more. He got up, pulled on his jeans, saw a T-shirt he'd left there at some point neatly folded on the dresser.

Grateful he didn't have to wear the shirt he'd sweated through the night before, he pulled it over his head—and discovered that whatever she washed stuff in smelled better than whatever he washed stuff in.

He'd had to tap Kevin and Jenny for the favor—then persuade Naomi to drive with them to Union for a couple of hours. He'd liked seeing her there—and more, he'd liked knowing Kevin would make sure she got home, got in the house, locked up safe until he'd made it back.

She'd given him a key and the alarm code, though he wasn't sure if it had been for the single night or what. He didn't think she was sure either.

The . . . arrangement would be easier if he could leave a few essentials at her place. He wasn't sure of his ground there—brand-new territory.

He'd never lived, even half lived, with a woman before. He'd been careful not to. His space might not have been as big as Naomi's, but he liked his space all the same.

Yet here he was, getting out of her bed again, wearing a shirt she'd washed, and thinking about hitting her up for coffee.

This thing between them had a lot of moving parts, and he'd yet to figure out how they all fit.

But he would, he told himself as he walked out to find her—and coffee. He always figured out how things fit.

He heard her voice, pitched low, so he changed directions from the pursuit of coffee and walked to her temporary work space.

She had the windows wide open and the dog sprawled under her makeshift worktable.

The sun flooded her hair, turned it into a hundred shades of gold and bronze and caramel as she used a long tool to cut some mat board while she muttered to herself. Nearby a big, slick printer hummed while it slid a poster-size print into a tray.

It took him a minute to realize the poster-size print was of his hands holding the Austen book.

He saw himself again, already framed and matted and tipped against the wall. That shot she'd taken in the early morning, with the sunrise at his back and his eyes on her.

She had other poster prints—his book wall, his hands again, sunrise over the inlet—clipped to the arms of some sort of stand and a stack of smaller prints in a tray.

The dog's tail thumped good morning, and since hope sprang eternal in Tag, he uncurled himself and brought Xander a ball.

Distracted, Xander laid a hand on the dog's head and just looked at Naomi.

Immersed in her work, immersed in sunlight, slim hands competent with her tools, dark green eyes focused on her art. That long, slim body in a pale blue shirt and khaki pants that stopped above her ankles, her feet bare.

So this was what it was, this was how it fit. How his half fit anyway, he thought. It fit, all those moving parts, because he was in love with her.

Shouldn't the universe have given him a heads-up on that? He needed a little time, needed to adjust, regroup, needed to—

Then she glanced over, and her eyes met his.

It blew through him, that storm of feeling, all but took his breath. For an instant he wondered how people lived this way, how they could carry so much for someone else inside them.

He crossed to her, yanked her up to her toes, and took her mouth like a man starving.

This. Her. His life would never be just what it had been as of that moment. And he would never be only what he'd been.

Love changed everything.

Thrown off balance, she gripped his shoulders. He made her head spin, her heart race, her knees weak. Overcome, she held on, rode the hot, fast wave with him.

When he eased back, she laid her hands on his cheeks, let out a long breath. "Wow, and good morning."

He rested his forehead to hers a moment while tenderness twined with heat.

"Are you all right?" she asked him.

No, he thought. He might not come down to all right again for years.

"You should always wear sunlight," he told her. "It looks good on you."

"I think you should always sleep in."

"No one in the actual world considers eight on a Sunday morning sleeping in."

To give himself a moment to settle, Xander turned to the prints. "You've been busy."

"I've got orders. The gallery, the Internet, Krista."

"So you were right about the hands."

"Oh yeah. Many hits on my website, and a nice bunch of orders for downloads and prints and posters on that and the book wall. I have to order more supplies."

He looked around at boxes and stacks. "More."

"More. I can't set up in here as efficiently as I will when they have my studio done. I might break my own rule and nag Kevin on that. But for now I can make do. You got in late," she added, and took the finished poster print out of the tray.

"Yeah, I got here around two, I guess. Woke the dog up."

"I heard him—and you."

"Sorry."

"No, it's reassuring that he barks and runs down like he'd rip an intruder to shreds. Though I suspect he'd run the other way if it was someone he didn't know. You all sounded good last night."

"Yeah, we had it down."

She clipped the poster in place, moved over to her tray. "What do you think of these?"

He started to tell her he'd look after coffee, as the need for it reared up strong, but he saw the print of the band, one with the tools, the broken windshield. Taking the stack, he paged through.

"Jesus, Naomi, these are great. Really great. Dave keeps saying how he can't decide what to use, which for what. On and on until you want to punch him."

"That's why I printed some out. You've all seen them on the computer, but sometimes prints help the choice."

"I don't think so. They're all great. You did some black-and-white."

"Moody, right?" As if checking for herself, she looked over his shoulder. "A little dangerous. You should all pick one for yourselves. I'll frame them for you. And you should pick one to go in Loo's."

"Yeah, maybe. Yeah. This black-and-white for Loo's, because it fits the atmosphere better."

"I agree."

"Dave's going to develop a nervous tic trying to decide." He set the prints back in the tray. "I need coffee."

"Go ahead. I've got a couple things to finish up, then I'll be down. You could let the dog out," she added. "It's too nice a day for him to be inside."

"For anybody. We could take a drive along 101. GTO or bike, your choice."

"If we did that, took the convertible, I could take some equipment. And the dog."

"We'll go by my place and pick it up."

Even as Xander started out, Tag raced ahead of him.

He'd take the day off—from work, from shaving, from thinking about what to do, or not, about being in love.

He knew people who fell in and out of love more regularly than they came in for an oil change. But he wasn't one of them.

He'd fallen into his share of lust, even into serious like, but this ground-just-shifted-under-my-feet feeling? A whole new experience.

He'd just let it all sit for a while, he decided. Make sure it wasn't some sort of momentary aberration.

Halfway down the steps Tag let out a low growl and bulleted the rest of the way to the door. He snapped out two sharp barks, then looked back at Xander as if to say, *Well? Let's take care of this.*

"Yeah, yeah, I'm coming. Why didn't I go for coffee from the jump?"

Xander opened the door, saw the black Chevy Suburban pull beside Naomi's car. And walked out as a tall man with light brown hair stepped out.

He wore sunglasses, a dark suit and tie—and a nebulous official air that said *cop* to Xander.

Not a local badge, but some sort of badge. And it pissed him off that Naomi would have her Sunday spoiled by more questions about Marla.

The man looked at the dog who stood by Xander's side, then at Xander.

"Who the hell are you?"

"You're the one who drove up here," Xander countered just as abruptly, "so I get to ask who the hell you are."

"Special Agent Mason Carson. FBI."

Mason took out his credentials, held them up—and wasn't subtle about the hand that flipped back the suit jacket to rest on the butt of his service weapon.

"Now, who the hell are you?"

"It's all right." Xander set his own hand on Tag's head. "He's okay. Xander Keaton."

The sunglasses might have blocked Mason's eyes, but Xander knew they narrowed and assessed.

"The mechanic."

"That's right. Naomi's in the house. Upstairs finishing up some work. I'd appreciate it if you took your hand off your gun. I haven't had coffee yet, and it's starting to piss me off."

Since Tag sidled over to sniff at Mason's FBI shoes, Mason gave his head a rub. "Do you usually have coffee here?"

"It's gotten to be a habit. If that pisses you off, it has to wait until after coffee."

"I wouldn't mind coffee."

Tag raced off, raced back, ball in his mouth, dropped it at Mason's feet.

And when Mason smiled, Xander saw Naomi.

She didn't smile all the way often enough, in his opinion, but when she did she shared that same slow build to blinding with her brother.

"She's going to be really glad to see you."

Xander waited for Mason, who wasn't so official he couldn't throw a ball for a dog, then started back into the house.

"If we drive north," Naomi began as she came downstairs, "I could get some . . . Mason. Oh God, Mason!"

She flew.

Mason caught her, swung her around, then swung her around again.

That, Xander thought, was a connection, a bond, a love that went as deep as they ever get.

She laughed, and he heard the tears in it, saw them sparkle in the jubilant sunlight that pumped through the open door.

"What are you doing here? Why didn't you tell me you were coming? You're wearing a suit! You look so— Oh, oh, I *missed* you."

"I missed you, too." Beaming right back, Mason held her a few inches away. "You have a house. And a dog."

"Crazy, isn't it?"

"It's a hell of a house. Great dog. And you've got . . . a mechanic."

"A . . . oh." She laughed, gave Mason another squeeze. "Xander, this is my brother, Mason."

"Yeah, we met outside. I'm going for coffee."

"I'll get it. I'll show you the house," she said to Mason. "We'll start with the kitchen. Right now it's the best part."

"It's a big house."

"With plenty of room for you and Seth and Harry to visit. And I've talked Gram and Pop into coming out, at least by the fall. Your rooms aren't finished yet, but we'll figure something out. How long can you stay?"

"Mmm."

"Have you eaten?"

"Had a bagel on the ferry."

"We can do better than that. The ferry? Where'd you come from? I thought you were in New York."

He made another noncommittal sound, one that put Xander on alert. It didn't bump against Naomi's delight, not yet. And Xander changed his mind about getting a coffee to go, and leaving the siblings to themselves for a while.

He'd stick around.

"I set up a FaceTime with the uncles for later today. They didn't say a thing about you being out here."

"I had to come to Seattle." Mason stopped, looked over the kitchen space, out to the view. "Wow. Nome, this is amazing."

"I really love it. Xander, maybe you could take Mason out on the deck. I'll bring coffee."

"Sure."

"Sweet," was Mason's opinion when Xander opened the accordion doors. "Yeah, this would grab her. The first time she saw the ocean, she fell for it. I always expected her to end up on the East Coast, but yeah, she'd fall for this. How long have you been sleeping with my sister?"

"That's a conversation you should have with her first, then we can have one. No problem. The quick one we should have now, before she comes out, is why you're here. Because it's not just a surprise visit to your sister. You've got business here. She doesn't see it," Xander added, "because she only sees you."

"I have a meeting with your chief of police in about an hour."

"If you've come to talk to him about Marla, is that FBI or the brother who's FBI?"

"My supervisor signed off on it. You knew her, Marla Roth."

"Yeah."

"Do you know Donna Lanier?"

A cold blade sliced into Xander's belly. "Yeah. What happened to her?"

"I don't know, yet, that anything has. I'd appreciate it if you'd let me get to this with Naomi in my own time."

She came out with three white mugs on a tray. "How about waffles? I bought a waffle iron," she told Xander. "We can have an early Sunday brunch, and toast the uncles. No champagne, but I've got OJ."

"Coffee works for now. Relax." Smoothly, Mason put an arm around her shoulder, rubbed the top of her arm. "You must have taken a million pictures right from this spot."

"It might be two million. And the town's a charmer. We'll have to take you through it. We could rent kayaks. I've been dying to. Xander, why haven't we rented kayaks?"

"Why would I want to sit in a hole in a boat with a paddle?"

"It's a whole new perspective."

"I like this one fine."

"For those who prefer land, there's plenty of hiking. You didn't say how long you can stay."

"I'm not sure yet. Seth and Harry are coming out."

"What? When? *Today?*"

"No, jeez, not today." Amused, Mason sipped his coffee. "They're probably going to spring it on you when you call later. A couple of weeks maybe—they're working on it."

"God, I have to get beds. And champagne. And serious supplies. If you think I can cook," she said to Xander, "wait until Harry makes a meal." Obviously buoyant, she jumped back to Mason. "Do you think you can put in for some time off so you can be here, too?"

"I'll look into it."

Sipping his own coffee, Xander saw it start to get through, when some instinct, some tone, maybe some body language told her something was off.

"Is something wrong?" The moment she asked, she went pale. "Oh God, Harry and Seth. Is something wrong? Is one of them sick?"

"No. No, they're both fine."

"Then what? It's something. You . . . you didn't tell me you were coming," she said, stepping back to look at him more keenly. "You aren't telling me how long you'll be here. You aren't telling me something else."

"Why don't we sit down?"

"Don't do that. Just be straight with me. Is this about Marla Roth? Are you here about the murder?"

"When someone's murdered near my sister, and my sister finds the body, I take an interest."

"So you're here to talk to Chief Winston."

"I'm here to see you, and to talk to Chief Winston."

"Okay." Though some of the shine dimmed, she nodded. "I'm sure he'll appreciate the assistance. You don't have to circle around telling me something like that, Mason. I know what you do."

"It's not just that. Another woman's missing. Another local woman."

"What? Who? When did— Did you know about this?" She whirled on Xander.

"No, and simmer down. Missing for how long?"

"Donna Lanier closed Rinaldo's restaurant at approximately eleven forty-five Friday night. She was the last to leave, and was last seen by two other employees, who left about the same time. According to statements, she was supposed to drive to Olympia to spend the weekend with her sister and a cousin. Her car's still in the lot, and she never met her sister and cousin or contacted them."

"She could have changed her mind," Naomi began.

"Her suitcase is in the back of her car. She'd planned to drive straight there after her shift. She hasn't been seen or heard from since eleven forty-five on Friday, she hasn't used a credit card, sent a text, made a call."

"Donna. She's the brunette?" Though she'd gone pale, Naomi's voice stayed steady when she turned to Xander. "Early forties, round, cheerful face?"

"Yeah. She and Loo are tight. Go back to high school together. You think whoever killed Marla wasn't passing through, didn't just grab her up because he saw an opportunity. You think whoever did that has Donna."

"I think it's a strong possibility."

"She calls everyone *sweetie*." Slowly, Naomi lowered to a chair. "I noticed that when I first moved here, and I'd go in for takeout, she'd say, 'I'll get that right out for you, sweetie.' Or 'How are you doing tonight, sweetie?'"

"She has a kid in college. She raised her mostly on her own. Divorced, no interest from him in the kid. She has a daughter away at college."

"I'm sorry." Naomi rose again, went to Xander. "You've known her all your life. I'm sorry."

"I've never known her to hurt anybody. She's nothing like Marla. Don't they go for a type? She's fifteen years older, brunette, settled, steady—and not the sort who'd catch your eye like Marla."

"I need to talk to your chief of police, get more information."

"How do you even know about it?" Naomi demanded.

"I contacted Winston after Marla Roth. Did you think I wouldn't hear about it, Naomi? Christ, I'm a federal agent, I'm going to hear about it when my sister finds a body in her goddamn backyard."

"It wasn't, and you're taking that tone with me to block me from taking one with you. I didn't tell you because there wasn't a point. I didn't want to worry you or the uncles. Is that why they're coming out here?"

"I haven't said anything to them about this. Yet."

Mason let the last word hang a moment.

"I talked to Winston about Roth, gave him my contact information, asked him to let me know if anything else came up. It came up."

"If you two want to snipe at each other about it, I'll stay out of the way." Xander shrugged. "But it's pretty pointless on both sides. I'm getting more coffee."

"You could have told me you'd called the chief, told me you'd come here to talk to him."

"You could've told me you found a dead body."

"Next time I find one, you'll be the first."

"Don't joke about it, Naomi."

"Oh, I'm not." She closed her eyes. "I'm not. I'm sick at the thought of it. I don't know how you do what you do. I know why, I understand why you chose to do what you do, but I don't know how you face it. Day after day, how you stand being faced with it. I've done everything I could to cut all of it out of my life, to put up walls. And you do the opposite. I can be proud of you, and I am, and still wonder how you stand it."

"Doing this is how I stand it. We can talk about this when we're alone, and when I have more time."

"Chief Winston knows who we are. He ran me after I found the body."

"Yeah, I figured as much."

"Xander knows. I told him."

"You—" Stunned, Mason stared at his sister, then Xander when Xander stepped back out. "Is that right?"

"Yes, so you don't have to worry about what you say."

"I can't say much more of anything because I need to go meet Winston. I'll be back." Mason took Naomi's shoulders. "I'll be back after I meet with him. You can show me the house, what you've been working on."

"All right."

He kissed her forehead, stepped back. "I'll be back," he said to Xander.

As Mason left, Xander sat on the glider. "Can we just sit here for a minute?"

"I should—"

"I need it. I have to hope this isn't happening to her. She's one of the best people I know, and she and Loo . . . I need to call Loo. She'd have heard. We'd have heard most likely but we had the out-of-town gig. She'll need to talk to me, but I need to sit for a minute first."

Naomi went over, lowered to the glider beside him, took his hand. "We'll just sit here, then you should go see her. It's better if you go see her than call."

"You're right, but I'm not leaving you here alone. Not until we know what the hell's happening."

Not the time to argue, she decided. "I'll go with you. I'll text Mason so he knows, and go with you."

Twenty-two

Mason's impression of Sunrise Cove jibed with Naomi's. It had charm, and its situation on the water added considerable appeal. He'd have enjoyed a few days downtime there, maybe renting some Jet-Skis, or that kayak his sister seemed so keen on.

He couldn't see making it his base, as Naomi was. He liked the city, where anything and everything could and did happen. He needed a quick pace, one that kept up with his own.

But then she preferred the quiet, prized her solitude. He needed movement, conversation, needed to be part of a team. Work drove them both—hers in art and imagery, capturing moments and making them speak. His in behavior, in rules, in an endless quest to find out why.

Compensations, he knew very well, for both of them, constantly on some level trying to weigh the scale against what they'd come from.

She tried, often too hard in his opinion, to erase it, to shove it away. And he couldn't stop studying it, aiming his life toward the pursuit of those, like his father, who lived to destroy, and found their only real pleasure in that destruction.

He didn't know what to think about Xander Keaton or Naomi's relationship with him. Yet. He'd study that as well.

The fact she'd told Keaton about Bowes indicated she'd formed a serious and he wanted to believe healthy attachment—something she'd avoided and denied herself all her life outside of their tight little family.

As for Keaton . . . on first impression Mason would tag him with one of Harry's terms. A cool customer. But he'd already observed a number of tells. The way he'd ranged himself in front of the house—with Naomi inside—before Mason had identified himself, the firm but casual order for her to "simmer down," and the fact that he'd told Mason to talk to Naomi when Mason had asked about sex.

Initial analysis? Mason thought as he parked in the tiny lot beside the station house. A confident man, and one who'd protect his sister. He could and would be grateful for that, for now.

And like any self-respecting brother who was also a federal agent, he'd run him.

Mason rounded to the front, noted the station had a small front porch, recently painted and swept clean as a parlor.

When he stepped inside, he had that instant déjà vu he experienced any time he went into a small-town cop shop.

Had Naomi been in here? he wondered. Would she see the similarities to Pine Meadows? Of course she would. Not the same, of course, not a mirror image, and the basic tools and equipment had advanced in the seventeen years since his father's arrest.

But the setup struck so similar, the *tone*. The smell of coffee and baked goods, plastic chairs, a trio of desks in what served as both a kind of lobby and the bull pen.

A uniformed deputy sat at one of the desks, gave Mason the eye.

"Help you?"

You already know who I am, why I'm here, Mason calculated. And don't like the idea of an outsider, especially a federal one, horning into town business.

The reaction was nothing new.

"Yes. Special Agent Mason Carson. I have a meeting with Chief Winston."

The deputy leaned back in his chair, sized Mason up with a faint sneer that clearly read *fuck you*. "Have you got identification?"

Even as Mason reached for it, a man came out of the back holding a big blue mug that read *CHIEF*. "Mike, you climb up any higher on that horse, you're going to get a nosebleed." Sam stepped forward, hand extended. "Sam Winston. Pleased to meet you, Agent Carson."

"I appreciate the time, Chief."

"Come on back. You want some coffee? It's not half-bad coffee."

"I just had some at my sister's, but thanks."

They stepped into an office with a window at the back. The wide sill held a scatter of trophies, some framed photos, and a wildly thriving philodendron.

The desk sat on the side wall, giving the Cove's chief views out the window and to the door. Two visitor's chairs—straight backs, no-nonsense—angled toward it.

"Have a seat."

Sam took the chair behind the desk that looked as though it had stood in that spot for a couple generations.

"I'm going to tell you straight off, we haven't got line one on Donna Lanier. Her sister, her daughter, and her cousin are all on their way here. No stopping them. Her car was locked, and we found the keys on the ground, just under it. It's clear whatever happened to her started in that parking lot."

Mason only nodded. "I'd like to see the lot, and her residence, if possible."

"We'll do that."

"You indicated Ms. Lanier lives alone, and is—to your knowledge—not in a relationship."

"That's right. Donna's been divorced and single for a lot of years. Now she and Frank Peters have a drink or dinner now and then, and I do believe a bit more than that. But it's a friendly sort of thing, and nothing serious on either side. And Frank was down at Loo's when Donna closed up Friday. He was with a couple of friends, didn't head out until nearly one."

Nodding again, Mason decided to keep his notes mental for the time being. "Is that usual?"

"More like clockwork. Frank and his buddies tend to hit Loo's on Friday nights, blow off the workweek steam."

"Would you object if I speak to him?"

"No, and neither would he. He and Donna have been friends a long time. He's scared for her, and I'll admit I am, too. She's not one to go off like this. She's a responsible woman with a daughter she loves, a job she loves. She's got friends. And let's cut through this, Agent Carson. She sure as hell didn't go willing out of that lot, without her car, keys on the ground, when she'd planned this get-together with her sister and her cousin for months now. All she could talk about was her trip, how they were getting hot-stone massages."

"I don't disagree, and I realize it seems as though I'm asking to cover ground you've already covered, and ground you know better than I ever could. Sometimes an outside perspective, a fresh eye, sees something overlooked."

Sam looked into his mug, grimaced a little, drank. "I'm not going to argue that, and you can cover the ground all you want. But I don't just know the ground, I know the people who live on it. And I know there's no one in this town who could do what was done to Marla. And I know we've got people who come here for a few hours, a few days, maybe longer, to use the marina, the shops and bars and restaurants, the hiking trails. They rent boats and kayaks and Sea-Doos." Sam set his mug down. "I don't know them."

"You believe an outsider abducted and killed Marla Roth."

"With every bone in my body."

"Tell me more about her."

"Marla?" Sam puffed out his cheeks, let the air out in a half sigh. "As different from Donna as they come—and I know that's not usual if this is the same person. Marla was thirty-one, on the wild side of things, and always has been. She divorced a good man who loved her, and still does. Who's grieving for her. You can talk to him, too, but Chip Peters would've cut off both arms before laying a hand on Marla."

"Peters." He already knew, of course, had already looked at the connections.

"That's right. Frank's Chip's uncle. Frank and Darren Peters—that's Chip's dad—have run the Sea to Sea Tours and Rentals for about sixteen years now. Chip's part of that. I'm telling you he's no part of this, and neither is Frank."

Sam seemed to pull himself back, took another sip from his mug. "But you need to look, see for yourself."

"Was the divorce acrimonious?"

"Ever had one?"

"No."

"Me either, but I don't know any that are pleasant activities."

"My information indicates Chip—that's Darren Peters, Junior—has a temper, often a violent one."

"Your information's wrong," Sam said flatly. "What Chip has is a code, and God knows a weakness where Marla was concerned. Yes, he had what you could call a confrontation with the dickhead Marla was hooked up with some years back. I've got a report, I'll get you a copy. This individual tuned Marla up, a couple times. Chip got word of it—from Marla—and gave the dickhead a taste of his own. Only took one punch to lay him out, and plenty of witnesses to that. Chip didn't keep at him, and he could have. He used his fists once or twice otherwise—over Marla. He's a big man, Agent Carson. One punch usually did the trick. A man prone to violence doesn't stop at one."

"No charges pressed?" Mason asked.

"No. In the case of the dickhead—one Rupert Mosley—I spoke to him myself. At that time he and Marla both sported shiners, and the fact was he'd given her hers. I said I'd be happy to charge Chip with assault, and they could share a cell, as I'd also be more than happy to charge him with assault on Marla. He opted against, further opted to relocate. He moved down to Oregon, outside Portland. I've checked his whereabouts on both nights in question. He's alibied tight, seeing as he's doing a nickel in CRCI for laying into another woman down there. But I'll give you that data, too."

"I'd appreciate it. Can I ask why Chip and Marla divorced?"

"She wanted out. She wanted more. More what, only God knows, but nothing was ever quite enough. She went at your sister at Loo's that Friday night shortly before she went missing."

"I'm sorry? What?"

Sam kicked back in his chair—not cocky like his deputy, but a relaxed, even amused body language. "You didn't get that part? Well, Marla was the type who wanted whatever she wanted—and she'd decided a while back she wanted Xander Keaton."

"Keaton."

"Yeah—apparently they'd hit a hot round or two back in high school, which was all Xander wanted. And added to it, Xander thinks a lot of Chip. Divorced or not, he'd never go with Marla. Added to that added-to, Xander had his eye on your sister—and that was clear to anybody who cared to look. Marla took objection, and being half shit-faced at the time, got pushy with Naomi. Literally."

"She put hands on Naomi?"

"A couple of times, making a scene, using we'll say strong language."

"At the bar?" Mason qualified, wanting it lined up tight. "At Loo's the Friday night she went missing?"

"That's right. Witness reports agree on how that went down. Marla started it, Naomi asked her to back off, a couple times. Marla shoved her again. Naomi grabbed her wrist—that's the one most agree on—twisted it in a way that had Marla going down on the floor. Then Naomi left. Marla stayed pissy, went and got sick in the toilets there, bitched at her best friend, and stomped on out. And that's the last anyone saw of her until Naomi found her under the bluff."

Despite the hot ball in his belly, Mason spoke evenly. "You looked into Naomi's whereabouts, her movements, her background."

"Yes, I did."

"You know Thomas Bowes is our father."

"I do."

"And that Naomi hasn't seen or spoken to him since the day he was arrested."

"I do. Just as I know you've visited him in prison five times to date."

"And likely will again. When your father is a serial killer, and you pursue serial killers, it's smart to study what you have easy access to."

"Can't be easy, but it's smart. I said I know the people in my town, Agent Carson. Naomi hasn't been here long, but I've got a good sense of her. She's not involved in any of this. I'm not looking at her."

"And Keaton?"

"Not in him." In an easy gesture, Sam lifted his fingers from the surface of the desk as if to brush the idea away. "I'm not a psychologist or a behavior specialist—or no more than any cop—but I've got a sister myself, and I suspect you'd like to know what kind of man he is. He works hard. He's got a friend he's kept close since they were in diapers—that says something to me. He's got a head for business, though you wouldn't think it right off. He doesn't flaunt that around. He reads like a scholar—never seen anybody with so many books. He's got himself a good bar band with other friends, and they're worth hearing. I've seen him with your sister a time or two, and I can say I've never seen him look at anyone else the way he looks at her. We're trained observers, Agent. In technical terms?" Sam smiled, just a little. "He's hooked."

Sam's chair creaked as he sat up again. "Xander's got a soft spot for Donna—most of us do. She's a sweetheart, and I'm sick knowing I'm sitting here without a goddamn clue where she is or what's happening to her. If you can bring in a clue, I'm going to be grateful. I'm going to throw this in the mix, as I just got this information. A young girl—pretty thing, Maxie Upton—worked that Friday-night shift with Donna. In the usual case her car would've been in the lot back where Donna parked, but she got a flat coming into work, caught Xander at his garage as he was closing. She told me this morning he wouldn't put the donut on—said all her tires were bald, and she needed new. He'd get them for her the next day, and he'd give her a ride in to work, but only if she called her father to come pick her up. She had to promise not to walk home, or even to her friend's just a block away. She came out just a few minutes before Donna, and her father pulled up almost right away."

"More the same type as Marla Roth?"

"Younger—Maxie's about nineteen, but more physically like Marla than Donna. Blonde and pretty. It's got me wondering if Donna was second choice. If Maxie's car had been in that same area, or if Xander hadn't made her promise not to walk alone after closing, would we be looking for her?"

"It's possible."

"Go out on a limb, Agent. I won't hold you to it if things change."

"It's possible," Mason repeated. "You may have an opportunist. No one could anticipate Marla Roth would walk home alone, and at that time. The killer saw an opportunity, took it. The odds of two women being taken by different people in this small an area and in this time frame are slim. Ms. Lanier was alone, in a remote area of the lot, and presented an opportunity to someone who knew the closing time, the shift."

"You'd know that after a day around here."

Mason had only had to drive through town to see that for himself.

"He has somewhere to take them—locally, within say twenty miles—somewhere private. He held Roth for two full days, during which time he raped and tortured her. He'd need a place, and since he dumped her body here, it's reasonable to assume that place is within a comfortable driving distance. He would need a car, a van, a truck to transport them. I'm not telling you anything you don't know."

"Not so far," Sam agreed, "but it adds weight. There are rental houses and cabins around town and more within that distance. We've checked with the closer ones, talked to the people in them, to the owner or manager."

"You might want to expand your area, ask the rangers to canvass cabins and houses inside the national park. It's not far, and a good area for what he does, a private, quiet place. He's white, between twenty-five and forty—probably closer to the younger end."

"Why the younger?"

"More mature would probably be more patient, take more time to stalk the prey. This one jumps on it. And it is likely he wanted the young girl instead of Donna, but he took her because she was there. More mature would be more likely to wait until he gets another chance with his target. Once he has her, it doesn't matter. She's whoever he wants her to be."

"Is she a surrogate? I've done some reading," Sam added. "Does she represent someone?"

"Possibly. It's too soon for me to commit to that, but I can tell you he's a sexual sadist, so he enjoys what he does. He's not impotent, but may only be able to climax through rape, through giving the victim pain, through feeding on that pain and the fear. He kept Roth for two full days, and as you haven't found a second body, he still has Donna Lanier. While the kill is the ultimate release, he knows when he takes it, it's over. So he prolongs it as long as he can."

Mason paused, half wished he had that coffee, and went on.

"Taking two in such a short amount of time indicates he's found what he believes is a prime location. It's a small town, but in a very open area. The people in the town and area have routines he can study quickly. In small towns with a low violent-crime rate people feel secure, don't worry about walking home alone, crossing into a dark area of a parking lot after closing. I suspect many here don't routinely lock doors and windows, lock their cars. I could walk around town, check visors, and probably find any number of keys."

"You're not wrong."

"He knows places like this and has certainly spent time studying them. He's killed before."

Once again Sam angled forward. "Yes. Yeah, that's what my gut told me. Not his first kill."

"His method was too efficient for it to have been his first. He dumped the body in the manner he did because he wanted her found. He enjoys the fear, the upheaval. He left her bound and gagged as it maintains his dominance. You found no prints on the tape or body. He's experienced enough to use gloves—and a condom. There's control, there's intelligence.

"He blends in," Mason continued. "If he isn't a local, he presents himself as a visitor, friendly but not too much."

Sam nodded, nodded. "Nobody that causes a ruckus, argues with a shopkeeper, has too much to drink at a bar."

"Exactly. Nothing about him sticks in anyone's mind. He most certainly ate in that pizzeria. It's likely his father was dominant, physically and emotionally, and his mother submissive. She took what was dished out. She did as she was told. This man has no respect for women, but can only dominate by force.

"The unfortunate reality is I will be able to tell you more if and when he dumps the next body."

Sam blew out a breath. "So unless we get lucky and find him in a rental, nothing you have helps Donna."

"If he sticks to the same schedule, he could kill her tonight, and leave her body somewhere in the open. I'm sorry."

"How confident are you in this? Your boss says you're good—good enough to be on the fast track for the BAU. I know what that is, I know what profiling is."

Mason considered. "You've been married more than twenty years, and you still love your wife. You've got two kids who center your world. You played football in high school, and you enjoy the memory of those glory days. But they're memories, and the now matters more. Your wife's trying to get you on a healthier diet, and you're going along with it. For now, anyway. You've got an organized and open mind, and this isn't just your job. This is your town, your people, and protecting and serving aren't just words. Your men like you. You run a tight ship, but not a constricting one."

Mildly embarrassed, more than mildly impressed, Sam went back to his mug. "That's accurate on short acquaintance. How do you get it?"

"You're wearing a wedding ring, and there are pictures of your wife, your wife and kids, on the windowsill. Your kids are teenagers now, but you've got some of them still up from when they were younger. You've got a football trophy—MVP—but it's not front and center. The softball and volleyball trophies—your kids'—are more prominently displayed. You're drinking green tea, and you want coffee. There's a yogurt bar in your inbox, and you don't strike me as the health-bar type."

"Who wouldn't rather have a donut?"

"That goes without saying. Your deputy's annoyed you're meeting with me, but when you gave him the brushback, he didn't sulk. He grinned. You agreed to meet with me because you'll use any source that may help. You ran me and my sister, but you don't consider us guilty by blood or association. Believe me, some would, some do."

"Some are fuckheads."

"Some are. You know the area, you know the people, and you don't believe anyone from here killed Marla Roth or abducted Donna Lanier. I'm willing to weigh that opinion if you're willing to weigh mine."

"And I am. Why don't you give me a few minutes? I'm going to work on getting those rentals checked outside the town limits, into the park. I'm going to make it twenty-five miles. Then I'll take you to Donna's, and the parking lot. We can walk around some. You get a better sense of a place walking it."

"Good enough." Mason rose. "Is that coffee still available?"

"Plenty of it in the break room." Sam smiled. "Green tea, too."

"I think I'll hit you up for coffee."

B ack home, Naomi read Mason's text.

"He says he'll be a couple more hours. Are you sure you want me to go with you? I don't want Loo to feel uncomfortable."

"If it seems like she is, I'll kick you out."

"Tough, but fair." She stepped back, looked at the scatter of pieces they'd carted up from the basement storage area. She hadn't collected a great deal yet, and none of what she had belonged in this guest room.

But, for now, they made the space feel less empty.

"I can't come up with a bed before tonight, but at least he's got a chair—that needs to be reupholstered—a table, a lamp. And the walls look good. Bare, but clean and freshly painted."

She turned to him, held out a hand. "Dog or no dog to Loo's? Your call."

"She'll like the dog. She was nuts for Milo."

"Good, because he has a comforting way. Just let me change and fix up a little, and we can go."

"What for?" Since he had her hand he pulled her out of the room, headed for the steps. "We're not going to a party."

"I don't have any makeup on."

"You're beautiful."

He caught the wide-eyed, surprised blink, aimed her down the stairs. "What? You've got a mirror. You don't need me telling you."

"It's nice to hear."

"You don't wear makeup most of the time anyway."

"When I go out I try to make some minimal effort."

Since the dog meant taking her car rather than his bike, he headed for that with Tag racing ahead of them in anticipation.

"I don't even have my wallet."

"I do. I'll drive." He opened the door for the dog, then got behind the wheel. "Huh, first time I remember getting in a seat after a woman and not having my knees hit my ears. You got legs, baby." Still, he adjusted the seat back a couple of inches before he glanced over, saw her frowning at him. "What?"

"Have you ever in your life waited five minutes for a woman with shorter legs to get ready, grab her purse?"

"You hardly ever have a purse. I admire that."

"That wasn't the question."

"Yeah, yeah, I've waited. Mostly I think women just like having guys wait. And the fact is, most of them could work a couple hours at it and not look like you. So why wait?"

She huffed, pulled on her seat belt. "That's one hell of a compliment mixed in with amazing arrogance. I can't decide whether to be seriously flattered or seriously annoyed on behalf of women everywhere."

"Slim, you're not like women everywhere."

"I'm not sure what that means, but I think you consider it another compliment. In any case, give me a clear signal if I should leave you and Loo alone. Where does she live?"

"Over the bar. She has an apartment up there. Owns the building."

"She owns the building?" Because she understood more pieces of him now, she took the leap. "The two of you own the building," Naomi deduced.

"It's an investment, and since she lives up there she doesn't have a tenant—or we don't—bitching about the noise from the bar. I don't know what the hell to say to her."

"You'll know. You've got a way, too."

"Yeah. Me and the dog."

He parked, drummed his fingers on the steering wheel as he studied the building. "She's in the bar. Lights are on down there, and we don't open until four on Sundays."

When he got out, she took the spare leash she stowed in the center box. But Xander came around, let the dog out before she could use it. She started to object, but Tag stood beside Xander, wagging and waiting.

"Isn't there a leash law?"

"I think we're safe for the next ten steps." Digging in his pocket, Xander pulled out keys, unlocked the door.

Music blared out of the sound system, hard-driving rock with screaming guitars Naomi couldn't identify. She'd never been in the bar in daylight or with the houselights on full. It looked bigger, she realized, especially with the chairs upended on the tables, the booths empty of patrons.

In snug cropped jeans and a black tank that showed off sculpted arms and shoulders, Loo attacked the floor with some sort of mop.

Because he was directly beside her, Naomi heard Xander mutter, "Shit," before he strode to the bar, behind it, and turned down the music.

Loo snapped straight, hefting the mop like a bat—and lowered it again when she saw Xander.

"You'll blow out your eardrums."

"Rock's meant to be loud."

"Why are you down here doing Justin's job?"

"Because I want it done right for a change. And why aren't you up on the bluff trying to get into the blonde's pants?"

"Because I brought her with me."

Loo turned, caught sight of Naomi, and hissed out a tired breath. Before she could say anything else, Tag decided it was time for introductions and trotted over to her.

"Is this that half-dead dog you found?"

"Yeah." Xander came from in back of the bar.

"Looks pretty healthy now. You've got some blue eyes, don't you?" She gave him a rub. "Okay, nice of you to drop by, but I've got work to finish. I oughta close down for a week, get out the whips and chains, slap some ass, and get the crew to clean top to bottom. If you're not on them every second, they'll give these floors a swipe and consider it done."

By the time she'd finished, her words tumbled together, rushed and breathless, with her arms pumping pistons on the mop.

Xander just stood for a moment, then dragged his hand through his hair. He walked to her, wrestled the mop away from her. Then just wrapped his arms around her.

"I need to finish! Damn it, I need to finish."

"Come on, Loo."

She struggled and shoved against him another moment, then gripped the back of his shirt in her fists. "Xander. I'm so scared. Donna. Where is she? What's happening to her? How can this be happening?"

When she began to weep, he just held on.

Twenty-three

Not sure of her role, Naomi decided to make herself useful. Quietly, she went behind the bar, studied the hot beverage machine. She checked its supplies, opted for coffee because Loo didn't strike her as the tea sort.

She found mugs, kept herself busy as Loo composed herself.

"I don't know what to do," Loo said. "I need something to do."

"Right now, we're going to sit down."

As Xander steered Loo to a booth, Naomi called out, "I'm making coffee."

Swiping at tears, Loo spun around. "That machine's complicated," she began.

"She practically grew up in a restaurant, Loo. Sit down."

"She breaks it, you bought it," Loo muttered. "And I'd rather have a whiskey."

"Irish coffee, then," Naomi said easily. "Xander?"

"Just a Coke."

As she sat, Loo snatched napkins from the holder, blew her nose. "They don't know *dick*. Sam came around here last night on the off chance she'd decided to stay home, was with me. Nobody knows squat about it, nobody's seen her, heard from her."

"I know, Loo."

The dog worked his way under the table, laid his head in Loo's lap.

He did have a way.

"She'd been talking about this trip for weeks—until you wanted to stuff a sock in her mouth. She tried to get me to go, nagged me brainless. I've got nothing against a couple days at a spa, but her sister's a pain in the ass. If I'd said I'd go with her, if I'd been with her . . ."

"That's bullshit, Loo."

"It's not." Her eyes filled to brimming again. "It's *not*! I'd've gone over there, picked her up."

"And maybe you'd be the one no one's seen or heard from."

"That's the bullshit." After she swiped at the tears, she balled up the napkins. "I can handle myself. Donna . . . She's just soft. She's soft."

Naomi came to the table with a glass mug of Irish coffee, expertly topped with whipped cream, and a glass of Coke.

"I'll take the dog for a walk, give the two of you some privacy."

"The dog's fine right here." Loo stroked Tag's ears as she studied Naomi. "And so are you. Sorry about the in-your-pants remark. It was rude."

"Well, he's been in them a few times, so not entirely."

Loo let out a bark of laughter, then went watery at the edges. "You're fine here, too. Get a drink, sit down."

"All right. I'm going to say something first. The only blame is on the person who took her. We can always say *if I'd done this, or hadn't done that*, but it doesn't change what is. The only person who could change what is, is the one who took her."

While Loo stared into her coffee, Naomi went to get herself a Coke.

"She's my closest friend," Loo said quietly. "Since high school. We didn't have a thing in common, but we just got to be friends anyway. I stood up for her when she married that asshole, just like she stood up for me when I married Johnny. And when he died, I don't know how I'd have gotten through it without her."

She sighed, sniffled. "And she told me not to marry Dikes. But when I did, she stood up for me again."

She sampled the coffee, arched eyebrows at Naomi. "This is damn good Irish coffee."

"I learned from the master." She slid into the booth beside Xander. "I don't know if it helps, but my brother's here, and meeting with Chief Winston right now. He's with the FBI."

"Sam called the FBI?"

"To tell you the truth, I don't know who called who—it got lost in translation—but we've got an FBI agent helping look for her."

"He's had her—whoever the bastard is—since Friday night. Word's gotten out on what was done to Marla. Donna . . ."

Reaching over, Xander closed a hand over hers. "Don't do that, Loo. We'll go crazy if we do that."

"I drove all over hell and back last night. Just driving the road, looking for her, for . . . something. With my baseball bat and my .32."

"Jesus, Loo. You should've called me."

"I nearly did." She turned her hand over, linked her fingers with his. "Who else do I call when I hit a wall? Not that I often hit one I can't bust through on my own. You'll find that out if you stick with this one," she said to Naomi. "If you hit that wall or your back's to one, you want this one with you."

"Come on, Loo."

"She should know you're not just a pretty face."

"I've seen prettier. I've had prettier," Naomi added, and earned that bark of laughter as she'd hoped. "You need some art on the walls in here, Loo."

"It's a bar."

"It's a good bar. I'm not talking frilly, fussy, fern-bar art. There's one coming in of the Wreckers—they have to buy that from me. But I've got one of Xander and Tag, a sunrise silhouette that I punched up so their blue eyes stand out. It'd work in here, and I'll give it to you if you like it. It'd be exposure for me."

"You're not going to put me up on the wall."

Loo arched those eyebrows again. "I will if I like it. It's my bar."

"It's half mine."

"So I'll hang it in my half." She gave his hand a squeeze, then a light slap, then went back to her coffee. "You've settled my nerves, both of you, and I'm grateful."

"You should get out of here. We'll go have lunch or something."

Smiling a little, Loo shook her head at Xander. "When I'm this worked up I clean, but I'll finish up here calmer than I was. If you hear anything from your brother, anything about where she is, you need to let me know."

"I will."

"All right. Go on now, and take this dog before I end up keeping him for myself. I'm all right now."

"If you need me for anything, you call me."

"I will. I'm going to hope I hear they found her, and she's okay. I'm going to hold on to that."

When they left her, she'd gone back to her mopping.

Since she'd decided to believe Mason would stay at least overnight, Naomi had Xander take her by the market—grateful they had limited Sunday hours. She picked up what she needed for one of his favorite meals.

Every local in the market had something to say about Donna, or would stop Xander to ask what he knew. She didn't take a clear, easy breath until they were outside again.

"I should've known that, and made do with what I had at home." She sat back in the seat, stomach knotted, headache brewing. "And it had to be harder on you than me. All the talk," she added. "The questions, the speculation."

"Everyone who lives here knows her, so they're worried."

"Maybe Mason will have something, anything, to add. I know he's my brother, Xander, but he really is ridiculously smart. He notices everything, forgets nothing, and he's studied for what he's doing since he was a kid. I caught him once—he wasn't quite fast enough to block my view of what he was looking at on his computer. Serial killers. I was so mad, so *outraged* that he'd do that, read about them. He just said he needed to know; the more he knew, the better he could deal with it."

"It sounds right to me."

"It didn't to me. Why couldn't we just be *normal*, live like everybody else? I was doing everything I could to be like everybody else, going to football games, working on the yearbook committee and the school newspaper, meeting friends for pizza, and he's studying the pathology of serial killers, thrill killers, spree killers. Victimology and forensic countermeasures."

"It sounds like you've read some yourself."

"Some because he was determined to make it his life's work, but . . . He's gone back to West Virginia. He's gone to see our father in prison. More than once."

"That bothers you."

"It did. Maybe it still does, a little, but I had to accept he wasn't going to put it behind him."

Better than therapy, she realized. Better this talking to a . . . *friend* wasn't quite right, and yet he was. He was her friend. It soothed rather than stirred to say what was in her mind and heart to someone who stood as her friend.

"Mason? He confronts it, and tries to understand it, so he can stop the next. I know that, and can still wish he'd found another way to save lives. Become a doctor—another kind of doctor."

"Has he saved lives?"

"He has. Did you hear about that man who was taking young boys— in Virginia? He'd taken five over a three-year period, killed two of them and dumped their bodies in a wooded area along a hiking trail."

"They called him the Appalachian Killer."

"Mason hates it when the press gives them names. But yes. He was part of the team that identified him, tracked him, stopped him, and saved the lives of the three boys he had locked in his basement. He saves lives, and to do it, he needs to understand the kind of mind that would take young boys, torture them, keep them caged up like animals, then kill them."

When Xander pulled up at the house, she got out. "I'm proud of him, so I have to accept that he lives a lot of his life in a dark place."

"Or he lives a lot of his life tearing down those dark places."

She'd reached for a market bag, stopped. "He does, doesn't he? And I should learn to turn it that way."

When they carried the groceries inside and to the kitchen, she got out a bottle of wine.

"I'm about to start some major cooking. Cleaning can work, but I lean toward cooking when I'm upset or stressed."

"Lucky me. I was going to head out when your brother got here, give you guys some catch-up time. But you bought pork chops."

"You bought them," she corrected. "And everything else in these bags."

"You have to contribute. I like pork chops."

"Do you like stuffed pork chops, Mediterranean-style?"

"Probably."

"Good, because that's what we're having, along with roasted herbed potatoes, sautéed asparagus, pretzel bread, and vanilla bean crème brûlée."

He wasn't sure he realized crème brûlée existed outside restaurants. "I'm definitely staying for dinner."

"Then I suggest you clear out."

"Give me a job."

"A kitchen job?"

"Definitely not a kitchen job."

He needed to work off the worry, too, she thought.

"Cecil's holding a table and four chairs—so far—for me. I was going to have Kevin pick them up, take them to Jenny, but if you brought them here, just cleaned them up, we'd have an actual table to eat this magnificent meal on. And don't say you don't want to leave me here alone," she added before he could. "I have the dog, I have an alarm system, and an excellent set of Japanese kitchen knives."

"You'll keep the doors locked until I get back—or Mason does."

"It pains me as it's a gorgeous day and I'd like the doors open, but for a dining room table, I'll keep them locked."

"Keep your phone on you."

"I'll keep my phone on me. Do you know how to lower the backseats in my car for the cargo area?"

"I'm a mechanic, Naomi. I think I can handle it. Let Cecil know I'm coming. It'll save time."

He hauled her in for a kiss, then pointed a finger at the dog. "You're on duty."

Naomi made the call, shoved the phone in her back pocket, then rubbed her hands together.

"Let's get cooking."

With the dog occupied with a rawhide bone, she focused in. It cleared her mind, pushed the terrible thoughts and worries away. The process, the textures, the scents and colors.

She had dough rising, potatoes in the oven, and the crème brûlée nearly ready to go into oven two when the dog scrambled up.

Maybe her heart tripped at first, maybe she glanced at the chef's knife on her cutting board, but she ordered herself to keep to the task at hand.

And was rewarded when she saw Xander haul chairs onto the back deck.

Swiping her hands on the dish towel tucked into her waistband, she walked over to at least open the doors.

"He swore—I almost made him take a blood oath—these were the chairs you wanted."

"That's right."

Xander looked at them—scowled at them. The faded, ripped, ugly patterned seats, the scuffed wood. "Why?"

"They're going to be adorable."

"How?"

"Reupholstered with this fabric I've picked out, painted. The ladderbacks a slatey blue, the armchairs a sagey green."

"You're going to paint them?"

"Jenny is. I've retired. They can be ugly until she takes them. I've got rags and wood cleaner. We can make them presentable for one meal."

"They look like presentable kindling to me, but it's your deal."

"What about the table?"

"I get the table—needs a little work, but it's a good piece."

"I meant do you need help getting it out of the car?"

"Eventually." Clearly unconvinced, he gave the chairs a final frown. "I'll be back in a minute."

"I'll get what you need."

She got the supplies out of the laundry room, filled a bucket with water, carted it out in time to see him coming back up the steps behind a forest of lilacs in a tall cobalt blue pitcher.

"There." He set them on the table on the deck. "I brought you flowers and something to put them in."

Staggered, she stared at them, at him. "I . . ."

"I stole the flowers, but I bought the pitcher."

"It's—they're . . . They're perfect. Thank you."

He stood there, scruffy, scowling at the chairs he obviously considered a waste of time and money—and she had to swallow, twice.

"This better be some dinner." After taking one of the rags from her, he dropped it in the bucket. "Are you okay?"

"Yes. Absolutely. I've just got things going inside."

"Go on, deal with that. I'll clean up these butt-ugly chairs."

She went inside, grabbed the wine on the way and took it with her straight to the powder room—the one that still needed lights, new fixtures, and a towel bar.

Her heart was tripping again. In fact it was tripping, stumbling, staggering all at the same time. Not a sensation she'd ever experienced before. Not a panic attack—not exactly, though she definitely felt considerable panic.

He'd walked up the steps with lilacs in a blue pitcher, set them down unceremoniously. Stolen flowers in an old pitcher, carried in big, callused hands.

And she'd fallen in love.

It couldn't be that fast. It couldn't be that simple. It couldn't *be*.

But it was. She didn't have to have felt it all before to know what tripped and stumbled inside her.

She breathed in, breathed out, took a good glug of wine.

What happened next?

Nothing had to happen next, she assured herself. Everything just continued, it just kept going until . . . something. But right now, nothing happened.

She had pork chops to stuff.

She heard him laughing, talking to the dog out on the deck. She saw the lilacs—so lush, so sweet. And had to press the heel of her hand to her heart, order it to behave.

But she pulled out her phone, angled herself, and took several shots of the flowers.

By the time she began making the stuffing, she heard Mason's voice and, glancing up, saw him step onto the deck from the stairs.

Xander moved into the opening. "We'll get the table. The chairs are clean, but they're still ugly."

"Their charm is simply yet to be released."

"Whatever. I'm going to want that food once we get the table up. It smells good."

"Food's an hour off."

"That'll do."

While she finished the stuffing, they hauled up the farmhouse table. Mason stepped in.

"Are those . . . stuffed pork chops!"

"I know how to soften you up."

He kissed her cheeks. "Thanks. Why did you buy such crappy chairs?"

"They won't be crappy when they're fixed."

"If you say so. I like the table. Is that barn wood?"

"It is."

"Built to last."

She finished stuffing the chops, slid them into the oven, and stepped out on the deck. "Oh, look how the cleaner brings out the grain. It just needed some tending."

"It's got some dings and scratches," Xander told her.

"It's called character. And Jenny said she could fix anything that needed fixing. I don't want to spoil anything, Mason, but I thought if we could talk about what you did, found out, think since meeting with Chief Winston, we wouldn't have it hanging over us at dinner."

He gave her a long look, then nodded. "I can't tell you much you don't already know. All indications are Donna Lanier was abducted from the parking lot shortly before midnight on Friday. Her car was locked, hasn't been moved since she parked it when she came on shift at four. Three other employees worked until closing. One, Maxie Upton, came out the back of the building alone a few minutes before Donna, Gina Barrows, and Brennan Forrester. Routinely Maxie parks in that same section of the lot, as most employees do, but her car was in the shop. Yours," he said to Xander.

"Yeah, she drove in on a flat just after I closed, and had four tires as bald as my uncle Jim. I wasn't going to let her drive around on them, made her a deal. I'd work the price of the tires down, take her to work—and she'd call her father to pick her up. She was going to walk, and after what happened to Marla, I wasn't having her walking home or to a friend's alone at midnight."

"She's lucky you provide such personal customer service."

"I've known her since she was . . ." Xander straightened from his slouch against the rail. "Are you saying he was looking to take her? Was waiting for Maxie to walk to her car?"

"It's possible. I lean toward probable. She's younger, blonde, more like the first victim physically than Donna. I talked to her when Chief Winston did a follow-up. Her father wasn't waiting when she came out, and she was alone out there for about twenty seconds—and now says she got nervous, thought about going back in. She thought it was because you'd spooked her about not walking, not being alone. Then her father came, and she didn't think any more about it."

"You said Donna came out with Gina and Brennan."

"Just after Maxie's father picked her up. And they walked off together—they're in a relationship—leaving Donna locking up."

"He took Donna because she was there?" Naomi asked.

"There's a reason we don't consider a serial until there are three like crimes."

"Mason."

"But I believe the same person took Donna. I believe he's an opportunist—he saw an opportunity with Marla Roth, took it. He saw one with Donna, took it. At the same time he was in that lot or close by, he was most certainly lying in wait, which tells me he'd observed the routine of that restaurant, and I believe he'd probably selected his target. Circumstances caused him to miss that opportunity. He took the next."

"Christ." Xander turned away, stared hard out over the water.

"There's a young woman, and her parents, who are never going to forget a set of bald tires or the man who demanded a promise. Chief Winston has already looked into like crimes, but I'm going to look again, narrowing the parameters, and adding in missings. He has deputies, and rangers, checking rental houses and cabins within a twenty-five-mile radius."

"Because he needs a place," Naomi stated.

Like a cellar, an old root cellar deep in the woods.

"Yeah. I'm not discounting a local, but I respect Winston's firm opinion that this is an outsider—and the low crime rate helps support it. Still, he'll take a harder look at individuals in the area."

"No one believes it's someone they know, someone they're close to," Naomi said. "Until it is."

"He's a good cop. Smart, thorough, and not so territorial he won't take help from outside. He's doing all he can do. For now, I can help him do more. I reached out to one of our geeks, and he's getting names on the rentals—owners, tenants. We'll run those in addition to the knock-on-doors. I'm sorry. I wish there were more."

"You came." Naomi went to him, put her arms around him, her head on his shoulder. "That's more. You'll stay a few days?"

"Tonight, at least. Maybe tomorrow. I want to get out of this suit. I've got a bag in the car, if you tell me where I'm bunking."

"It's not much more than bunking now. A real bed next visit, I swear. Let's get your bag, and I'll show you." She glanced at Xander. "I'll be right back, help you get the table inside."

Alone, Xander looked out at the water, into oncoming evening. Her brother agreed to stay the night, he thought, because he expected to find a body in the morning.

After the meal, and the fancy coffee Naomi made in her fancy machine, Xander rose. "I'm going to go on."

"Oh."

"You've got stuff. I've got stuff." And with an FBI agent sleeping down the hall, she'd be safe. "I'll see you tomorrow."

"Okay, but—"

He just pulled her to her feet, and into a hard, hot kiss. Maybe it was a little like marking his territory, with her brother right there, but he wasn't sorry about it.

"Thanks for dinner. Later," he said to Mason, and walked out.

"He didn't have to leave on my account," Mason began. "My sharp deduction skills ascertained he's sleeping here."

"He wanted to give us time alone, and he wants to go be with Loo. His business partner. She and Donna are close friends." Automatically, she began clearing dishes.

"Sit down a minute. Just for a minute," Mason said, taking her hand. "I've got to ask. How serious is it with you and the mechanic?"

"You say that like he doesn't have a name."

"I'm working on it. Give me some room. My vagabond hermit of a sister suddenly has a big house in the middle of rehab, has a dog, and is sleeping with a guy I just met. It's a lot in a short time."

"It doesn't feel as short when you're in it. I'm not going to get all"—she circled her index fingers in the air—"and say I recognized the house. But

I recognized the potential of it, and its potential for me. I didn't know I was ready to plant until I saw it, then I was ready. The dog wasn't going to happen, and then he did. Now I can't imagine not having him around."

"He's a great dog."

Even more, she thought, he'd become her family. "I'd have taken him to the shelter if Xander hadn't blocked me, every time."

"Why didn't he take the dog?"

"He just lost his."

"Ah." Mason nodded, understanding completely. "You haven't answered the actual question. We call that deflection."

"I'm not deflecting, I'm working up to it. It's more serious than I planned. More serious than I thought I'd want, and more serious than I'm sure I can handle. But he's . . ."

She wasn't sure she could explain it, to him or to herself.

"He makes me feel more than I thought I ever could or would. He figured out who I was. He had Simon Vance's book on his wall of books— you have to see that wall of books. I have pictures."

"Check out my shocked face," Mason said, and made her laugh.

"Anyway. Apparently I didn't hide my reaction to seeing Vance's book as well as I thought, and Xander figured it out. But, Mason, he didn't say anything to me, or change toward me. He didn't tell anyone, even his closest friend. Do you know what that means to me?"

"Yeah." Now Mason covered her hand with his. "And it goes a long way for me deciding he has a name. I liked him, and I know that matters to you. And I'm going to be up-front because you matter and tell you I ran him."

"Oh, for God's sake."

"You're my sister, you're my family. And we share something most don't, most can't understand, and shouldn't. I had to do it, Naomi. A couple of bumps in his late teens, early twenties, if you care."

"Which I don't."

He rolled over that. "Disturbing the peace, destruction of property— bar fight that reads like he didn't start it, but sure as hell finished it. No time—plenty of speeding tickets up until he hit about twenty-five. And that's it. I'm going to add I feel better knowing he had a couple of bumps, got them out of his system. I like knowing he can finish a fight. No marriages or divorces, no children on record. He's sole owner of the garage, half owner of the bar, and half owner of the building that holds the bar and an apartment. Winston thinks highly of him."

"Are you done now?"

"Yeah."

"Good. Now we're going to get these dishes done, FaceTime the uncles, then you get the grand tour."

"Okay. I've got one more thing, but I'm really done. Does he make you happy?"

"He does, and that was a shock to the system. And he makes me, or helps me, think beyond the moment. I'd gotten too much in the habit of only right now. I like thinking about tomorrow."

"Then I may start calling him Xander. But what kind of name is that anyway?"

"Really, Mason Jar?"

"Shut up," he said, and pushed away from the table to help her clear.

He waited until just after two in the morning to drive the quiet roads to the woods near the bluff. He parked on the shoulder.

Maybe they had patrols out at this hour, looking for the likes of him. But in his considerable experience it was far too early in the game for it, considering the two-bit town and half-ass police force.

And this wouldn't take long.

He had her wrapped in a standard sheet of plastic. Trial and error had proven this method worked best. He had to put some muscle into hauling her out and up over his shoulder—fireman's carry. He took some pride in being stronger than he looked, but she was a heftier package than he preferred.

All in all she'd been a disappointment. No fight or sass in her, not after the first couple hours anyway. It just cut into his fun when they didn't try to scream or beg, when they stopped fighting, and she'd gone downhill so fast he'd nearly killed her out of sheer boredom.

Too much like that scrawny old bitch he'd grabbed up in godforsaken Kansas when he couldn't get the one he'd had his eye on.

Or that fat-ass in Louisville. Or—

No point in dwelling on past mistakes, he assured himself as he shifted the dead weight on his shoulder and used the hunter's light on his hat to light the track.

He just had to stop repeating them, remember patience was a virtue.

He'd already scoped his ground, using Naomi's website pictures as a guide, and gratefully dropped Donna's body between the track and a nurse log. With practiced moves, he rolled it out of the plastic, studied it while he folded the sheet to take with him.

Waste not, want not.

He took out his phone, switched to camera mode, and took his last souvenir pictures of Donna Lanier.

Then he walked away without giving the woman he'd killed another thought. She was the past, and he had his path set for the future.

He cruised the road just far enough to bring the house on the bluff, its spreading silhouette against a starstruck sky, into view.

Sleep well, Naomi, he thought. *Rest up. I'll be seeing you soon, and we're going to have some fun.*

Twenty-four

A young couple from Spokane, with a baby in a backpack, found the body on a nature hike on Monday's sparkling afternoon.

Within minutes, Sam Winston stood over the body of a woman he'd known for three decades, and had liked every day of them.

Minutes later, Mason made his way through the woods to join him.

"I had to hope it wouldn't end this way."

"I'm sorry, very sorry, for your loss, Chief."

"She's everyone's loss. Well." Determined to do his best for her, Sam rubbed his hands over his face, shook it off. "Bound and gagged, naked, like Marla. Wounds are worse—he cut and beat her more severely."

"He may be escalating. Or . . . it may be frustration that she wasn't his first choice."

"He brushed out any footprints—you can see how he stirred up the dirt, the layer of pine needles. So he's careful. He had to carry her to this spot, most likely from the road—down the track. She's easily one-fifty, so he's got some muscle."

Careful to touch nothing, disturb nothing, Mason crouched down, studied the wounds, the position of the body.

"She's not posed, no attempt to cover or bury her. No remorse, nothing symbolic. He was simply finished, and dumped the body here, walked away."

"She didn't mean anything to him."

"No. The first victim, she was laid out differently—the way her arms reached out. And he left her shoes. She was more important—maybe a surrogate. Younger, blonde, attractive, slim."

"Like Maxie would've been."

"Yes. We're not that far from my sister's house. Is this trail popular?"

"It gets some use, yeah. A little farther west, toward the park, into the park, you get more hikers, but this area gets visitors pretty regularly. He wanted her found, and directly."

"I agree. Do you mind if I take some pictures?"

"Go ahead. We'll be taking our own—I wanted a minute with her first."

And, Sam could admit to himself, had to resist the gnawing urge to cover her. Once again, he shook it off.

"My deputy back on the road, you probably saw him, is getting the statements from the couple who found her. They've got a three-month-old baby with them. Their first vacation as a family." Sam sighed out air. "They won't forget it."

He looked into the woods, into the green deepening as spring slid toward summer. "We'll get this taped off, do what we do, and do what we can. And once we do that here, I'll go see her sister, her daughter."

"Do you want me to go with you for the notifications?"

"I appreciate the offer, but they know me. It'll be a little easier, as much as it can be, from somebody they know."

Naomi understood a process came with death, and with murder that process became official. But she wouldn't let Xander hear about his friend through a process.

She didn't see him through the main opening of the garage, so she walked inside the noise, saw one of his crew plugging coins in the soda machine.

"Is Xander around?"

"Yeah, sure. Back in the machine shop—straight back, to the right. Can't miss."

"Thanks."

She picked her way through, found she couldn't miss.

He sat on a stool behind an engine on a stand, a wrench in his grease-smeared hands.

"Bearings shot to shit, crankshaft shot to shit."

He took off another part, scowled at it, tossed it into a plastic tray with a dismissing thump. "Wonders why it's got rod knock."

"Xander."

She spoke quietly, but he heard her voice over the clanging, the thumping, the music. And the instant he saw her face, grief clouded his eyes.

"Ah, hell."

"I'm sorry, I'm so sorry."

She started toward him, hands out, but he shoved back on the stool and held his own up. "Don't. I've got grease all over me."

"It doesn't matter."

"It does." With sharp, angry moves, he snatched up a rag, rubbed it over his forearms, his hands. Tossed it down again, walked to a small, wall-hung sink that had seen its share of action.

With his back to her, he poured some sort of powder on his hands, dry-scrubbed them with a brush. "Where did they find her?"

"I'm not sure, I'm sorry. I just know the chief called Mason about a half hour ago and said they had. In a wooded area, was all he'd say. He was in a hurry to get there. I didn't want you to hear—just hear."

He nodded, kept scrubbing. "I knew it last night. If they hadn't found her by last night . . . but until they do, you have to figure there's a chance."

He worked the powder up to his forearms, then turned on the water. "I need to tell Loo."

Not the process, not procedure. And the hell with that. "Do you want me to go with you?"

"Not this time."

He yanked paper towels out of a wall unit, dried off, tossed them in a big, widemouthed trash can.

"They have to notify her next of kin. I don't know how long before they can."

"Loo won't want to talk to anybody. She won't get in the way of that."

"I'm so sorry, Xander. I wish there were something I could do."

"You did it. You came to tell me."

When she stepped toward him again, he looked at his hands.

"They're clean enough," she said, and moved into him.

"I guess they'll do." He got a grip on her, a tight one, held her in silence while the workday banged around them.

"Stay with Loo as long as you need, as long as she needs. But would you let me know if you're staying in town?"

"I'll be coming out, but I don't know when. If Kevin and the crew leave before I get there, before your brother gets back, stay home." He drew her away. "Stay inside, and lock everything. Tell me you'll do that."

"I will. Don't worry about me, just take care of Loo."

"I'll do that. I have to deal with some things here, get some coverage, then I'll do that."

When she got home she closed herself in her temporary office so she didn't have to talk to Kevin or any of the crew, so they couldn't sense what she knew.

Time dragged while she tried to lose herself in work. Feeling closed in, restless, she gave it up and took the dog out in the narrow backyard, thrilled him with a session of fetch the ball.

She saw Kevin start down the deck steps, and the expression on his face told her the news had gotten out.

"Xander called me. Ah, he said he'd be here within the hour, and look, Naomi, I'm staying until he gets here, or your brother does. I'll sit out in the damn truck if you—"

She went with instinct, stepped up to hug him.

"What the hell's happening? Jenny's got a couple of neighbors and their kids over at the house so I don't have to worry about her being alone.

We've never had to worry. Donna—God, Donna, of all people. I can't get ahold of it."

"I know. I know."

"He said Loo's pretty steady now, and she's going over to Donna's house. Her—Donna's—sister and daughter, and the family, I guess, are there. He had to make her swear she'd get the sister's husband to take her home, make sure she's inside and locked up. We never had to think about doing that. It's always been safe here. My kids can go all over the neighborhood and you never worry."

"I'll go inside." She stepped back. "I'll go inside, lock the doors. You need to go home, you need to be with your family."

His face went hard. "I'm staying. Until Xander gets here, I'm staying. Jenny's with a dozen people."

"Then let's go up, sit down."

"He said it was like Marla." Now that hardness faded into grief. "Word's going around." With the dog between them, they started back to the house. "On a Friday night, too, the same as Marla. He dumped her over there."

"Over . . ." She shuddered when he gestured toward the forest she thought of as her own.

"Just west of the bluff. You can't go walking there on your own anymore, Naomi." A friend, a brother, he grabbed her hand. "You can't do that. Not until they find him."

"I won't, don't worry. Sit down."

In her forest, she thought. At the foot of her bluff, and in her forest.

Because it was remote, she told herself. Because he could slip through the dark with no one to see. That was all it was, and what it was, was bad enough.

She sat in the chair beside him.

"Your studio's nearly finished," he told her, and threw her off balance. "After tomorrow, day after latest, you can set it up."

They'd talk of something else, she realized, of anything else but the unthinkable.

"Can't wait."

"We'll get the desk, the equipment in there for you. A couple more weeks, we're going to be out of here. Well, three. We should be out in three."

"You've brought the house back to life, Kevin."

"We have," he said just before the dog leaped up and raced off the deck.

"Xander," Naomi told him. "He just knows—the way the bike sounds, I guess. He doesn't bark anymore when it's Xander."

"He's nuts about you, you know—Xander. So's the dog, but I'm talking about Xander, who'd kick my ass for saying it, but I need something good to balance things out. I've never seen him nuts about anybody."

"Nobody?"

Shaking his head, Kevin smiled a little. "You're the first."

She got up and went to meet Xander as he came up the steps with the dog. "Thanks."

"How's Loo?" she asked.

"She took it hard. Really hard." Looking exhausted, he blew out a breath. "But she pulled it together, talked to Donna's daughter. She's over there now. Did you hear from your brother?"

"No, and I've had to stop myself from texting him a dozen times. He'll tell us what he can when he can."

"Would you let me know if there's anything?" Kevin pushed to his feet. "It feels like if you just knew *something* it would start to make sense. I'm going to go on, get home. Keep this one close, Xan."

"I intend to. Same for Jenny."

He sat when Kevin left. "Her daughter—you don't know her—she's inconsolable. I wasn't doing any good over there, so I got out of the way. She and Loo are better off huddling up together."

"Kevin said she was found in the forest—over there."

Eyes hard, Xander nodded. "Somewhere in that area—and too damn close to here. Like Marla."

"Likely for the same reason. It's out of town, hardly any houses, hardly any traffic on the road, or the water depending on how he comes in."

"That's probably what it is, all it is. But if what Mason said has weight, and if Maxie was the actual target, he has a type. Right? Young, blonde, attractive, slender. You're all of that."

"And I can promise you I know better than any young blonde woman in this town how to take care of myself. I can promise you, Xander, not to take unnecessary chances, and to take sensible precautions. I'll also point out that both women he killed lived or worked in town. I think he must stalk them, or at least watch their routines. I don't have a routine—and you have enough on your mind without worrying about me."

"Nothing that's on my mind is more important than you."

He turned to her, took her breath away with one long, steady stare.

And once again, the dog raced off the deck, this time leading with a bark.

"It's probably Mason." She laid a hand on Xander's tensed arm. "This son of a bitch comes at women in the dark, and I'll bet from behind like a coward. He doesn't walk up to them in the daylight."

"You're right. I'm edgy."

He relaxed a little when Mason rounded the house with Tag.

"I have to make a couple calls. I'll be down when I'm done and tell you what I can. Xander, I'm sorry about your friend."

"Yeah, we all are."

"I'm going to see what I have to throw together for dinner," she told Xander.

"I can call in for pizza or whatever. You don't have to cook."

"I'm edgy, too. Cooking helps."

"Have you thought about getting a grill? I can grill—you know, steaks, chops, even fish." He shrugged when she stopped at the opening. "Give you a hand with meals sometime."

"As a matter of fact, I've been looking at grills online."

"You can't buy a grill online." Sincerely appalled, he stared at her—with some pity. "You have to see it, and—"

"Stroke it?" She offered a bright smile. "Speak to it?"

Appalled pity turned on a dime to a cool disdain that made her want to laugh. "You have to see it," he repeated.

She made a humming sound, then went in to check her supplies and formulate a menu.

Moments later, he came in, grabbed a beer, sat at the counter. "I'm buying the grill."

"What?"

"I said I'm buying the grill."

Sauté some chicken breasts, she thought. Garlic, herbs, wine. Distracted, she turned to him. "The grill? Seriously, Xander."

"Grills are serious."

Now she did laugh. "I'd be the last one to say any cooking appliance or tool isn't serious, which is why I've been researching and eliminating and considering online."

"Have you ever bought a grill before?"

"No, but—"

"I'll take care of it."

It occurred to her he was thinking, and feeling, something other than grief. So she stretched it out. "You don't know the features I want, the brand, the size. We're having chicken, rice, mixed vegetables," she decided.

"You don't buy a grill online any more than you buy a car online."

Because she felt better herself, she took another poke. "Have you ever bought a grill?"

"Kevin has, twice, and I was with him both times. It's the same thing."

She began to assemble her ingredients. "Well, there's plenty of time to decide before summer."

"There's your first wrong turn—well, second since the whole online deal. You get the right grill, you use it year-round, especially when you can put it right outside the kitchen like you can here."

She got a pot for the rice, put it on the stove, then came to the counter so she could face him while she minced garlic. "I had no idea you were so serious about outdoor grills. The things you learn."

"I'm buying the grill."

They'd see about that.

"Do you know how to peel carrots?"

Frowning, he took a slow sip of beer. "Probably."

She pulled carrots out of the fridge, got a peeler, pushed them to his side of the counter. "Good, peel these."

"I thought you scraped them off with a knife."

It was her turn for pity. "Sure, if you want to take all day and make a mess out of it. You just . . ." She picked up a carrot and peeler and demonstrated.

"Okay, okay. I've got it."

Mason came back in to see Xander with a small pile of carrot peels, scowling at the carrot he worked on stripping. And his sister at the stove sautéing garlic.

Pretty homey, he thought. Maybe Xander looked out of his milieu, but altogether, pretty homey.

"Mason, do you remember how to floret a cauliflower?"

"Um—"

"Sure you do."

She handed him a knife, set the head on a cutting board.

"I don't even like cauliflower." But he sat, comfortable now in an old Harvard Crimson T-shirt and jeans, and picked up the knife.

"You do when it's disguised with butter and herbs. It's nice," she said, "having line cooks."

"It's like home." Mason cut away the thick stem, sliced through the core from the bottom, pulled the head into two halves. "Back in New York, only you're head chef instead of Harry."

"When they get here, I'll abdicate, but only after he lets me show off. That gives me a couple of weeks to devise a show-off menu, outfit guest rooms, and hope Jenny can redo those dining room chairs." She added chicken to the pan with a satisfying sizzle.

"I'm going to try to be here. I should be able to work out of the Seattle office temporarily."

After a long beat of silence, Mason set the knife aside, picked up his wine. "Okay. I'm going to lay this out for you—as much as I can. While the ME will determine, it's clear from the on-scene examination and the evidence gathered that Donna Lanier was abducted and killed by the same unsub as Marla Roth.

You don't need the details," he added, and went back to the knife. "It's my strong belief, shared by Chief Winston, that Lanier wasn't his first choice. She was simply there. As with the first victim, she was held and killed at another location, then transported and dumped where she would be found quickly. He wants us to know he's here, he's hunting. He's arrogant, enjoys both the attention and the fear he's generating. He's intelligent, organized, experienced."

"You mean he's done this before," Naomi replied. "That's what you mean by experienced."

"Yeah. It's unlikely a coincidence he took both victims on a Friday night, held them until Sunday. We can speculate he has his weekends free or has the privacy he needs during that time period."

"You still think he lives here." Xander finished the last carrot, waited for a reply.

"I can't eliminate someone who lives in town, works in town, or works or lives in the area."

"Why?" Xander demanded. "We haven't had any rapes or murders, nothing like this around here before."

"He may not have brought it home before. He may have taken a hitch-hiker, a hiker, someone passing through, and buried or concealed the body. He may recently have acquired, through purchase, inheritance, divorce, a place he can use to do his work. So far, most of the rentals have been checked and eliminated. We're also checking on seasonal workers, tenants, new residents, vacationers who've been in the area since the first victim was abducted. I'll continue to research and analyze like crimes. If I find a pattern, if I find more, we'll have the full resources of the FBI on this.

"I've asked a contact I have at the BAU to look over the files, to check my profile, to see if I'm on the right track or if I've gone wrong. But whether or not the unsub lives and works here or happened upon this location, he's still here. It's gone too well for him to move on."

"Naomi fits his type."

"Xander." Annoyed, she turned the chicken.

"Yes, she does. I believe he has a type, and Naomi fits it. I trust her to take all reasonable precautions."

"I said I would."

"I love you, Naomi."

She sighed, hugely. "I love you, too, Mason."

"So even though I know you're smart, you're careful, and you can kick ass, I'm going to worry about you."

"I worry about you, Special Agent Carson. Especially since I know you can't always take what civilians consider reasonable precautions."

"You could spend a couple weeks in Seattle," Xander suggested. "Hang with your brother there, do some shopping or whatever, do some work. It'd give them a chance to do the floors in this place."

"First, Kevin and I have a schedule and the floors are dead last. Second and all the other numbers after that, I'm not leaving here to run off to Seattle so my baby brother can look out for me."

"You've got two years on me," Mason objected. "That doesn't make me baby brother. She won't do it," he added to Xander. "I walked through the conversation about it with her in my head, and always hit the same wall. But this might make you feel better about it. Did you tell him about the mugger, Naomi?"

"I haven't thought about that in years." She picked up the wine, dumped some into the skillet, then trapped the steam with a lid and lowered the heat.

"What mugger?"

"In New York. Naomi was home on summer break from college, working at the restaurant. Decided to walk home one night."

"It was a nice night," she added.

"The mugger thought so, too. Anyway, this guy comes up on her— with a knife—wants her money and her watch, her earrings, her phone."

"I would have given it all to him, just like the uncles had impressed on both of us a million times."

"Maybe you would have." Mason shrugged. "But the asshole figured he had a defenseless woman, a scared one. And a pretty one. So he copped a feel."

"And he *smirked*," Naomi stated, and, remembering it all now, sneered.

"She bruised his balls, broke his nose, and dislocated his shoulder, called nine-one-one. He was still on the ground moaning when the cops got there."

"He shouldn't have grabbed my breast. He shouldn't have touched me."

"You broke his nose." Purely fascinated by her, Xander studied those slim, almost elegant hands. "You like breaking noses."

"The nose is a quick and reliable target—offense and defense. I like yours." She gathered up the carrots, the cauliflower, the broccoli she'd prepped herself, in a big strainer, and took them to the sink to wash. "So don't piss me off."

"Just let me know if you're not in the mood for me to cop a feel."

She laughed, then brought the carrots back to slice for steaming. "You'll be the first. Excellent florets and carrot peeling. You're both dismissed from duty if you want to take the dog out or whatever. You've got about thirty."

"Did you come over on your bike?" Mason asked Xander.

"Yeah."

"I wouldn't mind taking a look at it."

"Sure." Xander led the way out the back and around. "Just so you know, the landscape crew starts tomorrow. Early."

"Define early."

"By seven. Maybe a little before."

"As early as or earlier than the bang-and-clang crew inside. Oh well. I wanted to say I feel comfortable working out of Seattle, coming over a couple times a week, because you're going to keep an eye on her. And I didn't want to say that where she could hear me."

"I got that. I feel more comfortable knowing she can dislocate some asshole's shoulder. And still."

"Still. I don't know a goddamn thing about motorcycles." Head angled, Mason studied it. "Except it looks impressive."

"Okay."

"Both women were taken in town, so I have to consider that, for now, as his hunting ground. But Naomi's his type, and she shops and banks and has business in town. She's the sort he looks for."

"I got that, too. I'm going to be here every night. We play this Friday at Loo's. I'll make sure she comes, and make sure Kevin and Jenny stick with her until we close."

"If I can be here, I will be. She'll be careful, but I believe this guy works fast, takes his target quickly."

As he spoke, Mason studied the house as if looking for security breaches.

"No defensive wounds on either victim. They didn't have a chance to fight back. Anybody can be taken by surprise, even if they're careful, even if they've studied martial arts and self-defense, so she's going to have to deal with not having as much time alone as she likes for a while."

"She's doing all right with people around."

"Better than she imagined she would, I'll bet. She doesn't know you're in love with her."

Saying nothing, Xander held Mason's steady gaze.

"I'm going there because she's the most important person in my world. We lived through a nightmare you never come all the way out of, because he's sitting in a cell in West Virginia. Our mother wasn't strong enough to keep living on the edge of that nightmare. Naomi found her—came home to pick something up on lunch break from school, and found her, already cold."

"I know—at least some of it. I looked up what I could after I figured out about Bowes. And I found the piece she wrote back then, for the *New York Times*. I didn't want to hit a sore spot by accident, so I read what I could find. I'm sorry about your mother, man."

"It put another hole in Naomi. Me? Sure, I lived with it and through it, but I'm not the one who saw firsthand what our father had done. I'm not the one who helped pull a victim out of a hole in the ground and half carry her through the woods. I'm not the one who came home from school and found our mother dead by her own hand. Naomi has no degree of separation. And she might deny it—would," he corrected, "but there's a part of her that doesn't see herself worthy of being loved."

"She'd be wrong about that."

"Yeah, she'd be wrong. We had counseling, we had the uncles, but no one else has those images of what our parents did, to themselves, to others, to us, in their head the way she does. So there's a part of her that doesn't think she's capable of loving outside of me and the uncles, or worthy of being loved."

"Well." Xander jerked a shoulder. "She'll have to get used to it."

The simplicity, the carelessness of the remark, made Mason smile. "You're good for her. That irritated me a little when I first came into it, saw that. I'm pretty much over that now."

"Did you run my background?"

"Oh yeah, right off."

"I'd have thought less of you if you hadn't. I'm never going to hurt her. That's bullshit," Xander said immediately. "Why do people say that? Of course I'll end up hurting her. Everybody does or says something stupid or petty or acts like an asshole sometime and ends up hurting somebody else. What I mean is—"

"I know what you mean, and I believe you. So, are we good?"

"Yeah, we're good."

Mason held out a hand; they shook.

Then he studied the bike again. "How about you let me drive it?"

Considering, Xander rocked back on his heels. "Have you ever been on a bike before—at the controls?"

"No. But I'm an FBI agent, I should know how to drive a bike. Right? What if, in the pursuit of a criminal, I had to hop on a motorcycle, and due to lack of knowledge and experience, said criminal escaped justice? None of us would feel good about that."

Amused, Xander unclipped the helmet. "Okay."

"Really? Are you serious?" And beaming like a boy on Christmas morning, Mason took the helmet.

"Sure. You wreck it, you pay for repairs. You end up needing the ER, dinner's going to get cold. I can go with that."

"I don't have a motorcycle license."

"You're FBI."

"Damn fucking straight." Delighted, Mason swung a leg over, settled. "Now what the hell do I do?"

Before long, drawn by the revving engine and Mason's war whoops, Naomi came out the front door.

"Is that— Is Mason on your bike?"

"Yeah." Xander sat on the steps with the dog.

"When did he learn to drive a motorcycle?"

"Pretty much now."

"Oh, dear God. Get him off before he hurts himself."

"He's fine, Mom."

She huffed. "Well, get him off because dinner's ready."

"Done."

He got up as she went back in, and decided it was best all around that Mason waited until her back was turned to pop a wheelie.

Her brother was a quick study.

Twenty-five

Her house was full of people and noisy tools and machines. Now her front yard was full of people and noisy tools and machines.

She couldn't defy her brother, Xander, and her own common sense and take off to the forest or down to the shoreline for quiet. For a couple of hours she made the best of it by taking pictures of what was essentially demo—just like the interior—while Lelo uprooted old woody shrubs and ugly tree stumps she'd simply stopped seeing with a massive chain attached to a massive tractor.

The sounds of a wood chipper, of chain saws, of trucks, joined the sounds of nail guns and saws.

Tag loved every minute.

Eventually she escaped inside, popped in her earbuds, and drowned out most of it with music.

The tap on her shoulder had her nearly jumping out of her chair.

"Sorry," Mason apologized.

"God! I didn't know you were back."

"You couldn't hear a plane land on your deck with this noise—and with Lady Gaga blasting in your ears."

"Lady Gaga, and others, help me tolerate the rest." But she took out the earbuds and paused her playlist. "Did they—the autopsy?"

"Yeah. There's not much more I can tell you. She hadn't had any food, any water, since about eight, nine o'clock Friday night. That's consistent with Marla. The same type of blade was used on both. No prints, no DNA, no hairs but her own, that's also consistent. He's careful. Anyway, I'm going to work outside on the deck for a while, take advantage of the sun. I'm heading to Seattle tomorrow, and surprise, they're calling for rain."

"I don't know how you can work outside with this noise."

"My great powers of concentration. These are nice." He nodded toward the photos on her screen. "These were taken in the forest just west of here?"

"Yes. I was just checking downloads and orders. And I think I'm going to do more notecards—nature shots. They tend to sell."

Wanting his company just a bit longer, she began to scroll. "This one, then no, no, yes. This one. Then . . . maybe this."

"Hold that. That's a—what do you call it?"

"Nurse log."

"Right, right, because it nurses other stuff. Moss and mushrooms and lichen."

"And the younger trees. I love how they grow out of it, the way—in this one—their roots wrap around the mother."

"Pretty cool." With a hand light on her shoulder, Mason leaned in a little more to study. "When did you take that?"

"Oh, this one's been up for a couple weeks. Got some nice hits, decent downloads. I figured I'd crop it a little more, and it would make a nice notecard, for a variety set of eight."

"Yeah, I can see that. I like it. Anyway, I'm going to get to work, let you get back to your own."

She'd barely started up before someone tapped her shoulder again. At least this time she didn't jump.

"Sorry." Kevin gave her shoulder another pat. "I wanted to ask if you're ready for us to move you into your studio space."

"It's really ready for that?"

"It's really ready, and we can start working in here again first thing tomorrow."

"Then I'm ready. Let me shut down, unplug and all that."

"We can start hauling out the supplies, the mat board deal, and the rest."

"I need those worktables I bought. Downstairs storage."

"Already brought them up, and everything you had marked for the studio."

"I need to let Jenny know I'm ready for the desk whenever she can get to it."

"Oh, she knows. I keep her up-to-date."

"I'd better get moving."

"Jeez, almost forgot." As if jogging his own memory, Kevin tapped the side of his head. "Lelo and his dad need you outside. We'll get things moving for you."

"All right." She shut down, unplugged.

Taking the back stairs, she hurried through the house, out the front.

There were questions about colors, heights, naturalizing, grass seeds. She had to switch gears from studio space to curb appeal. While she answered, debated, questioned, she reminded herself how glorious it would feel to head into summer the following year with it all done, with the quiet surrounding her like a gift from God.

Switching gears again, she went back in, up the stairs. Found it odd that the door to her studio space was closed, and the crew nowhere in sight.

She opened the door and froze.

The desk she'd first seen piled in Cecil's barn stood gleaming, facing out as she'd wanted, with the leather chair she'd bought and stored behind it. Her computer, her in and out boxes, her desk lamp sat on it, along with a little squat vase of wildflowers.

Her tools, equipment, supplies were all arranged just as she'd diagrammed—and the sliding barn door on her new storage closet stood open to show everything inside organized on shelves.

The walls, a warm cognac, made a rich backdrop for some of her framed prints.

Jenny stood, her hands clasped between her breasts, all but vibrating beside a grinning Kevin.

"Tell me you love it. Please, please love."

"Oh my God. I . . ."

"Say the words first. Say you love it."

"Of course, I love it. I'd be crazy not to love it. You finished the desk. You didn't tell me."

Now Jenny threw up her arms in a V. "Surprise!"

"It's—it's exactly what I wanted. It's more than I've ever had. I've never had a work space like this. It's always been on the go, or jury-rigged." More than dazed, she wandered. "Oh! The floors! The floors are done in here."

"That was a trick." Kevin's grin just widened. "Shows you how the original wood's going to come back just right. I thought, hey, let's get it done in here—takes longer, but you won't have to haul out again when we do the rest of the floors. It's done."

"Not done," Jenny corrected. "She needs a nice love seat over there, a table—a comfortable thinking spot. And an accent rug, pillows, a throw. And—you'll find what you want. But you love it."

Incredibly moved, Naomi brushed her fingers over the petals of the wildflowers. "I've never had anyone go to this much trouble for me, outside of family."

"We're family now."

Eyes welling, she looked over. "Jenny."

Jenny flew across the room, grabbed her up in a hug, swayed, bounced, wept a little. "I'm so happy. I'm so happy you're happy."

"Thank you so much. So much. You're the best."

"I am!"

Laughing now, Naomi drew back. "Both of you."

"We are! We were worried Lelo wouldn't be able to keep you outside long enough for us to finish, but he did."

"That's what that was all about."

"We're the best, the sneaky best. I have to go."

"I'm driving her back home."

"He's worried about me even being in the car by myself. Everybody's so worked up . . . but we're not going to think about that now." Blinking at tears, Jenny swiped a hand through the air, erased sad thoughts. "You're going to sit down in your new chair and bask."

"I absolutely am. Thank you. Both of you. All of you."

Alone, she did just as Jenny told her. Sat and basked. Then got up and looked at everything.

Then, forgetting the noise, she gave herself the pleasure of working in her own space.

With Tag apparently preferring Mason's company, and all of her tools and supplies exactly where she wanted them, Naomi lost track of time in the best possible way. The productivity and the pleasure of working in a settled, organized space told her she'd been making do far too long, sacrificing all this for the pick-up-and-go she'd felt necessary.

No one chased her, she thought, but her own ghosts and neuroses. Time to put it all away, time to believe instead of doubt that the past was over and done.

She had a home, and in it, she'd watch summer roll in, then feel the change in the air, then the light change as fall painted the world. She'd have fires lit when winter blew, and be there, just be there when spring bloomed again.

She had a home, she thought again as she added the last of the new stock to her page. She had friends, good friends. She had a man she . . . All right, maybe she wasn't entirely ready for what she felt for Xander, but she could be ready to see what happened tomorrow, or next week or—Maybe a week at a time was all she could be ready for in that department.

But it was a hell of an improvement.

Most of all, she was ready to be happy—all the way happy. To hold on to what she had, what she was building for herself.

Now it was time—past time, she realized as she noted the time on her computer—to go down and put a meal together.

She took the back stairs, reminding herself to hit her list and pick out the lighting for that area, and, singing the Katy Perry that had been in her earbuds when she'd shut down, she all but danced into the kitchen.

To find Mason at the counter, laptop open, maps spread out, coffee steaming, a couple of legal pads scattered among the work debris.

"Hey. I thought you were working outside in the sunshine."

"I needed more room."

"I see that. No problem. I have enough room here for the shrimp farfalle I have in mind."

"I asked Xander to pick up pizza. He's on his way."

"Oh." Already in the fridge, she paused, glanced back. "That's fine, if you're in a pizza mood, and saves me the trouble."

Closing the fridge, she switched modes, decided they could eat on the deck. "Where's the dog?"

"He wanted out. Everyone's gone for the day."

"So I see—or rather hear. I worked later than I'd planned. You *have* to see my studio space." The thrill of it bubbled through her. "It's finished, and it's awesome. I'm going ahead with that darkroom space—in the basement. I don't do film that often, and Kevin said the plumbing would be easy down there. So it would be really quiet, out of the way, and make use of some of that space."

She turned, found him watching her quietly. "And I'm babbling while you're working. Why don't I take this outside, let you finish up in peace?"

"Why don't you sit down? I need to talk to you about something."

"Sure. Is everything all right? Of course everything's not all right," she said, shut her eyes for a minute. "I've been so caught up in my own space, my own work, I forgot about Donna and Marla. Forgot about your work."

She sat at the counter with him. "It didn't seem real for a little while. Donna's funeral's the day after tomorrow, and Xander . . . It's the second funeral since I've been here, the second terrible funeral."

"I know. Naomi—"

He broke off as the dog raced in from the front, danced in place, raced back again.

"That would be Xander and pizza," Naomi said, started to rise.

"Just sit."

"You found something." She put a hand on his arm, squeezed. "Something about the murders."

She swiveled in the stool when Xander came in, tossed the pizza box on the counter by the cooktop.

"What do you know?"

"Let me start with this. Naomi, this is the picture you took in the forest just west of here. This nurse log."

She frowned at the image he brought up on his computer. "That's right. Why did you download it?"

"Because this is one I took yesterday, when Donna's body was discovered." Carefully cropped, he thought, as he toggled to it. "It's the same log."

"All right, yes."

"Donna's body was dumped just off the track, beside this log. It's an eight-minute trek into the woods—and that's without carrying a hundred and fifty pounds. It bothered me right off. Why take her in that far? You want her to be found, why take her so far in—put in that time, that effort? Why that spot?"

"I don't know, Mason. Wanting a little more time before she was found?"

"No point to it. But this place, right here." He tapped the screen. "It has a point. You've had that photo on your site a couple of weeks."

The chill skipped along her skin. "If you've got some wild idea he . . . this photo inspired him or factored into where he left her, it doesn't make sense. For one thing, I've got a dozen photos up I took in that area."

"He had to pick one." Face grim, Xander studied the images.

"It's just a weird coincidence," Naomi insisted. "Disturbing, but a coincidence. I barely knew either of the victims. I've only been in this area since March."

Saying nothing, Mason brought up another photo—one she'd taken of the bluff—then brought up another side by side. "Yours, and the crime scene shot. Up on your site, Naomi, for a couple months."

And that chill seeped in, dug into her bones.

"Why would anyone use my photos to choose where they left a body? It doesn't make sense. It doesn't."

"Stop it." Clamping a hand on her shoulder, Xander spoke sharply. "Stop it and breathe."

Annoyance at the tone shoved the weight off her chest. "It doesn't make any goddamn sense."

"And doing what he did to Marla and Donna does?"

"No, no, but that's—that's a pathology, right?" She appealed to Mason. "I know enough about what you do to understand that. But I don't understand how you could take these pictures and begin to think this killer is, what, a fan of my work?"

"It's more."

Xander had both hands on her shoulders now, and though they kneaded at the tensed muscles, she understood that another purpose was to keep her in place.

"What's more?"

Mason took her hand a moment, squeezed it, then brought up another image. "You took this shot in Death Valley in February. I had the locals send me the shots from the body dump."

He brought it up, heard her breath shudder out. "The victim was midtwenties, white, blonde, lived and worked in Vegas. High-risk vic—stripper, junkie, hooker. It didn't pop on Winston's like-crimes search because the locals charged her pimp—who'd been known to tune up his girls—with the crime.

"In January, you took this in Kansas—Melvern Lake. The body of a sixty-eight-year-old female was left here." Again, he brought up the matching shot. "She lived alone, and as her house had been broken into, things taken, they put it down to robbery gone south."

"But it was the same," Naomi said quietly. "What was done to her, the same."

"There's a pattern. You flew home for Christmas."

"Yes. I left my car at the airport. I didn't want to drive that far for the week I'd be home."

"A shot you took in Battery Park, and the corresponding crime scene photo. Another high-risk vic. Working girl, junkie, early midtwenties. Blonde."

"Donna wasn't blonde. And the older woman—"

"Donna wasn't his first choice. Neither was the older woman. It's a pattern, Naomi."

The cold, a jagged ball of ice, settled in her belly. "He's using my work."

"There are more."

"How many more?"

"Four more I can connect through the photos. Then there are the missings, missing from areas I've been able to track you to through the photos. I need the dates—the dates and locations for the last two years. You keep track."

"Yes. I don't blog about a place until I've left it—I'm careful. But I keep a log of where I was, what date I took what shots. On my computer."

"I need you to send them to me. If you've kept a log further back, I want that, too."

She focused on Xander's hands, hands warm and firm on her shoulders. "I have a log from when I left New York, from when I left six years ago. I have everything."

"I want everything. I'm sorry, Naomi."

"He didn't just stumble onto my site and decide to use my photos. He's following me, either literally or through my blog, or my photos. How far back have you gone?"

"Those two years so far."

"And you think it's longer."

"I'm going to find out."

"He's not following, he's stalking." When her shoulders only went stiffer under his hands, Xander turned her around on the stool. "You'll handle it because you have to. She'll handle it," he said to Mason without taking his eyes off Naomi. "He's been stalking you for at least two years. His preferred victim is blonde because you are. And they're all you. That's what your brother's not saying."

"It's a theory, and I need more information."

Xander flicked a glance at Mason, barely a heartbeat. "You're trying to ease her into it because you're worried she'll break. But that's not the way for you, is it, Naomi?" His gaze met hers, held her. "You're not going to break."

"I'm not going to break." But a part of her was trying desperately to shore up the cracks. "He . . . He takes them, and he keeps them at least for a couple of days so he can rape them, torture them, gratify himself. After he's beaten them and raped them, kept them in the dark, cut them, choked them, kept them bound and gagged, he strangles them."

She drew a shaky breath, then another, steadier before she turned to Mason. "Like our father. Too much like our father now, too much like it to say there are other cruel, sick men who do this. He's killing like Thomas Bowes, and following me, the way I followed our father that night."

"I believe he's studied Thomas Bowes—he may have written to him, visited him, and I'm pulling that line. I believe he's studied you. He's here, and for the first time that I can verify, he's killed twice in the same place."

"Because I'm in the same place."

"Yes. From what I'm putting together, he's evolved. His method, while not exactly the same as Bowes's, has mimicked it."

No coincidence, no excuses, she ordered herself. The facts stood clear and straight. She had to face them.

"Why hasn't he come after me? The others are what you call surrogates; why hasn't he come after me? There have to have been countless opportunities."

"Because then it's over," Xander said, shrugged. "Sorry," he said to Mason. "It's what makes sense."

"And I agree. I still have more to do, more to analyze, but I can tell you I've got enough to have convinced Chief Winston and the coordinator of the BAU to send a team here. This unsub is smart, organized, mission-oriented, and tenacious. But he's also arrogant—and that arrogance, using those particular sites for his dump spots, is going to break this open. We're going to stop him, Naomi. I need the data from you. It's key."

"I'll go up, email you the files." She slid off the stool, went up the back steps without another word.

"She's telling herself she can't have this." Mason lifted his hands to encompass the house, the life. "Not now. What Bowes is, what she tried to leave behind, came here with her."

"Yeah, she's telling herself that. She's wrong."

With a nod, Mason started to get up, sat back again. "You go. The torch passed while I wasn't around. And we both came from him. She needs somebody who doesn't carry that."

"I'll take care of it."

S he sat at her desk, her beautifully restored desk in her beautifully designed studio. A space that, less than an hour before, had made her so happy, so hopeful.

Had she really told herself, really *believed*, the past was done? Never done, she thought now. Never over. The ghosts never exorcised.

And once again a killer's life twined and twisted with hers.

When she heard footsteps, she opened her computer, began to bring up the files.

"It's going to take me a few minutes," she said, very, very calmly when Xander came in.

"I got that." He wandered, measuring the space, the look and feel of it. "Swank, but not fancy. That's a hard note to hit."

"You should go down. You and Mason should get to that pizza before it gets any colder."

"Nothing wrong with cold pizza."

"There's nothing for you to do here, Xander."

"That's where you're wrong. You need another chair in here. How else is somebody going to hang out and bug you when you're working? Why don't you spit out what's circling around in your gut. I can figure some of it anyway."

"You want me to spit it out? Start with if I hadn't gotten it into my head I could stay here, live here, Donna would still be alive."

"So, straight to the cliché?" He shook his head. "I thought you'd do better. That's not even a challenge. If you'd moved on, how many others before somebody like your brother finally clued in on the pattern? And what are the chances anybody but him would've seen the connection with your photos?"

"I don't know the chances. But obviously the chances of me being connected to a serial killer for the second time are really good."

"Sucks for you."

Shock snagged her breath. "*Sucks* for me?"

"Yeah, it does. It sucks for you that some lunatic's out there obsessed with you and emulating your fuck of a father. But you're not the reason, you're the excuse. The reason's inside this sick bastard's mind, just like your father's reasons were in his."

"It doesn't matter. It doesn't matter: excuse, reason. It doesn't matter what's in their minds, what drives them to kill. It matters that for the first twelve years of my life I grew up in a house with a monster, and I loved him. It matters that where I spent those years is now best known as Thomas David Bowes's killing field. It matters that what I grew up with followed us to New York until my mother killed herself rather than live with it. It matters that it's followed me, leaving death behind, ever since."

She wouldn't weep. Tears were useless. But fury, full-blown fury, felt righteous. "It matters that I tried to convince myself I could have what the majority of the human race has. A home, friends, people I care about. A damn idiot dog. All of it."

"You have that, all of it."

"It was—is—a fantasy. I got caught up in it, let myself believe it was real, but—"

"So what, you'll pack up, take off, sell this place, dump the dog?"

The fact stood clear, she thought again. "Sometimes people have roots so corrupted, they shouldn't try to plant them."

"That's bullshit, and it's weak. If you want to feel sorry for yourself, I'll give you a pass, but that's weak. You've got better than that, baby."

"You don't know what I've got, *baby*."

"Hell I don't, and because I do, I know you're not going to let some son of a bitch send you running."

He put the palms of his hands on her desk and leaned toward her. "I know what I've got, and I'm damned if I'll let you run. You've got what you need right here, and you're going to stick."

She surged to her feet. "Don't tell me what I'm going to do."

"I'm telling you. You're going to stick because what you want, what you need is right here. What makes you happy is right here. You need me, and I make you happy. And I fucking well need you, so you'll stick."

"It's my life, my choice."

"Screw that. You want to try to run, I'll just bring you back."

"Stop telling me what to do. Stop yelling at me."

"You started it. Maybe you haven't worked it through your system, pulled it free from the I've-got-bad-blood excuses you fall back on, but you've got feelings for me."

"How can you say things like that? How can you minimize this?"

"Because you overinflate it, so it's easy to stick a damn pin in it. Because I've got feelings for you. I'm in fucking love with you, so you're going to stick. And that's it."

She took one stumbling step back, went pale.

Xander rolled his eyes. "Cut that out and breathe. Yell back. You don't panic when you're pissed. And maybe I'd have done that with more class if I weren't pissed right back at you."

Or maybe not, he thought, but either way.

"Sunlight in your hair. Morning light. You're standing there, working on a piece of plywood, sunlight all over you, and I feel like someone kicked me off a damn cliff. So you're not going anywhere, just check that off the list."

"It can't work."

"You should try to balance out that Pollyanna attitude of yours, season it with some cynicism. It has been working," he added. "For both of us. I know what the hell works and what doesn't. We work, Naomi."

"That was before . . ." When his eyebrows lifted, she dragged a hand through her hair, tried to find level ground again. "Can't you see what's going to happen? I pray, and I'll keep praying Mason's right. They'll find him, they'll stop him. And I'll hope with all I have they do that before he kills again. But when they do find him, it'll all fall apart again. Me, my father, whoever this maniac is, all tied together. And the press—"

"Oh, fuck the press. You'll stand up to it."

"You have no idea what it's like."

"You'll stand up to it," he repeated, without a hint of doubt. "And you won't be alone. You'll never have to be alone again. You can count on me."

"Oh God, Xander."

When he crossed to her, she tried to back away, shook her head, but he simply grabbed her, pulled her in. "You can count on me. And you're damn well going to."

He tipped her head back, kissed her more gently than he ever had. "I love you." Kissed her again, drew her in, just held. "Get used to it."

"I'm not sure that's possible."

"You don't know until you try. We're not going anywhere, Naomi."

She felt herself breathe in, breathe out. "I'll try."

"That'll do."

BALANCE

Still to ourselves in every place consigned,
Our own felicity we make or find.

SAMUEL JOHNSON

Twenty-six

I t felt like an interrogation. She knew better—she knew—but when Mason came into her studio in the morning, set up a folding chair, and sat, he turned the sanctuary into an interrogation room.

"You didn't sleep well," he said.

"No, not very well. Neither did you."

"Well enough, just not very long. I worked late."

"You didn't come down for breakfast."

"Because it's at dawn." He smiled a little. "I grabbed a bagel, had coffee, talked to the tile guys. The room you've earmarked for the uncles is really coming along. They're going to love it."

"I'm not sure they should come."

"Naomi, I know it has to feel like your life tipped sideways, but you have to keep living it."

"If something happened to them—"

He cut her off. "The unsub's not interested in men."

"He's interested in *me*, and they're mine. So."

"They'll come anyway. Put that away for a while. I'm heading into town shortly, meeting the team. We'll work out of the police station. He's never had an investigation focused on him like this, Naomi. It changes things."

"Whatever we do, it doesn't change what's already happened."

"No."

"And I know, Dr. Carson, dwelling on that, brooding on my part of it, however involuntary, isn't healthy or productive."

Knowing that, knowing *he* thought it, irritated the crap out of her.

"But I might need a couple days to dwell and brood."

All understanding, he simply nodded. "You should play to your strengths, and you've always been a champion brooder."

"Up yours, Mason Jar."

"Another strength," he went on, "is your power of observation. You see the big picture and the small details. It's going to be an advantage. It's going to help."

"My keen powers of observation didn't clue me in that I've been followed by a serial killer for a couple years."

"Longer, I think—and being clued in now, you can go back, remember things and people you noticed. You can go back, refresh those memories by going through pictures you took—the where, when, what was going on around you."

Longer, she wanted to dwell on *longer*, but pressed her fingers to her eyes, ordered herself to deal with it. "I don't pay attention to people when I'm working. I block them out."

"You have to pay attention *to* block them out. You know more than you think, and I can help you bring it to the surface."

Though she had to stifle a sigh, she decided if she had to take another trip into a therapy session, it might as well be with her brother in the chair.

"Let's go back first, and tell me how much longer you think this has been happening."

"Did you know Eliza Anderson?"

"I don't know." Already battling a vague headache, Naomi rubbed at her temple. "I don't think so. Mason, I've brushed up against dozens and dozens of people. On shoots, at the gallery on trips to New York. There are motel clerks and waitresses and gas station attendants, shopkeepers, hikers. Countless. The odds of remembering . . ."

But suddenly she did. "Wait. Liza—I think they called her Liza. I remember hearing about her at college, my sophomore year, after she was killed. But, Mason, it wasn't like this. And everyone said it was her ex-boyfriend. He'd been violent with her before, which is why he was an ex. She was beaten and raped, but she was stabbed to death, wasn't she? And—God—they found her in the trunk of her own car."

"What do you remember about her?"

"I didn't know her. She was a year ahead of me. But I recognized her when I saw her picture on the news, on the Net, after it happened. We didn't have any classes together, didn't socialize, but she came into the restaurant where I worked the first two years of college before I could intern with a photographer. I waited on her enough times to remember her face."

Now, she brought that face back into her mind. "Blonde, short, swingy blonde hair," she said, waving her hands just under her own ears. "Very pretty. Polite enough to actually speak to her waitress, say thanks. I understand she was blonde, killed where I went to school, but she wasn't held for any length of time, wasn't strangled."

"I think she was his first. I think he panicked before he could attempt strangulation. It was messy and quick, even sloppy—and he was lucky. If the investigation hadn't zeroed in so completely on the ex, he might not have gotten away with it. She'd had a fight with the ex that night."

"I remember reading that, hearing it around campus." She found her calm, pushed back for memories. "He—the boyfriend—tried to get her to come back, and they fought, he threatened her. People heard him tell her he'd make her sorry, make her pay. He didn't have an alibi."

"And they had no physical evidence, and no matter how hard and long they worked him, he never came off his story of being alone in his room, asleep—when she was grabbed and killed and put in the trunk of her car.

"She looked a little like you."

"No. No, she didn't."

"You wore your hair longer then, not dissimilar from hers. She wasn't as tall as you, but she was tall, slim."

And the way he paused, the way those warm brown eyes fixed on hers, Naomi knew worse was coming.

"Say it."

"I think he used her as a surrogate, his first, because of those similarities. It may be he couldn't get to you, so he substituted. And then found the high of the kill, of taking those substitutes. Along the way he evolved, he learned, he refined."

"Mason, that's ten years. You're talking ten years."

"Initially, his kills would be more spread out. Months, even a year between. He'd experiment with method, study you, study Bowes. He may be competing with Bowes, and Bowes had a twelve-year streak—that can be verified. You and I know it might have been longer."

Couldn't sit, couldn't, so she pushed away from the desk, paced to the window, drank in the view of the water.

The peace of it, the colors blooming in light and in shadow.

"I don't know why, but if I believe it's been ten years, it makes it less intimate. This isn't about something I did, something I didn't do—Xander was right. I'm the excuse. God, I asked myself so many times in the first couple of years after that night in the woods what I'd done or didn't do to make my father hurt all those girls."

"I did the same."

She glanced back at him. "Did you?"

"Yeah, I did. Of course I did. And the answer was nothing. We didn't do anything."

"It took me a long time to accept that, to push away any blame. It's not going to take me as long now. Not with this, not with him. And he's not going to get away with using me as an excuse to kill."

She turned back. "He's not going to get away with it."

"Brooding time's over?"

"Damn right, it is. Ashley. Liza would have been the same age as Ashley when I found her."

"I hadn't thought of that." Considering, Mason sat back. "It might have been a trigger. Not necessarily the exact age, but the college student.

You saved a college student. Now you're a college student, and he goes there to kill you, or a surrogate. To finish what Bowes had started."

Mason rose. "I have to get into town. What I'd like you to do, when you can, is go back over that period when Eliza Anderson was killed, the days before it happened. Try to take yourself back there, the routine—class, work, study, social life."

"I barely had a social life, but all right. I'm going to do whatever I can to help you find him. And, Mason, when you do, I want something."

"What?"

"Something I couldn't do, just couldn't do, with our father. I want to talk to him."

"Let's catch him first." But Mason went to her, wrapped his arms around her before stepping back. "You and Xander? Things are okay there?"

"Why?"

"You were yelling—both of you—when you came up here yesterday. And you were still off and upset when you came down again."

"He pisses me off so I won't panic. It works. Most of the time. He said he's in love with me. Well, he didn't say it, he shouted and swore, and worked it into that. And I don't know what to do about it."

"What do you want to do about it?"

"If I knew that, I'd do it."

"You know." He poked a finger in the center of her forehead. "You're still brooding on that one. I'll let you know if I'm going to be late."

Alone, Naomi considered brooding on that one a little longer. Instead, she sat behind her desk again, dug out files.

And took herself back to college.

She spent two hours, made notes before taking her camera and going outside for a break. Dirt-covered and joyful, Tag paused his love affair with the landscapers to race to her.

"Sorry about that!" Lelo called out. "He's sure having fun, though."

"It shows." Resigned to carving out time to bathe the dog, she took

pictures of the crew setting pavers. Another of the one she thought of as
Mr. Hunk—tall, golden, built, and currently sweaty, stripped to the waist
and leaning on a shovel.

Hunks at Work, she thought, immediately seeing a series of photos.
Maybe a calendar, she thought, remembering Xander working on an
engine, Kevin with a nail gun.

She spent longer than she'd intended, taking candids, devising poses.
Then she left the dirty dog with the exterior crew and went back inside.

Back in her studio, she grabbed a bottle of water, texted Mason.

> Give me the next in line, chronologically. I'll organize
> notes on the college years and have them for you tonight.

Within minutes he'd emailed her two names, two dates. One eight
months after Eliza Anderson he'd termed a possible, and the other, nearly
eight months after that, termed probable.

She went with the possible.

And spent her day in the past. In the brisk winds of November on a
college campus where Eliza Anderson had walked from the library to her
car, intending to drive back to the group house she shared with friends,
to the sweltering summer in New York where a runaway—only seventeen—
was found beaten, stabbed, and strangled in a Dumpster behind a home-
less shelter. To a bitter February weekend where Naomi had traveled with
her photography group to New Bedford, where a married mother of two
left her evening yoga class—and was found dead on the rocky shoreline
Naomi had photographed only that afternoon.

She skipped any excuse for lunch, fueling herself on water, far too
much cold caffeine, and sheer drive. When she'd ignored the headache as
long as she could, she popped some Advil and finished writing up her
notes in a way—she hoped—someone besides herself could follow.

Exhausted, she decided Jenny was right. She needed a love seat in the
studio. If she'd had one she'd have curled up on it right that minute for a nap.

Then again, if she had a love seat to take a nap on, she'd have a dirt-covered dog roaming the house. Best to wash the dog, then think about dinner. Because now that she'd stopped, she was starving.

She stepped out of the studio, stood for a moment in the absolute silence—and decided having the house to herself was nearly as refreshing as a nap.

So she'd grab a couple of cookies to fill the hole, wash the stupid dog, *then* think about dinner.

But she realized as she came down the back steps into the kitchen that she didn't have the house to herself. Seeing the accordion doors wide open would've stopped her heart if she hadn't heard Xander's voice.

"Jesus, go lie down, will you? Do I look like I have a hand free to throw that damn thing?"

She stepped out.

He sat on a rolling stool, assembling a stainless steel cabinet. The rest of the . . . *behemoth* was really all she could think, was spread out on a folding table behind him.

The dog—clean and smelling of his shampoo—managed to work his way under Xander's arm to drop the ball in his lap.

"Forget it."

"Is that . . . a grill?"

He glanced up. "I told you I'd get the grill."

"It's really big. Very really big."

"No point in puny." He fitted the bit of an electric drill into a screw, gave it a whirl.

"Don't they come already assembled?"

"Why would I pay somebody to put something together when I can put it together myself?" To buy some time, Xander heaved the ball over the deck rail.

For one heart-stopping moment Naomi feared the dog would leap off after it, but he went into a flying scramble down the stairs.

"You bought a grill—what looks to be a Cadillac of grills."

"I said I would."

"And you do what you say you'll do."

"Why say you will if you don't?" He shifted, watched her watching him. "What?"

"I had a headache," she said, thoughtfully. "And I was tired—brain, body, spirit, if you want to do the hat trick. I wished I had a couch in my studio so I could take a nap. But I needed to wash the dog."

"I washed him—for all the good it'll do since there's plenty of dirt out front for him to roll in again. Go take an aspirin and a nap."

"The headache's gone, and I'm not so tired. I earned the headache and the tired by forgetting to eat lunch and drinking too much caffeine."

"I don't get how people forget to eat. Your stomach says *feed me*. You feed it, move on."

She let out a sigh. It surprised her as it wasn't sad, frustrated, poignant. It was content. "Xander." She went to him, reached down to take his face in her hands, kissed him. "You washed the dog. You bought a grill—one that looks like it needs its own zip code."

"It's not that big."

"And you're putting it together. I'll go do the same with dinner."

"What are you talking about? This is a grill. In about forty minutes I'm going to fire it up and cook those steaks I picked up on the way home."

"You bought steaks? You're going to grill steaks?" She looked at the partially assembled behemoth. "Tonight?"

"Yes, tonight. Have some faith. I had them put a big-ass salad together, and if you want to be useful, you could wash the potatoes I'm going to grill."

Just as she started to prep, Mason came in. "Listen, I want to change, have what you're having. Then we'll talk. I saw Xander's truck out front."

"He's on the deck, assembling a gigantic grill."

"A grill." Mason stepped out and said, "Whoa," in tones of awe and delight. "Now that's a grill."

"It will be."

"I'll give you a hand."

"You've never been mechanically inclined," Naomi began, and got a stony stare.

"You don't know everything." Obviously primed, Mason stripped off his suit jacket, tugged off his tie, and then rolled up his sleeves.

Naomi stood in the kitchen, listening to them talk. There could be normal, she realized. There could be pockets of normal even in the middle of the awful.

She would prize it.

And she should've had faith. In forty minutes, despite what she considered Mason's dubious assistance, Xander did just as he'd promised. He fired up the grill.

"I'm duly impressed. And it's beautiful. Big, but beautiful."

"It gets covered." Xander jerked a thumb at the cover, still in its package on the table. "You use it, it cools off, you cover it. Every time."

"Without fail," she promised. "And the side burners will be handy, plus it has all this storage." She opened one of the doors. "That's a rotisserie attachment."

"Yeah. I'll show you how to use it when you want to."

"Restaurant kid. I know how to attach and use a rotisserie. And I will be. Let me get the potatoes ready."

"You scrub them off, toss them on."

"I'll show you a trick. If I'd known this was happening I'd have picked up some liquid smoke."

"I've got some. They threw in this thank-you package. There's some in there. Why?"

"Why—get it and see."

What he saw was her mixing up oil, the smoke, some garlic in a bowl.

"They're just potatoes."

"Not when I'm done with them." In another bowl, she mixed salt, pepper, more garlic. Then she took one of her little knives and cut wedges out of the potatoes.

"Why—" he began, but she just waved him off and put pats of butter in the wedges, then sprinkled the salt stuff in it before fitting the piece she'd cut out back on.

"It's a lot of trouble for—"

She made a warning sound, rubbed the potatoes with the oil mixture, used the rest of the seasoning on them, then wrapped them in foil.

"Have a little faith," she said, and handed him the three massive spuds.

When Mason came down, they were sitting on the glider with the dog at their feet.

"That's one beautiful bastard," he said, studying the grill.

He sat on the deck, back against the pickets. "Do you want me to wait until later?"

"No. I'm good. I've had a lot of time to think it through, work it out. We all need to know all we can."

"Okay then. We profile the unsub from late twenties to early thirties."

"More my age," Naomi said.

"He'd have blended on campus, we believe as a student."

"What campus?" Xander demanded.

"You're not caught up."

"He was in assembly mode when I came down. I didn't talk to him about it."

"Okay. We now believe, strongly, the first kill was a student at Naomi's college, in Naomi's second year."

He filled in the blanks quickly.

"I didn't get to all your notes, Naomi, but I did read the ones on that time period. You were part of a photography club, casually dating one of the other members. You were still living on campus, and you worked at a place called Café Café—coffeehouse, casual dining. You paid extra to have a single room—no roomie—in your dorm."

"I learned the first year I couldn't handle a roommate. They wanted to party when I wanted to work, and I still had nightmares off and on. I could put in extra hours at the café and pay the extra."

"And the night Eliza Anderson was killed you got off about nine."

"It was a Friday night—I looked it up, and I remembered. Most Fridays I got off at nine, walked back to my dorm, put in a couple hours on assignments or study. Even if the weather was bad, it was only about a ten-minute walk, on campus. But Justin came by right before I got off—the guy I was seeing. He wanted to show me some of the shots he'd taken earlier in the day, for this assignment. I liked his work, which is probably why I'd started seeing him, so he and another girl from our club walked back to my room together."

"Three of you—not what the unsub was expecting. He'd watched you, he knew your routine. And he couldn't move on you when you were in a group. So he took a substitute, an opportunity."

"Eliza."

"She left the library about nine thirty. Her car was in the lot—she lived in a group house off campus. She wasn't dating anyone, but they were having a party at the group house, so she was expected. We believe she was forced into her car—we know she was raped and killed in it—forced to drive somewhere remote enough to do what was done. Then he put her body in the trunk, drove it back, left it in the lot. He would've been bloody, so it's likely he had his own car close, he had a change of clothes, a place to stay. By the time she was found the next day, he was gone."

She imagined the fear, like the terrible fear she'd seen in Ashley's eyes.

"If he knew my schedule, he had to have watched me for more than a week."

"Possibly, or he asked. Just asked someone. But he took Friday, which has proven to be significant. He may have been in school himself, taken time off. He may have gone to the same university, and have developed his obsession with you there."

"I never felt unsafe there. You were right before about noticing things. I think I would have, I would have felt it if someone that close had been focused on me. Someone I saw routinely, on campus, in class, in the café. But I didn't."

"How did he know you went there?" Xander asked. "How did he know where to find you?"

"If he looked hard enough, had decent computer skills?" Mason shrugged. "You can find anybody. I'm exploring the possibility you knew him, Naomi. In New York."

"Knew him."

"Know him," Mason corrected. "Even casually. Someone who came into Harry's restaurant. You may have waited on him. He could have asked anyone, casually, about you. Especially if he's near the same age. They'd think he had a little crush maybe, something that innocent. And it's *oh, Naomi, she's studying photography*, or *Naomi's going off to college in the fall to study photography*. He says, *wow, at Columbia?* and it's *oh no, some college in Rhode Island. We're sure going to miss her.*"

"Yes," she agreed. "It would be easy."

"Bowes released another name and location the summer before your sophomore year. He was all over the press again. Vance's book got another bump back onto the bestseller list," Mason added. "The movie ran on cable."

"I remember. I remember," Naomi said again. "I was so afraid those first couple weeks back at school someone would connect me. But no one did. Or I thought no one did."

"Something like that could've triggered it. Bowes got a lot of attention, a lot of mail, more visitors—more reporters getting clearance to interview him from that July when he made the deal, right through to October when the attention waned again."

"And in November, this man came to Rhode Island, probably for me."

"We're checking all the correspondence, the visitors' logs—back ten years, the records aren't as easy to come by as they are now. But this is someone who keeps tabs, who's probably developed a relationship with Bowes—or believes he has. Just as he believes he has one with you."

"He does have one with me."

"Everything you remember helps. Your memory of that first Friday night, it helps, it gives us your movements, and with them helps us see his. You remembered something else from college."

"The club trip my junior year. Presidents' Day weekend. Cold as it gets, but we piled in a couple of vans and drove to New Bedford. Winter beach theme. We shot for a couple of hours on the freezing beach, then we went into town to eat. That's what I remembered. How this other student sitting across from me—Holly, I don't remember her last name—said something about how come guys stared at me, I already had a boyfriend. And she pointed toward the bar, kind of smirked. I looked around, but the guy she'd pointed out had his back turned."

As she had that afternoon, Naomi walked through it again.

"She got up—I guess she was feeling the beer—she was one of the seniors, and ordered a beer. She walked up to him. I even heard her say he could buy her another beer, that I was taken, but she wasn't. He just walked out. Didn't look back, just walked straight out, which annoyed her. And I did feel something. I felt uncomfortable, exposed. I put it down to embarrassment because she was a little drunk, and she said how Barbie dolls like me always got the attention, how he'd watched me on the beach earlier. We took some more shots around town, then drove to Bridgeport, spent the night at a motel, took more pictures the next day. We were supposed to keep at it, come back on Monday, but a storm, a bad one was coming in, and we opted to go back, finish up closer to the campus. I never heard about the woman he'd killed until you told me this morning."

"Who was she?" Xander asked.

"She worked at the restaurant where you had your early dinner. She got off at seven that Friday, had a yoga class in a studio in town. Her car was still in the lot the next morning, her husband frantic. They found her body Sunday morning on the beach where Naomi's club spent that Friday afternoon."

"It's not a coincidence. Did he use her car?" Naomi asked. "The way he did with Liza?"

"No. We believe he had his own vehicle. Incapacitated her or forced her into it."

"Middle of February," Xander speculated. "Cold, windy, storm coming in. He sure as hell didn't kill her outside. Maybe he rented a motel room, or had a van."

"A lot of motel rooms in that area. The locals checked every one, came up empty."

"He'd had time to think about it," Xander pointed out. "To prepare. You put down a tarp, do what you're going to do. TV or radio on, she's gagged, who's going to hear?"

"I wish I'd gotten up, gone to the bar, gotten a look at him. At least I could give you a description."

"This Holly did. Maybe she remembers."

Naomi just shook her head at Xander. "She was half lit, a decade ago. In any case, I don't remember her last name, have no idea where she is."

"Your brother's FBI. I bet he can find her."

"Yeah, we can find her. We will find her. She's the only one we know of who knows what he looks like. Or looked like, so it's worth a shot. Do you want a break from this?"

"No, keep going. You said a runaway in New York. In July—between these two murders."

He took her through that, plucking at her memories, then called it when Xander got up to grill the steaks.

"Just give me the next you have," Naomi insisted. "So I can think about the time and place, what I was doing."

"April of my sophomore year—your senior year. Spring break. You, me, the uncles, we road-tripped it down to South Carolina, stayed a week in that beach house Seth found."

"I remember. It rained four of the six and a half days we were there." Remembering made her smile. "We played a hell of a lot of Scrabble and rented movies. But . . . that's nine months, isn't it? Nine months between. Doesn't it usually escalate?"

"It does, and I think he practiced between July and April. Disposed of the body or bodies."

"It's going to be like . . . Bowes. Even when you find him, you might never know how many he killed."

"Let's worry about that when we get to that."

"But—"

"How do you want your steak?" Xander interrupted.

"Oh. Ah. Medium rare for me, medium for Mason." She sloughed it off, rose. "I'll go dress the salad."

They'd take that break, she decided, dig into that pocket of normal. Then she'd go back to that rainy week at the beach, and whatever came after it.

She wouldn't stop.

Twenty-seven

When she turned to him in the night, Xander came half awake. "Just a dream." He slid an arm around her, hoped she'd settle again. "You're okay."

"He was chasing me. Through the forest, along the beach, everywhere I went. Right behind me, but I couldn't see him. Then I fell into a pit. But it was the cellar. And when he put the rope around my neck, it was my father."

He lay quiet a moment. "I'm no shrink, but that's pretty straightforward, right?"

"I dream of that cellar more than anything else. I can even smell it in the dreams. I never get out of it, in the dreams. He always comes back before I can get away, get away from him."

"He's not going to get out."

"But he has an apprentice, a competitor, whatever this is. I can't be afraid, Xander. I can't live afraid. Before all of this, before that night, I used to dream of finding a puppy and being able to keep it, or riding the brand-new shiny bike I wanted so bad. I'll never go back to that, that simple, that innocent, but I won't live afraid. I did get out of the cellar. I got out. I got Ashley out. I won't live afraid of what didn't happen, or what's going to happen."

"Good. Smart. Can you go back to sleep now?"

"No." She rolled on top of him. "And neither can you."

Fisting her hands in his hair, she took his mouth aggressively, took her fill of it.

"I have purpose."

"Yeah," he managed as she ravished his mouth again. "I got that."

"Not that." Her laugh came low and husky. "Or not just that. Oh God, I love your hands on me, so hard and strong it feels like you could break me in half."

Those hard, strong hands gripped her hips. "You don't break easily."

No, she didn't. She'd nearly forgotten that. She didn't break easily. She scraped her teeth along his jawline, down his throat, reveling in the taste and texture, gathering pleasure and excitement from the rapid beat of his pulse against her lips.

His heart, a quick, thick thud against the press of her breast. He'd given that heart to her. She didn't know, not yet, couldn't be sure, not now, what to do with it, for it. But she wouldn't be afraid of being loved.

She wouldn't fear the gift.

Strong, she thought. He was strong, body and mind and will. She would never be weak, never forget her own strength. His strength would remind her, even challenge her.

She rose up. Moonlight again, she thought. Here was moonlight, as it had been the first time they'd come together like this. Light, dark, shadows, living together to tint the air, to somehow sweeten it.

She took his hands, brought them to her breasts, to her own heartbeat.

"I'm what you need."

"You are."

For a moment, she pressed her hands to his. "Everyone should have what they need."

She took him in, slow, slow, stretching the moment like a fine silver wire. "Oh, what being with you does inside me."

And she began to move, a gentle, sinuous roll. Torturously arousing, a smoky, smoldering fire in the blood. He fought to let her set the pace, that slow burn of a pace, to stop himself from simply clamping around her like chains, taking her, taking his release.

Pleasure, so acute it sliced. Desire, so intense it seared. And love, so deep and yet so new it drowned him.

As if she knew, she smiled. "Wait." Her eyes closed as she rolled her hips, kept him trapped and on the edge of torment. "Wait. And you can take what you need. Take what you want. How you want. Just wait."

While he watched, barely able to breathe, her head fell back, her back bowed. Her arms rose to circle her head. All movement stopped. She was a statue, bathed in moonlight, made in moonlight.

She made a sound, half sob, half triumph. Then she smiled again; her eyes, opened and slumberous, met his.

His tether snapped. He had her on her back, under him, her arms still over her head, his hands clamping her wrists.

All that need, all that want, all that torment rushed together inside him. He drove into her like a man possessed; perhaps he was. Her shocked, breathless cries only added fuel.

He took what he needed, what he wanted. Took until there was nothing left for either of them.

And that was everything, for both of them.

In the morning Xander scowled at a tie as if deciding whether to wear it or hang himself with it.

"I don't think Donna would care if you didn't wear a tie."

"No. But . . . I'm a pallbearer. Her daughter asked Kevin and me to be pallbearers."

"Oh. I didn't realize." How much harder would that be for him? she wondered, and walked to her closet—which needed organizing since most of the clothes shipped from New York remained in boxes.

"You don't have to go."

She stopped, her hand on the black dress. "Would you rather I didn't?"

"I don't mean that. I mean you don't have to. You don't have to feel obligated."

So much easier to stay home, she thought, to work in a quiet, empty house, as everyone in both crews would attend Donna's funeral. And he was giving her the out.

"I didn't know her very well, but I liked her. I know I'm not responsible for what happened, but I'm connected. I know you'll have more friends than I can count there, but we're together. It's not an obligation, Xander. It's respect."

"I'm pissed off." He tossed the tie on the bed, shrugged into the white dress shirt. "I'd shoved it down, but today I'm pissed off I'm going to carry a really good woman to a hole in the fucking ground."

"I know." She laid the dress on the bed, went to the dresser for a bra and panties. "You should be pissed off."

While she dressed he picked up the tie again and, resigned, slid it under the collar of the shirt. "Ties are for bankers and lawyers," he complained. "Or like Elton John said, the sons thereof."

In her underwear, she turned to him, finished the knot herself. "Uncle Seth taught me. He said every woman should know how to tie a man's tie, facing him. And I'd know why someday." She smiled, smoothed the fabric down. "And now I do. Look at you, Xander Keaton, clean shaven." She stroked a hand over his cheek. "Wearing a tie." She angled her head. "Who are you again?"

"It won't last."

"And that's fine, too." She pressed her cheek to his. "This time I'm going to help you through. Let me."

He let out a curse that ended on a sigh. Then put his arms around her. "Thanks. Tell me when you need to go. They closed Rinaldo's for the day. People are supposed to go there after, but if you—"

"Just let me help you through."

"Right. You're half—more than—naked, and I'm not. Something off about that."

"I'm about to be un-naked. Maybe you could let Tag out, make sure he does everything he has to do. I don't want to leave him outside alone while we're gone."

"We could take him."

"No, we're not taking the dog to a funeral. He'll be fine in the house as long as he has a rawhide and his stuffed cat. And a ball. I'll be down in ten minutes."

"You're the first and only woman I've known who says that and means it. Hey!" He snapped his fingers at the dog, who instantly grabbed his ball in his jaws and body-wagged. "We're going out the back, pal, and keeping out of that topsoil."

Xander grabbed his suit jacket, headed out the bedroom doors to the deck with the dog flashing ahead of him. "Lock this behind me," he told Naomi.

She did, then put on the dress she hadn't worn in . . . she couldn't quite remember, and finished getting ready for her second funeral in the Cove.

He waited just inside the forest until Naomi and the grease monkey she was doing it with drove by in her car. Then he waited five full minutes.

Sometimes people turned around and came back, forgot something. His mother did it all the time, and once nearly caught him digging in the fake coffee can she used to hide cash from thieves.

Not that she'd ever been robbed, except by her son.

So he waited, watching the road through the screen of trees before he began the hike to the house on the bluff.

He'd parked nearly a quarter mile away—in the opposite direction from town. Had even put a white handkerchief on the side-view mirror, like he'd had a breakdown.

Getting into the house would be a nice little bonus. He'd seen how she lived, what she had. He wanted to touch her things, her clothes. Smell her. Maybe take a little souvenir she wouldn't miss, at least not right off.

He knew about the alarm system, but he'd gotten through that sort of thing before. He'd done a lot of studying, put in plenty of practice.

She might have forgotten to set it—something else people did all the time. And he should know.

More than once, he'd walked right into houses, and right into the bedroom where some dumb bitch was sleeping.

He didn't always kill them. You had to mix things up or even brain-dead cops might start piecing things together. Like sometimes he used ketamine—a jab with that, and down she went. Chloroform took longer, but there was something so satisfying about the *struggle*.

Once you knocked her out, tied her up, gagged that bitch—blindfolded her if you figured on letting her live—you could rape the shit out of her. He really liked when they came out of it *while* he raped them.

Then you mixed it up. You killed them, or you didn't. He liked the kill even more than the rape, but sometimes you had to resist. You beat the crap out of them, or you didn't. Cut them up some, or didn't.

And you kept your mouth shut unless you were going to shut theirs, permanently. No DNA when you wore a raincoat, no voice to remember, no face.

When the time came to do Naomi—and that time was coming right up—he'd take his sweet, sweet time. Maybe even keep her a couple weeks.

Stupid bitch got lucky, got rich enough to buy herself a big house. And was dumb enough to buy one this remote.

He could've taken her before, and he'd thought about it, oh, he'd thought about it so many times. But the wait, the long wait was better. And now he was—Christ—an *aficionado*. Oh, the things he'd do to her.

But not today. Today was a little opportunity.

Who knew he'd end up killing the fricking town sweetheart? He'd heard the buzz—he always made sure he heard the buzz. Everybody was going to her send-off. He'd never have a better chance to get in the house, get a solid lay of the land.

He could take her there, he was nearly sure of it. Just had to get the grease monkey out of the way for a few hours—or altogether. Make sure her asshole little brother was off playing Special Agent.

But he wanted the lay of the land first.

He strolled right up the drive.

He had lock picks and knew how to use them. If she'd set the alarm, he had a reader that should break her code before the alarm sounded.

If not, he just locked up again, moved off. They'd figure it was a glitch, nothing more. But the reader rarely failed him. He'd paid good money for it.

He glanced at the pots of flowers on the front porch, thought *Home sweet home*, and wished he'd thought to bring a little weed killer or salt. Wouldn't she wonder *what the fuck* when her posies croaked?

He heard the dog bark as he got out the picks, didn't worry about it. He had a couple of dog biscuits in his pocket—and he'd seen the stupid dog playing around with the yard crew, the carpenters. He'd even seen Naomi walking around town with him, and how the dog let anybody who came along pet him.

But as he went to work on the locks the barks grew louder, sharper, and made way for throaty growls and wet snarls.

He had a knife—*Don't leave home without it*—but if he had to kill the damn dog it would spoil the surprise. And he didn't relish the idea of having the dog try to rip a chunk out of him.

He reconsidered.

He'd go around the back first, to the glass doors. Let the dog see him—and the dog biscuit. Make friends through the glass. She may have left them unlocked on top of it.

He circled around, making note of windows on this far side—ones he hadn't been able to study up close before. And the trees, the potential cover.

He took the stairs to the deck. More pots of flowers. Yeah, he might just come back with weed killer, give her plants a good dose for the fun of it.

Then, slapping on a big, friendly smile, he pulled out a dog biscuit and walked to the big glass doors.

The dog wasn't even there. *Some guard dog*, he thought with a snort, and pulled on thin latex gloves to check if the doors were locked.

The dog—bigger than he'd remembered—flew at the glass, barking, snarling, even snapping. Shocked panic had him stumbling back, throwing up his hands as if to protect his face. His heart banged in his throat, his mouth went dry. Infuriated him even as he trembled.

"Fucker. Fucker." Breathless, he tried the big smile again, though his eyes transmitted pure hate even as he showed the dog the biscuit. "Yeah, asshole," he said in a friendly singsong. "See what I got. Should've poisoned it, you ugly fuck."

But no matter the tone, no matter the bribe, the dog's relentless barking increased. When he made a testing move toward the door, the dog peeled back those canine lips and showed his fangs.

"Maybe I'll stick this down your throat instead." He pulled the knife, stabbed out with it.

Rather than cowering back, the dog leaped at the glass and stood on his hind legs, barking madly with eyes creepy blue and feral.

"Screw this." His hand shook as he shoved the knife back in its sheath. "I'll be back, you fuck, I'll be back. I'll gut you like a trout and make her watch."

Furious, shaken, hot tears, hot rage burning behind his eyes, he stormed off the deck. Hands fisted, he hurried around the side of the house, stomped back to the drive and down.

He'd be back. And she and that fucking dog would *pay* for ruining his day.

In Xander's opinion no one had ever wanted to get out of a suit as badly as he wanted out of his. And once he had, he decided, he intended to toss it into Naomi's closet, leave it there, and forget it for as long as humanly possible.

"I appreciate your staying," he told her as he turned up her drive. "I know it was long."

"People really loved her. I think when you hear as much laughter as you see tears it's a testament to that. People loved her, and won't forget her. I wanted to stay, which isn't something I say often about any sort of event that involves so many people, but I did want to stay. And I didn't realize until I did that I've become part of the community. Or at least crossed that careful border into the edges of the community."

He parked, then just sat a moment. "You bought this place, and nobody else was willing to put the time, money, and vision into it. You shop local, you hire local, and that counts a whole hell of a lot. You put your art at Krista's, and it's something people notice, take stock of. You're hooked up with me, and people notice and take stock of that, too."

"I bet they do. New York Naomi and Our Own Xander." She smiled now. "I've heard myself referred to that way, which is why it surprised me to realize I'd crossed that border."

"You might always be New York Naomi. It has a ring. God, I've got to get out of this suit."

"And I've got to let that poor dog out. We were longer than I thought we'd be. Where's Lelo?" she wondered.

Xander glanced over at his friend's truck. "Around somewhere. The rest will be coming along, get a few hours in yet."

He waited while she unlocked the door and deactivated the alarm— and the dog raced in from the back of the house to wiggle and wag and lick and lean.

"Okay, okay, I know we were forever." But when she started to open the front door, Xander stopped her.

"He'll be all over the dirt. He should go out the back."

Though he intended to go straight up and ditch the suit, he went with instinct when Tag raced toward the back of the house, ran back a few feet, raced back again.

Something's up.

"I'll let him out," Naomi began as Xander started back. "I know you want to change and get to work."

"I'll go up the back."

He relaxed when he saw the reason for Tag's actions. Lelo—already out of dress clothes and into work mode—stood on the other side of the glass doors, pouring potting soil into the first of two containers.

Grinning, Lelo shifted the bag, gave a thumbs-up.

"Hey," he said when Xander opened the door. "You're sprung!" He laughed, setting the bag down to rub the dog all over. "I'd've broken him out, but the door was locked. He was pretty upset at first. Weren'tcha, yeah. Shaky and whining, but he settled down pretty quick when he saw I was sticking around. Sorry about the nose prints on the glass."

"Yours or his?" Xander asked.

"Har. I couldn't stay anymore at the, you know, thing after the thing. The first time I've ever seen Loo cry, and that just . . . wow. The other guys'll be along, I guess, since you are. I got a jump."

"Yes, you did." Naomi studied the planters. Lelo had been exactly right. They might have grown out of the house, and were the perfect size for her needs, just steps from the kitchen. "They're perfect, Lelo. They're wonderful. I love them."

"Turned out pretty good. I've got some herbs and tomatoes, peppers, like that, out in the truck. I can plant them up for you."

"You got all that?"

Shuffling, he adjusted his battered straw cowboy hat. "I was going right by the nursery anyway. Anything you don't want, I'll take home. My mom will plug it in somewhere."

"Can I take a look? I'd like to change and plant them myself. It'd be nice to balance out the day making something grow."

"I hear that. These'll be ready for planting by the time you're ready. Oh, and Xander? It's been a while since you've put in time on my dad's crew, but you oughta know not to go stomping around on dirt just seeded."

"I didn't."

"Well, somebody did since we knocked off yesterday. No big. I'll have it raked out."

"Where?"

"Around the front side. No big, like I said. I was just ragging on you."

"Let's have a look. Naomi, keep the dog back."

"We're not going to put you—or whoever—in jail for tromping over the topsoil," Lelo said, but led the way down. "I'll get those plants while we're out there. You can carry a flat unless you're worried about getting dirt on your suit."

"I may burn this suit."

It took some doing, but Naomi managed to stop the dog from racing after them, pulled him inside long enough to clip on the leash.

By the time she came out the front door both Xander and Lelo had hunkered down to study the ground. And her nerves began to fray.

"Not only didn't I walk across here, but my foot's bigger than that, Lelo. Buy a clue."

"Yeah, I guess I see that, but I just figured since it's coming and going toward the back. I guess one of Kevin's guys."

"They knocked off before you did yesterday, haven't been back today." He looked up to where Naomi fought to keep the heroically straining dog from pulling her forward.

"Sit!" He snapped it out, and to Naomi's—and probably to Tag's—surprise, Tag sat.

"Your brother's got about an inch on me," Xander said. "I can't say I noticed his feet, but I'm betting they're close to my size. I take a thirteen."

"Yes. I know his size because he hit it in high school. It's not easy to find that size off the rack."

"Tell me about it. Give him a call, Naomi. Somebody's been out here, snooping around."

"Well fuck, Xan." Lelo pushed to his feet. "I never figured that. Maybe that's why the big guy was so upset when I got here."

Xander circled around, took the curving path of recently set pavers. "He's on here, right?" Taking the phone out of her hand, Xander pulled up her speed dial list. "Go ahead and take the dog around the back, but don't— Never mind. Lelo, take this dog around back and keep him away from that dirt."

"Sure. The back door was locked," he said as he took the same path as Xander. "Front, too, because I'm going to admit I tried it, thinking to let Tag out since he was so upset at first. The house was locked up, Naomi. I don't think anybody got in. Probably somebody just wanted to look and see what you're doing up here."

"Maybe." She surrendered the dog. "Thanks."

When she turned to go in the house, Xander gripped her arm.

"I need to see if anything's been taken or—"

He just shook his head, kept talking to Mason. "Yeah, they're pretty clear. Enough to see size and tread. Yeah. Yeah, we'll be here."

He handed Naomi the phone. "Just wait here. I'm going to check inside."

"It's my house, Xander. My things. I'm not going to stand here wringing my hands while you go look under the damn bed for me."

He'd have cursed if it wouldn't have been a waste of breath. "Fine. We'll go check inside."

They went upstairs first, and she turned straight into her studio. Even the relief of seeing, at a glance, that nothing had been touched didn't ease the anger.

Still, Xander checked the closet, the powder room, and began going systematically room to room.

"Nothing's been taken or moved," she told him. "I know where things are. When you're in the middle of deciding what you want where, and where to keep it until, you know."

"I'm going to check the basement." When she gave him that *look*, he did curse. "I'm not riding the white horse, okay? Nobody got in here past the locks, alarm, the dog, but I need to check."

He stripped off the suit coat, the tie. "Mason's going to be here any minute. I just want to go down, take a quick look. You can change out of that dress or not, but if you want to walk around outside, see what the hell, you're going to want to get out of those skyscrapers."

She stepped out of the classic black pumps. "I'm out, but you're right. No one got in here, and I appreciate your being thorough and checking the basement. I'll change."

"Good." He hesitated. "You know, Lelo's not as stupid as he looks."

"He doesn't look stupid—and yes, he's going to start putting things together when the police and the FBI come out here because somebody walked across the fresh dirt that's my lawn." She drew a breath. "You can tell him."

"Tell him what?"

"Whatever you think he should know. I'm going to tell Jenny and Kevin. I'm going to tell them all of it."

"Good." He took her face in a firm grip. "You crossed that border, Naomi, because you wanted to. This is part of being on the other side. I won't be long."

Alone, she changed into knee-length jeans, a T-shirt. She still intended to plant. Goddamn it, she'd plant her new containers. Maybe she was afraid—she wasn't stupid either. But over that fear ran a strong, hard line of anger.

And that she'd hold on to.

She went out on the deck, saw Lelo and the dog playing throw it/fetch it, and stood, just for a moment, looking out at the blue and the green she'd made her own.

She didn't have to tell herself she'd do whatever she had to do to keep it. She already knew.

Twenty-eight

She didn't know the other agents in their dark suits and sunglasses, but she doubted they were much different from the ones who had swarmed over the house, the woods in West Virginia seventeen years before.

She hadn't stood with them, as she did now, but had watched the news reports in the safe house when her mother slept.

Now she wasn't a child; now it was her house, her ground.

So she brought out cold drinks and started a jug of sun tea on the deck because it reminded her of summers in New York and how Harry had added mint from his kitchen garden.

She didn't interfere, didn't ask questions—yet—but she was present.

If somehow he watched, through a long lens, through field glasses, he would see that she was present.

Sam Winston stepped over to her, adjusted his ball cap. "I'm sorry about this, Naomi. The fact is somebody could've taken advantage of the house being empty just to satisfy curiosity. Point Bluff's got a lot of people curious."

"But you don't think that."

He inhaled through his nose. "I think we're going to take every precaution and turn over every stone. The FBI has people who can study those footprints, give us a sense of height, of weight, give us the shoe size, even the make. If this is who we're looking for, he made a mistake."

"Yes, he did."

Maybe not the same mistake the chief meant, Naomi thought. He'd made one by coming into what was hers. He'd made one by helping her pump that anger over the fear.

She went over to Lelo's truck. They'd be sending him away—as they had the others who'd come to work. She'd get the plants, at least take them around to the containers.

When she found none, she decided Lelo had taken them around for her already. With the dog again on a leash to keep him from rolling over the evidence, she took him around the far side of the house with her, and onto the deck.

Tears swam when she saw the flats and pots lined up on the deck, and her own garden gloves, spade, and rake beside them.

"He's a sweet man," she told the dog. "Remind me to stock some Mountain Dew. That's our Lelo's drink."

Though Tag objected, she tied the leash to a picket. "You need to stay with me, let them do what they have to do around front." To soften the insult, she got him a bowl of water, a biscuit.

Then she crouched, rubbing the spot between his ears that made his eyes roll back in bliss. "Was it you? Did you chase him off—big, fierce dog? Did some good fairy put you on the side of the road that day for me?" She laid her head on his. "Did you scare him as much as he scared you? Well, we're not going to let him scare us. We're going to take a bite out of him, you and me, if he tries it again."

She pressed her lips to his muzzle, looked into his wonderful eyes. She'd fallen in love with the dog, just as she'd fallen in love with Xander. Against her better judgment.

"There doesn't seem to be a thing I can do about it."

She rose, then walked to her pretty new containers to plant.

Xander found her tamping the dirt around a tomato plant while the dog stretched out full-length in the sun, half snoozing.

"They're pretty much done out there, and said there's no reason the landscapers couldn't get back to it tomorrow. Kevin's crew, too."

"That's good. That's fine." She picked up a pepper plant. "Do you know why I'm doing this?"

"It looks obvious, but tell me."

"Besides the obvious, I'm planting these herbs and vegetables. I'm going to water them, watch them grow, watch the vegetables flower and watch the tomatoes and peppers form. I'll harvest them and eat them, and it all starts with what I'm doing right here. It's a statement. I need to do some research, but I think you can plant things like kale and cabbage in the fall."

"Why would you?"

"I can make some very good and interesting dishes with kale and cabbage."

"You're going to have to prove that to me."

She kept planting while he went in, came out, and stood watching her.

"He ran away," Xander began, and she nodded.

"Yeah, I saw that."

"Saw what?"

"The footprints. You don't have to be an expert to conclude, or at least speculate. The ones going toward the house, toward the side are different from the ones leading away. Leading away they're farther apart, and with a kind of skid—moving fast, even running.

"I bet he *strolled* around the back here. The son of a bitch. Cocky, confident. I don't know if he'd intended to break in or just look, but he wasn't feeling cocky and confident when he left. The dog scared him."

Tag thumped his tail at her quick glance.

"I think he came around here, and would've gone in if the door hadn't been locked—or maybe planned to get in anyway, but the dog scared him off, defending his territory. Defending what's ours."

"You ought to know that the scenario you just outlined is the one those trained feds and cops outlined a few minutes ago. It's how they see it."

"Well, aren't I fucking clever?"

He arched an eyebrow. "I think so."

"I'm so pissed off. I should probably level that out before I plant any more. I don't think you should plant living things when you're so incredibly pissed off. You'll probably end up with bitter tomatoes."

She yanked off her gloves, tossed them down. "He used her again, Xander. He used Donna, used the fact that everyone who's usually here would be at her funeral. That makes me sick inside."

"Then think of this instead. That stray, that dog who wandered from place to place as much as you used to, stuck, like you stuck. And scared the bastard off. He didn't leave here strolling, Naomi, just like you said. He left with his heart knocking and his knees shaking."

"Damn right, he did. Damn right," she repeated, and strode up and down the deck. "If he tries it again, he won't get to leave, heart knocking, because he's going down bloody. If he thinks I'm an easy mark, that he can come for me whenever he damn well pleases, he miscalculated."

"I get the value of mad, as long as it doesn't walk with stupid and careless."

She whirled to him, eyes dark green fire. "Do I look stupid and careless?"

"Not so far."

"And that's not going to change." She calmed a little, told herself to keep the mad in a back corner until she needed it. "Do you think Kevin and Jenny can get a sitter? I'd like them to come over, I want to tell them sooner rather than later, but not with their kids around."

"I'll make it happen, if you're sure."

"I am."

"What time?"

"Whatever works for them will work for me. I'm going to finish these containers, clean up, so any time that works for them."

Where did you confess your blood ties? Naomi wondered. The scarcity of furniture in the living and sitting rooms made that difficult. Sitting around the dining room table on folding chairs seemed too uncomfortable.

She opted for where she herself felt most relaxed and brought more chairs out to what she thought of as the kitchen deck.

"Do you want me here?" Mason asked her.

"You have work?"

Did she serve food? Naomi wondered. What sort of canapé suited the moment, for God's sake?

My father's a serial killer. Try the crab balls.

"I mean, of course you have work, but something specific?"

"The team's meeting for a briefing, but I can catch up with it if you want me here. This is hard for you."

"Why hasn't it ever been as hard for you?"

"I wasn't in the woods that night. I didn't go down into that cellar. I didn't find Mom. She was his last victim."

"You never were."

She remembered that day in the coffee shop, after she'd bolted from the movie theater. How young he'd been, and how strong and steady.

"You resolved so early on not to be, to be everything he wasn't. And however much I denied it, ignored it, shoved it back, I let myself be his victim. I'm done with that. Go to the briefing. Find a way to end this, Mason."

She put a tray together—cheese, flatbread crackers, olives. It kept her busy until Xander got back from a roadside call and Mason left.

"Do you know how many people don't pay attention to, or just don't believe the fuel gauge?"

"How many?"

"More than you think, so they end up paying more than double what the gas would've cost in the first place, so they bitch about that—like you should make the service call as a fricking favor. Are these any good?"

Look at him, she thought, *heading toward scruffy again.* Annoyed with some stranger who'd neglected to get gas, unsure what to make of sesame and rosemary flatbread. Idly scratching the dog's head as he decided whether to risk the fancy.

"You brought me lilacs."

He looked over, frown deepening. "Yeah. Was I supposed to do that again?"

"Sometime. But you brought me lilacs in an old blue pitcher. That was when."

"When what?"

Not really listening, she thought. She'd grown up with a brother. She knew when a male wasn't really listening.

All the better.

"You told me when, and I'm telling you."

"Okay."

"Stolen lilacs in an old blue vase."

"It wasn't that big a deal."

"You're wrong. It was a very big deal, the biggest of my life, because that's when. That's when, Xander, I knew I was in love with you. I didn't know what to do about it," she said as—oh, he was paying attention now—his gaze snapped to hers, hot blue and intense. "I've never felt what I feel for you before, never believed I could feel it, so I didn't know what to do about it. I have a better idea now."

"What's the better idea?"

"To be glad you're in love with me, too. To be grateful, really grateful it happened now after I'd already realized it was time to stop running. Or at least try to. To be happy it happened here where we both want to be. And to hope. To be brave enough to hope you'll want to stay with me here."

"Lilacs?"

"Lilacs."

"Lelo needs to work one into his design."

"It's going out back, so we can see it from the deck. I told him I wanted to plant it myself."

"We'll plant it."

Her throat closed; her eyes brimmed. "We'll plant it."

He stepped to her, caught her face in his hands. "I'm moving in. You're going to have to make room."

The first tear spilled over. "There's plenty of room."

"You say that now." He kissed the tear away, then the second as it trailed down her other cheek. "Wait until I tell Kevin to build a garage."

"A garage."

"A guy's got to have a garage." He brushed his lips to hers. "Three-car garage, north side of the house, put a side door on the laundry room."

"You've given this some thought."

"I was just waiting for you to get used to it. I love you, Naomi."

She lifted her hands to his wrists, squeezed hard. "You do. I know you do. Thank God you do. I love you so much we're going to build a garage. Wait, a *three*-car—"

It was as far as she got before his mouth took hers, before the kiss swept her up, swept her away. Then to the delight of the dog, he lifted her off her feet, spun her around.

"You're what was missing," he told her. "Not anymore."

"You told me you made me happy, and you do. But it's more than that. You helped me understand I deserve to be. A thousand hours of therapy never got me all the way there."

She sighed, drew back. "I'm still screwed up, Xander."

"Who isn't?"

The dog let out a yip, then raced toward the front of the house.

"Early-warning system says Kevin and Jenny are here."

She drew a breath. "All right."

"It's going to be okay. Have some faith."

"I'm going to borrow some of yours. My supply tends to run low."

"Try regular fill-ups. I'll let them in."

She took the tray out, set it on the folding table, went back for glasses, plates, napkins, heard Jenny's laughter.

As she opened a bottle of wine, Jenny came in.

"Great timing! Oh, Naomi, every time I get out here there's more done. It must be crazy living in the middle of it, but it's amazing to see it off and on."

"I'm glad you could come. I know it was last-minute."

"Worked out great. We had my parents over for dinner, and they took the kids back with them for a sleepover. Fun for all." She moved in for a hug. "I'm sorry you've had trouble. Kevin told me somebody was poking around out here while we were at Donna's funeral. I'm sure it was just some kids trying to get a look in the house."

"I think it was . . . something else. That's part of what I wanted to talk to you about."

"All right. You're really upset. I shouldn't make light of it."

"I thought we'd sit outside."

"Perfect. Oh! Look at these planters—Lelo built them? They're wonderful. You're really making this deck a wonderful outdoor living space. Kevin, look at these containers."

"Nice," he said as he came out with Xander. "How are you doing?" he asked Naomi.

"I've had better days. Then again . . ." She looked at Xander. Love, given and received, outweighed everything. "Let me get you some wine, Jenny. Then I'm going to dive right into this, get it done."

"It sounds serious."

"It is."

"Oh God, are you sick?" Immediately, Jenny grabbed her arm. "Is something wrong, or are you—"

"Jenny." Kevin spoke quietly, drew her back. "Come on, sit down."

"Sorry. I'm sorry. I'll shut up."

Naomi poured wine for Jenny, for herself, but couldn't sit. "Okay, straight in. Carson was my mother's maiden name. It's my uncle's name. Mason and I had our names legally changed a long time ago. From Bowes. Our father is Thomas David Bowes."

She wasn't expecting blank, quietly expectant looks, and it threw her off.

"Not everybody knows who that is, Naomi," Xander pointed out. "Not everybody gives a damn."

"It's familiar," Kevin said. "Like I ought to know."

"Thomas David Bowes," Naomi continued, "killed twenty-six women—that he's admitted to—somewhere between 1986 and 1998. August of 1998, when he was arrested."

"Bowes. Yeah, I remember some of that," Kevin said slowly. "Back east somewhere."

"West Virginia. He raped and tortured and eventually strangled his victims."

"Your father?" With one hand gripping Kevin's, Jenny stared at her. "Is he alive?"

"Yes. They don't have the death penalty."

"Did he escape? Is that what's happening now?"

"No. No, he's in prison. He's been in prison for seventeen years. We changed our name, we moved away. But it doesn't change the reality of it. You've been friends to me. You're helping me make a home here. I needed you to know."

"I remember some of it, I think. We were just kids," he said to Xander. "They made a movie. I caught it on TV a few years ago." His gaze shifted to Naomi. "You found that girl he had. Is that true? You found that girl and helped her, got her to the cops."

"I never saw the movie, or read the book. I don't know how accurate they were."

"Close enough," Xander said. "She followed Bowes into the woods one night, went into the cellar by a burned-out cabin, found the girl."

"Her name's Ashley," Naomi added.

"Ashley. Found her, got her out, walked miles through the woods, and got her help. That's how they found him. That's how they stopped him."

"Seventeen years?" Jenny repeated, eyes huge, face pale. "But you'd have been . . . Oh God, Naomi." She sprang up, shoved her wine at Kevin, threw her arms around Naomi. "Oh my God, poor little girl. You were just a *baby*."

"I was nearly twelve. I—"

"A baby," she repeated. "I'm sorry, so sorry. God! Did he hurt you? Did he—"

"He never touched me. He was strict, and sometimes he'd leave for days at a time. But he never laid a hand on me or Mason. He was a deacon in the church. He worked for a cable company. He mowed the lawn and painted the porch. And murdered women."

Jenny tightened her grip, swayed them back and forth. "You never think about the families of . . . You never really think about them, and what it's like for them. You didn't have to tell us," she said as she drew back. "It has to be hard for you to talk about."

"I didn't plan to tell anyone. Just to live here, just to be here. But . . ." She looked at Xander. "Things changed."

"She figured you'd probably pull back," Xander commented. "Look at her different."

"Xander—"

"Shut up. Some people put it together, one way or the other, and did that or went the other way and salivated for all the nitty-gritty details, so she'd pack it up and take off."

"Some people aren't worth spit. Is that what you thought of us?" Jenny demanded. "That's insulting."

"I—"

"You should apologize."

"I . . . I'm sorry?"

"Accepted. Kevin, accepted?"

He half smiled at his beer. "Yeah."

When Naomi covered her face with her hands, fought for composure, Jenny stabbed a finger at Xander, then at Naomi. Fisted her hands on her hips until he stepped over, put his arms around Naomi.

"Cut it out."

"Oh, give her a minute," Jenny snapped. "Where's my wine?" She swung back to Kevin to take it, and swiped at tears. "I need a minute, too, and all I can see is a little girl only a few years older than Maddy dealing with what no little girl should even know exists. If you don't want anyone else to know, Naomi, no one will. You can trust us." On a huff, she pulled Naomi from Xander. "Hell, men are no good at times like this. We're going inside for a few minutes. I'm taking the wine."

"She's one in a million," Xander said as Jenny pulled Naomi into the house.

"Which one of them?"

"Looks like both. We're lucky bastards."

"Yeah, we are. Now tell me what Bowes has to do with Marla and Donna, and whoever was around here today."

"I'm going to."

Xander sat down, and did.

I n the morning, Naomi set a mug under the coffee machine when she heard Mason coming down the back stairs. And turned to take the plate she'd already prepared out of the warmer when he stepped into the kitchen.

"Coffee and a hot breakfast? I may have to relocate. Whoa, eggs Benedict? Seriously?"

"I was in the mood to cook, and Xander's fond. You're wearing your suit again."

"It's what we do in the Bureau. I know I got in late. Since Xander's going to be here, I may bunk in town off and on. More on than off probably until we finish this. Thanks."

He took the coffee, drank. "But I'm not going to get eggs Benedict and coffee this good at the diner."

"Will you finish it, Mason?"

He looked at her, those clear brown eyes—like their father's. Nothing like their father's.

"I won't stop until it's finished. He wears a size ten Wolverine Sentinel. Some wear on the treads so he's had them awhile."

"You found that already, from a boot print."

"It's what we do in the Bureau," he said again. "We figure him for between one-sixty and one-sixty-five, between five-ten and six feet. Going by shoe size, depth of print, stride. He's white, he's most likely around thirty. That's a hell of a lot more than we had a few days ago."

"Now we just have to figure out who I know who's average height and weight, about my age, and wants to kill me." She held up a hand before Mason could speak. "I'm not being sarcastic. It's something I'm racking my brain over."

"You may not know him. Or not realize you do. But he knows Bowes. I'm going to be going over all the visits and correspondence today—starting that. Then I'm going to go see him."

"You're . . . You're going to West Virginia."

"It's unlikely anyone's obsessed with Bowes's daughter, has been killing in a way that mimics Bowes, and hasn't had contact with him."

She braced herself. "Should I go?"

"It may come to that, Naomi, but no. Let me make the first pass. If we get to the point that we believe you talking to him could help, can you do it?"

"It's something I've thought about, asked myself. Yes. I can go back, I can see him. I can do that to save myself, and any other women this pseudo Bowes might target. Mason, it hasn't been fear of Bowes—or not primarily that—keeping me from going back. It's been the need to deny it. Maybe I had to keep denying it, in my way, until I could accept, fully. I let it define me in too many ways. I'm not going to let it define me anymore. I told Jenny and Kevin last night, and it's okay."

"It's a hell of a good step toward defining yourself. You made the first one buying the house. You shifted your lines then, Naomi. You've kept shifting them, and making your own. You did what you needed to do until you could."

"Xander loves me."

"I noticed."

"You would. I'm adjusting to having a man who loves me, and enough to wait until I'm ready to shift the lines. Last night I was able to tell him I loved him. As desperately as I wanted normal, I never believed I'd have someone who knew everything about me and loved me. Someone who could get past the blocks so I could love him. It feels . . . miraculous."

"He's who I'd pick for you, if I had a vote."

"Even though you don't, it means a lot. He's moving in. Not just staying here, but moving in. God." With a hand pressed to her heart, she blew out a breath. "It's huge for me."

"How do you feel about it?"

A shrink question as much as a brother's, she thought. But even that was okay.

"Nervous. Not scared, just nervous. And happy. And baffled as apparently we're now building a three-car garage."

"The uncles are going to go nuts."

"I know it. I'm going to wait until they meet him. They should meet him first. Probably. Mason, get this finished before they come. Get this finished."

"I'm working on it."

Twenty-nine

Within a day Xander moved everything he wanted into the house on the bluff. The books presented the biggest challenge. The library wouldn't hold all of them.

"I never imagined this house would be too small for anything."

He shrugged, studying the shelves, now filled with books. And the tubs on the floor, still full of them.

"You don't want all your books in one place anyway. We should scatter some around."

"There are too many to scatter."

"Don't even think about saying I should get rid of some."

"Wouldn't think of it."

Maybe she had—just for an instant—and had just as quickly rejected the idea.

"I just don't know where to put them. They don't deserve to be stuck in tubs either. How will I know what's in there I want to read?"

"Kevin could do another wall of books."

"I'd love a wall of books," she considered. "But I don't know where."

"Basement. You're putting in a darkroom down there, right?"

"Yeah, sooner or later."

"I could use some office space. Don't need much, but somewhere for a desk and some files."

"You don't want an office in the basement."

"Works for me," he countered. "You're out of my way, I'm out of yours, and there's a hell of a lot of space down there. Plenty for a wall of books. They're okay in tubs until. I'll spring for the office and the wall, whatever goes with it."

Which included, to his mind, doors leading out to the yard. But he didn't see the point of front-loading that on.

"I've got money, Naomi. Investing it here instead of another rental—I've been looking at that—makes more sense right now. Plus I just got another rental since Jimmy's moving into the apartment over the garage. Gangly guy with the pitiful goatee deal? He works for me."

"Yes, I met him. You . . . You've already rented it."

"Jimmy graduates from trade school in June, wants his own place. And I like having someone over the garage. It's a good deal on both sides as it comes mostly furnished. You don't want the crap I had in there."

"But don't you?"

"I want the books. They're nonnegotiable," he said, idly picking up a worn paperback copy of *The Illustrated Man*. "Did you ever read this?"

"I saw the movie."

"Not the same." He pushed it into her hand. "It's good. Anyway, unless you've got other plans or want to think about it, I can get Kevin thinking about office space and a wall of books."

"Other than the darkroom, I didn't and don't have any plans for the basement."

"Good. We'll get on that. Worrying about what you've gotten yourself into?" he asked her.

"No. More wondering why I'm not. And I guess since I have some actual furniture coming tomorrow, we could scatter some books. Or at least consider their final location."

She stuck the book in the back pocket of her jeans for later and would have picked up a tub, but he beat her to it. "They're heavy," he said.

"The little sitting area off the living room. That's a good start."

She led the way through the quiet house. Just the man and the dog, with all the workmen gone for the day. It didn't seem smaller, she realized, now that she lived with a man and a dog. It seemed that was always what the house had in mind.

It seemed natural.

She mentally rearranged the sitting room furniture she'd yet to buy as she studied the space—added a funky plant stand with some interesting houseplant. And . . .

"There's this open cabinet—four shelves—in the basement. I was going to use it outside for plants, but it would work right here for a bookcase—with knickknacks worked in. Books and maybe a couple of photos, some whatever. Metal frame, wood shelves."

"I guess you want me to get that."

"What's the point in having a man around if he doesn't get things from the basement?"

"Right."

"Oh, you know, now that I see it here—in my head—Cecil has this old radio. You know, the dome-shaped vintage style. How cute would that be on the top of the case? It doesn't work, but . . ."

"Doesn't work doesn't mean it can't work."

"And what's the point in having a mechanical man around if he can't fix a vintage radio that would be perfect in the sitting room? I think, yes, I think I'm getting used to it already."

"I'll get the case. How about if I see if I can get used to drinking your wine while we set it up?"

"An excellent idea."

They drank wine, loaded books on shelves.

"Did you talk to Loo?"

"Yeah. She's pissed. Not at you," he said, reading Naomi's face clearly. "Jesus, give her some credit. She's pissed this bastard's been stalking you since college. Pissed he killed Donna. And now she's aware. A lot of people go into Loo's. A lot who aren't local, who stop in for a drink, some easy food. Or like they will Friday night to listen to the band. She'll be looking."

For a thirtyish guy with an average build in Wolverines, Naomi thought, but let it go.

"Mason's going to West Virginia, to the prison, with someone from the BAU."

"It couldn't hurt."

"They have some names."

Xander dropped the book he'd just picked up. "Why didn't you tell me?"

"I didn't recognize any of them. But they're going to interview anyone who sends up a flag—who's corresponded with or visited Bowes multiple times, or whose correspondence sends up those flags."

She picked up the book, set it on the shelf. "They'll look into all of them. Lifestyle, travel, occupation."

"Good. Nobody's ever looked for him—not like this. And I'm not buying he's so damn smart he'll slip through now that they are."

"Mason agrees with you. I'm working on getting there, too. He could be gone—from here, I mean. He could have moved on, at least for now."

But when they found the body of Karen Fisher, part-time waitress, part-time prostitute from Lilliwaup, on the side of the road a half a mile from Point Bluff, they knew he hadn't gone far.

The best thing about a press pass—and his was legit—was how it got you where you wanted to go. The little whore from nowhere stirred things up again, brought reporters from Seattle back. Even some national stringers.

And he was right there with them. Hell of a story *that* would be, he thought. If he wrote it himself he'd win the fricking Pulitzer.

Up yours, *New York Times*, *Washington Post*, and all the other creaky dinosaurs who wouldn't give him the time of day when he'd wanted a job.

Now papers were the dodo of news, and blogging was the way to go.

He could work anywhere, and did. He'd actually doubled back and covered some of his own work before, but this marked the first time he'd been right on the spot before, during, after.

While he found it tremendously satisfying, and knee-slappingly funny, he knew he couldn't stay in the area much longer.

Getting too hot, he thought as he recorded the droning chief of police (asshat) and the media liaison from the FBI (arrogant bitch).

Time was coming—he could *feel* it—to wind up the odyssey. Time to take Naomi for a ride, have some long conversations, a hell of a lot of fun.

Then end her.

After that, maybe he'd take his show on the road. Maybe up to Canada for the summer, down to Mexico for the winter.

Footloose, fancy-free. And plenty of targets to shoot when the mood struck. In memory of Naomi Bowes.

And one day he would write the story. He'd write a book—not for money. He'd have to wait until he settled somewhere. Like Argentina. He'd write and self-publish the book that rubbed everything he'd accomplished in the faces of the asshats and arrogant bitches.

He took notes on his tablet, took some pictures. He liked focusing in on Mason, he especially liked that.

Hey, over here, fuckhead. I'm going to kill your sister soon. I'll rape her every way there is to rape first, then strangle her like your old man should have.

Maybe send old man Bowes a picture of her. There were ways to smuggle things in—and he'd made a point of finding them. He thought that would be the whipped cream on top.

Yeah, he'd do that, and go one better. He'd publish all the pictures online, every one of the bitches he'd done. God bless the Internet.

Then everyone would know he'd outdone Bowes. Outdone them all. The Green River Killer, the Zodiac? They were nothing next to him.

Deliberately he threw out a question during the Q&A, wanting to draw eyes to him.

Look at me, look at me, look at me.

He would've asked a follow-up, but the ugly bitch beside him tossed a question out first.

Later he wrote up the story for the bullshit Daily Crime blog he free-lanced for, working on his laptop in the pizzeria because most of the media types retreated to the motels or the coffee shop that looked out over the marina.

"Can I get you anything?"

He looked up, saw the pretty blonde he'd targeted and lost. He thought: *You should be dead.*

"I'm sorry, what did you say?"

"Ah, gotta get out of my head." He offered a big smile. "Forgot where I was for a minute."

"I can come back."

"No, that's okay. I could use a Coke, and, yeah, I could eat. How about the calzone—loaded."

"Sure."

She brought the drink in under two minutes. "Are you staying in the area?" she asked. "You've been in before."

"For now, yeah. I'm a reporter."

"Oh." Her eyes went sad and blank.

"Sorry." Immediately he coated himself in sympathy. "I guess you knew the . . . Donna Lanier. She worked here."

"Yes."

"I'm really sorry. If there's anything you want to say, want me to write about her—"

"No. No, thanks. Enjoy your Coke."

When she scurried away, he had to hide the smile.

Maybe he'd snatch her up after all. Maybe he'd just circle back for her, then make Naomi watch while he did the little bitch with her tight ass and tight tits.

Can't save this one, he imagined saying. *Not like Ashley this time. And when I'm done with her, when I'm done with you, I'm going to pay your good friend Ashley a visit, too. Finish what your old man couldn't.*

He worked right through the calzone, putting together another piece on spec, and listening to the chatter around him.

Small towns, the same everywhere, he thought. If you wanted to know what went on, you just had to sit in the same place long enough.

He learned the mechanic was moving in with the photographer, into the big house on Point Bluff. He learned people were scared, and some of them impatient with the police.

Why hadn't they caught him? they asked.

Because he's smarter, better, more *than they are,* he wanted to answer.

He learned that some people speculated the killer lived in the national forest, like a survivalist.

And thought: *No. He's sitting right here, asshole.*

He heard that Naomi's new fuck buddy was playing at the bar on Friday night.

So he began to make his plans.

Lucas Spinner." Mason tapped the photo on the kitchen counter again. "You're sure, no bells?"

"Not even a muffled gong." But she studied the face—young, a lot of disheveled brown hair, a beard that needed shaping. "Why do you keep coming back to him?"

"He had press credentials, a small paper in Ohio, visited Bowes six times between July 2003 and August 2004. Corresponded with him for another eighteen months afterward. Then he's reported missing, presumed dead while covering a brush fire in California in 2006."

"Well, if he's dead—"

"Presumed," Mason qualified. "And shortly after, correspondence begins between Bowes and a Brent Stevens, initially with a Queens return address and postmark. But there's no Brent Stevens from Queens during that time period. And I've read the correspondence, Naomi. I'd swear the same person wrote Stevens's and Spinner's letters. There's an attempt to change it up, but the syntax, the terminology. We're having an expert analyze the letters."

"If they're the same person, you think this is the man you're looking for." She picked up Spinner's photo again.

"Some of Stevens's letters were postmarked from areas you were in, and the timing jibes. Then he drops off the grid. It all stops."

"And that worries you."

"Because it wouldn't stop. He's found another way to communicate. Smuggled cell phone, smuggled snail mail. Somebody looking the other way when Bowes gets his supervised computer use. It happens."

"Maybe without all the hair, the beard." Naomi shook her head. "I'm going to scan this onto my computer, work on it. I'll work on it while you're flying to West Virginia. That way if I have any luck, you'll be right there with Bowes. You could push on it."

"He'd be older now. Remember that, too."

"You said he blends. He wouldn't blend with the hair and the beard, so let me work on seeing him without them. First thing tomorrow," she promised. "We need to get going. I promise you'll have a good time."

While she checked the locks on the back door and got Tag a rawhide bone to keep him busy, Mason checked his watch.

"A bar, a rock band, a Friday night. Yeah, I'll have a good time, but only a couple hours, max. We're leaving at seven thirty tomorrow morning."

"Will you let me know when you're on your way back? After you've talked to him?"

"I'll text you. I'll call if there's anything you need to know. You do the same," he added when she set the alarm, stepped outside.

"We haven't done this in a long time. Gone to a bar together."

"My twenty-first birthday, you flew home to surprise me."

"Not since then?"

"Not since. We went to the bar at the Spot, so I had my first legal drink with you, Seth, and Harry, then you took me to that weird little place."

"The Hole in the Wall, in Chelsea. And that girl hit on you."

"I might've hit back, but I had a date."

Laughing, Naomi closed her eyes, let the wind blow over her face as Mason drove. "Let's make a pact. Once a year, wherever we are, we meet somewhere and have a drink in a bar. Even when we're a hundred and ten."

He held out his hand, pinky crooked. She hooked hers with it. "Even when you're married with five kids," he warned.

She snorted. "That'll be the day."

Yes, he thought. *Yes, it will.*

He saw her come in. He'd been watching, waiting, and felt a tightening in his loins when she stepped into the bar. Pale yellow shirt, snug jeans.

Had her kid brother with her, and after one look at the stage where the mechanic and his grease monkeys hammered away on some ancient Rolling Stones bullshit, the kid brother began to scan the room.

So he angled away, picked up his beer.

Grabbing a stool at the end of the bar hadn't been a problem. Most people wanted tables—and he didn't. A solo at a table drew attention. A guy sitting at the bar drinking a beer didn't.

He shifted on the stool just enough to keep them in his line of sight as they worked their way through the tables to sit with the asshole carpenter and his asshole wife.

He'd thought about killing the wife—Jenny—just for the hell of it. But she really wasn't his type.

Maybe, if he ever decided to come back this way, just for the memories, he'd pay her a little visit. But he didn't have time to play with her now.

Now, it was all about Naomi. So he'd watch awhile, finish his beer, leave a decent tip. Nobody remembered a decent tipper, just the lousy ones or the big ones.

Then he had things to do. It was going to be a big night.

Y ou said they were good," Mason shouted at Naomi. "You didn't say
they were really good."

Delighted, she nudged him toward the table. "They're really good!"
She locked eyes with Xander and thought: *Oh yeah, I'm with the leader of
the band.*

After laying a hand on Jenny's shoulder, she leaned down. "We're a
little later than we planned. I'm going to the bar for a round. Are you
guys ready for another?"

"We could be."

She gave the shoulder a squeeze, started toward the bar. Because she
wanted to connect with Loo, she aimed for the middle, idly scanning as
she went.

She saw a man at the far end, bill of a ball cap pulled low, head down
toward the nearly empty beer glass in front of him. And *felt* him watching her.

He rubbed his fingers up the bridge of his nose, shouldered away from
her. Something shivered up her spine like a warning. Despite it, or maybe
because of it, she changed directions, started toward the other end of the bar.

"Hey, Naomi!" Krista popped up from her table, grabbing Naomi into a
hug. "We sold the print of Xander with the dog. Ten minutes before closing."

"That's great."

"We need more!"

"I'll get you more."

"Can we have a sit-down next week, talk about it?"

"Sure. Email me. We'll set it up."

She broke away in time to see the man in the cap walking casually
toward the exit.

Nothing, she told herself. Probably nothing. Changing directions
again, she walked up to the bar and Loo.

"Guy walking out was giving you the eye," Loo said before Naomi
could speak.

"I saw that. He was sitting alone, end of the bar."

"Didn't like the look of him."

"Why?"

Loo shrugged, continued to mix a dirty martini. "Warmed that seat nearly two hours, nursed one beer—and had his eye on the door half the time. Kept his head down, wouldn't look you in the eye." She shrugged again, added a spear of two fat olives to the glass. "But he watched you, all the way to the table."

"I couldn't get a good look at him. Did you?"

"Not much of one. Suz! Order's up! Kept his head down, like I said. Early thirties, I'd say, looked like brown hair under that cap. Long, skinny fingers. Couldn't keep them off his face. Nervous like, if you ask me."

She pulled the next ticket, set two beer mugs under taps, drew them both at once.

"Or maybe it's me who has the jitters, between one thing and the other."

"Are we all right? You and me?"

"No reason for us not to be. Terry! You're up. Are you here to chat or drink?" she asked Naomi.

"Both, I guess. A round for the table. Kevin's beer, Jenny's wine, and I'll have the same. A Corona with lime for my brother. I'm so sorry, Loo."

"There's nothing to be sorry about. If you want to talk, we'll talk when I don't have to yell back at you. My boy up there loves you. Anything else is just noise."

"I'm really going to try not to screw it up."

On a bark of laughter, Loo set the two glasses of wine on a tray. "Aren't you the positive thinker?"

"That's pretty positive for me."

She carried the tray to the table, served the drinks. Suz breezed by, grabbed the tray, kept breezing.

"Jenny says they've got a CD." Mason hefted his bottle. "I'm going to buy it. You know the uncles are going to love this." He drank some beer, sighed. "Thought you'd never get back with this."

"They're busy, and I was talking with Loo. There was this guy . . ."

Immediately Mason set down his beer. "What guy?"

"Just a guy at the bar. We both felt he was watching me."

"Where?"

"He left."

"Did you get a good look at him?"

"No. Mason—"

"Did she?"

"Not really."

He got up, left his beer, and headed toward the bar.

"Hey! I was going to talk him into dancing with me."

"He'll be back—and he can dance." Wishing she'd said nothing, Naomi picked up her wine.

When Mason came back, he leaned in close and spoke directly in her ear. "She says early thirties, white, short brown hair, average to slim build, about five-ten."

"Yeah, that's what I'd say. And I can pick out twenty more guys in here that more or less fit that."

"But you had a feeling, both of you. Feelings count. I'm going to have someone work with you tomorrow."

"Mason."

"People see more than they think they do, especially observant people. It can't hurt."

"Okay, okay. Now dance with Jenny. She wants to dance, and Kevin has to be cattle-prodded onto the dance floor."

"I could dance." He took another swig of beer, then got up to grab Jenny.

With Kevin grinning after them, Naomi turned her attention back to the stage. Xander watched her—and that gave her a feeling she could live with.

Pleasantly tired, absolutely relaxed, Naomi settled into Xander's truck.

Ky leaned in the window. "Sure you don't want a postgig brew, man?"

"I'm on call, as of ten minutes ago."

Ky shook his head. "One beer isn't going to impair you, son."

"One beer could cost me my license. I'll catch up with you guys later."

"You shouldn't feel like you can't decompress because I'm here," Naomi began.

"We go that same round after nearly every gig when I'm on call. Plus, I'm ready to head home."

"I bet the dog's more than ready to get out."

"And there's that. And there's another way to decompress."

She smiled. "Is that so?"

"I'll show you."

After the dog went out, made his rounds, and settled down for the night, he showed her why home and bed was a much better idea than a beer.

When his phone went off at four fifteen, Xander sincerely wished he'd stuck Jimmy (first night in his new apartment, and with a female companion) on the graveyard shift.

"Shit, fuck, shit." He grabbed the phone, stared blearily at the readout. "Keaton's. Uh-huh. Right. Okay, got it. About fifteen minutes."

"You have to go."

"Dead battery—probably. Between here and town, so I'll check it, jump it if that's it, and be back in a half hour."

"You want coffee?" she mumbled.

"Like I want to breathe, but I'll get it. Go back to sleep."

"Don't tell me twice," she managed, and did just that.

Even the dog didn't get up. Xander saw Tag's eyes gleam as he pulled on clothes, but the dog didn't stir or follow him down to grab that coffee before he headed out.

He used a travel mug, downing the coffee as he walked out to his truck.

Thirty, forty minutes, he thought as he gave the house one last long look. He'd be back. The doors were locked, the alarm set, the dog right there.

She'd be fine.

Still, he wished he'd dumped the shift on Jimmy. He knew about the guy at the bar—had noted him himself. The way he sat alone, head down, the way he'd kept a bead on Naomi when she'd come in.

Then again, he'd noted a guy sitting alone at a table, one who fit the basic nondescription, and who'd given Naomi a long study when she'd walked through the bar.

Until a woman had come in, hurried over, and snuggled up with him.

This murdering bastard didn't break into houses anyway, he reminded himself. But he flicked a glance in the rearview as he drove away.

"2013 Ford Escape towing a 2006 Fun Finder RV," he muttered. "Can't miss that."

He slowed rounding the turn, and indeed couldn't miss it. SUV and camper both sat on the shoulder, emergency flashers blinking.

Xander slid in, nose to nose, and watched the man get out of the driver's seat.

Another reason he hadn't dumped on Jimmy. The murdering bastard liked hunting on Friday nights. Women, but why take chances?

The man lifted his hands, waving one, blinking against the headlights. Then he turned back to the SUV and spoke to someone inside as Xander got out.

"Keaton's?"

"That's right."

"Mike Rhoder. You were really quick. It just won't start. I got my kid in the back, and we were heading to Olympia to camp for the weekend. I just pulled over—he had to pee—and it wouldn't start back up. Just clicks. No, we're not there yet, Bobby." He rolled his eyes. "Just go back to sleep."

Xander hit his own flashers. "Go on and pop the hood. I'll take a look."

"Thought I'd be stuck here till morning, then I'd never hear the end of it from my ex. Hope like hell I don't need a new battery."

With the hood latch released, Xander went around to the front while the man leaned into the SUV again. "We're fixing it right now, and it shouldn't take long. It's an adventure, right, buddy? And we're nearly there. Promise."

"Why don't you try to start her up?" Xander said with his head under the hood.

"Sure, I can do that."

There was just the faintest hint of . . . excitement in the tone to have Xander pushing back, bracing. But the blow to the side of his head flashed pain, flashed lights, then shut out into the dark.

"Or I could do that. How about a couple more, for good measure?"

He lifted the crowbar over his head just as he caught headlights beaming ahead of the turn.

Swearing, he lowered the crowbar and gave Xander a shove with his boot to roll him off the shoulder.

The car slowed. The Good Samaritan rolled down his window.

"You all right there, pal?"

"Sure am. Getting a jump, but thanks for stopping!"

"No problem. Have a good one."

As the car pulled off, he swiped sweat from his face. Too close, and one good crack would have to do. No time for more. He slammed the hood, got back in the SUV, and drove toward the bluff.

He checked the time, smiled to himself. Right on schedule. He'd pull the camper off the road, just far enough up her drive so any cars passing wouldn't give it a thought, but not so close that she or that damn dog would hear.

He'd thought about poisoning the dog, even researched methods. But they all took too long, were too unpredictable. He needed fast.

He'd thought about shooting the dog, which, while satisfying, would be noisy and give her a chance to run or hide.

And the knife? That meant getting too close to those teeth.

So he'd keep back, and let her go through the routine he'd watched countless times already.

She'd let the dog out the bedroom doors, then head down to the kitchen.

All he had to do was wait.

The dog woke her, predictably, at five. She reached out first, hoping Xander had come back. Then she reminded herself he'd only been gone about a half hour.

"I'm up. I'm up," she grumbled as the dog did his predawn dance.

She let him out, then considered crawling back into bed. But the routine was too ingrained. She grabbed cotton pants and a tank, pulling the top on as she walked out of the bedroom.

She'd make waffle batter—after coffee. If Xander hadn't gotten back by that time, she could text him, get an ETA.

Was it clingy or smothering to text about that?

She didn't feel clingy or smothering, so she'd text, if necessary.

In the kitchen she hit the lights, put a mug under the machine, and punched the button for a shot of espresso in the coffee.

While it brewed she got out a bowl, eggs, milk, flour, sugar—and stopped gathering ingredients the minute the coffee was ready. And taking it, she walked to the accordion doors.

She wanted to smell morning.

Even as she started to open the glass, she heard movement behind her.

Thirty

She whirled, saw him, threw the coffee, mug and all. The mug hit him dead center of his chest; hot coffee splashed into his face. He shouted, dropped the rag in his hand, and gave her enough time to leap toward the knives.

She grabbed one, spun back. And slowly lowered it.

"Yeah, you know what they say about bringing a knife to a gunfight." He gestured with the .32 in his hand. "Put that down. You ruined this shirt. Let me tell you, you're going to pay for it."

"They're closing in on you."

"Yeah, you'd like to believe that, but the fact is, this is all just the way I pictured it."

"Why?" she demanded.

"We'll talk about it later. We'll have plenty of time." He grinned, pushed his fingers up the bridge of his nose.

"I'm not—"

It clicked, the gesture, the sarcastic quirk of his mouth.

"Chaffins."

"Took you this long." Obviously pleased, he grinned. "Well, I had

Lasik—ditched the glasses. And a nose job. Decent haircut, bulked up a little. It's been a while, Carson. Or should I say Bowes."

"How could you . . . We were friends."

"Bullshit. You wouldn't—didn't—give me the time of day until I headed up the yearbook committee, cleared you onto the school paper."

"This is because I didn't pay enough attention to you? In *high school*?"

"Please, like I carried a torch. I've had plenty of women. Girls. Old ladies." He bared his teeth in a smile. "All of that. I figured out who you were. *I* figured it out, and I made a deal with you. You lied, and you sent that fucking cop over to tell me to keep it zipped."

How had she missed the madness in his eyes all those years ago? How could she have not seen what she saw now?

"I didn't make any deal."

"You fucking did, then you took my idea. You wrote the story yourself. It should've been *my* byline. It was my story."

"It was never yours."

"Because you're Thomas David Bowes's daughter?"

If he lowered the gun, just lowered it, she thought, she had a chance. She'd have to be fast, but she'd take the chance.

"It's always been about my father."

"Maybe, maybe he kicked it off because I knew, way back, I'd put your father in the shade. It's more about your mother."

"My mother."

"I said we'll talk later. Get moving."

"My mother." He didn't want to shoot her, didn't want to kill her fast. So she planted her feet, took a stand. "You tell me what my mother has to do with any of it."

"Fine. I'll give you another minute. But give me any trouble, I'll shoot you in the knee. It won't kill you, but it'll hurt like hell."

"My mother," she said again, and checked the time on the oven clock behind him. And thought: Xander. Where was Xander?

"Your mother? Other than birds, some stray cats I killed, she was the first dead body I'd ever seen. Man, it was a revelation! She was cold, and her eyes. Man, her eyes. I got *such* a boner." He laughed at the look of disgust on her face. "It's just wiring, Carson. I was born for this, just like your old man. I've studied up on it, researched it. I bet your kid brother and I could have a hell of a conversation about it."

"You stay away from him."

"He doesn't interest me. It's always been you. I knew when we were on the floor with your mother's cold, dead body, I'd do you one day. Then I figured out who you were, and that made it so fucking sweet. Now move, or I'll kneecap you. Maybe I will anyway. I've never started out that way be—"

He jerked back when the dog charged the door like a bull.

The wild barks and Chaffins's shouts exploded in the air.

When he swung the gun toward the door, Naomi threw up her hands. "Don't. Don't. I'll go with you. I'll go." She positioned herself in front of the door, hands up.

There was still time, still a chance, she thought desperately. Xander would come back. She could get close enough to try to fight, to get the gun away. Or far enough away to run.

"Out the front, and fast, or I swear to God—"

Tag shoved the opening wider, gathered himself, and leaped.

As the gun swung back, Naomi threw herself over the dog.

The shock of pain dissolved her legs. She heard the dog's sharp yip as fire burned in her side, as the room spun, as she fell, the dog beneath her.

"Bitch! Stupid bitch, stupid bitch."

She saw his face swimming over her, the mad fury in his eyes. "This is the way you want it? You want a bullet in the brain? Maybe that's how it was always supposed to be."

She stared at the gun, mildly puzzled. Why did it look so small? Like it was a hundred miles away.

Then it was gone. She heard shouting, thought something crashed, but it was all, again, so far away. Nothing really to do with her. Not when she was floating away.

Look at me! Damn it, Naomi, open your eyes. You fucking stay with me."

Pain seared back, like a brand in her side. She cried out against it, her eyes wheeling open.

"That got your attention. I'm sorry. I'm sorry. I have to keep pressure on it." Xander fixed his mouth on hers. "I have to hurt you. I'm sorry."

"Xander." She lifted a hand that didn't feel like her own, touched his temple. "You're bleeding. You're bleeding a lot."

"Yeah. You, too. Help's coming. You just look at me. You talk to me."

"Were you in an accident?"

"No. You're going to be okay. Everything's going to be okay."

"I can't . . ." Memory flooded back, washing through the pain. "Tag. The dog. The dog."

"Stay down, stay still! He's okay. He's going to be okay, too. Hear that? Hear the sirens? Help's coming."

"He was in the house. He was going to shoot the dog. I couldn't let him shoot the dog. He . . . the gun. He has a gun."

"Not anymore. Don't worry about him. Broke his nose for you," Xander murmured, laying his brow to hers.

"I was going to fight. Going to try, but the dog—he came to save me. I need to close my eyes."

"No, you don't. You need to look at me. You need to stay awake. Back here!" he shouted. "Hurry, for Christ's sake. I can't stop the bleeding."

"High school nerd."

"What?"

"Chaffins. Anson Chaffins. Tell Mason," she said, and slid away.

She went in and out in the ambulance, caught snippets of words, mixed voices. She felt Xander's hand clutching hers, and once turned her head and swore she saw the dog on a gurney beside hers.

"Anson Chaffins," she said again.

"Got it. They got it. They got him. Just take it easy."

She surfaced again, moving fast, lights blurring overhead, voices, more voices shouting out medical terms like an episode of *Grey's Anatomy*.

She heard, "I'm going to give you something for the pain."

And said, "Oh, yes. Yes, please."

Furious they'd blocked him from going with Naomi, Xander argued with the burly nurse who stood in his way. If she'd been a man, he'd have decked her.

He considered doing it anyway.

"You need to get that dog out of here, and you need that head wound examined."

"The dog's hurt. He's been shot, for God's sake."

"I'll give you the number for an emergency veterinary clinic. But you have to—"

"You're going to take care of this dog."

"That's exactly right." Mason, face set, strode up, his ID held out. "The bullet is evidence, and needs to be removed. The dog is a material witness, and needs to be treated immediately."

"He's a fucking hero."

"That's right. I suggest you get a doctor, get this dog prepped for surgery, or I swear, I'll arrest you for obstructing a federal investigation."

They wouldn't let him in with Naomi, but loosened up enough to let him sit with the dog while they removed the bullet, treated the wound. And while they cleaned his own wound, stitched up his scalp.

"He's going to be fine."

The surgeon who'd volunteered for the procedure neatly closed Tag's wound.

"It's going to be sore, and he'll limp for a few days. I've given him some antibiotics, and I'll write up a report for your vet. She should do a follow-up."

"Thanks."

"He'll sleep another hour, I'd say. He looks like a good dog."

"He's a damn good dog. Please, God, somebody find out about Naomi. Naomi Carson. Just—shit!"

"I need you to hold still." The intern doing the scalp stitching looked at the surgeon.

"She's doing a good job, just give her a few more minutes. I'll check on Ms. Carson."

Before he could, Mason came in. "How's it going?"

"Both patients are doing well. One more cooperative than the other."

"Where is she? How is she? Fuck! Are you mining for gold in my scalp?"

"They're working on her. But she's going to be fine. It was through-and-through. Through her, into Tag."

"Your evidence, Special Agent."

"Thanks." Mason took the dish with the spent bullet.

"She lost a lot of blood, and a bullet never does you a favor, but it didn't hit any organs. Just the meat. They're going to want to keep her overnight. Probably want to do the same with you."

Xander readied for battle if need be, because his mind was set. "I'm staying with her. So's the dog."

"Already arranged. Are you up to giving me a statement? It can wait."

"I'm okay. Just tell me, where's this Chaffins now?"

"In a cell in Sunrise Cove, but officially in federal custody. He's been examined by a doctor, and his injuries treated. Among other things, you broke his nose, knocked out three of his teeth, cracked a couple ribs."

"Did I?" Xander looked down at his hand, flexed his aching fingers, his raw and swollen knuckles.

"Thanks. I know you love her, but I loved her first, so thanks for saving my sister's life."

"No problem."

Mason pulled up a stool. "Okay, tell me what happened."

He ran it through.

"I should've seen it coming. I did see it, but too late. I actually bought the little-Bobby-in-the-backseat bullshit. And when I came to, I knew he'd gone after her. I called you while I drove back. Pulled in behind his damn camper, ran for the house. I heard the gunshot."

He stopped, closed his eyes. "I heard the shot. I heard her scream. When I ran in he was standing over her, ranting, had the gun pointed at her head. I pulled him off, beat him unconscious. She and the dog were lying there, bleeding. So much blood. I grabbed a couple of dish towels and put pressure on her side—like they always say you're supposed to. It hurt her. I hurt her."

"He hurt her," Mason corrected.

She dreamed she swam, slow and lazy, through the palest of pale blue water. Surfaced and floated, skimmed under to glide. Up and down, in and out, with everything warm and watery.

Once in the dream, beavers cut down trees with chain saws, deep, rhythmic buzzing. She surfaced, thought she saw the dog snoring away on a cot beside her.

She laughed in her sleep—heard Xander's voice. *Wouldn't mind some of whatever they gave you.*

And smiling, slid under again.

She thought of moonlight falling in slants over the bed, how it felt to make love with him over and under those moonlit slants.

Opening her eyes, she saw it was sunlight, sliding through the slats over the window.

"There she is. Are you staying with me this time around?"

She turned her head, met Xander's eyes.

He looked so tired, she thought, and pale under the scruff. Bruised—badly—on the temple.

"We . . . had an accident."

"Not exactly."

"I can't remember what . . ." She turned her head again, saw Tag watching her from a cot. "He is sleeping on a cot. And we're . . . we're in the hospital. He shot me. He shot us."

"Simmer down." Xander pressed a hand on her shoulder, kept her in place. "Anson Chaffins."

"Yes. Yes, I remember. I remember all of it. He got in the house."

"Bedroom. You let the dog out, he waited, came in that way, caught you in the kitchen. Mason said you went to school with him."

"Yes. He was a year ahead of me. I only got to know him for a few months—yearbook committee, school newspaper. But he was with me when I found my mother. He said—he told me—it was his revelation. He said it was wiring, he and my father, both born to be what they are. And seeing my mother's body opened things up for him. Excited him. All this time . . ."

"Don't worry about it now."

"How bad am I hurt? Don't sugarcoat it."

"Well, baby, they did the best they could." And laughed when her mouth fell open. "That ought to cure some of that pessimism. You're fine. As fine as anybody who's been shot. Hit your left side, just above the waist, pinched right through, and straight into the dog's right hindquarters. He's fine, too. I'm saying right now, no Cone of Shame, not for him."

"No Cone of Shame." She reached out, stroked the dog. "Not ever. He can have the Pants of Heroism."

"You jumped in front of the dog, didn't you? He was going to shoot the dog, and you jumped in front of him."

"Wouldn't you have done the same?"

"Yeah." Shakier than he wanted to be, Xander blew out a breath. "Yeah, probably. Idiots."

"How did you get hurt? Your head. You were covered with blood."

"Head wounds bleed a lot."

"He was the call—that's it. The breakdown. It was him. He could've killed you."

"He didn't."

"He could have—"

"He didn't. Get used to it." He pulled her hand to his lips, held it there, rocked for a moment. "I've still got to get used to him nearly killing you—but not. We're both right here. Jesus, Naomi. Jesus, I didn't know I could be that scared and live through it. I didn't know how bad it was. I couldn't tell, just you lying there, and the blood."

"Did you save me?"

He pressed his lips to her hand again. "You'd have done the same for me."

"Yeah. Probably. We're both right here." She smiled as Tag nosed under her other hand. "We're all three right here. And Chaffins?"

"In custody. I don't know where they're taking him, probably later today. News is all over. I spent some time reading on my phone last night. It's all over the news. They broke your connection to Bowes. I'm sorry."

"I don't care. It doesn't matter anymore. I should never have let it matter so much. How long do I have to stay in here? I want to go home."

"They'll want to look you over, but they said you could probably go home today."

"I need to go home, Xander, but I need to see him first. I need to see Chaffins. I never saw or spoke to my father, but I'm going to see and speak to Chaffins."

"Okay. Let's see about getting you out of here, and see what Mason can do."

It took two hours, a lot of paperwork, a lot of warnings, and she had to leave in a wheelchair, use a side entrance where Mason had a car waiting.

He helped her stand, then just held her. "You've looked better."

"I've felt better."

With his help she eased into the car while Xander and Tag took the backseat.

"The press are all over town. If you do this, you can't avoid them completely."

"It doesn't matter."

"He had a press pass," Mason said as he drove. "He came to briefings, booked a motel room—though he stayed in the camper, too. Even when he wasn't using it for other reasons."

Just a smart, nerdy kid who'd gone to a school dance with her, who'd put a couple clumsy moves on her, easily brushed off.

And a monster, all along.

"He held his victims there—like Bowes and the cellar."

"Yeah. Different campgrounds, different names. He's collected several IDs over the last several years. He's got skills, computer skills."

"He always did."

"He kept a log of his victims—names, locations, dates. He has photos of them. We've got enough evidence to put him away for a dozen lifetimes. You'll never have to worry about him again."

"I'm not. I won't. You've told the uncles I'm okay."

"Yeah, I talked to them. Don't worry."

"I don't want them to. I'll call them as soon as I get home."

"Then you're taking one of those pills," Xander said, "and zoning out."

"I probably won't argue about that one. Are you still going to see Bowes?"

"I will." Mason nodded. "But it can wait."

He drove into town, pulled into the slot closest to the station house they'd cleared for him. The minute Xander helped Naomi out of the car, reporters rushed toward them, shouting.

"Tag, too. He should see the dog, too."

Sam Winston opened the door for them, stepped out.

"Every one of you keep back, and stop yelling or I'll have every last one of you arrested for disturbing the peace. This is my town, and I'll do it."

He closed the door, took Naomi's hand. "This is your town, too. Are you feeling up to this? You're certain?"

"Yes. It won't take long."

Not so different, she thought, no, not so different, from that police station so long ago. They'd have put her father in one of the cells in the back, behind the steel door.

"Mason, Xander, and Tag. All of us."

It hurt to keep her back straight, but she'd deal with it. She needed to walk in, unbowed. When she did, Chaffins rolled off the bunk where he'd sprawled. And, despite the blackened eyes, the bruised, swollen, and taped nose, the split lip, he smiled, showing gaps from missing teeth.

"Kid brother, grease monkey, and your little dog, too. Afraid of me, Naomi?"

"Not in the least. I just wanted us all to have a look at you in what's now your natural habitat."

"I'll get out," he snapped as Tag growled low in his throat.

"No, you won't."

"I'll get out, and come for you. You'll always look over your shoulder."

"No, I won't." She laid a hand on Xander's arm, felt it vibrate. "Would you give us a minute?"

"Sure." But Xander stepped up to the cell first, whipped a hand through quick as a snake, rapped Chaffins against the bars. She couldn't hear what Xander murmured in his ear, but it drained the color from Chaffins's face.

"Fuck you! I should've beat you to fucking death."

"But you didn't," Xander said easily, and, stepping back, looked at Naomi. "You don't move from this spot unless it's back."

"Don't worry." She took his hand, kissed his bruised knuckles. "You, too, Mason. Just for one minute."

"I'm on the door," he said.

Naomi waited, studying Chaffins, seeing the boy he'd once been, the monster he was.

"They might write books about you."

"Damn right, they will."

"Even make movies. You can have the sick glory your kind enjoys. I'm fine with that. But you and I, and everyone else, will know that when you came for me, you lost. You lost, Chaffins. I put my father in a cell, and he once meant something to me. Now I've put you in one, and you mean nothing."

"You got lucky. Next time—"

"Dream about it. I hope you do. Every cold, dark night, dream about me."

"You'll dream about me."

"No. I'll forget you, just like I forgot you years ago. I'm the daughter of a monster. Monsters don't scare me. Come on, Tag. Let's go get you a Milk-Bone."

"Come back here! You come back here, I'm not finished with you."

"But I'm finished with you."

She kept walking.

"Feel better?" Xander asked her.

"Yes. Yes, I do. But oh God, I'll feel better once I get home and take that pill."

She closed her eyes on the drive so she could focus on pushing through the pain. She had only to get home now, let everything go.

She breathed out relief when the car stopped. "Definitely drugs, but I'd really like to sit—sprawl out on the deck for— Whose car is that?"

Before Mason could speak, the front door of her house flew open.

"Oh God. Oh God." Tears spilled as Seth yanked open her door.

"Don't you think about getting out by yourself. I'm going to carry you."

"You came, you're here. You're both here. How? No, you can't carry me. I can walk."

"You're not walking anywhere." Harry eyeballed Xander. "You're Xander?"

"Yeah. I've got her."

To settle it, Xander slid his arm under her legs, wrapped the other around her back, gently lifted her.

"Take her right up to bed. We've got it all ready for her."

"No, please. I'm okay. I'd really like to sit out on the deck. I need to hug both of you."

"I'll get pillows." Seth rushed off.

"I made pink lemonade, remember?"

"With crushed ice." She took Harry's hand as Xander carried her. "When did you come? How did you get here so fast?"

"Private jet. We've got connections. My baby girl," he murmured, kissed her hand. "Your people said we could come in, Mason. They'd cleared it. And you'd gotten a crew in to . . ."

"Yeah. It's clean," he said to Naomi.

By the time they got her to the deck, Seth was fussing with pillows, with a light throw. And had a little vase of flowers on the small table.

"There now, set her right down." As Xander did, Seth went down on his knees, wrapped arms around her. "My sweetheart, my baby."

"Don't cry, don't cry. I'm okay."

"She needs a pill. I'm sorry," Xander added, "but she really needs the pain pill."

"I'll get you some lemonade to wash it down. Do you want lemonade?" Harry asked Xander.

"I'd about kill for a beer."

"I'm going to get you a beer. Mason?"

"I have to go. I'll be back, but I have to go right now."

"You be here for dinner. I'm going to make something spectacular."

As Harry hurried inside, Seth pushed to his feet. Still weeping, he turned, enfolded Xander.

"Ah." Xander looked into Naomi's wet, smiling eyes. "Okay."

"You are now and forevermore a hero to me." Sniffling, Seth stepped back. "She is the light of my life. She and Mason are the lights of our lives."

"She brightens up mine, too."

"I've got to go." Mason kissed Seth's cheek. "Sit down. Take a breath."

"Not yet. This boy—handsome," he added with a wiggle of his eyebrows for Naomi. "He needs some ice for those knuckles. I hope you beat the crap out of that vicious little shit."

"Broke his nose, knocked out three teeth," Naomi said.

"Well done."

Harry came out with a tall glass filled with crushed ice and frothy pink liquid and garnished with a twist of lemon. He handed it to Naomi, then handed a beer—in a pilsner—to Xander. Then, as Seth had, he wrapped his arms around Xander.

"I'm Harry, and this is my best girl. It's very nice to meet you, Xander."

"Nice to meet you." He pulled a pill bottle from his pocket, tapped one out. "Take this."

"Actually, I want to hold off just until—"

"Take it."

She sighed, but swallowed the pill. "Oh, Harry, nobody makes pink lemonade like you."

"Could you eat? Something soft and soothing. Cheesy eggs on toast?"

Tears just flooded up again. "My favorite sick-day meal, Harry."

"I'm going to make you some eggs, both of you. And I'm going to fix this amazing dog something special. No kibble for you today, my brave boy."

Tag sent him a look of adoration, laid a head on Harry's leg. "Some beef. We'll call it Beef à la Tag."

When Harry went in, Tag limped after him. Before Xander could sample the beer, Seth bustled out with a zip-top bag of ice.

"Here now. Why don't you sit on the glider? Naomi can put her legs in your lap. You'll ice that hand, drink your beer. And look at this beautiful view. It's the best day of our lives. How's your pillow, honey?"

"It's fine. I'm fine."

"When you're ready, Xander's going to carry you upstairs so you can sleep awhile. We'll all be right here. Just right here."

"I'm so glad you're here."

"I'm going to help Harry. You call if you need anything."

She smiled, sipped lemonade when he went inside. "It's starting to feel like a dream. Did you know they were here?"

"Mason told me. They flew in early this morning."

"You're going to like them."

"I already like them. What's not to like? I've got a beer and I'm getting cheesy eggs." He had to set the ice aside to dig the phone out of his pocket. "I'll answer later. I've been getting calls and texts for hours. Everybody wants to know how you're doing, come see you. Bring food, flowers, Jesus knows."

"Everybody?"

"Name somebody. I bet they've called or texted."

Like family, she thought. Friends and community could be like family if you let it happen.

"We could have some over—Harry loves to cook for people. It's nice they want to. I'm just tired. Pill's already kicking in."

"Tomorrow. They can come tomorrow if you're up for it."

"That's probably better. It's okay now."

"Is it?"

"Yes. I'm not going to ask what you said to him, but thank you for whatever you did say that drained the blood from his body."

"You finished him off."

"I finished." She nodded. "I'm where I want to be, with who I want to be with, and I'm done worrying about blood ties and how people I don't care about react."

"Good."

"And I love this spot. I love looking out at the water, and knowing I will day after day."

"It's a good spot. We ought to get married down there in the backyard."

"It's a good spot for— What?"

"Fall's nice, all the color." Contemplatively he sipped the beer. "October. That'd give you time to do what women think they need for it. Flowers and the dress, whatever."

"But married? That's—"

"How it ought to be." Casually, he rubbed his big hand up and down her calf. "You've got until October to get used to it. That's long enough."

"You actually consider this a proposal?"

"I think it's perfect," Seth said from the doorway, then wiped his eyes and stepped back inside.

"I'll get you a ring. We'll make a good life here."

"I haven't said I'd—"

"You will," he said easily. "I love you, Naomi. That's the start, the finish, and everything in between." He looked at her, those strong blue eyes. "You love me."

"I do. I really do. I just never thought about getting married." She took his injured hand, laid the ice over it again. "But I think I could get used to it."

"Good. October. Anything else is negotiable."

"The uncles are going to want one hell of a show."

He shrugged. "Why wouldn't they? Shows are fine, as long as there's this."

He leaned over, touched his lips to hers.

As long as there's love, she thought, sighing into the kiss. And the good, strong place to build a life together.

A life of sunrises and lilacs, of friends and quiet moments.

And a really good dog.